James H. Graff, James Grant

Jack Manly

His Adventures by Sea and Land

James H. Graff, James Grant

Jack Manly
His Adventures by Sea and Land

ISBN/EAN: 9783337341572

Printed in Europe, USA, Canada, Australia, Japan

Cover: Foto ©Andreas Hilbeck / pixelio.de

More available books at **www.hansebooks.com**

BY JAMES GRANT

Price 2s. each, Fancy Boards.

THE ROMANCE OF WAR.
THE AIDE-DE-CAMP.
THE SCOTTISH CAVALIERS.
BOTHWELL.
JANE SETON; OR, THE KING'S ADVOCATE.
PHILIP ROLLO.
LEGENDS OF THE BLACK WATCH.
MARY OF LORRAINE.
OLIVER ELLIS; OR, THE FUSILIERS.
LUCY ARDEN; OR, HOLLYWOOD HALL.
FRANK HILTON; OR, THE QUEEN'S OWN.
THE YELLOW FRIGATE.
HARRY OGILVIE; OR, THE BLACK DRAGOONS.
ARTHUR BLANE.
LAURA EVERINGHAM; OR, THE HIGHLANDERS OF GLENORA.
THE CAPTAIN OF THE GUARD.
LETTY HYDE'S LOVERS.
THE CAVALIERS OF FORTUNE.
SECOND TO NONE.
THE CONSTABLE OF FRANCE.
THE PHANTOM REGIMENT.
THE GIRL HE MARRIED.
FIRST LOVE AND LAST LOVE.
DICK RODNEY.
THE WHITE COCKADE.
THE KING'S OWN BORDERERS.
LADY WEDDERBURN'S WISH.
ONLY AN ENSIGN.
JACK MANLY.
THE ADVENTURES OF ROB ROY.
THE QUEEN'S CADET.

GEORGE ROUTLEDGE AND SONS,

THE BROADWAY, LUDGATE.

His Adventures by Sea and Land.

BY

JAMES GRANT,

AUTHOR OF
"THE ROMANCE OF WAR," "OLIVER ELLIS,"
ETC. ETC.

LONDON:
GEORGE ROUTLEDGE AND SONS,
THE BROADWAY, LUDGATE.
NEW YORK: 416, BROOME STREET.

LONDON :

SAVILL, EDWARDS AND CO., PRINTERS, CHANDOS STREET,

COVENT GARDEN.

CONTENTS.

JACK MANLY.

CHAPTER I.

WHY I WENT TO SEA.

IT was the evening of the sixteenth of March.

Exactly six months had elapsed since I left my father's snug villa at Peckham, with its walls shrouded by roses and honeysuckle; and now I found myself two thousand three hundred miles distant from it, in his agent's counting-room, in the dreary little town of St. John, in Newfoundland, writing in a huge ledger, and blowing my fingers from time to time, for snow more than ten feet deep covered all the desolate country, and the shipping in the harbour was imbedded in ice at least three feet in thickness; while the thermometer, at which I glanced pretty often, informed me that the mercury had sunk twelve degrees below the freezing point.

While busily engrossing quintals of salted fish,

B

by the thousand, barrels of Hamburg meal and
Irish pork, chests of bohea, bales of shingles,
kegs of gunpowder, caplin nets, anchors and
cables, and Indian corn from the United States,
with all the heterogeneous mass of everything
which usually fill the stores of a wealthy merchant
in that terra nova, I thought of the noisy world
of London, from which I had been banished, or, as
tutors and guardians phrased it, "sent to learn
something of my father's business —*i. e.*, practically
to begin life as he had begun it;" and so I sighed
impatiently over my monotonous task, while melting
the congealed ink, from time to time, on the birch-
wood fire, and reverting to what March is in
England, where we may watch the bursting of the
new buds and early flowers; where the birds are
heard in every sprouting hedge and tree, and as we
inhale the fresh breeze of the morning, a new and
unknown delight makes our pulses quicken and
a glow of tenderness fill the heart—for then we
see and feel, as some one says, " what we have seen
and felt *only* in *childhood and spring*."

"Belay this scribbling business, Jack," said a
hearty voice in my ear; "come, ship on board my
brig, and have a cruise with me in the North Sea.
I shall have all my hands aboard to-morrow."

I looked up, threw away my pen, closed the gigantic ledger with a significant bang, and shook the hand of the speaker, who was my old friend and schoolfellow, Bob Hartly, whose face was as red as the keen frost of an American winter evening could make it, albeit he was buttoned to the throat in a thick, rough Flushing coat, and wore a cap with fur ear-covers tied under his chin—a monk-like hood much worn in these northern regions during the season of snow.

"I don't think your cruise after seals and blubber will be a very lively affair, Bob," said I, rubbing my hands at the stove, on which he was knocking the ashes of his long Havannah.

"Lively! if it is not more lively than this quill-driving work, may I never see London Bridge again, or take,

'Instead of pistol or a dagger, a
Desperate leap down the falls of Niagara!'"

"I am sick of this Cimmerian region!" said I, stamping with vexation at his jocular mood, when contrasted to my own surly one.

"Cimmerian—ugh! that phrase reminds me of school-times, and how we used to blunder through Homer together, for he drew all his images of Pluto

B 2

and Pandemonium from the dismal country of the Cimmerii.   By Jove! I could give you a stave yet from Virgil or Ovid, hand over hand, on the same subject; but that would be paying Her Majesty's colony a poor compliment."

"Well, Bob, I am sick of this place, in which evil fate, or rather bad luck, has buried me alive— this frozen little town of wood and tar, without outlet by sea or land in winter, without amusement, and, at this time, seemingly without life."

"It forms a contrast to London, certainly," said Hartly, assisting himself, uninvited, to the contents of a case-bottle of Hollands which stood near; "but there is a mint of money to be made in it."

"The first English folks who came here were re- duced to such straits, we are told, that they killed and ate each other; and those who returned were such skeletons that their wives and mothers did not know them."

Hartly laughed loudly, and said—

"But that was in the time of King Henry VIII., and people don't eat each other here now.   But to resume what we were talking about——"

"Old Uriah Skrew, my father's agent, and I are on the worst terms; he keeps a constant watch over me. I go from my desk to bed, and from bed to my desk—so passes my existence."

" Why not slip your cable and run, then ?"

" Skrew being a partner in the firm," I continued, warming at the idea of my own rights and fancied wrongs, " cares for nothing but making money from the riches of the sea, and thinks only of cargoes of fish to be bartered in Lent, at Cadiz, for fruit and wine, oil, seals, and blubber; and really in this cold season——"

" Ah, but summer is coming," interrupted Bob, drily.

" Summer ! How is the year divided here ?"

" Into nine months of winter and three of bad weather."

" A pleasant prospect! If I were once again at Peckham——"

" Well, Jack, I have a grudge at old Uriah Skrew, for, like a swab, he played me a scurvy trick about a cargo I had consigned to your father and him, from Cadiz, last year—a trick by which I lost all my profit and tonnage.

" Likely enough; this ledger is Uriah's bible— and his God——"

" Is gold ! So I care not a jot if, for the mere sake of provoking him, I lend you a hand to give him the slip, for a few months at least. Ship with me to-morrow—as a volunteer, passenger, or whatever you please."

"I shall," said I, throwing my pen resolutely into the fire.

"Your hand on it! I like this. Get your warmest toggery sent on board; you'll need it all, I can tell you! I can give you a long gun, and bag for powder and slugs; and then, with a bowie-knife in your belt, a seal-skin cap with long flaps, and a stout pea-jacket, you will make as smart a seal fisher as ever sailed through the Narrows! By this time to-morrow you may be forty miles from your ledger, running through the North Sea with a flowing sheet. By Jove, I know a jolly old Esquimau who lives at Cape Desolation under an old whale-boat. He will be delighted to make your acquaintance, and give you a feed of sea weed and blubber that will make your mouth water, though we eat it when the mercury is frozen in the bulb."

This cheerful prospect of Arctic hospitality might have persuaded me to remain where I was, but soured by the treatment I experienced from Mr. Skrew, who misrepresented my conduct and habits to my family at home, and tired of the monotony

of his counting-room, I looked forward with eager-
ness to an anticipated escape.

How little could I foresee the consequences of my
impatience, folly, and wayward desire for rambling!
Ere a month was past, I had repented in bitterness
my boyish repugnance for steady application and
industrious habits.

My friend, Robert Hartly, who was eight years
my senior, was master and owner of the *Leda*, a
smart brig of two hundred and fifty tons register—
a craft in which he had invested all his savings.
Last year he had lost a wife and two children,
whom he tenderly loved; he had come to St. John
from Cadiz, missed a freight and been frozen-in,
and now, with all a sailor's restlessness and dread of
being idle, even for a month or two, he had resolved
to sail for the spring seal fishery, as a change of
scene, and a trip which he hoped would not prove
unprofitable, as his vessel was one of a class far
superior to those which usually venture into the
region of ice, being well found, well manned,
coppered to the bends, and, in short, the perfection
of a British merchant brig.

"By the bye," said he, "talking of powder and
slugs, we may need both, for other purposes than
shooting seals."

"How ?" I asked.

"I mean if we came athwart the *Black Schooner* which has been prowling and plundering about the coast for the last six weeks."

"Are there more news of her ?"

"No; but here is a placard given to all ship-masters yesterday," said he, unfolding a paper surmounted by the royal arms, and running in the name of "His Excellency the Governor and Commander-in-Chief over the Island of Newfoundland and its Dependencies," offering 500*l.* to the crew of any ship that would capture "the vessel known as the *Black Schooner*," &c. "She is a queer craft," continued Hartly, "and said to be a slaver, bankrupt, and out of business ; though Paul Reeves, my mate, maintains that she is the *Adventure* galley, which sailed from London in the time of King William III., and that her crew are the ghosts of Kidd and his pirates; but ghosts don't steal beef and drink brandy."

Hartly's father had been in the navy; thus he had received a good and thorough nautical education, but early in life had been left to work his way in the world ; so he made the watery portion thereof his home and means of livelihood. He was a handsome, hardy, and cheerful young fellow, and the *beau idéal* of a thorough British sea-man.

On the third finger of his left hand he wore a curious ring of base metal, graven with runes or strange figures. This was the gift of an old woman to whom he had rendered some service when in Iceland, and who had promised, that while he wore it, he could *never be drowned;* consequently Hartly was too much imbued with the superstition of his profession to part with it for a moment.

"But how am I to elude old Skrew, and get on board," said I, after we had concluded all our arrangements, over a glass of hot brandy-punch, in Bob's lodgings in Water-street.

"True—the brig lies frozen-in at the end of his wharf, the hatches are all locked, and the hands ashore."

"If he sees me on board, there will be an end of our project, for I have no wish to quarrel with him in an unseemly manner; but merely to 'levant' quietly, leaving a letter to announce where I am gone, and when I may, perhaps, return."

"All right—I have it! I'll send an empty cask to Skrew's store to-morrow. Paul Reeves, the mate, and Hammer, the carpenter, will head you up in it, and so you may be brought on board unknown to

all save them—ay, under the very nose of old
Uriah.   Will that suit you?"

"Delightfully!" said I, clapping my hands.   The
whole affair had the appearance of an adventure,
and though there were a hundred ways by which I
might have joined the brig, when the *cutting-out* of
the sealing fleet took place next day, like a young
schoolboy—for in some respects I was little more—
I accepted the strange proposal of going on board
in a cask, and retired to bed, to dream of adventures
on the high seas ; for being young, healthy, and
active, I could always have pleasant dreams without
studying the art of procuring them—an art on
which Dr. Franklin wrote so learnedly in the last
century.

CHAPTER II.

ADVENTURE IN A CASK.

ON the next day (17th of March), when the fleet
of adventurers departs for the spring seal fishery,
the little seaport town of St. John's presents
an unusual aspect of bustle and gaiety. On that
anniversary, at least one hundred vessels, having
on board three thousand seamen, batmen, and
gunners, sail to seek their fortune in the ice-
fields; but on the day I am about to describe,
the number of craft and their crews far exceeded
this.

The day was clear and sunny, not a speck of cloud
was in the sky, whose immensity of blue made the
eye almost ache, while the intense brilliance of the
snow, which covered the hills and the whole scenery,
made them seem to vibrate in the sunshine, and
caused a species of blindness, especially on entering
any apartment, however large or well-lighted; for

after being out of doors in that season and region for an hour or so, a house usually seems totally dark for a time.

For some days previous there had been that species of drizzle which is termed locally "a silver thaw," thus, all the houses of the town, the roofs, walls, and chimneys ; the trees, the shipping in the frozen harbour, every mast, yard, and inch of standing or running rigging, were thickly coated with clear ice, which sparkled like prisms in the sunshine, making them seem as if formed of transparent crystal. Then, there was a glittering in the frosty atmosphere, as if it was composed of minute particles, while the intensity of the cold made one feel as if a coarse file were being roughly applied to one's nose or cheek-bones on facing the west, the point whence the wind came over the vast and snow-covered tracts of untrodden and unexplored country which stretch away for three hundred miles towards the Red Indian Lake and the Bay of Exploits.

The keepers of stores and shops—who in St. John are usually dressed like seamen, in round jackets and glazed hats—with all idlers, were pouring through every avenue and thoroughfare, and spreading over the harbour. All the ships displayed their colours, and the sound of music, as bands perambulated the ice, rang upon the clear and ambient air, mingled with the musical jingle of the sleigh bells, as the more wealthy folks, muffled and shawled to the nose, galloped their horses with arrow-like speed from side to side of the harbour.

The latter and the town (but especially the grog-shops) were crowded by the seal fishermen, who had come in from all parts of the coast, and bore bundles of clothing slung over their backs, each having his carefully selected club wherewith to smite the young seals on the head, and also to be used as a gaff or ice-hook. Many of these men were also armed with long sealing-guns, which are twice the size and weight of an ordinary musket, and resemble the huge, unwieldy gingals of the East Indians, having flint locks of a clumsy fashion.

They are generally loaded with coarse-grained powder and pieces of lead, termed *slugs*, to shoot the old seals, who frequently prove refractory, and dangerous when defending their young.

Those fishers who are thus armed as gunners rank before the mere clubmen, and receive a small remuneration, or are remitted some of the "berth money" which is usually paid to the storekeeper or merchant who equips the vessel for the ice; "the outfitting," says one who is well-informed on these matters, "being always defrayed by the receipt of one-half the cargo of seals, the other half going to adventurers, with these and other deductions for extra supplies." But, as Captain Hartly fitted out his own vessel and shipped his own crew, gunners, and batmen at stipulated salaries, he expected to reap the whole profits of the expedition.

In addition to the project I had in view, I was particularly anxious to witness the gaiety of this the only and yearly colonial gala day—the shipping of the crews, (who always proceed in procession along the ice,) with the cutting-out and departure of the sealers; but old Mr. Uriah Skrew, with his clean-shaven face and small cunning eyes, was in the counting-room betimes, and piled work upon me thick and fast, to anticipate any application for a day's leave.

"May I not go out for an hour, sir, and see what is going on in the harbour?" I asked, gently.

"No, sir," he replied, sharply; "such nonsense only leads to idleness—idleness to dissipation, and dissipation to ruin! That is the sliding-scale, young man——"

"Oh! my good sir, you are too severe,"

"Severe! Mr. Jack Manly!——"

"Well, sir?"

" I have always been kind and indulgent to you."

" Kind—hum."

" Yes; more kind and indulgent than your father, my worthy partner, wishes—and more than he would be."

" Query ?"

" What do you mean by 'query'?" he demanded in a bullying tone, for he intensely disliked me, fearing that I should soon be admitted into the firm.

" Because I have my doubts on the subject, and your refusal to grant me leave to-day confirms my opinion of you, Mr. Skrew."

" Very well; enough of this, not a word more, or by the first ship for Europe I will write what you'll wish had not been written. Not a word more."

" I am mute as a fish."

" Engross these papers—but, first, go to the store on the wharf, and tell the keeper to speak with me; and look sharp !"

I put on my cap and left the counting-room, feeling assured that many a day would elapse ere I stood within it again, as I caught a glimpse of Paul Reeves, mate of the *Leda*, and two seamen, loitering outside; but near the window, wherein stood my desk, under the leaf of which I deposited a letter addressed to Mr. Skrew, informing him, in the parlance of Bob Hartly, that "I had slipped my cable and gone to sea."

"Captain Hartly's friend, sir?" said the mate, touching his hat, and winking knowingly.

"Yes."

"All right, sir! here is the cask, step in, and Tom Hammer, our carpenter, and his mate, will head you up in it comfortably in less than a minute."

"No one is near?" said I, anxiously glancing round the courtyard.

"Not a soul, sir: in you go, on with the head, Tom, and be quick, for the ice channel is cutting fast to the fairway; the jib and foretopsail are loose, and the lashings all but cast off."

The counting-room of Messrs. Manly and Skrew stood within a courtyard, which was entered by a gateway from Water-street; and from this court— which was formed by four large wooden stores, all pitched, tarred, and now coated with snow and ice— a path led down to the wharf, at the end of which, as at the end of all the others that jutted into the harbour, a mercantile flag was displayed from a mast. In this court were piles of old barrels, hampers, boxes, an anchor, a spare topmast or so, half buried under the usual white mantle, on which a flock of poor little snowbirds were hopping and twittering drearily.

"Do you feel snug, sir?" inquired Paul Reeves, through the bunghole.

"Yes ; but please to lose no time in getting me through the crowd on the wharf, and on board the *Leda*," I replied, in a somewhat imploring tone of voice ; for the cask, though a roomy one, was the reverse of comfortable, and *already* I longed to stretch myself.

"The *Leda* lies just outside the Bristol clipper."

"She that was overhauled and plundered, and had three of her crew shot by the *Black Schooner ?*"

"Yes, sir," replied Reeves, as the two seamen hoisted up the cask ; and I soon became aware by the clamour around me that I was being conveyed down to the wharf, where Mr. Skrew, in a full suit of Petersham and sables, was walking to and fro till his sledge arrived.

"Hallo, what have you fellows got in the cask?" he demanded as I was borne past him.

"Some of the captain's stores, sir," replied Reeves.

"His grandmother's best featherbed," added the carpenter.

c

" Very good," said Uriah, as I was deposited almost on his gouty toes.

Men often stumbled against my cask, and swore at it or pushed it aside. Once a fellow seated himself *on* it, and kicked with his heels till I was nearly deranged, and the impulse to scare him by a shout became almost irrepressible. For a time, I dreaded that it might be tumbled off the wharf into the sludge and broken ice alongside!

Ere long the wharf was cleared; I heard the clanking of the gates, as the keeper, by order of Mr. Skrew, locked them, doubtless to exclude me therefrom on this great gala day; and then followed the jangling of bells, as he stepped into his sledge, and departed upon the ice. Thus I was left to my own reflections on the solitary wharf.

Before this, a great commotion had taken place at the extremity thereof, as the Bristol clipper by some mismanagement ran foul of the *Leda*, and the usual volleys of threats, oaths, and orders incident to such collisions in harbour were exchanged from the decks and rigging of both vessels, while, by using boat-hooks aloft and fenders below, the crew strove to keep the rigging clear and the hulls apart.

Amid this unexpected hurly-burly, I was *forgotten* in my cask!

The wharf stood near the western extremity of the town, which lies along the basin of the harbour. The sounds in my vicinity seemed all to die away, as the crowd along the shore and upon the ice followed the ships, which in succession were warped along their ice-channels into the fairway, and each was greeted by a tremendous cheer as the sails fell, their head canvas filled, and they broke into blue water; but hours seemed to elapse, without a person coming near the horrible cask in which I was imprisoned, and the agonies I endured are beyond description!

The sense of oppression and of being cramped amounted to intense bodily torture; thus a perspiration alternately burning hot and icy cold burst over me. The interior of this now detested prison seemed hot as a furnace; yet there was in my soul a deadly fear of perishing by cold, as I should assuredly do, if left all night on the locked wharf, in such a climate, with the thermometer at twelve degrees below the freezing point!

How fruitlessly I repented me of the silly project of thus escaping, and alternately longed to be back again in Skrew's snug counting-room, or on board the departing brig—of being anywhere, instead of being thus " cabin'd, cribb'd, confin'd," and forgotten.

A terror of being conveyed on board, and left, perhaps, in the hold—left undiscovered till dead of suffocation, gave me wild energy; madly I strove to kick or beat out the head of the cask ; but my legs were powerless, as if suffering from paralysis, for my aching knees were wedged under my chin, and I might as well have attempted to escape from a block of adamant.

Faintness and delirium were fast coming over me! I screamed like a madman ; but my hoarse voice was lost in the hollow of the cask. Though a perspiration bathed all my aching limbs, my tongue clove to my palate, and soon became hot and dry. Starry lights seemed to flash and dance before me in the darkness ; my brain reeled ; then I gasped, as sense and pulsation ebbed together, and after enduring three hours (as I afterwards learned) of such agony as those who were confined in the stone chests of the Venetians, or in the iron cages which Louis XI. placed in the Bastille, alone could have known—1 fainted.

CHAPTER III.

THE NARROWS OF ST. JOHN.

On recovering, I found myself in the cabin of the *Leda*, with Captain Hartly hanging over me, and chafing my hands and temples, in anxiety and solicitude, with hartshorn and vinegar; for being a kind-hearted fellow, he was seriously alarmed.

In these friendly offices he was ably assisted by Cuffy Snowball, his black cook, who burned several grey goose-quills under my nose, and who brought me a rummer full of brandy-punch steaming hot from the galley. On swallowing this, which they forced me to do at two draughts, I became considerably revived and invigorated.

"Why did you leave me there, Hartly—it might have been, to die?" I asked, reproachfully.

"I did not leave you, my dear boy, at least not a moment longer than we could help," he replied. "It cost us no small trouble to get clear of that lubberly barque. I wish the *Black Schooner* had sunk her, when athwart her hawse! We had to clap on all hands to warping into the fairway, and once there, we had to keep constantly forging a-head, as other craft were crowding into the channel astern of us."

"Then I was pretty near being left till the wharf-keeper came next morning. My heaven! I should have been stiff enough by that time!"

"I sent Paul Reeves and Hans Peterkin to bring off the cask on a sledge, and you may imagine the fright we were in on finding you cramped up and lifeless as a pickled herring!"

"Oh, Hartly," said I, "the torture I endured was frightful! I now repent of my undertaking, and wish myself back again."

"Repent—bah! It has been a stupidly managed job, but it is over now, and there is an end of it. Take another sip of the hot brandy-and-water, and come on deck; we are abreast of the Crow's Nest now, and in ten minutes more will be in blue water; then hurrah for the ice-fields!"

I followed him on deck, and found that we were, as he said, abreast of a high sugar-loaf shaped rock, crowned by a little battery named the Crow's Nest, and that around us a very exciting scene was passing.

The *Leda* was now in the fairway, or main channel, which was formed through the ice in the centre
of the harbour, and into which there were cut more
than fifty canals, or connecting links, along which
the sealing ships were being warped from the various
wharves at which they had been fitted out. All
were gaily decked with their owners' private colours,
and had their courses, or lower sails, cast loose, and
were accompanied by crowds, who were conversing,
laughing, and expressing their hopes of a successful
fishery to the crews, whose voices rang cheerily as
they tripped round the capstan or wrenched at the
windlass, till they came abreast of the kedge anchor
which was wedged in the ice ; and then it was
torn up, and carried off a-head towards the Narrows,
when the cheering, warping, and tripping began
anew.

Thousands of persons, many of them on skates,
covered all the glassy expanse of the frozen harbour,
which from some points of view appears land-locked,
so closely do the mountains of rock converge at its
entrance ; and hundreds of sledges (Mr. Uriah
Skrew's among the number), with round Russian
bells at their horses' collars, or on the circular iron
rod above their ears, with the drivers muffled in
furs, swept to and fro ; while bands of music

playing the air invariable on this occasion, "St.
Patrick's Day," marched alongside of the departing
fleet.

Flags of every fashion—square, triangular, and
swallow-tailed—were streaming everywhere; on the
mastheads of the shipping, on the black-tarred mercantile stores, and on the dwellings of their owners
—a passion for a display of bunting being one of
the peculiarities of this our most northern colony in
America.

The aspect of its capital, which covers the
northern slope of the harbour, is rather pretty,
though the country beyond is nearly as wild and as
dreary as when, in the words of Hakluyt—" in the
yeere of our Lord 1497, John Cabot a Venetian, and
his son Sebastian, with an English fleet from Bristol,
discovered that land which no man had before attempted, on 24th June, about five of the clocke,
early in the morning. That island which lieth out
before the land, he called of *St. John*, as I think,
because it was discovered upon the day of John the
Baptist."

During the brief summer, this harbour, the entrance of which is so narrow that two ships can
scarcely pass in the dangerously deep mid-channel,
is smooth as a mill-pond, and presents a lively

scene, for there the smart Clyde-built clipper, the
dark and battered Sunderland collier brig, the
smart Yankee liner,. with her gaudy stars and
stripes, her snowy decks, and gear so taut ; the
Pomeranian, with her grass-green hull and fur-
capped crew ; the Dutch galliot, all brown varnish,
and shaped like a half cheese, or like the old craft
that bore the Crusaders to Palestine ; the huge ship
of Blackwall, redolent of guano, all blistered, rusted,
and turned yellow by the sun of the fiery south ;
the sharp Spanish brig, which had run her cargo of
slaves in South Carolina and escaped here, to go
quietly home, with her brass nines hidden in the
hold, and with fish in Lent for the pious at Cadiz or
Oporto—during the brief season of summer, I say,
all these had been here ; but now when a snowy
mantle covered the land, and black ice locked the
harbour, its basin or bosom presented a very different scene.

Floundering through sludge and water, a thousand
of those men who are England's real pioneers in
the Far West—Irish emigrants—in long boots, were
cutting the thick ice with ponderous saws, and
pushing the blocks under the solid mass on either
side, to form a fairway or clear channel for the
shipping ; and this channel, though at least

twenty feet broad, would certainly be frozen hard and fast ere morning dawned.

On this occasion there passed out with us, as I have elsewhere stated, more than one hundred sail of sealing craft. There were brigs, brigantines, and schooners, ranging from fifty to two hundred and fifty tons, all following each other through the fairway, warping ahead, till beyond the Chain Rock, where they got into open water.

Many of the smaller craft are miserably adapted for the dangers they have to encounter, and thus are frequently crushed or lost in the ice by being swept off among the floes and fields to the far north, from whence they never return. Some, I have observed, had only a box lined with fire-brick placed on edge, lashed aft the foremast, for a caboose, and an iron cauldron on three legs placed therein for boiling the wretched mess of old salt pork and doughballs which form the daily food of the crew, who, with such apparatus, would be unable to cook anything in foul weather or a heavy sea.

The wind was southerly for a time, but gradually veered a little to the west as we neared the harbour mouth. After passing the Chain Rock, where a cable of Cyclopean aspect, that now lies a mass of rust thereon, was wont in times of war and alarm to be stretched across to the Pancake Rock to secure the harbour at night, we found ourselves in the deep water. With a loud cheer we brought the kedge anchor and hawser on board. Paul Reeves took the wheel; we sheeted home the foresail and gib, let fall the fore and main topsails, and brought the starboard tacks on board when we were clear of the Signal Hill, and the Dead Man's Bay— a dreary inlet of the sea—lay on our quarter.

This hill is a stern and precipitous mountain of sandstone and slate-rock, nearly six hundred feet in height, with batteries that rise over each other in tiers, to the highest, which is named " The Queen's." Opposite, towers an equally abrupt mountain of similar height and aspect, having at its base a little promontory defended by Fort Amherst.

The slender gut between is named the Narrows of St. John.

The breeze came more and more round upon our quarter as we ran past Signal Hill, ploughing through a somewhat heavy surf; past the Sugar Loaf, and a little creek where, in the clear summer sea, I have seen the guns of an ancient and forgotten wreck lying like black dots on the smooth white sand many fathoms below; for in these regions, when a brilliant sun shines upon the ocean, its waters become transparent to a wondrous depth; thus giant corals, dusky weeds, and the snow-white bones of mighty fish,

"With the rainbow hues of the sea-trees' bloom,"

may be seen distinctly at the depth of a hundred and fifty feet from the surface.

There, too, I have seen the bright yellow sea anemone, with its long fibrous leaves, that close and shrink into the rocks from view when touched.

Cape St. Francis, one of the eastern promontories of Avalon, was soon upon our beam; Cape Spear light had sunk into the waves astern, and night was coming down upon the wintry sea, when we hauled up a point or two to the north and west, and stood right away to the icy regions of the North; and that night merrily at supper we sang in the cabin—

"'Twas in the year of 'sixty-one,
Of March the seventeenth day,
That our gallant ship her anchor weighed
And to the North seas bore away,
                    Brave boys," &c.

CHAPTER IV

THE BRIG "LEDA."

WE had twenty-four hands on board; twelve of these were landsmen, being gunners and batmen, half agriculturists and half fishermen, who, at times, in summer, left their families to till the scanty soil, while they fished in open boats among the countless creeks and bays which indent the peninsula of Avalon; and now in winter, when all out-of-door operations were suspended, and the land was buried under fourteen feet of frozen snow—and when the sea, even to the distance of two hundred miles, would soon be bound with ice, they became seal-fishers; and, like others, had shipped in the little fleet which, on St. Patrick's Day, always departed from this Iro-American isle for the stormy seas that lash the Labrador.

All these men were Irish and oft at sea; I have heard the poor fellows, when seated under the leech of the foresail, with the icy spray flying over them to leeward, singing the sweet or merry songs they had learned at their mothers' knee, in the brave old land they were fated never to see again—for the story of our crew is a sad one!

We had a negro, who was our cook (of course), Cuffy Snowball—I never heard him named otherwise; and his adventures had been somewhat singular.

Cuffy had been a warrior of Congo, and dwelt in a hut on the banks of the Zaire, where, by dint of "his spear and shaggy shield," he had amassed a wealth of baskets, gourds, carved calibashes, and wooden spoons from cowards who could not defend them. He could tell, with great simplicity, innumerable stories of his combats with other tribes, and with lions, leopards, buffaloes, crocodiles, and hippopotami; and in evidence of his prowess, he wore on his left arm a bracelet formed entirely of lions' teeth—which form a kind of "Order of Valour" in Congo. He had been very happy in his wigwam, till the daughter of a Chenoo or chief—a beautiful damsel, with her teeth painted blue and the bone of a shark through her nose—espied him one day, and desired to have him for her husband, as it is the right of these ladies to do.

The chosen, of whom she becomes absolute mistress and proprietress, dare not refuse, so poor Cuffy was married to the Chenoo; there were great rejoicings, and three prisoners of war were devoured at the marriage-feast.

But his sable fair one tired of him in a short time, and by certain artful means decoyed him one evening to the mouth of the Zaire, and there sold him into slavery

The slave-ship was wrecked; but Cuffy got ashore on the island of Jamaica, where he was very much surprised to see some of his countrymen, dressed and armed like white men, in coats of a red colour, with light blue trousers; so he enlisted as a soldier in one of her Majesty's West India Regiments.

Ere long Cuffy was made a corporal; and though he ground his sharp teeth now and then when thinking of his wigwam in Congo, and the treacherous Chenoo his wife, he was very happy, for he had plenty of rice, yams, and sangaree, and as a corporal, carried his black snub nose very high indeed!

From Jamaica his company was ordered to Trinidad, and the whole, a hundred in number, were shipped on board of a Yankee barque which had been freighted for the purpose. Her skipper, on seeing such a choice lot of tall and handsome young negroes, proposed to their captain (a reckless fellow, who was steeped to the lips in debt and all kinds of West Indian dissipation) to bear away for the Southern States of the Union, and there sell the whole as slaves. Singular as it may seem, the captain, who owed more money in Trinidad than he could ever hope to pay, accepted the proposal, and the soldiers of this company of H.M. West India Regiment, instead of garrisoning the isle where the "mother of the cocoa" blooms, were duly landed at Charleston in South Carolina, where they were all sold to the highest bidders. The skipper and captain put the money in their pockets, leaving the astonished lieutenant and ensign to get back to headquarters in Jamaica as they best could.

Cuffy's new master proved a severe one, and under his lash he often sighed for the rice, yams, and his quiet duty as sentinel under a sunshade, or the high authority he could wield as corporal over Scipio, Sambo, or Julius Cæsar, in the days when he was the white man's comrade; but one day Cuffy lost his temper, and gave his master a tap on the head with a sugar-hoe!

Then, without waiting to see whether or not he had killed him, he fled into the woods—crossed the Savannah river, and getting on board a British vessel became a sailor, and within one year thereafter, was shipped, as cook, on board the *Leda*.

The rest of our crew were all steady and hardy men, and Paul Reeves, the senior mate, was the model of an English sailor.

The wind had changed during the night; thus, when next day dawned, we were still in sight of Cape St. Francis—a snow-covered headland, which shone white and drearily, as the sun came up from the blue sea.

Hartly expressed some impatience at our progress as we trod to and fro aft the mainmast in the clear, cold, bracing air of the morning, while the odour of a hot breakfast, which Cuffy was preparing, came in whiffs from the galley.

"Never mind," said I; "the wind will soon change again—I can see by the clouds there are contrary currents overhead; and when once among the ice, we shall have great fun!"

"Fun! I don't know much about that," said Hartly, who, like every seaman, was put in a sulky mood by a foul wind.

"We shall have perils to encounter!"

"Perils may be fun to one so young as you, Jack," said Hartly, pausing thoughtfully; "however, in our trade, I have ever found that peril and

D

profit go together. Think over all we have read of what Parry, Ross, Scoresby, Franklin, and Kane underwent in those regions of ice and snow; and I do not remember the word *fun* occurring once in their narratives."

"Well," said I, abashed by his monitory tone, "we shall have excitement, at all events."

"Both excitement and danger, I grant you," said he, as we resumed the usual quarter-deck step and trod to and fro again: "it is a well-paying speculation, a sealing expedition; and, by Jove! it would need to be so to compensate poor fellows for all they undergo in such a rigorous season, and in such seas as those which sweep round the frozen rocks and shores of Newfoundland and the drearier Labrador in the blustering month of March. Some crews are frozen in, far at sea, for months and months, till all perish of starvation; others are lost in detached parties on the ice-fields, in fogs, and are never found again. Some are swept out to sea on broken floes, or fall through holes in the ice, and are never more seen. Then the strongest ships are often crushed, as you would crush an egg upon an anvil, by the ice-fields, masses of which, perhaps a hundred miles in extent, are whirled, dashed, and split against each other by opposite currents, with a sound so frightful, that one might well imagine the last day was at hand, or that chaos had come again! Ah, we should have some profit, after encountering all that!"

" I should think so," said I while glancing at my watch, and reflecting that Mr. Uriah Skrew would, about this time, find the farewell letter I had left for him on my desk in the counting-room.

" But I do not say all this, Jack Manly, to cast you down," said Hartly, laughing ; " for you will always be safe with me, as you know I never can be drowned, while wearing *this* ring."

" Do you really believe in it ?" I inquired.

" Why, I dont know, Jack ; but I should not like to lose it now : we sailors have strange fancies at times, but, with all our alleged superstition, are, I cannot help thinking, more religious than you landsmen. One who finds his daily bread upon the waters, and is for ever struggling with the wild elements by night and day, must at times think solemnly of the mighty Hand and Will that fashioned them out of thin air."

" But your ring ?"

" She who gave it me was a strange old woman, whom we called Mother Jensdochter—a kind of Norna of the Fitful Head, who lived, or for aught I know, lives still, in a hut at the base of Mount

Hecla, in Iceland. I was wrecked there, when on a voyage in the *Princess*, of Hull, bound for Arch-angel, five years ago. This witch occupied a regular Icelandic hut. It was built of wreck and drift wood, caulked with moss and earth, roofed with rafters of whale-ribs covered with turf, and having in the centre a hole for a chimney. Her bed was a mere box of seaweed, feathers, and down; but I seldom saw any house of a better kind in Iceland."

" Well ?"

" She used to sell fair winds or foul, blessings or maledictions, as the matter might be, to the fisher-men of the fiords. She would give, as the simple folks believed, a fair wind that would carry a craft as far as Cape Horn without lifting tack or sheet; or a curse that would sink the *Royal Albert* line-o'-battle ship, for a loaf of ground codfish, or a bottle of hockettle oil for the iron cruse that hung from her whalebone rafters; but she conceived a strong regard for me, because I had saved her miserable life in a snowstorm one night, and carried her in my arms— ugh! what a precious armful she was!—to her wigwam. She used to assure me that whenever there was a battle being fought anywhere in the world, the terrible mountain that overhung her dwelling vomited black ashes and stones; and then, as she sat at her door, with her long grey locks hanging over her fierce red eyes, she could see troops of infernal spirits carrying the souls of the damned, shrieking through the air, towards the flaming crater. The noise of the ice-floes dashed against the shore, she alleged to be the groans of others, who were doomed to endure excess of cold for eternity, even as those in Hecla were to endure excess of heat; and she had many other fancies wild enough to make a poor Jack Tar's hair stand up on end!

"Near her hut stood a conical knoll, covered with fine green grass, and thence named the Grœnbierg. There, she asserted, by putting an ear to the ground, she could hear the large-headed gnomes and little bandy-legged dwarfs, who dwelt in it, busy at work, fashioning trinkets and curiously carved goblets—especially at Yule, where the clink of their tiny hammers rang like chime-bells on little anvils; and the puff of their bellows and forge could be heard, with the jingle of gold and silver coins, and opening and shutting of quaintly-carved and iron-bound treasure-chests, which they were shoving to and fro, and hiding in the bowels of the mountain. She fell asleep there one evening, and dreamed that the Grœnbierg opened, and there came forth a little man in a red cloak and pair of puffy breeches, with a white beard the entire length of his body (that is, about two feet,) and he bestowed this ring upon her, with a promise that whoever wore it was free from all danger hereafter. He then vanished into a mole-track on the hill-side. Mother Jensdochter awoke, and found the ring upon her finger, where it remained, until, in a burst of gratitude, she bestowed it on me, with the comfortable assurance (I give you the yarn, Jack, for what it is worth) that I 'could never be drowned while it remained on my finger.' Hans Peterkin—forward there!"

"Ay, ay, sir."

"Brace those foreyards sharper up; set the fore and main staysails and foretopmast staysail; and keep her a point or so further off the land.—And now, Jack, come below, for Cuffy has gone down with the bacon and coffee, piping hot, too."

Leaving Hans, the second mate, in charge of the deck, with orders to announce the slightest indication of a change of wind, we descended to breakfast with the appetites of hawks.

On this morning only two of our sealing companions were visible, and these were at the far horizon to the eastward; so as we were forced by change of wind to hug the land, we soon lost sight of them, and, ere noonday, were alone upon the sea.

CHAPTER V.

KIDD THE PIRATE.

WE had scarcely lost sight of Cape St. Francis when the wind became light and variable, and one of those dense fogs peculiar to that region settled surely and slowly, densely and darkly, over land and sea. We shortened sail, and sent ahead the jolly-boat with four hands in her, to feel our way as it were; while Paul Reeves kept sounding ever and anon, for in that ocean of strong currents, with a slight wind from the eastward, and a shore of reefs and shoals upon our lee, every precaution was necessary.

The raw cold of a fog upon a wintry sea in that latitude of ice and snow must be *felt* to be understood. The clear bracing frost, however intense, may be endured; but this chill and murky dampness made one intensely miserable.

As we crept along, a strange sound reached us from time to time.

" What is that ?" I asked.

"The voices of the penguins," replied Hartly—
" the Baccalao birds. We are off that island ; and
their cries are as good as fog-guns to people situated
as we are. See ! the fog lights a bit ; and now
there is the land about two miles off, on the lee
bow !"

As he spoke, the dense bank of vapour which
shrouded sea, land, and sky, parted for a few
minutes ; a gleam of brilliant sunshine fell upon the
rough and precipitous rocks of the wild and desert
isle named Baccalao, which, in summer and winter,
are alike ever whitened by a species of guano, deposited there by the auks or penguins, which we
could see hovering above them in countless myriads,
uttering shrill cries while they soared, wheeled, and
flew hither and thither, as if to warn us of our
danger in being so near those treacherous reefs,
which are a source of terror to mariners. Their
dangers are only seen, however, by the daring egg-
gatherers, who come from the mainland in summer,
and sling themselves by ropes from the summit of
the cliff, to rifle the nests ; although these poor
birds are specially under the protection of Government, by a proclamation, being sea-marks, or danger-
signals (as we found them) in foul or foggy weather.

With some interest I surveyed the stern cliffs of Baccalao, as they were the first land seen by Cabot, the Grand Pilot of England, after ploughing the mighty Atlantic in his little caravel; and he named them in his joy *La Prima Vista*, though a "vista" grim enough.

"The shore is dark, dreary, and sterile," said I to Hartly.

"Yes," said he, "but there are many strange stories of treasure being buried there by the pirates in old times."

"Do you see that deep chasm in the rocks in the north end of the isle?" said Paul Reeves, lowering his voice impressively as he pointed to the land.

"Yes, it seems quite black among the snow."

"That is *not* snow, but the deposit of the Baccalao birds," said the mate. "In the old buccaneering times, the pirates are said to have buried their treasure there; and a cask branded with the King's broad arrow, and the name *Adventure*, was once found in it. Now all the world knows that the *Adventure* was the ship of the famous Captain Kidd, who cheated King William out of the finest craft in the English navy."

"How?" said I.

"Let us hear," added Hartly.

"At a time when all the seas about the coasts of North and South America and the West India Islands were swarming with buccaneer craft, manned by desperadoes of every country, who made war upon all ships that sailed the ocean and were unable to resist them, the Government of King William III. selected a mariner of doubtful reputation, named Captain William Kidd, who volunteered to root out those sea-hawks, who persecuted the thrifty traders of New Amsterdam."

"King William acted on the principle of setting a thief to catch a thief."

"Exactly so, Jack," said Hartly, "for Kidd, though ostensibly a merchant-mariner, was something of a smuggler, and had done a little in the way of picarooning. He was always heard of in out-of-the-way places, departing on voyages no one knew whither, and coming from places never heard of before. Then he was always followed by a crew of well-armed, black-muzzled, drinking, swearing, tearing fellows, who were as flush of money as if they had been at the overhauling of Havannah. But go a-head, Paul."

"Well," resumed the mate, "in 1695 Kidd sailed down Channel in the *Adventure* galley, of forty-four guns, with a royal pennant flying, duly commis-

sioned by King William to fight all buccaneers, and
his crew were all selected by *himself*. But Master
Kidd was barely off the Lizard when he hauled
down the King's pennant, hoisted the skull and
crossbones, and bore away for the East Indies. He
burned two towns in Madeira, and after plundering
and sinking every craft he could overmatch, reached
the entrance of the Red Sea, where he captured a
Queda merchantman, the cargo of which lined the
pockets of himself and his followers to their complete satisfaction.

" Queda is a town of Asia, situated on the western
coast of the peninsula of Malacea; and so Kidd was
cunning enough to attempt passing-off this capture
as a crusade against the enemies of Christianity; but,
unfortunately for him, the ship was commanded by
a Scotchman, and people did not believe in crusaders
under Orange William.

" A year or two after this, he was cruising off the
American coast, and in dread of the King's ships,
which were all on the look-out for him, he ran
north as far as Newfoundland, and was alleged to
have buried on its coast all the treasure amassed on
his long and rambling voyage; but *where*, no one
could exactly say, until the old barrel head, marked
Adventure, and bearing the King's broad arrow,

found in yonder cavern, seemed to indicate Baccalao as being the place. Moreover, he is known to have run up Conception Bay in quest of the gold and silver rocks which Frobisher and Sir Humphrey Gilbert averred were to be seen there."

"Rocks of gold and silver!" said I, incredulously.

"They are only the fire-stones of the Red Indians, and emit sparks when struck together," said Hartly.*

"His treasure," continued the mate, "if he had any, was never found; though *he* was, for Richard Coote, Earl of Bellamont, and Governor of New England, caught him one day in 1701, when swaggering about the streets of Boston, and sent him home to King William, who lost no time in hanging him. But he died as hard as he had lived, for the rope broke with his weight in Execution Dock, so he was reeved up again with a new one.

"He was hung in chains on the banks of the Thames, but his body disappeared in the night, and

---

* They were the solid iron pyrites which deceived the early navigators who visited these barren shores. In the " List of H.M. Royal Navy for 1701," we find among the " fifth-rates, the *Adventure,* 120 men, 44 guns."

the sailors in London declared that he could neither be hanged nor chained, as he had a *charmed* life, having sold his poor soul to the devil. Be that as it may, on the *same night,* in 1701, my Lord Bellamont was found dead in his bed at Boston, and many affirmed that this event had some connexion with Kidd's mysterious disappearance from the gallows, as he was said to have been seen by some of his old shipmates near the dead Governor's house.

" Fishermen when jigging or trawling off Baccalao in the clear moonlight nights, often saw a solitary man sitting on the rocks at the mouth of yonder cavern, but his figure always seemed to melt away into the moonshine when any one approached; so a story went abroad that the island was haunted by the ghost of a drowned man. However, a stout fellow, named Tom Spiller, who was rather bolder than the rest, and who lived alone at Breakheart Point, where he had a little hut and stage for drying the fish he caught, went off to the island one night, when there was little cloud and a bright moon. The sea was calm, for there was but a puff of wind off the land from time to time.

" Tom Spiller was a brave and devil-may-care kind of fellow, whom I knew well, for he was an

old man when I went to sea with him first as a boy,
so I have often heard him tell the story without
variation or leeway, or shaking out a new reef by
way of a change.

"On approaching the island, he saw the solitary
figure sitting on the rocks at the mouth of the deep
black chasm, motionless, with his head resting, as it
were, sorrowfully on the palm of his right hand, and
his eyes fixed apparently on the sea that rippled to
his feet, though it boiled and roared in white foam
over the reefs that lay a few fathoms off outside.

"Tom steered his boat straight for the cave, and
now, when the towering rocks of the desert isle
were over his head, covered with thousands upon
thousands of wild auks, screaming, whirling, and
flapping their wings, as if to scare him away ; when
the deep black chasm in which the sea was gurgling
and moaning yawned before him, and everything
seemed so weird and wan in the pale moonlight, he
did feel queer, and more so when the solitary man,
instead of melting into thin air as usual, turned his
white face towards him, and arose, just as he let go
the halyards, lowered the brown flapping sail, and
running his boat into the cave, adroitly noosed a
rope over a large stone to moor her, and stepped
ashore.   Tom's heart was beating wildly and

strangely, for he was determined to discover whether this figure, which he had so often seen from the sea, and which had so invariably eluded his brother fishermen, was man, ghost, or devil.

"He perceived that the stranger was clad in an old-fashioned dress, his coat having large metal buttons, broad pocket-flaps, and deep cuffs. He was ghastly pale, his glassy eyes glistened in the moonlight, and dark crimson blood was flowing from what appeared to be a pistol-shot in his left temple.

"'What seek you here?' he asked, in a voice so hollow that the terrified fisherman, who now repented sorely of his rashness, knew not whether the sound came from the spectre's white lips, from the depth of the dreary chasm, or from the sea. 'Speak,' continued the figure, with mournful earnestness; 'what seek you?'

"'To discover who and what you are,' said Tom.

"'May you never be what I was, or what I am,' replied the other, sadly.

"'But what are you?'

"'A restless spirit.'

"Tom's knees bent under him, for the pale eyes of that cold white visage seemed to pierce his soul.

" ' A wretched spirit—left here by a fiend to guard his ill-gotten spoil—so begone, I charge you.'

" The fisherman shrank back on hearing these strange words, while the gloomy terrors of the scene —the screaming of the Baccalao birds that whirled in a cloud about him, the dashing of the waves upon the reef, and the mournful gurgle of the backwash within the vast cavern, with the weird glimpses of the moon as the white clouds sailed swiftly past her face—all combined to make this interview a dreadful one.

" Suddenly there was a sound of oars to seaward, the spirit seemed to become excited, and clasped his thin white hands.

" ' See ! see ! he comes !' he exclaimed. ' Kidd the pirate ! Kidd, my murderer ! But he comes, blessed be God ! to release me after a hundred years of restless watching and penance !'

" For you must know that this occurred, as Tom Spiller told me, in 1801.

" ' Land ho !' cried a deep hoarse voice from the sea, while Spiller, overcome by terror, shrank behind a fragment of rock.

" ' Hilloa !' answered the spirit, in nautical fashion.

" ' Clouds and thunder ! why the devil don't you

show a light?' cried the strange voice, as a large barge full of men shot round a promontory, against which the waves were dashing in foam. On it came—on and on—at every stroke of the oars, till they were all triced up in true man-o'-war fashion as she sheered into the creek, and a man sprang on shore, uttering a tempest of oaths and maledictions.

"Tom Spiller now fancied that they were all dressed in the fashion of a hundred years ago, with deep square-skirted coats, long flowing perriwigs, and little three-cocked hats, and that all were pale, silent, and spectral; in short, it was a boat manned by unquiet spirits! Strangely enough, he felt less afraid of tchm *all* than of *one*, and continued to gaze at them like a person in a dream.

"The man who sprang ashore was a short, squat fellow of ferocious aspect; his battered visage was covered with cuts and patches of black plaster; a hellish spark glittered in each of his eyes. He wore a coarse perriwig with long curls, a three-cocked hat, an old-fashioned blue coat, covered with tarnished lace, and brass buttons; he had also a pair of brass-barrelled Spanish pistols, and a hanger sustained by a broad belt.

"*Two* ropes were knotted round his neck, which was bare, and pieces of rusty chain were dangling

E

at his wrists and ankles. Then the marrow froze in the bones of Tom Spiller, for he knew that he looked upon William Kidd, the pirate, who had been *twice* hanged a hundred years before in Execution Dock.

" 'Now, you canting, cowardly lubber, why the henckers didn't you hang out a light?' he bellowed in a hoarse voice.

" ' I have been in the dark these hundred years,' replied the spirit, meekly.

" 'Likely enough; seas and thunder! you were the faintest-hearted fellow in the *Adventure.'*

" ' I suffered sorely at your hands since you captured the ship of Queda, of which I was captain, and made me a prisoner in yon galley.'

" 'Bah !' thundered Kidd.

" ' I have repented me of my sins in life,' said the spirit, mournfully.

" ' 'Sblood and plunder!' shouted the other, with a diabolical laugh ; ' I shot you through the head, as a canting Scotsman, on this night one hundred years ago, and buried you here—you know for what purpose.'

" 'That my unquiet spirit might watch your buried treasure,' moaned the other.

" 'Right,' chuckled the pirate ; ' I shot you as I

would have done my lord the Earl of Bellamont, though he was Governor of New England and Admiral of all the seas about it, for that long-snouted Dutch lubber, William of Orange, who sent him to lord it over the Yankees.'

" ' I have waited and watched your treasure long, and now am anxious for the repose of the grave.'

" On hearing this, Kidd and his boat's crew laughed, and gnashed their teeth; but a few there were who wept and wailed heavily, and the sound of their lamentation was fearful as it mingled with the chafing of the surge.

" ' I have some fine things stowed away here in Baccalao,' said Kidd; ' but I have some that are better still in the haunted Kaatskill Mountain, and at Tapaan Zee, up the Hudson.'

" The spirit-watcher groaned.

" ' Since I saw you last, brother, I have been twice hanged and strung in chains on the banks of the Thames—ha! ha! at Gravesend Reach.'

" ' Hanged!'

" ' Yes, by all the devils in New Amsterdam!— HANGED! Hanged by order of him of pious, glorious, and immortal memory—by Orange Billy, who assassinated the De Witts in Holland, who murdered eighty men, women, and children in cold

blood in Scotland; who abandoned his soldiers at
Steinkirk; who boiled and burned women alive in
London for coining a few brass halfpence; and who
departed this life amid the prayers of canting hypo-
crites and lawn-sleeved parasites, on the 8th day of
March, 1701! He roasts now, for some of his
pranks, I can tell you! But heave a-head, brother!
we must ship our cargo, and be off to-night for Cape
Cod at New Amsterdam (or New York, as the folks
call it now-a-days), ere the moon wanes or the tide
falls. Where is the plunder?'

" The sad spirit-watcher pointed to a place which
seemed to have opened in the rocky cavern; and
there Tom Spiller could see, by the beams of the
moon, heaps of gold and silver vessels, sparkling
jewels and trinkets, with veritable pyramids of gold
and silver coins of every nation and of every size,
piled up in confusion.

" Bewildered by this sight, he permitted rather
too much of his figure to be seen; for suddenly a
yell of rage came from the spectre boat's crew; and
Kidd, drawing one of the long brass pistols from his
broad buff girdle, uttered a dreadful oath—

" ' A spy!' he exclaimed; ' take *that* and perish !'

" He fired full at the head of Tom, who felt the
ball pass through his brain like a red-hot arrow, and

he sank upon the rocks—where he found himself
lying stiff enough when he awoke next morning,
and saw the Baccalao birds wheeling about in the
sunshine."

"So the whole affair was only a dream!" said I.

"I cannot say," replied Reeves; "for strangely
enough, an old Spanish pistol, with a strong smell
of powder about it, and 'W K.' on the butt, was
lying on the rocks by his side. Tom lost no time,
you may be assured, in jumping into his boat, and
clapping on all sail to leave the island astern; but
after that night the spirit was seen no more at
the mouth of the cavern, for Kidd had come to
release him, or to take away his treasure."

"And Tom Spiller?"

"Forsook his hut at Breakheart Point, and went
to sea for many years: he felt unhappy, for the
parsons say that folks always are so who have con-
versed with ghosts; but his mind dwelt for ever on
the treasure in the cavern, and he never ceased to
spin yarns about it, and express hopes that some, if
not all that he saw, might yet remain. He returned
to Breakheart Point about twenty years ago, an old
and white-haired man; and one night, accompanied
by three men armed with picks and shovels, sailed
in search of the treasure; but they never reached

the island, for a tempest came on and drove their
boat to the northward. He tried to fetch Ragged
Harbour, but was blown right across Conception
Bay for more than thirty miles, and was drowned
at La Cabo Bueno Vista, on a rock called, to this
hour, Spiller's Point.

"As for Captain Kidd, he has never been seen
since, though some folks hereabout say he commands
the *Black Schooner*, which has overhauled so many
of our merchantmen and escaped the Queen's
cruisers. So that is my yarn, Mr. Manly."

"Steady, Paul, steady," said Hartly; "the fog
has concealed your haunted island again."

"Steady it is, sir; but we had better take a pull
at these larboard tacks, otherwise we may not be
able to clear the three rocks that lie to the northward of Baccalao; and I think we can hear the
breakers already!"

CHAPTER VI.

THE BLACK SCHOONER.

LONG ere the mate's story was concluded, the dense fog—chilly, white, and drenching—had shrouded the dreary isle of Baccalao, and the voices of the penguins alone indicated its locality ; but they became fainter, until we lost the sound altogether as we ran further to the north.

Now a furious snow-storm came on ; thick and fast the white flakes fell ceaselessly aslant through a dark-grey sky upon the winter sea (for in that region there is *no* spring), covering the rigging, the decks, and storm-jackets of the watch, who shrank to leeward, while the wind, which blew keenly from the N.N.E., and thermometer, which had sunk very low, made me begin to reflect that there were more unpleasant places in the world than the counting-room of Mr. Uriah Skrew.

This snow-storm continued for three or four days,

during which the whole seamanship of Hartly, Reeves, and Hans Peterkin was required to prevent the *Leda* being driven upon a lee shore. By chart and soundings they were constantly at work, to keep her off a land which was veiled in obscurity, for the wind was dead and strong against us; and frequently through the blinding snow, and grey hazy drift to leeward, we could hear the sullen booming of breakers, as they rolled in foam that froze upon the granite rocks and islets about Cape Freels.

This foul weather lasted for several days, and weary of beating fruitlessly to windward, when the storm abated, and the sky became again blue and serene, we found ourselves under easy sail, at the rate of four knots an hour or so, passing the Twillingate Isles, which lie between the Bay of Exploits and the vast Bay of Notre Dame. They were covered with snow, and are desolate, bleak, and little known, as on that part of the coast there are only about one hundred and fifty inhabitants—poor people—who, after fishing for cod and salmon in summer, quit their wigwams in winter to live in the sheltered woods, or sail south towards St. John. And now we began to get ready our boats and guns, and with telescopes to sweep the snow-clad shore for seals, and the open sea for ice-floes.

It was about the hour of six; the sun had just set, and the western sky was all a-blaze with fiery-coloured light, which tinged with roseate hues the waves that rolled upon the bleak and snow-clad shore. Captain Hartly took the wheel, and Reeves stood anxiously close by the binnacle, for we had to weather a long, sharp, and lofty promontory which abutted like a wall of rock into the ocean, and round which there eddied a swift and dangerous current. The wind, though now off the land, was too light to enable us to make headway against the stream.

On the brig we had but little "way," and a general exclamation of satisfaction rose from the hitherto silent crew, when the *Leda shaved*—as they phrased it—past the promontory, and we saw a deep cove of blue water opening beyond it; but lo!

There lay at anchor a schooner—a long, low, sharply prowed and rakish-like craft—with her hull painted black as jet could be, and with a number of rough-looking fellows crowding along her gunwale. We were not three hundred yards apart.

"Reeves, take the wheel," cried Hartly, in an excited voice. "The glass, Cuffy, the spy-glass!" he added with sharp energy, snatching from the hands of Snowball the telescope which usually hung on two hooks in the companion; "a row of ugly dogs they are that man her. By Heaven, she is the *Black Schooner!*"

"The *Black Schooner!*" we all exclaimed with something of dismay in our varying tones ; and I felt, that with Paul Reeves's grim legend about Captain Kidd fresh in our memory, we had some cause for alarm in meeting with this robber ship upon those solitary seas.

"Are you sure, Hartly?" I asked.

"Not a doubt of it! see, Reeves—she is a two-topsail schooner!"

"What does that mean?" said I.

"A brig without tops, in fact."

A kind of growling cheer, mingled with wild and insolent halloing, rose from her crew on beholding us suddenly come round the abrupt promontory, from the brow of which a fringe of gigantic icicles over-hung the sea. A commotion was instantly ob-servable on deck ; a man in authority sprang up the companion-ladder, and we heard him in a loud and clear voice ordering sail to be instantly made on the schooner as we altered our course.

"Man the windlass-bars—up anchor—rouse it to the catheads with a will, my boys! Shake out everything fore and aft—every stitch that will draw. Stand by the jib and flying-jib halliards," he shouted.

After a pause, during which we heard the clanking of the windlass pauls, as her anchor was started, and would soon be a-cockbill, and dangling by its ring, we heard his voice again.

"Up with the jib and flying-jib now—sheets to starboard! Heave and away—presto! my Jack Spaniards. Stand by topgallant and topsail sheets and halliards. Bear a hand, you French devils! Well done, my Kentucky rowdies!"

In less than three minutes the swelling of the jib and other head-sails, as well as the motion of the schooner when her bows fell round, proved that she was under weigh. These orders, which were obeyed with skilful alacrity, seemed to indicate alike the mixed character of her crew and the hostility of their intentions.

"Ready a gun there forward! sheet home and hoist away, topsails and topgallant sails!"

This alarming order, uttered in a loud voice, rang distinctly upon the clear frosty air, and, on the other hand, Captain Hartly was not slow in his preparations to avoid her.

"By Jove!" he exclaimed, "this is the very craft we have heard so much about, and for the capture of which the Governor offers 500l. I have no wish to be caught by these fellows—see, they are shaking out a couple of reefs in her fore and aft mainsail already! Hands make all sail—Reeves, set every. thing that will draw—square away the after yards."

"Ay, ay, sir," said Reeves, jumping about and setting all the men to the yards, braces, and halliards ; " port the smallest bit—keep her full—so—• steady !"

" Maldito los Inglesos renegados !" ("Curse the English runaways !") cried a Spaniard, shaking his clenched hands at us over her starboard bow.

" Caramba !" cried another.

"Sangbleu !" added a Frenchman, " stop hare— lie to—or it vill be ze vorser for you."

" Will it, you rascally thief !" shouted Hartly, as his eyes flashed and his cheek glowed with excitement: "Manly, look alive, my lad! load all the double-barrelled rifles in the cabin. Snowball, get up the kegs of powder and slugs. We shall not be overhauled by a pirate without having a skirmish first."

" Luckily for us the wind is off the land, and it freshens too," said Reeves : " we shall beat her when running before the wind; but she would come up with us hand over hand on a taut bowline. It was *on* a wind she overtook the Bristol clipper."

In the red glow of the winter sunset, we saw the

foam flying on each side of her sharp bows as the breeze freshened, and she rolled heavily from side to side; while the *Leda*, being square-rigged, had a greater spread of canvas, and caught more of the wind: thus, notwithstanding that our dangerous pursuer was built for sailing fast, as Paul Reeves foretold, she was no match for us, when running right before the wind.

Our crew, half of whom were only poor seal-fishers, became very much excited; but inspired by the example of Hartly, Reeves, and myself, they proceeded to load all the sealing guns and muskets, lest the schooner might lower her boats to overtake us and attempt to board.

The stern and confident order to get "ready a gun," was repeated more than once before we got beyond hearing; but as no gun was ever fired, we believed this to be a mere bravado to frighten us into shortening sail, till she might run alongside and board us, when a ruinous scene of plunder, if not of bloodshed, would be sure to ensue.

"She sails with the speed of an arrow," said I, while carefully loading and capping my rifle.

"This *Black Schooner* was one of the craft employed in protecting the French fishery of Miquelon, on the south side of the island," said Hartly; "but

her crew mutinied, shipped some runaways of all
countries and colours, and turned slavers. These
rascals have committed several outrages hereabouts
by sea and land, but have always escaped our cruisers,
as she alternately shows a British, French, and
Yankee ensign, and runs all kinds of paint-strokes
along her bends."

On, on, we bore; and on, on, she came after us,
with the still freshening breeze, the foam flying
before her bows and ours; but ere long we were
evidently half a mile apart.

She was a handsome clipper-like craft of about
two hundred tons' burthen, coppered to the bends;
her lower masts were long and heavy, so as to carry
fore and aft sails of immense spread upon a wind,
with a square sail, top and topgallant sail aloft.

"Massa Hartly—Massa Captain—look out!"
exclaimed Cuffy Snowball, who had armed himself
with a musket, and stood in soldier-fashion at "the
ready," grinning over the taffrail at the rolling
schooner.

"Look out for what?" said Hans Peterkin.

"Something make you all look white as de
debbil."

"What do you mean by *white*," asked the carpenter, "when we all know the devil is black?"

" In my country him white, sare," replied Cuffy, angrily.

" Then," said Hartly, to keep up the spirits of his crew by jesting, " what colour do you think he is, Cuffy ?"

" I tink him *blue*," replied the prudent negro ; and then he added with a yell, " dere come something will make you look blue too, Massa !"

As he spoke, a puff of white smoke rose from the bow of the *Black Schooner ;* the report of a musket rang in the air, and a conical rifle-ball whistled past the ear of Hartly, and sank with a heavy *thud* into the mainmast.

CHAPTER VII.

CUFFY SNOWBALL fired his musket at our pursuer, whether with or without effect we know not; but, in reply, a confused discharge of firearms followed, and the balls pattered among the rigging, and knocked little splinters from our spars and gunwale.

"Now, my lads," said Hartly, "let fly at her with everything you have—sealing-guns and rifles!"

This order was executed with alacrity. We had four good rifles and ten long-barrelled and wide-muzzled sealing-guns, each of which sent ten or twelve slugs of lead *whirring* through the air at every discharge, and we blazed away right valiantly at the crowd of rascals in the schooner's bows; but so great was the distance between us, that I am certain our fire fell harmlessly into the sea—the rifle shots alone could have told with effect.

On first deliberately levelling my rifle (a fine Enfield, presented to me by my father on leaving Peckham) at a man in the starboard bow of the pirate, a strange sensation came over me !

I lowered my weapon and paused; but a shot that struck one of the davits at which the stern-boat hung, removed my momentary, and at that unpleasant crisis most unnecessary scruple.

I levelled again—fired and reloaded, and without considering whether or not I had killed a man, continued to pepper away with all the coolness and precision of Cuffy Snowball, the ex-corporal of H.M. West India Regiment.

"Run up our ensign, and let her rascally crew see it while there is light," said Hartly. "Paul Reeves, rig out the lower studding-sail booms forward, and bring aft those two carronades and the small anchor, to trim her more by the stern. Tom Hammer, see to this !"

"Ay, ay, sir," was the ready response.

The orders were promptly obeyed. The small anchor and two little guns, for which we unfortunately had only powder for signals, were brought aft; the sharp bows of the *Leda* thus rode more easily over the water. The lower studding-sails were rapidly spread and hoisted up; and then we flew through

F

the darkening sea till its water seemed to smoke alongside, and bubbled in snowy froth under the counter, leaving a long white wake, like that of a steamer, astern.

Closely in this long wake followed our pursuer, with deadly pertinacity.

It is impossible to convey in words any idea of the excitement of this chase—this flight and pursuit—this race of rivalry, of life and death! The daring ruffians who manned the schooner had committed several murders and robberies on sea and land. They had overhauled and rifled several merchant ships, carrying off compasses, charts, provisions, watches, money, and everything of value: thus, to have undergone such a ransacking at their hands—even if our lives were spared— would effectually have marred our expedition for that year.

They were evidently well armed, for their rifle-balls flew thick and fast about us. The cracking report, and the *pingeing* sound of the conical shot that followed every red flash which broke over the sharp bows of the schooner, added considerably to our anxiety to escape, and to our exasperation at being thus molested on the high seas, and within two hundred miles of where we had left one of her

Majesty's sloops of war in the harbour of St. John, but frozen in, unfortunately.

Though these missiles struck the brig's stern and rigging incessantly, we had only one man hit—an Irish seal-fisher, who had left a wife and family at Dead Man's Bay, to try his fortune with us in the North. A ball pierced his shoulder, smashing the collar-bone; and the poor fellow sank on the deck with a shrill cry of agony. A lad named Ridly had his cheek grazed by another shot.

The dusk was fast increasing; but the red flush of the winter sunset yet lingered in the western sky; the snow-clad islets that stud the Bay of Exploits had assumed a dark purple hue, and the sea through which we were careering, northwest, towards the Bay of Notre Dame, wore a deep and sombre blue.

Clearly defined against the dusky and ruddy sky, we could see the pursuing schooner, her tall slender spars swaying from side to side, with every stitch of snow-white canvas spread upon them; and she tore through the waves like a giant bird, swimming in the wake of dead water that ran like a long path astern of us.

We had everything set aloft and alow; to her very trucks the *Leda* was covered with swelling canvas, and she was a beautiful sight! The keen and anxious eyes of Hartly, who was at the wheel, scanned ever and anon the taut cordage, the bending masts, and then he would cast a fierce glance astern.

"We are leaving her fast, sir," said Paul Reeves, confidently; "in another hour we shall be far enough apart to feel comfortable."

"Bravo, my little *Leda* !" responded my friend; "she is trimmed and masted to perfection ! You see, Jack, how a square-rigged craft has the advantage over even a sharp little serpent with a floating sheet, like that rascally schooner !"

Her crew still continued to blaze at us with their rifles; but ere long the bullets fell far short, for we were now more than a thousand yards apart, and with cheers of derision we continued to surge through the darkening ocean.

"If we had only possessed a few round-shot, we might have knocked some of their sticks away with these two useless carronades," said Hartly, as he now relinquished the wheel to Hans Peterkin, his second mate, and ordered glasses of grog to be served all round. "Corporal Cuffy, do you think you could have knocked her mainboom away, when the sea is so smooth ?"

"Like to knock all him brains out !" replied the

Congo-man with a savage grin; for, inspired by some of his old African instincts, Snowball was the only person on board who regretted that we had not enjoyed a hand-to-hand conflict with these outlaws.

But now the darkness of the descending night, together with the gathering clouds and haze, concealed the schooner from us.

We extinguished all lights on board, and ere long when a red spark about seven miles astern indicated that she was still tracking us, Hartly took in his studding-sails, reduced the canvas on the brig, brought his larboard tacks on board, and bore up for Cape St. John, the boundary of the French shore, to land our wounded man, who was suffering great agony from his compound fracture, and with whom, as we had no medical officer, it would have been impossible to pursue our voyage.

This rencontre, chase, and escape, formed a staple topic for conversation to all on board, and till the night was far advanced no one thought of turning in.

When day broke we found ourselves close in shore, on the northern side of the great Bay of Notre Dame, with Cape St. John bearing about three miles off on our lee bow. We swept the sea with our glasses, but not a sail was visible in the offing, nor all along the snow-clad coast. Save Cuffy Snowball, all expressed their satisfaction at this; but we were not yet entirely done with our sable acquaintance, the *Black Schooner.*

CHAPTER VIII.

OUR REVENGE SCHEMED.

WE came to anchor, handed our topsails, but merely hauled up our courses, so as to be ready for sea at a moment's notice. We were in a little sheltered cove, abreast of a small village of wooden huts, surrounded by fences that were buried deep in the frozen snow.

These huts, like all others in this wild terra nova, were built of fir-poles with the bark on, braced or pegged closely together, and having chimneys of rough stone built without mortar. Bark and sods formed the roofs, and all the crevices were carefully caulked with moss and mud.

There, in a wretched and dreary region, dwelt— and, I presume, still dwell—a little Irish colony of fifty or sixty poor souls, who fished for cod in summer and seals in winter, each family herding

together for warmth in the same apartment with
their pigs, fowls, and the shaggy dogs which dragged
in harness the stunted trees that formed their fuel,
and which were cut in the adjacent bush—the desolate place which once formed the summer hunting-
grounds of the extinct Red men of the island.

Our anchoring in the cove was a great event—
the entire population came forth to gaze and their
dogs to bark at us.

Though Newfoundland is larger than England
and Wales together, it is indented by broad bays of
deep water, which run for forty or fifty miles into
the interior, and are but little known.   On some of
these solitary shores are little stations of Europeans,
such as this we visited, so remote from all inter-
course, and so secluded, that their reckoning of time
has become confused as to days, months, and even
years; thus Sunday is frequently held by them in
the *middle* of a week.

To the care of these pioneers, or squatters, we
consigned our wounded man.   By the intensity of
the frost mortification had commenced, so the poor
fellow died a few days after being landed.

We had scarcely conveyed him ashore, when a
man arrived from the bush with a large tree, which
he had cut down, and which his dogs had dragged

easily over the snow (after it was denuded of its
bark and branches) in the usual manner, by having
their traces secured to his hatchet, which was
wedged in the broad end of the log. He informed
us that a schooner—by his description, our identical
Black Schooner—was then at anchor under the lee
of the Gull Island, about five miles distant; and
added that the poor French people at La Scie com-
plained bitterly of the rifling they had undergone at
the hands of her crew, which consisted of forty well-
armed desperadoes, of all nations, but principally
English and Frenchmen.

Here was startling intelligence!

"Only five miles distant, say you?" reiterated
Hartly.

"Yes, sir; and you may see Gull Island from the
mouth of our cove here."

"You are sure she is a schooner?"

"Yes, with masts raking well aft."

"All black in the hull, with slender spars and
double topsails?"

"Sure as I now spake to yer honour," replied our
informant, who was an Irish fisherman and squatter;
"her crew have let go both anchors to make all
snug, and gone in a gang to enjoy themselves, or
rob—which you plaze—I suppose it's all one to

them, at La Scie; bad luck to them, and may the devil fly away with them all!"

"Are they all gone?"

"All except six rapparees, whom I could count from the bush where I was hiding."

"Six—left as a deck-watch, I suppose?"

"Just so; yer honour's right again."

"How long have you lived here?" I inquired, for his brogue was as strong as if he had only left his native Kerry yesterday.

"I have lived here, plaze yer honor, five-and-forty years this last St. Patrick's Day, and have niver had an hour's illness, glory be to God!"

"Five-and-forty years!" I reiterated, with a shudder, while surveying the snow-clad wilderness amid which the wigwams stood.

"How far is La Scie from the Gull Island?" said Hartly, after a pause.

"Six miles, capthin."

"Then by Heaven I'll burn her to the water-edge, or sink her at her anchors!" exclaimed Hartly, who, with all the rapidity of his nature, at once conceived and prepared to execute a very daring scheme.

While the quarter-boat was got ready, and four oars, with as many rifles loaded and capped, and a case of ammunition, were put into her, Hartly, with Paul Reeves, proceeded in the most simple and methodical manner to prepare their apparatus for burning the piratical schooner.

He took a common ship-bucket, and secured an iron ring to the iron handle, for a purpose to be afterwards explained. He filled this bucket with pieces of rope and spun-yarn, well steeped in tar and grease, mixing them with rosin and gunpowder. They were nearly three hours in getting these combustibles prepared to their complete satisfaction; and so impatient were they to put their scheme in execution, that they would scarcely wait until dusk to make the attempt. But the moment the sun set, Hartly issued orders to Paul Reeves and Hans Peterkin to heave short on the anchor to get it apeak, to cast loose the topsails, and prepare the jib for hoisting; and while he started along the coast in the quarter-boat, to follow him under easy sail, keeping pretty well to windward of Gull Island, and out of sight of the schooner. If the night became obscure, on hearing the report of a rifle a blue light was to be burned on board the *Leda*, to indicate her whereabouts.

While Paul Reeves got the brig under weigh, and, favoured by a very light breeze, crept slowly out of the cove, Bob Hartly, with Hammer the carpenter, Cuffy Snowball, and I, started in the sharp little quarter-boat, and aided by a current which there runs north to Cape St. John, pulled swiftly along the shore towards Gull Island, which lies beyond the extremity of the headland.

CHAPTER IX.

OUR REVENGE EXECUTED.

THE evening, as it deepened into night, was calm
and beautiful : as yet the moon had not risen, but
the sky was clear, with an intensity and purity
of blue that can only be found in the icy north, and
studded by ten thousand sparkling stars. Some of
these were so bright as almost to cast our shadows
on the smooth water as we stretched to our oars,
and swept along the snow-white coast.

The latter being nearly destitute of inhabitants,
after we left the cove was voiceless, silent, and
desolate. Not a light was visible, and no sounds
broke the stillness save the booming of the surf on
the rocks of Cape St. John, our own hard breathing,
and the clatter of the oars in the rowlocks. Then
(as that is a species of noise which the water con-
veys to a vast distance) we proceeded to muffle them
by our handkerchiefs, and once more we stretched
out vigorously.

Notwithstanding the intensity of the cold, so invigorating was the exercise of rowing, and so full were our minds of excitement and of our project for destroying the pirate schooner, that we all felt in a glow of heat, and almost uttered a shout when, after pulling about three miles, on clearing the bluff Cape of St. John, on the flinty brow of which the spray was frozen white as it was dashed up by the sea, we saw the steep rocks of Gull Island; and at anchor, half a mile to leeward of it, the dark hull and tall spars of the *Black Schooner !*

The increasing light at one part of the horizon showed that the moon would shortly be up, so we pulled with might and main to get close under the lee of the island, and out of the long brilliant track the Queen of Night would shortly send across the rippling ocean.

"I might have brought an auger and bored a hole or two in her sheathing under water, and so have scuttled her quietly at her anchors," said the carpenter.

"But that boring would have kept us alongside too long," said Hartly; "and the rascals might have got some of their plunder out before she went down; moreover, your auger would have made too much noise. But, hush! we are seen—two fellows are looking over her side !"

"All her boats are gone," said I.

"Yes, to La Scie, except one at the stern."

"They are hailing us, sir," said Hammer.

"Hush! I'll weather the ruffians yet," said Hartly.

We spoke in whispers, while our hearts beat like lightning, as we knew not the issue of our attempt, or the moment we might be fired on from her deck. The schooner rode with both her anchors out, to make sure of her holding-ground in case a squall came suddenly on. Her canvas was neatly handed, her fore and aft foresail and boom mainsail were tightly brailed up, and her topgallant yards sent down.

Though black and sombre, with nothing light about her save her copper, which shone brightly as burnished gold in the clear and starlit sea, she was a beautiful little vessel; and Hartly almost sighed on thinking that he was about to destroy instead of capturing her.

"She is a lovely craft!" said he, "sharp at the bows as a needle below the water-line, clear at the counter, and coppered to the bends. What a glorious yacht she would make!"

"In sheering alongside, take care, sir, they don't scuttle us—by a cold shot, or a large stone," said Hammer.

"Well," replied Hartly, "my friend the Greenland witch said I should never drown; but that does not prevent me from being shot, or hung from the schooner's topsail yard."

As we pulled round across her bows to starboard, keeping pretty well off, we were hailed again.

"Boat—boat ahoy! what are you?"

"Fishermen," replied Hartly.

"From where?"

"La Scie, where all your fellows are enjoying themselves."

"Got any feesh?" asked a Frenchman.

"No—not at this season."

"Any zeels?"

"Seals—no."

"Then prenez-garde, messieurs."

"Which means, in plain English, sheer off, d—n your eyes!" growled the first speaker; but by this time we were close under her starboard counter.

"Sheer off, or it may be the worse for you!"

"What the devil are you lubbers about under the counter?" exclaimed another; "Baptiste, hand me a musket——"

"We have dropped an oar, and our boat has run foul of yours," replied Hartly; adding, in a whisper, "The gimlet, carpenter—quick, the gimlet!"

In less time than I have taken to write these last half-dozen lines, Hartly had screwed the long gimlet into the vessel's side, under her counter, and hooked on the bucket, through the iron ring which he had secured to its handle, and there it hung close to the rudder and stern-post. By the swift application of a single lucifer-match he fired the touch-paper that was to light the carefully-prepared combustibles, the gathering flame of which shot upward from the bucket, and began at once to lick and flicker on the newly-painted planking of the schooner.

"Shove off, and give way—for your lives, give way!" said Hartly, in a hoarse whisper.

"Cut away stern-boat—let hims all burn—agh! agh!" grinned Cuffy, who, by a slash of the knife which hung at his neck, cut adrift the boat which was moored astern. We had not intended thus to destroy the retreat of the wretches on board, but the African was merciless to his enemies, and we had no time to repair his severity.

" Give way," shouted Hartly, as soon as we were clear of her; "clap on dry nippers! By Jove! those lads of the knife and pistol will never come athwart the hawse of the *Leda* again!"

We had not pulled ten strokes from her, ere a flame seemed to play on the water beneath her counter!

G

It spread rapidly between the rudder and stern-post, burning through outer and inner sheathing; penetrating the rudder-case, and reaching the cabin, which was unoccupied, as all the crew were ashore save the six already mentioned, whom we saw loitering amidships.   One was provided with a musket, which no doubt he would have discharged at us, had we lingered another moment alongside.

Suddenly they raised a shout; then we saw them rush aft, when they immediately discovered the vessel to be on fire, and that their only boat was adrift !

He with the musket took a long aim at us, and fired; but as we were now three hundred yards from the schooner, and our boat was alternately rising and falling on the long rolling swell that heaved between Gull Island and Cape St. John, his shot fell far from us.

By this time the schooner was hopelessly on fire; her whole quarter-deck, stern, and cabin, forward to the mainmast, were sheeted with red and roaring flame.   It spread along the deck; it leaped up the well-greased masts like a fiery corkscrew, round the tarred rigging and over the handed canvas, till every-thing was in a blaze; the great fore and aft sails fell from their brails like fiery curtains; then we saw her two tall, slender spars, the long boom of her mainsail, her towering gaffs and topsail yards, all swaying to-and-fro, as the decks fell in and the shrouds sank smouldering into the sea. Then everything went to cinders fore and aft—aloft and alow!

A lurid glare that outshone the light of the rising moon, overspread the calm blue sea, casting a ruddy glow upon our faces as we paused upon our oars, close to the island, where the weird illumination scared all the sea-birds ; thus we heard the shrill scream of the wagel or great grey gull, as he rose with booming wings and flew to seek the darker waters of the offing or the frozen bluffs of Cape St. John, on which the thundering breakers as they reared their heads, gleamed in the double light of red and silver, like showers of diamonds and rubies.

" Jack—see how she burns !" said Hartly : " there goes her mainmast crash into the sea—and now the foremast, a mass of whizzing sparks, with all its top-hamper ! Pull for the island, till the brig comes abreast of it ;" and then cheerily he sang—

> " Haul away, pull away, pull, jolly boys !
> At the mercy of fortune we go,
> *We're in for it now*, and 'tis all folly, boys,
> To be faint or downhearted, yeho !"

By this time the schooner was a mass of fire, and burnt down nearly to her bends. Through the flames we could see the blackened stumps of her timber-heads, standing in a row from stem to stern. Suddenly there was an explosion, and a mighty column of red and blue sparks and burning brands shot into mid air, arching over in every direction as they fell hissing into the sea.

A quantity of powder had exploded on board!

Just at that moment we beached our boat upon Gull Island, and ascended the rocks in haste to view the result of our handiwork.

A great cloud of smoke was now settling over her, as the flames approached the water; and beyond this cloud we could see a little boat with some men in it, pulling in the direction of Cape St. John. Hartly was pleased on seeing this; for although he had resolved to destroy the schooner, his heart reproached him for leaving six of the pirates to perish in her. One, no doubt, had swum after their drifting boat, and brought her alongside in time to save his five shipmates; and then we laughed on thinking how cold his swim would be in the wintry waves, and of the baffled rage of the ruffians at La Scie, left there without a vessel or any means of escape from a desolate fishing-station, which in a week or two more would have, perhaps, three hundred miles of field-ice between it and the sea.

A faint hurrah now came from seaward. We turned, and saw the smart and saucy *Leda* with her foresail backed flat to the mast, and her maintopsail full and swelling—her straight sharp hull, and her taut rigging, in all its details, clearly and distinctly defined against the vast silver disc of the moon, which seemed to linger as it rose from the flat horizon of the distant offing. There was no need of showing lights on board the brig, as we could see each other distinctly, and also the burning pirate. No flame rose from her now ; but a vast black pall of smoke enveloped all her hull.

From the centre of this, there came a sound like a deep sob, as she filled and went down. Then when the smoky pall arose and melted into thin air, not a vestige could be seen of the *Black Schooner !*

" And now, my lads, away for the brig," said Captain Hartly, as we descended from the highest part of the island to reach our boat, passing through deep snow, among thickets of dwarf firs and great juniper trees—over rocks covered with savin and frozen furze, where, in the short season of summer, the wild Indian tea called *wisha-capucoa* grew plentifully, and where the beaver and the musk-rat had their holes.

As we floundered down to the creek, a yell from Cuffy Snowball, who was behind, startled us all. A wild cariboo deer had rushed past him. How it came on the island puzzled us, for usually in winter these animals seek the forests of the interior, till the sun of the brief summer melts the snow, and enables them to browse on the scanty herbage of *the barrens,* as the cleared patches of moorland are named by the squatters.

" If the Governor adheres to his proclamation, this night's work adds five hundred pounds to our profits," said Hartly, as the crew received us with hearty cheers; the headsails were filled, and we at once stood off the shore.

Next morning, when day broke, we could see by our glasses a band of men assembled on the snow-covered summit of Cape St. John.

These were evidently the outwitted crew of the schooner; so, hoisting the ensign at our gaff-peak, Paul Reeves dipped it to them thrice, ironically bidding them farewell, as we stood away to the eastward to make up for the time we had lost in being driven, by their attack and pursuit, so far out of the course our captain first intended to steer.

CHAPTER X.

THE SEAL-FISHERS.

SOME days after this event, we saw the dark blue of the sea flecked at the horizon by white spots. These increased in size as we approached, and proved to be the floes, or detached portions of a vast field of ice, coming down from Davis' Straits, and with them came masses of strange sea-weed, uprooted from the bottom of the ocean, as some writers aver, by the mighty tusk of the male narwhal when searching for food.

We were soon amid the floes, and after passing through them, Paul Reeves from the fore-crosstrees announced that he could discern the field of ice, extending along the whole line of the horizon; and we soon became sensible of its vicinity by a very perceptible increase of the cold, which ere long became almost unbearable. But our seal-fishers prepared with alacrity for the great work of our little expedition,

by getting up their wooden clubs, their long sealing-
guns, and shot-pouches ; their knives, sledges, and
rue-raddies or collar-ropes, by which to drag the
loads of skins to the brig, as they might have to
pursue and slaughter the seals for some miles from
where she would anchor by the outer edge of the ice.
The *inner*, Hartly knew by his observations, partly
rested on Wolf Island, off the coast of Labrador.

On the detached flocs, we saw a few seals like black
dots ; but on the ice nearing the brig they always
disappeared.

"There they go, souse into the water, tail up
for old Greenland!" said Hans Peterkin. "Now.
Cuffy, get your fiddle in order."

"A fiddle !" said I ; "for what ?"

"That you shall soon see, Jack," said Hartly.
"Paul Reeves, get ready a gang with the ice-anchor
and cable !"

As we neared the scene of our operations, we
passed ten or twelve gigantic icebergs, the bases of
which were merged deep in the icy sea. Solemnly
still, and intensely cold and pure they seem, to those
who first behold these voiceless floating mountains,
so terrible in their form and whiteness, the shades of
which are blue.

By a telescope, I perceived that some of them

bore masses of gravel, frozen mud, and even enormous boulder-stones, torn from the shore—but from
what shore?

From unknown and untrodden lands beyond the
Arctic Circle—shores where, perhaps, the last of
Franklin's fated crew are lying unburied save by the
eternal snow ; and while I gazed on these floating
islands, so awful in their aspect and solitude and so
mysterious in their formation, there came to memory
the oft-quoted words of the Psalmist, how "they
who go down to the sea in ships, and occupy their
business in great waters, see the works of the Lord,
and His wonders in the deep."

No small care, skill, and seamanship were requisite
to avoid those perilous "wonders ;" but ere long we
were close to the mighty field of ice which covered
all the ocean to the far horizon—a white and desolate expanse, like a snow-covered moorland—varied
only by the incessant hummocks, as those ridges of
broken ice formed by the collision of ice-fields, are
named; or by the wavy outline or sharp spiral
pinnacles of bergs which were wedged in the floating mass, and seemed to form the crags and mountains of this white and desolate world of ice and
snow.

We considered it singular, that up to this time

we had not seen a single ship bent on the same errand, either of those which sailed with us on St. Patrick's Day through the Narrows of St. John, or any of the steam sealers which leave the northern ports of Scotland about the same season of the year.

Now the quarter-boat was lowered, and Paul Reeves with her crew took off the cable and ice-anchor, which is formed like a pick-axe; the courses were hauled up, the fore and aft mainsail brailed, the topsails and topgallant sails handed, and we warped close to the ice-field, fairly coming to anchor alongside its edge, just as we might have warped close to a quay or wharf.

This was about ten in the morning of the 25th of March, and after receiving a glass of stiff rum-grog per man, the whole of our seal-fishers "landed," as they phrased it, on the ice, with all their apparatus, including Cuffy with his violin; and, after three hearty hurrahs for Captain Hartly, proceeded in quest of their prey, scores of which were seen dotting the white ice-scape (if I may so term it) within the distance of a mile from the brig.

Seals of every species live or consort in droves along those desolate shores where the bergs and ice-fields float; and they are often found basking in

the rays of the sun. Thus, when falling asleep they
easily become a prey, though, when reposing, the
seal is cunning enough to open its large black eyes
from time to time, to see whether all is quiet around
it. The female produces two or three at a litter,
and feeds them for a fortnight or so on the shore
where she has brought them forth, suckling them in
a position nearly upright, till the fattened cubs
depart to see the Arctic world upon the ice-floes,
and are old enough to search the waves for food.

Armed with my double-barrelled rifle and a
sheathed knife that dangled at my shot-belt, and
well prepared to encounter the cold by a suit of the
warmest clothing (Flushing lined with English
blanket), I set out alone in quest of adventures, feeling a strange emotion of mingled alarm and delight
on finding myself afoot upon that frozen sea. The
intense purity and rarity of the atmosphere carried
the voices of our scattered men to a vast distance.
I could hear Cuffy vigorously scraping a hornpipe on
his violin half a mile off; and thus won by the lyre
of our sable Orpheus, the seals with their hairy
paws (usually known as flippers), their round black
heads, soft gleaming eyes, and spotted skins, from
which the brine was dripping, began to appear in
herds from subtle holes in the ice—holes through

which I was frequently in terror of vanishing from mortal ken ; and as these strange amphibious animals rolled upon the field, turning up their full round bellies, which reminded me of those of gorged swine, I could see their bodies steaming in the frosty sunshine, for being warm-blooded they emit at times a vapour.

Seated on a sledge, under the lee of a hummock, Cuffy played vigorously ; but how his black fingers could handle his instrument in such an atmosphere was beyond my comprehension, for though the glare of the noonday sun, as he shone through a cloudless sky, was almost blinding, the degree of cold was indescribable. Ere long Snowball had a numerous auditory, for music allures and fascinates these animals, as it does many others ; we are told how

> " Rude Heiskar's seal through surges dark,
> Will long pursue the minstrel's bark ;"

but the moment our treacherous musician replaced his violin in its canvas bag, an appalling scene of butchery began.

The batmen rushed about as if a frenzy had seized them, striking the seals on their round bullet-like heads, knocking them over, stunned and motionless. Others followed, with long sharp knives, by *five* slashes of which the expert hunter will denude the largest cub of his smooth glossy skin, to which the thick white fat adheres, and after being thus denuded, on more than one occasion I have seen the miserable animal, bared to its slender ribs, when stung, as it were, by the intense frost reaching its vitals, revive for a minute, and make efforts to crawl along the ice, or drop into the sea!

The whole ice-field, which a moment before had been so white in its spotless and untrodden purity, now, within the radius of a mile, presented the aspect of a battle-field, strewn with gashed carcases and heaps of bloody skins that were steaming in the sunshine. Cuffy seemed in his element—in his glory! Flourishing his long knife, he uttered yells as if every seal he stripped had been the Chenoo wife who sold him into slavery, or the Yankee taskmaster whose whip had skinned *him* more than once.

This wholesale butchery sickened me.

The attachment of the mother-seal to her offspring is very great; and here I saw a great hooded one carrying off a little wounded cub in her mouth toward the edge of the ice-field, where they dropped into the sea, escaping Cuffy, who pursued them. There are times when the mother turns fiercely with tusks and claws upon the destroyers of her young,

and then the long gun with its charge of slugs is
brought into action; for on the *old* seals (Buffon
avers that some of them live for more than a hundred years) the sturdiest batman's arm would swing
the knotted club in vain. The membrane of the
hooded seal can be drawn over the nose, and in-
flated, so as to protect the head like a helmet of
gutta-percha.

Leaving our people engaged in the work of
slaughter, halloing, shouting, and encouraging each
other, as they threw their bloody and greasy spoil
upon little sledges, to be dragged by ropes alongside
the brig, I proceeded over the hummocks in search
of—I scarcely knew what.

Our men seldom fired their guns, as shot destroys
the skin, which, after the cargo is brought into
port, has the fat or blubber carefully removed and
placed in the great wooden tanks or vats of the oil-
merchant; while the pelts are cleaned, spread, and,
after having layers of coarse salt placed between them,
are packed in bales for transport to other countries.

CHAPTER XI.

COMBAT WITH A SEA-HORSE.

WE continued to fish, or rather to hunt, the seals here with considerable success, warping the brig from day to day along the outer edge of the ice, between which and her side we placed strong and soft fenders ; and the satisfaction of Hartly and his crew increased in proportion as the piles of pelt and blubber replaced in the hold the stone ballast which we had brought from the island of Newfoundland.

I had shot a few refractory seals, but one evening, when the atmosphere was singularly clear, I rambled far along the ice-field, floundering and scrambling among the hummocks, in the hope of finding worthier game. I was accompanied by one of the crew, a smart and intelligent lad from North Shields, named Ridly, who was armed only with an ice-gaff.

One who has been among the countless waves

and ridges of a frozen sea can alone have an idea of the toil of travelling, even for a mile, on an ice-field.

But on this vast floating waste we failed to discern anything worth powder and shot, and so, worn with our fruitless and desultory hunt, after wandering about for an hour or two, we turned our steps towards the brig, which still lay at anchor by the edge of the field, about three miles off, and the masts and yards of which formed the chief and sole feature in the flat and dreary prospect.

The sun had set, but there was a dusky red flush in the sky which marked the place of his declension ; and now the ice began to assume the cold green tints of salt water when frozen, as the shadows of night stole over the sky from the eastward like a crape mantle, and one by one the stars came out in the deep blue dome above us.

Sliding, toiling, and scrambling on, we were endeavouring to reach the brig, when suddenly Ridly and I uttered a mutual exclamation of alarm, paused, and shrunk back.

In our front we heard an astounding roar, as of an earthquake, and lo! between us and the brig— between us and our friends, our home upon the waters—there yawned a mighty fissure of zigzag

form, that ran east and west, and was about fifteen
or twenty feet wide, as the ice-field split under the
influence of some atmospheric change!

We stood and gazed blankly into each other's
faces on beholding this terrible barrier to our pro-
gression, and fearing that the ice might yawn as
suddenly under our feet.

"Separated from all succour from the ship—
alone upon the ice, and with night coming on,
what will become of us?" said I, thinking aloud.

"God only knows, sir," responded my companion;
"but we must endeavour to reach the brig somehow."

"There goes a lantern up to her mainmast-head,"
said I, as a light was hoisted swiftly by the ensign
halliards.

"The captain is showing a signal to indicate her
whereabouts. He has heard the noise of the splitting
ice."

"If a fog should come on!" said I.

"Don't think of it, sir," said my companion,
hastily; "the night is as clear as if day were overhead. So let us find the end of this crack; it cannot
be very far off."

We proceeded westward for more than a mile
being compelled to make many détours to avoid

H

falling into the water among the ragged floes or
pieces of ice that lay along the margin of this
zigzag fissure ; but, as it extended far away beyond
the range of our vision, and seemed to widen, we were
compelled after long consideration, and suffering
great anxiety, to retrace our steps and proceed eastward, in the hope of gaining the *east end* of it, or
at least of discovering a place so narrow that we
might leap across without the danger of immersion,
which, in such a season and at such an hour, would
have been fatal, as our entire clothing would in an
instant have become a casing of ice.

To favour our efforts the moon now rose, ascending slowly from the edge of the vast plain of ice,
and notwithstanding the peril of our situation, her
beauty filled me with a glow of pleasure and
hope.

Far over that waste—so wide, so desolate, and
mysterious—fell her flood of silver light, so bright
in its intensity, and redoubled by reflection from
the snow. It glittered on every rounded hummock
and splintered berg, and formed strange fantastic
figures in their cold green shadows, elsewhere
making prisms that seemed like fairy crystals, or
gemwork of rubies, emeralds, and silver. Clouds of
fleecy whiteness came up with her from the sea, and

as she *waded* among them, I recalled the words of Sir Walter Scott :—

"There is something peculiarly pleasing to the imagination in contemplating the Queen of Night when she is wading, as the expression is, among the vapours which she has not the power to dispel, and which on their side are unable entirely to quench her lustre. It is the striking image of patient virtue calmly pursuing her path through good report and bad report, having that excellence in herself which ought to command all admiration ; but bedimmed in the eyes of the world by suffering, by misfortune, and by calumny."

While I felt something of the poetry of our situation and the beauty of the night, my more practical and prosaic companion was sensible only of the danger we ran, and after a minute reconnaissance, assured me, with an exclamation of joy, that the split in the ice was narrowing.

We were then four miles from the brig, the crew of which had sent more lanterns aloft, and ever and anon burned a brilliant red or blue light, for Cuffy Snowball was a great pyrotechnist.

"What is that ?" said I, as a strange sound reached us.

"I cannot tell," replied my comrade, as he toiled

on, supporting himself with his ice-gaff; "I never heard it before, and don't like it at all, sir. I wish we were on board," he added, shuddering alike with cold and superstitious fear, as the sound came again and again from among the hummocks, and it was as weird and mournful to the ear as their aspect was to the eye.

It was a strange *mooing*, and gradually swelled into a bellowing as we proceeded; thus it evidently came from the throat of a large animal—but *what* species of animal could it be in such a place?

We were not left long in doubt, for on the centre of a narrow isthmus of ice, *over which lay our way to the ship*, as the fissure beyond it opened wider than elsewhere, sat a huge, dark monster of the deep, in which, on approaching it, I recognised (from pictures I had seen) a sea-horse, or walrus, which the reader must remember is *not* a seal, but a ferocious animal that can defend itself and frequently destroys its assailants, and this one manifested not the slightest intention of making way for us.

He was fearfully pre-Adamite, or antediluvian, in his proportions, being fully twenty feet in length, and having a pair of tusks thirty inches long protruding from the mass of quill-like bristles which covered (like a thick moustache and whiskers) his upper lips and cheeks. Grimly and ferociously he regarded us with his deep-set eyes, which glittered in the moonlight amid the square mass of his elephantine visage, and on beholding us, his hollow mooing turned into a species of grunting bark.

Finding that he obstinately barred our way, and, moreover, seemed inclined to attack us, I levelled my rifle full at his grizzly front and fired, while Ridly rashly and fatally charged him in the smoke with his ice-gaff, which was armed with a sharp pike

My ball had pierced his great sloping shoulder, pricking him as a pin might have done, and serving only to incense him, for his bark changed to a mighty roar, and when the smoke cleared away, I saw poor Ridly, who had fallen, lying under one of his gigantic fore-flippers. The foam of rage was frothing on the bristles of the sea-horse, and with his two enormous tusks, which stood upward through them like two crooked sabre-blades, he was alternately rending the limbs and body of his assailant and then great fragments of ice, which he dashed into the water on each side of him.

Ridly had only power to utter a faint cry, when he expired.

Appalled by this sudden and terrible catastrophe, I reloaded my rifle, and full of mingled rage and

fear—a combination which made me no longer feel
the intensity of the cold—I fired again and again at
the horrid front of the walrus; but every shot
seemed only to redouble his wrath, and he continued
to rend to pieces the clothes and body of Ridly,
till in less than five minutes the ice around him was
covered by the blood of his victim and that which
gushed from his own wounds. Ridly's left leg he
wrenched completely off, and cast into the sea.

Rolling about in his wrath, and in his lubberly
efforts to reach me, he at last fell into the water;
I then rushed across the narrow isthmus where my
poor companion lay. As I did so, the walrus made
many ineffectual efforts to reach me, grasping the
ice with his forepaws, or dashing his vast shoulders
madly against it, while he plunged and bellowed
and covered all the water in the chasm around him
with mingled blood and foam, and, in his impotent
fury, tore great blocks off the ice by the tusks of
his lower jaw.

I fired ten shots into his body, point blank,
without his strength or wrath appearing to di-
minish in the least.

On perceiving this, a species of superstitious
dread came over me, and turning away, I hastened
towards the brig, which, as I have stated, lay about

four miles distant, leaving my walrus to flounder, bellow, and drown in the moonlight.

Anxiety to reach the vessel, lest I might be overcome by fatigue, or that fatal drowsiness caused at times by intense cold, made me strain every energy; and thus in a much shorter time than could have deemed possible, considering the alternately rough or slippery and laborious nature of the ice-field to be traversed, I found myself among the carcasses of our slaughtered seals, and within hail of the *Leda*.

Furnished with ice-gaffs, a bottle of rum, a sledge, and plenty of blankets, so as to be prepared for any emergency, Captain Hartly, with Hans Peterkin and ten of the crew, met me, just as I was sinking with fatigue, half sleepy and half delirious with cold. Thus a considerable time elapsed ere I could relate the story of my adventure and our shipmate's death.

They had heard the roar of the splitting ice, and knew why we were wandering so long and so deviously among the hummocks, but the sound of firing puzzled them extremely; and thus, while Paul Reeves with a gang was hoisting out the jolly-boat upon a sledge, to have it launched in the chasm for our conveyance across, Hartly had come

on in advance, and he met me just in time, for in
ten minutes more I must have perished of fatigue
and cold !

On returning next morning to collect poor
Ridly's remains and commit them to the deep, we
found his great destroyer dead, but floating by the
margin of the ice, to which he was literally anchored,
or hooked, by his two longest tusks.

By this, and the affair with the *Black Schooner*,
we had lost two of our crew.

CHAPTER XII.

ON AN ICEBERG.

SOON after this, in a dark and howling night, we were blown from our moorings, and forced to run before the wind, with our topmasts struck, and only our jib and a close-reefed foresail set, as we were in the dangerous vicinity of innumerable broken floes, or masses detached from the field-ice: the decks were so slippery that one could scarcely keep afoot; and amid the arrowy sleet and snow that rendered all so murky and obscure around us, and which stung the face like showers of sharp needles, we were hurried on, expecting every moment a collision which would stave our bows or snap the masts by the board.

We were repeatedly frost-bitten in the ears, nose, or hands; but snow scraped up in the scuppers and promptly applied, soon brought a hot glow in the benumbed member, and proved our best, indeed our only remedy.

All who could cultivate beards had permitted them to grow in Crimean luxuriance, as any attempt at soapsudding in those latitudes produced a coating of ice in a moment.

Surging on through blinding drift and pitchy darkness, amid the howling of the fierce tempest, the *Leda* went bravely! Her spars and cordage straining and groaning, her timbers creaking, while wave after wave broke over her decks and hardy crew, each leaving its legacy of ice upon everything. From time to time we were conscious of a rude shock, or a furious scraping sound, as she grazed upon the passing floes; and now, to add to the gloomy horrors of that tempestuous night, Paul Reeves, who was keeping an anxious look-out forward, shouted back through his trumpet—

"Icebergs ahead! Hard to port, or we are foul of one!"

"Hard to port," echoed the two men at the wheel; sharply it revolved, and in a moment we swept under the frowning cliff of a stupendous iceberg, the cold white mass of which was discernible through the gloom, as the arm of the main-yard *grazed* it!

We passed on and it vanished in the darkness astern.

" Thank Heaven !"

" Thank God !"

" A narrow escape !"

Such were the muttered exclamations of our half-
frozen crew ; but at that instant an icy sea broke
over us, and two men were swept into a watery
grave, without the possibility of our rendering them
the least assistance.

A minute had scarcely elapsed before we were
sensible of a fierce concussion; the masts reeled and
the icicles fell in a shower as they were shaken
from our stiffened top-hamper. Then the brig's
head was tilted up and her stern correspondingly
depressed; but still impelled by the fury of the
wind, she continued to advance upwards and *out of
the water,* as if she was being steamed up a landing-
slip, or into a dry dock.

" We are ashore—beached !" said some one,
beholding this phenomenon.

" We are foul of an iceberg," exclaimed Hartly,
while the brig continued slowly to ascend till little
more than the sternpost and counter were in the
water; then she heeled over to port and remained
there, wedged, with her jib-boom broken off at the
cap, and dangling in the jib-guys, her canvas bellying out so furiously that we thought the masts

would be carried away before the benumbed fingers of the seamen could get it handed.

In a trice the *Leda* was under bare poles, while around us the tempestuous wind was bellowing, the surf was roaring, and vast blocks of ice, many tons in weight, were crashing against each other, adding to the dread horrors of this bewildering catastrophe!

It is impossible to depict the dismay of all on board, when finding the vessel in this situation—high and dry upon a berg; for, influenced by the storm, by the wind, or the slight additional weight of the brig and her cargo, we felt the monstrous mass on which we were wedged, *oscillating* and gradually heeling forward ahead; thus the stern of the *Leda* was raised until her hull remained in the air horizontally, just as she usually sat in the water.

In blank horror we endured the gloomy hours of that northern night, amid the drift, the sleet, and a darkness so dense that we could in no way discover our real position, or how to extricate ourselves from it.

One fact, we were alarmingly alive to. It was this:—The sea no longer dashed against the hull of our vessel, which lay on her side, well careened over to port; and though we could *hear* the roaring of the waves, amid the oppressive gloom that enveloped us, we could no longer *see* them.

As day broke the tempest gradually lulled, and the sleet, the snow, and wind passed away together. Then the increasing light enabled us to see the perils of our situation.

We were nearly eighty feet above the ocean, on the flat, table-like summit of a mighty iceberg; which, though it had presented a sloping face *up* which we had run last night before the furious wind and sea, had now changed its position by heeling over, as icebergs always do, from time to time, when their base in the ocean becomes honey-combed and decayed.*

The sky was clear now to the horizon; the ice-field on which we had pursued our hunting so successfully was no longer visible; but about half a mile distant lay the island of floating ice we had escaped last night; and around for miles, far as the eye could reach, the sea, still perturbed by the past storm, was flecked by white floes, the ruins probably of a third berg, which had been

---

* Her Majesty's steam ship *Intrepid*, when commanded by Captain Cator, was similarly carried bodily *up* the face of a berg, and left high and dry in air, without injury.

shattered by the waves or by being dashed against others.

Both these icebergs were several miles in circumference. The summit of ours was flat as a bowling-green; but that portion on which the brig rested was soft, pulpy, and rotten by its long immersion in the sea.

The other had many spiral pinnacles, some of them being several hundred feet in height; and, save for the peril in which we were situated, I could have admired the sublimity of that cold and silent mass—so dazzlingly white when the beams of the rising sun fell on it, so indigo-blue in its shadows—for it resembled a fairy isle, which had steep hills, deep valleys, and chasms all fashioned of alabaster; while around its base was a thick fringe of frozen foam of snowy brilliance.

While we were gazing upon it that morning, one of its loftiest pinnacles, with a mighty crash, fell thundering into the sea.

The *Leda* was soon frozen into the bed she had ploughed by her keel in the ice; and *how* to get her launched again, *how* to descend from our perilous eminence, were the questions we asked of each other, and which no one could answer.

The summit of the berg was nearly a mile in circumference, and, as I have said, was more than eighty feet from the water. This we ascertained as a fact, though there was no small peril in venturing from the ship upon its surface, which was so glassy and smooth that in some places the lightest among us would have slipped off, as if shot by a catapulta, into the sea below.

Council and deliberation availed us nothing. Even Hartly, Reeves, and Hans, with all their united skill, foresight, and seamanship, found their invention fail in suggesting any means of release.

"There is nothing for it but to wait the event," said Hartly, after a long and solemn council.

"But suppose that we waited a month, captain," asked Reeves, gloomily, "where would our provisions be?—where our fresh water?"

"We may be driven south into warmer latitudes where the bergs melt rapidly in the sunshine."

"But we may be drifted north into latitudes where the bergs freeze harder, and where ice may close around us for ever," said Hans Peterkin.

"Or," said one of the seamen, who all crowded anxiously to this conference, which we held around the capstan-head, "the berg may *capsize*, and what will become of us then?"

"Hold hard, my lads," exclaimed Hartly, "hold

hard, and be stout of heart and cheery. Remember that however miserable we may deem ourselves, there is one Blessed Eye upon us—the eye of a kind, good God," he added, uncovering his head reverently to the bitter frost, "One who will never forget the poor sailor, if he is true to himself. Think of the ' sweet little cherub that sits up aloft,' as the song says, and rail not at fate, for fate guides man neither at home nor abroad, at sea or on shore. Put all your trust aloft, my boys, and hold on by poor Jack's best bower anchor !"

This harangue was exactly suited to his hearers. We tried to feel hopeful and trusting, and to have patience. But we longed very much, nevertheless, to be free of the iceberg, and to have the blue sea dashing alongside once more.

CHAPTER XIII.

ON THE ICEBERG—THE MASSACRE AT HIERRO.

IN this appalling situation we remained for ten days before any alteration in the position either of the brig or of the two icebergs was perceptible.

We missed our lost companions sorely, for the death of a shipmate in his hammock, or by falling overboard, makes a great impression on the secluded survivors at sea. His watery grave is in itself a fearful mystery, the depth of which we cannot realize or fathom. No stone or mound marks the place where he lies; he is hurled, as it were, soul and body into eternity, and blotted out of existence like the bubbles that break round the place where he sinks.

During these ten days Hartly was indefatigable in his efforts to keep his crew employed, and their spirits from depression. Lest provisions might become scarce, and our water fall short, he had

I

portions of the seals, the hideous paws especially, cleaned, prepared, and pickled, while the snow and ice which adhered to the rigging was boiled down, and added to our supply of fresh water. To save our fuel, the fire for these purposes was fed with the fat of the seals, and the blubber (so long as it lasted) of the gigantic walrus I had slain.

The seal "flippers," hairy and bloody, like the claws of a baboon hewn off at the wrist, made a very cannibal-like repast when fricasseed. Remembering how I had shuddered on seeing such repulsive carrion sold at a penny per bunch in the streets of St. John, I could scarcely digest such a meal; though Cuffy Snowball, when he made them into sea-pies, rolled his eyes and grinned from ear to ear while declaring his handiwork "de berry best dish in de 'varsal creation!"

Our rigging was carefully inspected and prepared for any emergency, as if we expected to make sail on the brig at a moment's notice; but *how* was she ever to reach her natural element again?

On this subject, though we were wearied of it, conjecture became utterly *lost!*

Still, like a brave fellow, Hartly left nothing unsaid or undone to keep up our hopes, though his own sank at times. Save the watch on deck, he

nightly assembled all hands in the cabin for com-
panionship and also for warmth.   There he sang
songs, (while Cuffy accompanied him on the violin,)
and told stories, or read aloud, and spoke again and
again to the poor crest-fallen seal-fishers (who
thought only of their wives and families) of their
profits on the voyage, and the reward they would
receive from the Governor of Newfoundland for destroying the obnoxious *Black Schooner ;* and of that
affair he drew up a statement, to be attested by all
on board.

His example was invaluable, for he had somehow
acquired the greatest influence over all his crew.   " It
is pleasing to see a family, a farm, or establishment of
any kind (says Lorimer, in his " Letters to a Young
Merchant-Mariner") when, from long servitude, the
assistants and domestics are considered as humble
friends or distant relations ; and independently of
the kind feelings thereby occasioned and cherished,
all seems to prosper with them.   Such a state of
things is by no means unfrequent in this happy
country, Britain ; and I see no good reason why the
same attachment to the master and to each other,
should not be more frequent on shipboard ; indeed,
considering the dangers they are continually sharing,
one is almost surprised that they can *separate* so

readily. How to obtain a kind but powerful influence *over*, and a devoted attachment *from*, a crew,
is a secret worth our deep consideration;" and
Robert Hartly eminently possessed this secret,
which, in the desperation of our circumstances,
proved a priceless gift to him and to us.

Every night one story or yarn produced others,
and so the time passed on, and peril was half
forgotten.

Most of these narratives were gloomy enough,
however. They told of ships whose crews were all
poisoned save one man, by partaking of a mysterious
fish, or whose crews turned pirates, and slaughtered
all who opposed them; or of men who were marooned on lonely isles, and left to perish miserably.

Hans Peterkin, an Orkneyman, could tell us of
queer shadowy craft, manned by spectres, demons,
and evil spirits, who displayed lights to lure vessels
ashore on Cape Wrath and the rocks of Ultima
Thule, like the wreckers of Cornwall and Brittany.

Then Paul Reeves matched them by a curious
tale of an enchanted island in the Indian Seas, on
which the lights of churches and houses could be
seen at night, and where the tolling of bells and
the song of vespers could be heard, with many
other sounds; but lo! as the ship approached, the

isle would seem to recede till it sank into the sea and reappeared *astern !*

Then Tom Hammer, the carpenter, gave us a yarn of an ice-cliff in Hudson's Bay that long over-hung a whaler he was once serving in.   One day the cliff was changed in form, for a mighty piece had fallen from it into the sea ; and wonderful to relate, there was seen a man's figure among the ice—a man imbedded up there a hundred feet above the sea.   Telescopes were at once in requisition, and they made out that he was frozen—dead—hard and fast ; but by his dress—a red doublet, trunk-hose, and a long black beard—they supposed he was some ancient mariner ; and some there were on board who vowed he was no other than the famous voyager Hendrick Hudson, who discovered the bay, and was marooned by his mutinous crew in 1610.

But one night, when we were all nestling close together, muffled in our pea-jackets, and smoking, to promote warmth, a narration of Hartly's far ex-ceeded all that preceded it in interest, being a veri-table occurrence, and by its barbarity singular.

" My grandfather," said he, " as thoroughbred an old salt as ever faced a stiff topsail breeze, was skipper of the *Dublin*, a smart little ship of three hundred and fifty tons, pierced for twelve six-pounders, being a letter of marque that fought her own way when the way upon the high seas was somewhat more perilous than it is now.

"About the autumn of the year 1784—now a long time ago, my lads—she was chartered as an emigrant ship for Canada, and sailed from the Mersey with one hundred and eighty poor folks, half of whom were women and children, going to seek their bread in another land; and a troublesome voyage the old gentleman had with them, for foul weather came on; many of his spars were knocked away, and then a heavy sickness broke out among the emigrants. Their little ones died daily and were hove overboard, till those whose children survived became wild with fear and apprehension that theirs would follow next; and, to make matters worse, there was no doctor on board; for this was in 1784, as I told you, and the lives of the poor were not worth much to any one, save themselves, in those old times.

"Well, my grandfather was a soft-hearted old fellow, and his heart bled for the poor people. His sick bay was crammed, and the sailmaker's needle was never idle, but made one little shroud after another till the man's heart sickened of the dreary task. So, when foul weather mastered the *Dublin*, and blew her out of her course, the old gentleman put his helm a-lee and bore up for the Canaries, which were once called the Fortunate Isles, and came in sight of Hierro, the most westerly of these islands, on the 6th December, 1784. He had his ensign flying; but knowing well what slippery devils the Spaniards are, and that the *Dublin* had rather a man-o'-war cut in her spars and bends, he hoisted a *white* flag at his foremast head, and so came peacefully to anchor about sunrise.

" The morning was beautiful; the shore was desolate, but fertile and green. The poor emigrants were mad with joy at the sight of land, and in an hour or two he set them all ashore, about a hundred in number, on the smooth sandy beach. Many of them were women with infants in their arms or at their skirts—men supporting their young wives or old parents ; and new life and health seemed returning to them as they rambled on the sunny shore, or drank of the pure springs that gushed from the rocks, and as they pulled the green leaves and aromatic flowers, or the broad plantain leaves which always flourish best near the sea.

" Meanwhile, my grandfather had triced up his portlids, and a gang with buckets and swabs were busy cleaning, airing, and fumigating every place fore and aft, ere the live cargo were shipped again at night, when an unforeseen catastrophe took place——"

"A catastrophe!" said I; "the ship was blown out to sea?"

"Not at all," said Hartly, refilling his pipe.

"What then?"

"His poor people were all dead ere nightfall."

"Murdered?"

"Aye, in cold blood, as you shall hear. They were all enjoying themselves — the children were playing, gambolling and tumbling over each other in heaps on the warm sands; the women were busy washing, dressing and arranging each other's hair; the men smoking their pipes, and talking, perhaps regretfully, of that jolly old England they had left for ever and, it might be hopefully, of the new shores they were bound for, when a long line of bright bayonets that glittered ominously in the sunshine, appeared suddenly upon the steep rocks which completely enclosed the sandy cove, and three companies of lubberly Spanish militia commanded by Don Juan Briez de Calderon, encircled them on all sides, save towards the sea, where the *Dublin* lay at anchor about three-quarters of a mile off. The reason of this military display I shall explain.

" False rumours of a plague said to be raging in Europe had reached these isles, and filled the selfish and superstitious Spanish colonists with such alarm, that Señor the Governor, fearing, or pretending to fear, the strangers might bring it among them, instantly convened la Mesa del Consejo—his council-board, as they call it in their lingo—and quietly proposed to cut off all these voyagers root and branch!

" Some of the councillors vigorously opposed a course so revolting, and pled the cause of the poor Inglesos, the rights of religion and humanity, and called upon Don Juan to remember the honour of the king he represented, and that he was the lineal descendant of that adventurous Don Diego de Hierro, of Old Castile, who had captured the island in the days of Ferdinand the Catholic, King of Arragon, bestowing in memory thereof his own illustrious name upon it, and so forth.

" Señor Don Juan did not reply, but knit his fierce black brows, lighted a cigar, and puffed away with true Castilian imperturbability.

" ' Señor el Gobernador,' urged a venerable Spanish friar, ' these poor people who have landed on our shores, after a long voyage apparently, we know not from whence, have been forced hither, as our mariners aver, by those recent storms which have swept over the Canary Isles———'

"'What is all this to me?' growled Don Juan.

"'Simply, Señor, that it will be alike cruel and unjust to inflict the penalty of death upon them all for this.'

"'Padre, they have transgressed the laws of Hierro,' thundered the Governor.

"'Laws temporarily made by *yourself*—laws with which they can in no way be acquainted. If they have sickness among them, let us send tents and supplies; but guard the avenues to the ground we may allot them, until they are all re-embarked with their wives and little ones. I will myself go among them,' continued the old friar, warming in his merciful advocacy, 'and say that you will graciously afford them succour, until the orders of the most illustrious señor, our Governor-General at Teneriffe, can be obtained.'

"'*Silencio!*' thundered Don Juan, and rudely threw the remains of his cigar in the old man's face; 'order out our troops—we shall march instantly and exterminate these dangerous vermin!'

"The drums were beat, and the militia, three hundred strong, with the valiant Don Juan at their head, marched to where the poor visitors, ignorant of the horrors that were impending, were still amusing themselves upon the beach. Some were gathering the brilliant shells, flowers, and leaves; others were filling little kegs and jars with the pure spring water that poured over the ledges of rock. The women were sitting in groups, with their children gambolling about them; others were gazing sadly on the evening sea, as if calculating the number of miles that lay between them and their old home; or the miles they had yet to traverse ere they found a new one amid the forests of the western world.

"To gather them all together, the villanous Briez de Calderon procured an empty sugar puncheon, and tossed it over the summit of the cliffs on which his men were posted. From thence, with a loud noise, it rolled to the beach below. Curiosity made all the loiterers rush towards it, as many of them thought it contained food, clothes, or other necessaries for them. The men gave a hurrah, and waved their hats in hearty English jollity to the crafty Spaniards, and gathered with the women and children around the puncheon.

"'Fire!' cried Don Juan.

"Savage as they were, the Spaniards paused a moment; but Don Juan was the first to fire a musket, and observing that his men were still reluctant, he knocked one down with the butt-end, and threatened the rest with death if they disobeyed him.

"'Fire!' he shouted again, and then on the unsuspecting crowd there was poured the concentrated volley of these three hundred miscreants; thus, in ten minutes the dreadful massacre was complete. On the beach all were lying dead and drenched in blood—husband and wife, parent and child—all save one woman, who, with her infant, concealed herself in the rocks, and her husband, who, with a ball lodged in his arm, sprang into the sea and endeavoured to swim to the ship.

"Failing in this, faint with loss of blood, weary and despairing, he turned about and sought the shore, where he was hewn to pieces by sabres as he clung to a seaweedy rock. On beholding this dreadful sight, his poor wife, who was concealed in a cleft of the cliffs not far off, uttered a shriek of dismay, which drew the murderers, now flushed with blood, towards her.

"She was soon dragged out, and with his own dagger Don Juan stabbed her to the heart, and then killed the child, which he tossed into the sea beside its father!

"Paralysed by rage and astonishment, my grandfather and his crew saw all this from the deck of the *Dublin*. They could see the red musketry flashing from the rocks, filling all the little cove with slaughtered corpses and smoke. They could hear the shrieks that were borne over the water on the evening wind; and after a time, when all was still, they could see the beach strewn with dead bodies, and in possession of the Spaniards, who were stripping them, and who brought up field-pieces to fire on the *Dublin*.

"He hoisted his anchor and bore away; but on coming abreast of the capital with British colours flying *above* the Spanish ensign *reversed*, he pitched a few shot into it from his carronades, sunk three craft at their anchors, with all their crews on board, and then bore away for England, and there was an end of it. We were at peace with Spain; but I never heard that satisfaction was given, or the atrocity revenged. That is *my* yarn, lads." *

---

* The papers of the time fully corroborate Hartly's story. "The news of this barbarity," says the *Annual Register* for 1785, " has been received at Teneriffe by all ranks of people with the deepest concern and regret, and by none more than the Governor-General, who deplores it extremely. He could not at first give credit to it; but was at last convinced of the fatal truth, by letters from the wretch Briez de Calderon himself. Exasperated to the highest pitch, he has given a commission to an officer of rank to go over to Hierro to take cognizance of this tragical affair,"—of which we hear *no more.*

CHAPTER XIV.

ESCAPE FROM THE ICEBERG.

THOUGH our apprehensions were great, our chief sufferings were from cold in that lofty and listless situation; yet our dread of impending dangers was so keen, our hope of a change so great, that even the oldest seamen on board never turned into their berths or bunks at night but with their clothes on, "to be ready," as they said, "to turn up with all standing at a moment's notice."

Hartly, who was rather scientific and was wont to expatiate upon the theory of storms, and so forth, endeavoured to account for the intensity of the frost, which I deemed a somewhat unnecessary illustration to us who were on the summit of an iceberg.

"The thermometer—" he would begin.

"Ugh! don't speak of the thermometer, Bob," said I, one day, when trembling in every fibre, as we endeavoured to tread to and fro on the sloping deck.

" It is so cold now, that the atmosphere can never be colder!"

" So you think; but wait until—"

" When ?"

" —we are a few degrees further north, perhaps in the centre of an ice-field, and then you will know what cold is! But the *degree* of it depends upon the power of the wind, after passing over snow-covered wastes, rather than the actual state of the mercury ;—that was all I was about to remark."

I was too miserable to thank him for the information, but said:

" I do not think our vicinity to that other atrocious iceberg adds to the pleasantness of our temperature."

" Of course not—but see," he added, raising his voice, " by Heaven, it is oscillating!"

Just as he spoke, the cold, glistening, and splintered peaks of the mighty berg seemed to topple over and sink into the sea, as it *reversed* with a stunning roar—its former base coming upward, and imparting an entirely new form to it.

All on board stood gazing at this reversal, which is a common occurrence with icebergs ; but it filled us with a horror of what *our* fate would be should a similar capsize occur with us, for now the berg on which we were wedged heaved and surged in the foaming eddy made by the other.

"Icebergs have usually nine times as much of them below water as appears above it," said I.

"Yes, and at that ratio, if this one of ours reversed, we should find ourselves in a moment somewhere about six hundred and forty feet below the surface of the sea," replied Hartly, with a grim smile.

"Ay," added Paul Reeves, "and our poor little *Leda* would be adhering, keel upmost and trucks down, like a barnacle at the bottom of this vast floating island."

On the tenth day of our imprisonment, as I have elsewhere said, after rain had been falling all night in such torrents that we had battened all the hatches fore and aft, on day breaking, we found a very perceptible alteration in the position of the brig. From careening over to port, she had gradually righted, and now rested fairly on her keel, with her masts upright. The summit of the berg had again become soft and pulpy on its surface, and the *Leda* seemed to sink lower by her own weight every minute, while the ice on each side sloped upward, leaving her in a kind of valley; and so rapidly did this state of matters go on, that in four hours the sides were nearly eight feet above our deck, and suggested a new terror, that they might collapse—close over, and freeze us in more hopelessly than ever.

As the rain abated, the berg began palpably to oscillate, that portion of it which lay under the brig's head, however, became depressed, and then the rain-water and *sludge* that had collected in the valley where we lay, poured over its icy brow like a cataract, and we heard it thundering, as it fell into the sea below.

"She moves—the brig moves! she forges ahead!" exclaimed Hartly, in an excited voice, as the berg careened over more and more, and we all stood pale, breathless, speechless, and rooted to the deck, expecting a capsize that would bury her masts downward in the sea.

This change of position continued to progress, but very slowly.

There were about sixteen feet of ice from the cutwater of the *Leda* to the edge of the berg, and about forty from her stern-post to the edge in the other direction.

"If this depression forward continues slowly," said Hartly, " we shall be floating in the blue in two hours, my lads; clear away two hawsers, an ice-anchor, and kedge. Stand by with the capstan-bars, cast loose the jib and foretopsail, to lift her head a

K

bit, if the wind serves when she slips off, and then stand by the braces to sheet home!"

These orders recalled us to life, for they filled us with hope, and inspired us with activity.

Led by Hartly, Hans Peterkin and two other adventurous fellows named Abbot clambered along the soft ice astern, and fixed there a kedge with our strongest hawser, which was to be eased gently off the capstan, as the brig continued to forge downward and a-head, for her motion was a double one. It was perilous work for these four brave men, as the rain had rendered the face of the berg slippery as wetted glass; but Hartly was full of inherent courage, and in the excitement of the moment forgot all his superstition about his ring, the gift of the reputed witch Jensdochter.

He was scarcely on board again, ere the depression continued so rapidly that the entire hull of the brig lay at an angle of forty-five degrees from the line of the water below—her bows being yet twenty feet distant from it.

This was a momentous crisis for us all!

A deathlike stillness was everywhere on board; on our pale lips, as we grasped the shrouds or belaying pins to preserve our footing; on the mighty isle of ice, from the shelving summit of which we were about to be precipitated; and from the lonely sea below, there came no sound; at least, we heard only its wavelets rippling against the cold, glistening, and glacial sides of our prison.

Slowly the brig moved, as if to protract that time of agonizing suspense. Every man compressed his lips and stifled his breathing. We seemed to speak our thoughts in silent and expressive glances, for all had the certainty now that in *three* minutes more, we should be floating on the free waters of the ocean, or foundered and sunk, headforemost, far beneath them.

Foot by foot she forged ahead, as the berg continued to heel over, and ere long our bowsprit projected in the air over the edge, and then the bows, headboards, and cutwater! The angle at which the *Leda* lay was fearful; we could no longer work the capstan; I clasped it with my arms, and shut my eyes. Then a heavy sob seemed to escape from me, as Reeves, by one slash with a sharp axe on the taffrail, parted the stern warp, which recoiled with a crack like a coach-whip. Then followed a rushing sound—a mighty plunge, and the waves dashed in foam on each side of us, as the *Leda* shot off the berg, and went souse, bows foremost into the sea; but rising up again, and snaking all the spray off her, as a duck would have done.

K 2

There was a deep silence after the shock and escape of this launch, and all seemed to await the signal to utter a hearty hurrah of joy and thankfulness for our miraculous preservation. Ere long it burst forth, but Hartly cut it short by his orders to sheet home the jib and foretopsail, to set the foresail, fore and aft mainsail and maintopsail.

Rapidly he was obeyed, and just as the *Leda* fell off, and bore away from the dangerous vicinity of the ice-island, it capsized, as its companion had done, and with a roar, as if defrauded of its prey.

CHAPTER XV

UNDER WEIGH ONCE MORE.

THE chainbobstay under the bowsprit was snapped, our rudder was split and its pintles were started, but these defects were soon repaired by the carpenter; and next day, at noon, Hartly and Reeves on comparing their observations, discovered that, unknown to ourselves, we had drifted nearly one hundred miles towards the western coast of Greenland, so a lookout was kept for the field-ice, as they were anxious to complete their interrupted seal-fishing, to haul up for St. John's, and then freight for Europe in the spring.

Poor fellows! . . .

We seemed to have returned to life once more. Again we were dashing through the blue sea with a free sheet, with the white canvas bellying full upon the breeze; again, on waking in the morning, the first familiar sounds that met the ear were the decks undergoing their customary ablutions, by bucket and

swab, and the rasping holystones; Cuffy singing
some Congo melody as he lighted the cabin fire, the
wind whistling through the rigging, the patter of
the reef-points on the bosom of the swollen sails, the
dashing of the spray over the sharp black bows, the
occasional order issued on deck, the clatter of the
rudder in its case, and the bubble of the water as it
frothed past under the counter.

All these spoke of our wonted life of activity, and
of the *Leda* being under canvas.

In a day or two we descried the slender white line
of an ice-field, stretching for miles along the horizon
towards the north, and approached it under easy
sail, as the fields usually drift southward at this
season. By the appearance of the ice and the state
of the thermometer, we concluded this to be a much
larger field than that from which we had been blown
by the gale of wind.

While Reeves got ready the ice-hooks, sledges,
warps, and gangs of seal-hunters, with their bats,
guns, and other apparatus, Hartly and I were
treading to and fro talking of various matters. I
can remember that he was relating to me, how, in
his last voyage with the *Leda* up the Mediterranean,
St. Elmo's blue and phosphorescent light had enveloped fully three feet of her masts below the

trueks, to the great terror of Cuffy Snowball, and others who were ignorant of the cause of that phenomenon, which lasted nearly an hour. He was proceeding with his narration, when Tom Hammer, who was repairing something aloft, hailed the watch.

" Deck—ahoy !"

." Hallo ?" responded Hans Peterkin.

" There is a craft wedged in the ice, sir."

" Where away ?"

" About twenty miles off."

" How does she bear ?"

" On our lee bow."

" And what do you make her out to be ?"

Hammer stood on the main-crosstrees, with his left arm embracing the mast, and through his telescope took a long and steady glance with a somewhat perplexed air at this vessel, which we could not see from the deck.

" She is a brig with her topgallant masts struck."

" Indeed !"

" No," stammered the carpenter.

" What then ?"

" A ship with all her canvas unbent."

" Unbent ! that is strange," said Hartly, shading his eyes, and peering away to leeward.

" No—now, sir, she looks like a brigantine, or

hermaphrodite brig, with her yards topped up in different ways."

" Do you wish your nightcap sent up to you, Tom ?" said the mate, drily ; " look again, perhaps she is the *Flying Dutchman*."

" Or the ghost of the *Black Schooner*," said one.

" Or a whale," added another.

But on nearing the edge of the ice-field—so close that we sent off the mate in the jolly boat with the warps, and handed our canvas, preparatory to resuming the war against the seals—we could all see the vessel which Hammer had discerned, lying among the ice about fifteen miles off, and various were the discussions on board as to her rig and nation. Even our oldest seamen were puzzled. Her hull was scarcely visible, so high were the hummocks around her. She had two masts, but her spars were, as Tom said, topped up in various ways and at various angles, and seemed covered by long-accumulated ice and snow, from which we augured that she had been long beset.

We hoisted our colours and displayed the private signal of Messrs. Manly and Skrew, but received no response, by which we supposed that she had been deserted by her crew, or that her signal halliards had given way

Some averred stoutly that they could distinguish a flag flying at her gaff peak; others that she had no gaff peak whatever, but had *one* man seated in her fore rigging.   Hartly ridiculed these fancies, saying that the intensity of the cold, and the dazzling glare of the sun shining on a sea covered by white ice, bewildered the vision of most men; and so, full of vague conjectures as to what our neighbours might be, we saw the sun set and night close in upon us.

Next morning another large field of ice was discovered on our larboard quarter, closing in upon us with considerable rapidity.   It extended along the offing for twelve or fourteen miles, and increased to the eye as it was borne towards us by an undercurrent.

Hartly conjectured it had drifted down Hudson's Strait from the Bay, and to avoid being *beset* like the unfortunate craft we had been observing, he brought off the ice-anchor and made sail on the brig, steering due west and keeping her close hauled with his starboard tacks on board; but the field of ice we endeavoured to leave kept close alongside, as if it sailed or floated *with* us, which I have no doubt it did.

Thus both fields verged towards each other rapidly,

one before the wind, the other before a current ; and
so, ere sunset, we were closely wedged in a frozen sea
—BESET, amid a wilderness of pack-ice, of bergs, and
hummocks, which extended, as far as the eye could
discern from the main-crosstrees, in every direction,
and probably far beyond the horizon.

Though this predicament was not without great
peril, still it was preferable by many degrees to our
last situation ; for here we could pursue the object
of our expedition, and hoped to have our cargo complete, the hatches battened down, and all ready for
our return to Newfoundland when the ice broke up,
amid the warmer water of more southern latitudes,
towards which we expected the field, like others,
would be borne by the currents.

Alas ! how little did we then foresee how long we
and our desolate neighbour, whose disordered aspect
and bare spars made her resemble a withered bush
or bunch of reeds at the horizon, were to remain in
sight of each other.

CHAPTER XVI.

BESET WITHOUT HOPE.

I CARED little about the slaughter of the seals,—
indeed, I rather disliked it—and for several days my
attention was excited solely by the vessel which was
beset so far from us.

My imagination drew many painful scenes.   I
endeavoured to picture how long she had been
there—weeks, months, it might be years !

Where was she from ?   What had she been—a
ship, brig, or schooner ? for by the confusion of her
rigging, and the distance at which she lay from us,
there was a difficulty in discovering this, even by
by our most powerful glasses, or whether the smoke
ever rose from her galley funnel.

How many of her crew were alive, or had she a
crew at all ?   If so, what were their sufferings—if
abandoned, amid that world of ice, whither had
they gone, and where had their perilous journey

ended ? On Greenland, on the Labrador, or in the grave ?

These queries were for ever recurring to me, and that old beset ship—I had made up my mind that she *was* old—was the first object to which my eyes turned when coming on deck in the morning, and the last at night. Fogs—the dense fogs of the Arctic seas—came on and shrouded us for days, till one's lungs almost filled with icy vapour, and the pulses of the heart seemed to freeze. The wind blew a gale at times, but the ice remained fast as adamant around us ; but when the obscurity passed away, there lay the beset ship in the dim distance, wearing the same lifeless aspect as ever, so dreary and forlorn amid that waste of cold white glistening ice, with its endless vistas of hummocks and splintered bergs.

We became somewhat alarmed on discovering by observations that instead of drifting into southern latitudes, where the ice-fields are usually broken into floes, and a ship becomes free to shape her course in any direction, we were being borne almost due west, and with considerable rapidity By this the temperature remained nearly the same, and our besetting, like that of our unfortunate neighbour, became a permanence, and would probably continue so, unless we weathered Cape Farewell, of which Hartly had some doubts at that season.

We had now reached the first week of April, and could only look forward to the early days of May, when the field-ice breaks up, and from the unknown seas and inlets of the north, floats southward in masses so mighty, that a girdle of ice, sometimes two hundred miles in breadth, environs the coasts of Newfoundland and the Labrador.

Ere long we became sensible of a tremendous pressure upon the sides of the brig, a pressure so great that her timbers in some· places became distorted, and Hartly was seriously alarmed lest she might be crushed and destroyed.

This unwonted pressure rendered us very anxious, and inspired many with dread.

One night when it was greater than usual, I was on deck, and from thence ascended into the main-rigging a little way to contemplate the snow-covered scene—so vast, so silent, and so terrible in its beauty !

Spreading far as the eye could reach—far beyond the old deserted ship, for such we deemed her now —lay the hummocks in uncounted myriads, ascending here and there into bergs and mountains, so impressive in their cold purity, so solemnizing in their silence and monotony, their spiral peaks glistening and vitreous against the blue immensity of the sky —an accumulation of ice and snow that would seem to have lasted since the will and hand of God had first separated the land from the water, and marked the limits of both.

While lost in reverie, and surveying this scene, a strange sound, like that which might be caused by the rending of a vast rock asunder, fell upon my ear; then there was a shock which made every fibre in my body tingle. A mighty power below us seemed to be hoisting the brig out of the ice, while her masts and hull began to sway to and fro.

"Aloft, lads—all hands aloft!" cried Hartly; "we are about to be crushed—God help us! for all is over with us now!"

All our men rushed into the rigging on hearing this terrible announcement, and at the same moment there was another crashing shock, and lo! about a league from us, there ascended slowly and vertically into the air, a sheet or wall of ice, perhaps twenty feet thick, nearly a hundred feet in height, and several miles in length!

Erect it stood for some moments, like a giant rampart, and then broke into fragments, and as the field collapsed below, these fell with a roar as if heaven and earth were coming together.

How many *millions of tons* might have been in that erected mass no man could conceive, but the thunder of their fall, as they crashed and glittered in the moonlight, caused one's soul to shrink with awe and wonder at the grandeur and sublimity of such a scene.

The ice around us cracked and rent in every direction, but though there was a vibration, a seeming heaving of the icebound sea, the brig settled down again into her bed, and we were only relieved of that intense pressure which had threatened us with immediate destruction.

"We are saved—for this time," said Hartly.

" Have the currents caused this?" I inquired.

"Partly: and the east edge of the ice-field has crashed upon a western shore."

"Greenland?" suggested Paul Reeves.

"Of course."

" Then we are to the *north* of Cape Farewell!"

I gazed wistfully towards the east. Hartly saw the glance, and smiled.

"You wish to snuff the land," said he; "but whether the land on which this mass of ice that imprisons us and our neighbour—a floating mass perhaps as large as Ireland—be just below the horizon, or two hundred miles distant, I have no means of ascertaining until I make a correct observation at noon."

The morrow came duly, and at twelve o'clock, Hartly, on consulting the sun and his chart, declared that we were at least one hundred and seventy miles due westward of Cape Farewell, on the coast of Greenland. We had thus drifted before the wind many hundred miles with the ice. The cold had now rendered the action of our compasses sluggish; but, situated as we were, that was of little consequence.

Our anxiety increased as our provisions diminished; we were placed upon a scanty allowance; symptoms of scurvy became visible among our seal-fishers; and how shall I find words to describe the intensity of the cold?

As we huddled together in the cabin at night, the ice actually came down the funnel of the stove, and formed a little arch above the fire. Our breath froze on our beards and whiskers, and on the blankets of our beds. The barrels of salted junk had to be dashed to pieces ere the food could be separated from the brine and staves. Stiff grog froze as hard as our beer; and every day a smoky haze rose from the sea, and freezing as it rose, when blown about by the wind, seemed to scrape the very skin off one's face. This *frost-rime* frequently enveloped us like a dense fog for days, and when it cleared, the wearied eye had no object to rest on but the everlasting ice and the old ship in the dreary distance.

Chancing to stumble one day against the anchor, my bare hand touched the fluke, and a portion of skin adhered to it as if it had been hot iron.

We hunted diligently for seals, as they formed our staple food, when cooked on a fire of blazing blubber. The flesh of the cub, especially the heart and liver, when hashed, and well seasoned with pepper, was not unacceptable to appetites sharpened by the northern blast that came from the Arctic circle.

The middle of April came and passed away without a change, save that the sun shone with a brilliance which somewhat alleviated the cold. One day, at noon, I saw Hartly form a piece of pure fresh-water ice from the scuttle-bucket into a lens, through which he concentrated the rays of the sun as through a burning-glass, and thus igniting little puffs of powder on the capstan-head, to the great astonishment of our seamen, and the terror of Cuffy, who began to consider him a species of Obi man.

So day followed day of captivity!

Seal-hunting and idling over, we would assemble, and sit for hour after hour, crouching close together for warmth, around our little fire, watching the glowing embers and the upward sparks; often in dreamy silence, mentally wondering where, when, and *how* this monotony, misery, and suffering were to end!

At times each almost fancied himself the last man in the world—and certainly we were the last men to be envied. Then terrible sensations crept over us, and horror filled our souls—the horror of being the *last survivor*, when famine and death came together among us.

As a relief from this intolerable monotony, a party of us resolved to visit the other ship. All were anxious to go; but Hartly said we could never know the moment when the ice would partially break up; thus half the crew at least must remain with him for the safety of the whole.

Furnished with a sledge, on which we placed a supply of such provisions as the *Leda* could afford, a small breaker, or gang-cask of stiff grog, hatchets, guns, a compass, plenty of blankets, and tobacco, so as to be ready for any emergency or detention, twelve men—Paul Reeves, Hans Peterkin, Tom Hammer, Cuffy, and myself inclusive—departed one bright morning about an hour after dawn, resolved to overhaul the stranger, and if we found her deserted, to cut away her masts, and drag them to the brig for fuel, though she lay now at least fifteen miles distant.

CHAPTER XVII.

THE DEATH-SHIP.

INURED though we were to the cold, we felt the toil and peril very great when traversing the ice for fifteen miles ; but fortunately the day was clear, and not a speck of cloud appeared upon the blue immensity of the sky.

The crew of the *Leda* cheered us from time to time until we were at some distance, when they hoisted a red flag at the mainmast-head ; but in the hollows between the hummocks and vast blocks of ice which were jammed and piled upon each other by the recent concussion and compression of the field, we lost sight of both ships at times, and could only discover them while surmounting some of the frozen ridges.

We toiled bravely, anxious to attain the object of our journey ere night came on, as we were assured of quarter on board, whatever might be the circumstances of this strange-looking craft, the attention of whose crew our colours by day, and our lanterns by night, had totally failed to attract.

Fifteen miles over an ice-field—especially *such* an ice-field as that which inclosed us, rent by chasms in some places, and piled in giant blocks elsewhere— were equal to the toil of traversing forty miles on land; thus about two P.M., we found ourselves only eight miles from the *Leda,* but rapidly gaining on the hull of the strange craft, which seemed to rise out of the ice as we approached, and the aspect of which puzzled us more than ever. We halted for a brief space; then each man partook of a biscuit and piece of seal's flesh boiled, a ration of rum, and in ten minutes more we pushed on again, four dragging our sledge, laden with stores, by shoulder-belts made for the purpose, and relieved by other four at every two miles or so.

Our expedition was not without several dangers. Fog might come on and conceal both ships from us; a blinding storm of snow might have the same effect, and pile its drifts above our corpses for ever. The ice-field might break up, and separate us from our ship so long that when our slender stock of necessaries was expended, we should infallibly perish. Each man among us thought of these possible and

terrible contingencies as the distance increased between us and the *Leda*—our home amid the icy
waste—but none spoke of them *then;* all sang
cheerily, and pushed on to overhaul the strange
craft; thus about five in the afternoon we found
ourselves alongside, and all paused to survey her
with deep and undefinable emotions of awe in our
breasts, for she had evidently been long deserted,
and now wore a most chilling and desolate aspect.

She was an old-fashioned pink-built barque, of
about six hundred tons, with bulging ribs and bluff
bows; broad and clumsy in the counter and deep in
the bends—all fenced about with iron bands; she
looked like a whaler of George the Second's time,
for, with a fiddle head, she had the remains of a
jack-staff and spritsail yard upon her bowsprit.
Her hull and spars were thickly coated with ice.

Her fore and main topmasts were gone; her mizen
was broken off at the crosstrees, and hung, truck
downward, in its gear.

The topping-lifts and braces of the yards had
long since given way, and tatters of them swung
mournfully on the wind. Many of the yards had
dropped from their slings, and lay athwart the deck
or among the ice alongside, where the gales had
tossed them.

Her ironwork was red and corroded; almost every

vestige of paint and tar had long since disappeared, as if she had been scraped by the ice; beaten, battered, and washed by Arctic storms, American fogs, and Greenland showers of sleet and rain, for many, many years must have elapsed since the keel of this old craft had last been in blue water, and first been frozen in the treacherous ice; years of drifting to and fro in the far and frozen regions of the north, where perchance not even the eye of the Esquimaux had seen her.

We seemed all to read and know her history instinctively at a glance; but her crew—what had their fate been?

Inspired by a strange emotion, we hung back, while gazing at her, as she stood like a silent ruin, or the ghost of a ship in the frosty sunshine of the April evening; but no man attempted to board her, till Paul Reeves, taking a hatchet from the sledge, exclaimed,

"Come on, shipmates—we'll overhaul her!" and proceeded at once to mount from the ice into her mainchains. As he grasped the starboard shrouds about the upper dead-eyes, the whole gave way from their rotten cat-harpings and crashed about him, with a shower of the ice that had coated them for years.

"By Jove! lads, 'twas not yesterday this craft left the rigger's hands!" said he, as we clambered after him, and at length stood upon her deck, which was coated about two feet deep with hard frozen snow, on the pure whiteness of which no foot-track was visible.

Sailors are ever superstitious; but theirs is an honest and reverential superstition, very different from that of the landsman; thus in breathless silence our party paused upon her deck, as if it had been the lid of a huge coffin.

"Go on—go on!" said several; yet no man moved, for there was a deathlike silence in and around her.

Her main-hatch was battened down; but we could see that the companion aft and the fore-hatch were partly open. Her long-boat was turned keel upmost on deck, aft the foremast; and by other indications it had doubtless formed a species of round-house. Various large white bones, fragments of broken casks, coils of old bleached ropes, and rusty harpoons were strewn about, and served to indicate that she had been a whale-ship.

Urged by curiosity, I proceeded towards her cabin, my eleven shipmates following closely at my heels.

The skylight was covered with snow; yet through a broken pane I could perceive the figures of men below: then I turned to descend into her

dark, gloomy, and slimy cabin, on entering which
I beheld a wondrous scene of horror, such as can
never be forgotten by me, nor was it by those who
accompanied me.

The red glow of the sun, now setting beyond the
distant waste of ice, shone from the west through
her two square stern windows, pouring athwart her
cabin a sombre and dusky light. Its sides were
covered by a damp mould, which was green and thick
as moss. Nearly three feet of snow, which had
drifted down the companion-hatch, was lying upon
its floor; half buried among it and huddled close
together in a corner, lay the bodies of three
emaciated men, with fur caps tied under their
wasted jaws.

A blue and ghastly hand that hung over one of
the cabin berths announced that a dead man lay
there; and seated at the table was another, whose
arms, head, and back were half covered by the snow
that had drifted over him after he had sunk into the
sleep of death. His coat was old in fashion, with
large brass buttons and square pocket-flaps. Amid
the snow that covered the table, and amid which
his face was hidden, there appeared the necks of
one or two square case-bottles—empty.

A quill was also standing amid the snow, and
seemed to indicate that the dead man had been

writing, for it was still in the pewter inkhorn, and near it stood a lamp, used by him probably to keep his ink from freezing. Close by appeared the corner of a book, which I drew with difficulty from amid the frozen snow, and then impelled by a horror, of that cold dark floating grave, like frightened school-boys we rushed up the cabin-stairs, and regained the deck, just as the last segment of the sun's red disc went down beyond the frozen sea.

We stood in a group near the mouldering main-mast, gazing at each other awe-struck, for we had looked on the faces of men who had been dead for years—how many, we knew not.

" There is *something moving* in the forehold!" exclaimed Tom Hammer, the carpenter, while his teeth chattered alike with cold and fear.

" Something ?" I reiterated.

" Ay, sir, and alive, too! Do you hear *that?*" added old Hans Peterkin, in terror.

It was a strange, croaking sound ; and then, as we approached the half-open hatch of the forehold, we heard the flapping of large wings.

Though almost paralysed by hearing such an unwonted sound in such a place, one of our seal-fishers fired his gun in his confusion. I crept forward and peeped fearfully down, but could not distinguish anything amid the gloom below.

Then we heard another *croak*, which sounded so loud and so dreadful to our over-strained organs of hearing that it nearly made us all scamper over the side; when suddenly two giant ravens, who had doubtless long made the empty wreck their home, rose through the fore-hatchway on their black booming pinions, and soaring high into the clear air, winged their way directly to the east, and so swiftly t'a t they soon disappeared.

"The land lies where they are flying to," said Reeves.

"And it is not far off, as their presence here would indicate," added a seaman.

This idea encouraged us all very much, as we forgot that they might have floated with the ice-field for years. We were about to descend into the forehold, but on lifting the other half of the decayed hatch, we found the frozen remains of a man hanging there by the neck, and half devoured by those obscene birds. A capstan-bar had been placed athwart the combing, and to this he had suspended himself by a well-greased rope.

Was this unfortunate the last survivor, who, in desperation, had thus awfully ended his misery?

His situation seemed to say so.

CHAPTER XVIII.

LEAVES FROM THE LOG.

WE repaired to our sledge alongside, and dragging it a little way from the deserted barque, took a ration of grog (of which we stood much in need), and then I proceeded to examine the volume we had brought away. It proved to be the mouldered fragments of a log-book or diary kept by the mate—doubtless the dead man, who was seated on the stern locker, and whose body was reclining on the snow-covered cabin table.

From this book we could gleam that she was the *Royal Bounty*, a Peterhead whaler, which had been beset in the ice off Cape Desolation in 1801, and that one by one all her crew had perished of cold, hunger, and despair!

The thick and crystalline coat of ice which covered every portion of the ship, from her tops to her chain-plates—a coat that had never melted or been disturbed—had protected her rigging, spars, and hull from the natural progress of decay; so let none suppose it marvellous that in a region or atmosphere of eternal snow, bodies are also thus preserved; for frequently the remains of elephants and mammoths which lived before the flood, and of pre-Adamite monsters, are found buried in the Arctic ice, unchanged, undecayed, and entire.

At the mouth of the Lena, in Siberia—a river which traverses the vast and uninhabited plains of Asiatic Russia—there was discovered, in 1805, a mammoth entire, with the hair on its skin four inches long, and all of a reddish-black; and so frequently are similar discoveries made along the shores of the Frozen Sea, that the poor Russians believe that race of animals to be still extant in their country, but existing like moles which dwell underground, and cannot endure the light of day; and their exhumation from the ice is ever deemed a forerunner of calamity, as it is said that all who see them die soon after. But to resume.

The book was much mouldered and decayed; only a few entries here and there could be traced, as its leaves, now soft and pulpy, perished in our fingers when we attempted to turn them over. A few passages ran thus:—

" March 3rd, 1801 ; a brisk breeze from the S.W
The Faroe Isles bearing about twenty miles off on
our starboard quarter.

" At 7 P.M., took in the topgallant sails, and all
fore and aft canvas   set the

" April 4, 8 P.M. Set more canvas—out reefs—
set foretopmast and maintopgallant studdingsails.
Ice-floes a head. Compasses not working well. The
captain ordered   . and Cairns

" 9 P.M. Land ahead—supposed to be Cape Farewell. Weather squally. Beset by an ice-field in a
strong current running N. and by E. Took in
everything fore and aft—sent down the topgallant-
yards, and brought the masts on deck   "

After a successful whale fishing in latitude 76°—
77°, they had been again, or were still, beset.

" 1st May, 1801 ; hoisted a garland of false
flowers, made by our wives and sweethearts at home
in Scotland, between the fore and mainmast   "

Then followed days and weeks, to the effect that
they were *still beset.* These memoranda were in
the handwriting of various persons, and were frequently mingled with earnest prayers for release.
Then scurvy appears to have broken out among
them, and disease was quickly followed by death.

" 1802. Birnie from Buchan-ness, off duty, unwell—Birnie's teeth fell out of his head. Willie Cairns from Southhouse Head, off duty, unwell. Poor Birnie died, and was buried in the ice, where the *others* lie, half a mile off, on the starboard bow God rest them!

"May 6th. Jobson ill with scurvy and blindness— Cairns died, and was buried beside Birnie   ."

Many leaves totally illegible followed, till we deciphered a passage like this—

"1802, 4th Dec. The captain died in his berth this day at 8 A.M., and we are too weak to move him. Smith, Arthur, and the cook are dead, or dying of hunger on the cabin floor! We have now been beset two years and twenty-one days. In that time twenty-four men have died out of a crew of nine-and-twenty—no hope! no mercy! My God! where is all this to end? We sailed upon a Friday, and this   "

I shut the book abruptly, for I could perceive in the twilight a blank horror stealing over the pale features of my companions as we stood beside that old vessel—a frozen tomb; and favoured by the light of the rising moon, we proceeded to regain the *Leda*, with all the speed we could exert; for to some it appeared as if *our* future fate was fearfully foreshadowed in the story of this old doomed whale-ship.

Half a mile distant, on her starboard bow, an ice-coated pole was visible. It seemed to indicate where her dead were buried.

Hans Peterkin and three others strapped the collar-ropes over their shoulders for the first " spell," and proceeded briskly in front with our sledge of blankets, &c. The rest followed in silence, and only turned from time to time to cast a backward glance at the old whaler, whose decaying spars, coated with ice, glimmered darkly against the starry sky. The moon arose in her full northern splendour—clear, glorious, and wondrous ! The sharp summits of the bergs (the ice-mountains that rose from the plains of ice) gleamed and glittered like mighty prisms, or spires, pyramids, and obelisks of crystal and spar.

After all we had seen, the dead, the awful still-ness of the frozen sea—that snow-clad plain, " the silence of which seemed to come from afar and to go afar," impressed us with deep and solemn emotions. Thus, for several miles we trod gloomily on, equally desirous of reaching the *Leda* and of leaving far behind the scene of gloom I have described.

The spirits of our party were sorely depressed ; but Paul Reeves and I did everything in our power, by cheerfulness and anecdotes, to divert the gloomy current of their ideas; though poor Paul was not without fears that a day might come when he would be inserting in the log of the *Leda*, entries similar to those I have quoted from the mouldering volume we had brought away.

"We have found a ship of the dead," said he, "but that is nothing! What think you, shipmates, of a whole city full?"

"A city full!" reiterated our men.

"Not exactly a city like London—but a city, nevertheless."

"And where was this?" asked Hans, doubtfully.

"I read of it in a book—a real printed book— when I was in South Carolina. There was one Lionel Wafer, an English surgeon, who, having nobody to physic at home, took a voyage with the old buccaneers to the South Seas. Well, on one occasion, his craft was cruising off Vermijo, at the mouth of the Red River, in Peru. It was a wild and solitary place; but he went ashore with a boat's crew, and travelled four miles up the stream in quest of adventures; and there, from the margin of a fine sandy bay, a plain spread inland as wide as this ice-field, all covered with the ruins of streets, built of mighty blocks of stone carved with wonderful sculptures, like those of the Egyptians—only more terrible and

M

quaint; and among these crumbling streets and
mansions were thousands of graves half open, with
the dead bodies of men, women, and little children in
them, all mummified and light as cork, for they had
been dead two hundred years or more.

"His men were terrified, and fled back to their
boat; but on the way they met an old Indian, who
related that, in the days of his forefathers, this arid
plain had once been fruitful and green as the greenest
savannah, and the country so populous, that a fish
of the Red River could have been passed through
the land from hand to hand, till it was laid at the
foot of the throne of the Inca (that was their king,
shipmates); but the cruel, murdering Spaniards came,
with their guns and bloodhounds, and laid siege
to the capital city. Its defence was long and desperate; and rather than yield, the inhabitants slew
themselves, and buried each other in the sand, till
there was only one man left, and *he* drowned himself
in the Red River.

"In after years the stormy winds had blown the
dry sand aside, and there the grim Mexicans lay in
thousands—the women with the pearls of Vermijo
at their ears and round their necks, their little
children, their distaffs and hand-mills by their sides,
and their long black hair filled with coins and

precious stones. There, too, lay the warriors, with their flint axes and broken spears, and the war-paint yet traceable on their mummies. Lionel Wafer brought away the body of a child, but the buccaneers would not admit it on board lest it might bring a plague or a curse upon them; so he threw it into the Rio Grande."

This yarn produced others equally lively, of course; but while conversing we got over the dreary waste of hummocks more rapidly, and some time after midnight were welcomed on board the *Leda*, where those whom we had left were burning with curiosity to learn the result of our expedition.

The impression of all we had seen was so vivid, that a horror lest the same fate should befal us, made our men suggest and revolve every rash plan for release.

The flight of the two ravens eastward indicated that land could not be far off. Hans Peterkin, a hardy Orcadian, who was suffering from scurvy, proposed that if matters grew more desperate, we should travel over the field, taking with us the longboat upon sledge-runners. Some urged that we should bore through the ice with canvas set, while gangs went ahead blasting it up with gunpowder.

"Bore and blast through ice twenty feet thick,

for a hundred miles, perhaps!" said Hartly, with sorrowful irony.

But scurvy continued to increase among us; and on the eighth day after our visit to the ship one of our crew died, and was buried in the ice; while the brig was thrown in mourning, her colours half-mast, her running-gear cast in loose bights, and her yards topped up variously.

After his funeral, which had a most depressing effect upon us all, I remarked to Hartly, that either by a strange coincidence or by an irresistible fatality, we had interred him *half a mile distant on the starboard bow*, exactly as the crew of the old whaler had interred *their dead !*

CHAPTER XIX.

THE GRAVES ON THE STARBOARD BOW.

THE last of our stone ballast had long since been thrown overboard on the ice, and was replaced by seal skins. We had now a valuable cargo, over which the hatches were barred and battened; but Hartly's hopes for an honest profit on his adventurous expedition were forgotten, or merged in the overwhelming desire for freedom and the safety of our lives and of the brig.

Already five deaths were recorded in her log; and Hartly vowed that if ever again her bows cut blue water, he would never more tempt Dame Fortune in *the region of ice.*

By this time our monotonous detention had so far exceeded every expectation and contingency, that our beer, rum, and other spirits, our salted beef, preserved meats, and lime-juice were consumed; and though our biscuits were doled out in very small rations indeed, grim starvation was before us, or food composed of seal and blubber alone ; so scurvy in its worst forms assailed us all more or less. Our strongest seamen were the first who sank under it : their complexions became yellow, with swollen gums, loosened teeth, and fetid breath. These symptoms were accompanied by a difficulty in respiring, which, on the least exertion being made, amounted almost to suffocation.

Two of our gunners died one evening within an hour of each other. We wrapped them in blankets, and buried them quickly, under cloud of night, lest the survivors might be affected by the scene.

Hartly, Hans Peterkin, Cuffy, and I performed this melancholy office, when we had no lamp but the twinkling stars and the sharp streamers of the northern lights, shooting upward from the icebergs that edged the plain, over which the wind blew keen and bitingly.

Grim seemed the pale faces of the dead in that wavering gloom, as we lowered them into their last home, heaped the ice above them, and returned to the *Leda*, leaving them to sleep the sleep of death among their shipmates *half a mile distant on her starboard bow.*

And now with each day there sank a deeper horror

over us—the horror that, like the old whaler at the horizon, the *Leda* was a ship foredoomed! Yet, like her, we had *not* sailed upon a Friday.

We were without a surgeon; but Hartly was a skilful fellow, and by administering such simples as we possessed, he endeavoured to ameliorate the condition of his suffering crew.

Common potatoes he washed, cut into thin slices, and gave raw to some, for the cure of their swollen and bleeding gums—usually a sovereign remedy in this case. To others he gave decoctions of tamarinds, scraped from an old gallipot, and boiled with cream of tartar; or a ship biscuit pounded into a panada, and sweetened with sugar; or gargles made of honey of roses and elixir of vitriol; but, ere long, even these remedies failed us; and we had Reeves, Hans Peterkin, and more than half our remaining crew, unable to raise their heads or hands, sick and despairing.

The miserable Esquimaux, by scraping the snow from their native rocks, can find coarse berries, sorrel, and cresses, with which to correct their blubber food; but in that world of ice we had no such boon accorded us.

Armed with our rifles and knives, I set forth with two of our healthiest men, Dick and James Abbot, two brothers, in search of a few fresh seals, as they had learned to shun our locality, and had ceased to venture through their holes in the ice for some time past.

We left the brig about two o'clock, P.M.

On this day the wind was blowing hard, the white scud was flying fast through the blue sky, and for the first time we felt a heaving motion in the ice, which warned us instinctively *not* to venture far from the *Leda*. After a ramble of three hours, we had only shot one seal and knocked two cubs on the head with our rifle-butts, when we sat down on a hummock to rest, at the distance of two miles or so from our ice-bound home.

" I wonder much how the masts of that old craft the *Bounty* have stood these many years?" said Dick Abbot, breaking a long silence.

"The coating of ice has saved them, as it has preserved everything on board--from decay, at least," replied his brother.

" Always thinking of that ship," said I, with an air of annoyance. " Come, let us talk of something more cheerful. You know that she—but *where is she ?*" I added, as we swept the horizon in vain for her—the sole object on which our eyes had rested for so many dreary weeks.

" Sunk, by Jove! or can her old spars have gone by the board at last?" exclaimed James Abbot, starting up.

In great excitement we clambered to the summit of a mass of ice, and looked around us. Not a vestige of the old barque could be seen, but dense clouds that came heavily up from the north were overspreading the sky, against the blue of which her crystal-coated spars had so long been visible.

" We shall have foul weather," said Dick Abbot.

" And so they seem to think, sir, aboard the brig," added his brother: " see—they've run the ensign up to the gaff peak as a signal for us to return, Mr. Manly."

" But our three seals——"

" We must leave them where they are—that big hummock will mark where they lie till to-morrow."

" James is right, sir," said Dick Abbot; "let us get back to the brig as fast as we can."

" She is two miles distant, at least," said I.

" The sky darkens fast ; and see—see !" he added, with wild joy expressed in all his features, his eyes, and voice ; " the captain expects something—they've cast loose the courses, and are hoisting the topsail-yards—THE ICE IS BREAKING UP !"

These words made every pulse quicken, and as if

in corroboration of his surmise, we felt the field on
which we trod agitated by convulsive throes, and
these increased as the fierce and darkening blast,
armed with showers of hailstones large as peas, that
fell aslant the cold grey sky, deepened the atmosphere
around us.   Madly we toiled, scrambled, and rolled
—fell, rose, and fell again—shouted and cheered to
each other, as we surmounted the endless succession
of glassy hummocks and snowy hollows to reach
the *Leda;* but the gloom increased so fast, that in
less than half an hour we could no longer distinguish where she lay.

We did not feel cold—our brains seemed on fire,
our bloodshot eyes were wild and eager in expression, as we toiled on and on—but *where* was the brig?

A misty veil of hail and snow—an atmosphere
dark as the twilight of the Scandinavian gods—enveloped us like a curtain.   We paused at times in
our desperation, and uttered a simultaneous hallo;
but no voice replied, no sound responded, save the
hiss of the hailstones as they showered on the hard
hummocks.   Then we heard from time to time a
stunning crash, as the field was rent asunder into
floes, that were surged and driven against each
other with such force as the waves of an irresistible
sea can alone exert.

To us this crisis was, as I have said, maddening. We tossed away our rifles, shot-belts, knives, bats, and everything that might impede our progress, and toiled in wild despair in search of the *Leda*— but alas, alas! the *Leda* was nowhere to be seen!

"Can we have passed her?" we asked repeatedly.

To return was to acknowledge still more that we were at fault.

Left upon the breaking ice, with night deepening, and a tempest, perhaps, coming on together; the ice-field rending into floes, and the *Leda*, when last seen, with her topsails loose for sea, and now we knew not where, but assuredly not within call of our united voices, which the envious wind, the very spirit of the wintry storm, swept from our trembling lips, as if in mockery of efforts and struggles so feeble as those of man when contending with the warring elements of God,—how terrible was our situation!

Inspired either by the activity of youth, or a greater dread of perishing, I left my companions some twenty yards behind me. In this race for life and death poor Dick Abbot was failing, and his younger brother was loth to leave him a single pace behind.

"Mr. Manly," I heard him cry, "take time, please; do you see anything yet, sir—of the brig, I mean?"

"Not a vestige," said I, turning to wait until they joined me.

The ice was bursting in every direction, and the waves seemed to boil through the yawning rents in snowy foam; vast pieces, like bergs, arose from the water, and were dashed against each other, to sink into the deep, to arise, and then be dashed together again. Add to this the darkness of the gathering night, the roar of the biting wind, and the dense murkiness caused by the hail as it swept through that mighty waste, and the reader may have an idea of the scene when I paused and looked back for my two companions.

At that moment the ice heaved beneath my feet, I was thrown forward on my face and almost stunned. There was a terrific splitting sound as the field around us broke into a thousand floes: I found myself separated from my two friends, upon a piece of ice about half a mile square, and borne away with it, despairing and alone, into the mist and darkness of the stormy night.

CHAPTER XX.

ADRIFT ON THE DEAD FLOE.

ALL was obscurity around me—a chaos of tumbling waves, of crashing ice and hissing hail.

I shouted wildly, fiercely, as the dying or despairing alone may shout.

A faint response seemed to come through the drift and the hail that was sowing the ice and pathless sea; but it might have been fancy, or my own cry tossed back by the mocking wind. And now from time to time I was covered by the icy *spoondrift*, as the water which the wind sweeps from the wave-tops is named by seamen.

For a time I felt the impossibility of realizing the actual horrors of such a situation, and murmured repeatedly—

"Oh, this cannot be reality; if so, it must soon come to an end, and I shall be dead!"

The floe on which I sat surged and rolled heavily,

as it was rasped, dashed against others, and whirled round in the eddies they made. On its slippery surface I was driven hither and thither, even when seated; and at last, on finding myself among some large stones which were frozen into the snow, and which I knew to be a portion of the brig's ballast, I shuddered with instinctive dread when discovering that I was adrift on that portion of the ice in which our dead were buried, and which had lain on her starboard bow. Thus I learned that at the moment of my separation from the Abbots, I had been within half a mile of the *Leda.*

There was agony in this now useless conviction !

" Am I to find a grave here, after all ?" was my thought.

If I could live till dawn, the crew of the *Leda* (if she, too, survived the night) might see and save me ; but who could live on an ice-floe through so many freezing hours ?

After a time the wind lulled, the hail ceased, the clouds were divided in heaven, and a star or two shone in its blue vault. The ice-blocks ceased to crash against the floe, thus its motion became steadier, and under the lee of a hummock, I endeavoured to keep myself as warm as my upper garments, which were entirely composed of seal-skins, would enable me.

The moon was rising, and its fitful light added to the chaotic terrors of the scene around me. To be alone—*alone* upon a floe at midnight, with the open sea rolling around me! All seemed over with me now. I felt that my sufferings could not last long, as I should certainly pass away in the heavy slumber of those who perish by exhaustion and intensity of cold. In spite of this horrible thought, I gradually became torpid.

I had been, perhaps, an hour in this situation, when I seemed suddenly to start to life, as a bank of vapour close by parted like a crape curtain, and the moonbeams fell upon the white canvas of a vessel. She was a brig—she was the *Leda*, under weigh, and distant from the floe not more than one hundred yards!

She was under sail, with her foreyards aback to deaden her way, as she was rasping along a lee of ice-floes and *brash*, as the smaller fragments are technically named. The weather had now become so calm, that her canvas, which glittered white as snow in the moonshine, was almost, as the sailors say, *asleep*, there being just sufficient wind to keep it from waking.

I endeavoured to shout, but my tongue was paralysed as if in a nightmare; sobs only came from my heart, and I thought all sense would leave me, as the brig, like a spectre, came slowly gliding past. Again and again I endeavoured to hail her, but in vain.

I rushed to the edge of the floe, at the risk of slipping off it into the sea. Then a faint shout reached my ear, and made my heart throb with joy. Those on deck could not hear my voice, but they had seen my figure in the moonlight; and in a few minutes I beheld a boat shoved off from her, and heard the cheerful voice of old Hans Peterkin, crying with his Orkney *patois*—

"Quick, my lads—lay out on your oars!" as they pulled through the rack and drift towards me.

I was soon dragged on board the boat, and on reaching the deck of the *Leda*, fainted, after all I had undergone, and the joy of escaping a death so terrible. The last sounds I remember were the voice of Hartly welcoming me, and the jarring of the yards and braces, as the foreyards were filled, and the brig payed off bravely before the gentle breeze.

Of my unfortunate companions, no trace was ever seen!

CHAPTER XXI.

CAPE FAREWELL.

For three days our course was encumbered by masses of broken ice, which seemed to crowd upon and follow us; thus the brig was constantly being put about or thrown in the wind, backing and filling to avoid the large floes and calves, as those treacherous pieces of sunken or detached ice which suddenly rush to the surface are named. To avoid the lesser floes, we had often to carry a warp to a large one, and track along its side. The cheerful voice of Hartly might always be heard encouraging the faint and weary on these occasions.

"Now, my lads—tally on! bowse away upon the guess-warp!"

"Hurrah!" the men would answer, as they pulled together vigorously.

"Once more we are afloat, Jack," said he to me, on the third morning. " I began to fear we should

N

berth all our ship's company in the ice that lay on
the starboard bow; but now we may sit cosily in
the cabin, as of yore, and learn how her head lies by
the *tell-tale* compass that swings in the skylight."

Again at sea, our sick recovered as if by a miracle;
but still many antidotes against scurvy were requisite before we could haul up for the long voyage
that lay between us and St. John.   I caught a few
fish, and they formed a delicious change for Cuffy's
fricasees of odious blubber, served up half cold in a
greasy mess-kid.

Once more there was a reckoning to keep.   For a
few cloudy days we had merely kept a dead one, by
log and compass; but on making a solar observation,
Hartly and Reeves found that they were many
hundred miles eastward of where they expected to
be; and this was a circumstance over which they
had no control.

It is well-known that a current which comes down
Davis' Straits eddies round the east coast of Greenland.   By this we had been borne towards its
western shore with great rapidity.

In 1818, the *Anne*, of Poole, when beset by an
ice-field, was thus drifted at the rate of two hundred
and twenty miles per day!

Early on the morning of the fourth day, the sea

was pretty clear of floes; but a dense and dusky fog-bank came down like a curtain, and seemed to float upon the water, about twenty miles from us. We had suffered considerably in our besetting, and by concussions among the floes; so, as the morning was calm and sunny, Hartly had all hands at work, tarring, painting, and repairing our various damages. A spare jib-boom was shipped, and it was soon taut with its heel-rope and jib-guys; our rudder was finally repaired, and two new staysails were being bent, when there was a cry of "land" from aloft.

"Land in sight!" shouted Hans Peterkin, who was out on the arm of the fore-topgallant yard, re-pairing something.

"Land!—where?" asked Hartly, snatching his telescope from the companion.

"On the lee quarter, sir."

"You must have deuced good eyes, Hans," said the captain, sweeping along the fog-bank with his glass; "for nothing like land can I see!"

"The bank is rising, sir," replied the Orcadian, as he sat jauntily astride his lofty perch, and pointed to the east. "I see either an island or headland."

Even while he spoke, the dense mountain of vapour, behind which the morning sun was shining, rose slowly from the surface of the sea, and with the naked eye we could see, at the far horizon, a low dark streak, that ended in a bluff or promontory Hartly sharply closed his telescope.

"Luff, Paul—keep your luff," said he ; "lie closer to the wind, while I prick off our place on the chart." He hurried below ; but soon returned, saying, "That is either Cape Farewell, or I am bewitched."

"Off the coast of Greenland ?" said I.

"No, *on* the coast of Greenland," he replied, laughing. "And now, as the ice and current have driven us so near it in spite of our teeth, we may as well stand in for the shore, and get some fresh provisions, before bearing up for Newfoundland."

A careful examination of the chart proved that we had drifted, or been driven (in our endeavours to avoid the floes) to latitude 59° 48′ North, and were in longitude 43° 54′ West of Greenwich, consequently, the land we saw was undoubtedly Cape Farewell, a lofty promontory which forms the most southern extremity of Greenland.

With considerable satisfaction we stood in towards the shore, in the hope of obtaining supplies from some of the Moravian settlements.

About four hours after, some of the natives who were fishing came about us in their strange boats, which are made of whalebone covered with seal-skin, and shaped like a weaver's shuttle, so that they may be rowed any way.

By sunset we were close upon the land, and came to anchor several miles north of the cape in a little cove of Nennortalik, or the Isle of Bears, where, as Reeves said jestingly, we had no *groundage* to pay for letting go our cable; and there the wondering population of the little Moravian colony received us with acclamation. The canvas was handed and most of the crew were allowed to go on shore, with instructions to return with as much scurvy-grass as they could collect; for with this herb, like Baffin, the voyager of old, Hartly proposed to brew scurvy-beer for his patients.

CHAPTER XXII.

THE MUSK-OX.

REJOICING that we trod on firm land once more, Paul Reeves, Hans Peterkin, and I set off to shoot on the great Island of Sermesoak, which is divided from the mainland of Greenland by the Fin Whale Strait, while Hartly arranged with the Danish resident at the village for such supplies of fresh food as a place so poor could afford.

Leaving the Isle of Bears, we ran our boat into a creek called Cunninghame's Haven, from John Cunninghame, a Scotsman, who was Admiral of Denmark, and who, on his return from Davis' Straits, in 1605, appeared off Greenland with three ships, and carried away some of the natives, whom he presented to Christian IV., together with a chain weighing twenty-six ounces, formed of fine silver, found by him among the rocks at a place still named Cunninghame's Fiord.

With all our anxiety to add to the fresh provisions on board, we were not without a desire to encounter some of the bears with which one always associates the name of Greenland; and ere twenty-four hours elapsed, I was certainly gratified to the fullest extent in that way.

The people of Sermesoak were then in consternation, owing to the depredations of a fierce herd of Bruins which had crossed the strait from the mainland, and devoured many of their children, dogs, and reindeer.

These bears are as revengeful and subtle as they are savage. "Some years ago," says a traveller, "the crew of a boat belonging to a ship in the whale-fishery shot at a bear and wounded it. The animal immediately uttered the most dreadful howl, and ran along the ice towards the boat. Before he reached it a second shot hit him; this, however, served but to increase his fury. He presently swam to the boat, and in attempting to get on board, placed one of his fore-feet on the gunnel; but a sailor, having a hatchet in his hand, cut it off. The animal still continued to swim after them, till they arrived at the ship; several shots were fired at him which took effect, but on reaching the ship he ascended to the deck; and the crew having fled into the shrouds, he was actually pursuing them *thither* when a shot laid him lifeless on the deck."

Allured by the odour of the seal oil, they had surrounded and broken into the dwellings of the natives in herds, and devoured them in their beds ; and numerous stories of these terrible *raids* were told to Hans (who knew something of the language) by the people of Sermesoak, as we set out on our expedition.

We shot several white hares, and consigned them to a large canvas bag which Hans had slung over his shoulder. In our sporting ardour we penetrated several miles into the country, and in making a détour to beat up for nobler game, I lost my companions among the furze-covered rocks of a ravine. Dusk was coming on, and, wearied with halloing, I sat down to look around me. I was quite alone and in a strange place, but more safe and comfortable in every way than *when* I was alone on the ice-floe. Though in a foreign and barbarous country, this reflection set my mind completely at ease.

A wild and dreary scene lay around me.

Mountains piled on mountains of stern rock rose on every side, covered with snow unmarked by foot-step, track, or road. No trees were growing there and no verdure was visible, save some patches of short grass and moss where the wind had torn the snow from the rocky surface. It seemed as if the icy breath of the Northern Sea, when it swept through the Fin Whale Strait, destroyed all vegetable nature ; and as for the flowers of spring, one might as well have looked for them on an iceberg.

Why that country was named the *Green*land, Heaven only knows!

In 1610, Jonas Pool, a whaling captain, called it King James' Newland, from James VI. of Scotland; but that name was soon forgotten.

Above me impended a bluff of sullen aspect, the rifts of which formed the eyrie of myriads of white sea-gulls and birds like the great Solan goose of the Scottish isles ; and these were whirring, screaming, and booming on their broad pinions, as they came home from the shore.

As the shadows deepened, even these sounds ceased, and nothing met the ear but the croak of a lonely raven which sat on a granite boulder.

Far away in distance, down below me, stretched the headlands which jutted into the deep blue waters of the Whale Strait—starting up in fantastic pinnacles and precipitous ridges, like the towers and turrets of crumbling castles. These walls of rock were black and sombre, though their summits were crowned by eternal snow.

From the mountains the sleet and melting snows of ages have long since washed away every grain of earth; hence, no verdure can spring there, and their rugged fronts present the most harsh and singular outlines. The higher ridges are rendered inaccessible by glaciers; and when the snows melt from their gloomy lichened fronts, long and silvery runnels, that seem like threads in the distance, trickle down the precipices; then winter comes again, converting these runnels into ice, which splits and rends the hardest rock to fragments, that roll with the sound of thunder down the steep glaciers into the valleys below.

Leaning on my gun, I was surveying this wild and dreary scene, and careless alike of the cold and the coming night, was lost in reverie, when a sound aroused me, and on looking up, I saw close by an animal of strange form, such as I had never seen before, even in a menagerie.

It was larger than a pony, but had singularly short limbs, which were almost entirely concealed by the long dark hair that covered all its body, and reached nearly to the ground. It had a short tail, and large crooked horns of powerful aspect, with a mass of hair like a horse's mane hanging beard-wise under its throat.

A very strange sensation comes over one on beholding an unknown animal for the first time, and on this musk-ox—for such it was—approaching, with its large projecting eyes glaring, and while shaking those formidable horns, by which it can encounter and slay the bear and walrus, astonishment soon gave place to alarm, and I regretted more than ever the absence of my two comrades.

The ox was only a pistol-shot distant, so, with my heart beating quickly—as I knew not what the sequel might be—I levelled my gun, and fired full at its head. The animal uttered a bellowing roar, bounded furiously forward, and fell motionless on its side.

The ball had pierced its brain.

With a thousand echoes, the report of my gun rang among the hills of rock, peak after peak seeming to catch the sound and toss it from one to the other, until it died away on the wind that blew through the Fin Whale Strait.

I was not without hope that the sound might reach Reeves and Hans Peterkin, and guide them towards me; but I hoped in vain.

The ox I had slain was one of the largest of the Musk species, and might have weighed, perhaps, seven hundredweight. It would, I knew, prove a most acceptable addition to our scanty stores on board the *Leda;* moreover, I was not a little vain of having slain, by a single ball, an animal so large and so little known by Europeans; but *how* to get it conveyed to the brig, or how to guide any of our crew to the spot where it lay, were puzzling queries.

I observed that at the distance of a hundred yards from it, there rose a steep and rugged rock, cleft into three singular peaks, so lofty as to be visible from a great distance. Conceiving this to be a sufficient landmark, I reloaded my gun, and re-solved, if possible, to discover Cunninghame's Haven, where our boat lay. Without a track, a road, or native to guide me, I toiled over the steep and rugged mountains, and through ravines and hollows half filled with drifted snow, steering my way by the stars in that direction which I conceived might lead me to our boat.

To enhance the wildness and gloomy grandeur of the scenery, there now came a wondrous and fan-shaped light over all the clear cold blue of the north-ern sky—a glorious Aurora Borealis. This light, sent by Heaven to cheer the lone denizens of that

frozen wilderness, spread a rich and wavering glow
over all the northern firmament, playing in streaks
or lines that alternately faded away, and resumed
their dazzling brilliance.   These alternations fill
with awe the simple Greenlander, who calls them
the *Merry Dancers*, and who deems,

" By the streamers that shoot so bright,
The spirits are riding the Northern light."

At times, the whole sky seemed a blaze of diamond-
like light, tinged with rainbow hues, and in front of
these, the stern rocks, crags, and mountains stood
forth in sharp black outline.   Ever and anon, an
electrical meteor shot athwart the sky, leaving, as
these falling stars always do, a train of momentary
light.

Frequently the long streamers played across this
luminous white radiance as if a mighty fan were
being opened and shut, or like the spokes of some
revolving wheel whose axle was at the Pole.   Then
a burst of glory would open in the zenith, and for a
moment every feature in the desolate landscape and
the far-stretching vista of the Whale Strait between
its walls of rocks would be distinctly visible.

Alone in that sterile solitude, I gazed upon the
Aurora with emotions of mingled awe and wonder,

turning again and again to the north, as I stumbled over rocks and frozen snow piles in my efforts to discover a path that led to Cunninghame's Haven: so the result was this—that after more than an hour of toil, I found that I had been proceeding in a circle, and came back to the place from whence I had set out, the bluff with the three pinnacles, at the foot of which my musk-ox was lying; but there a very singular scene presented itself, for my property had already been converted into a banquet by two denizens of the wilderness.

CHAPTER XXIII.

THE FOUR BEARS.

On first approaching, I imagined that a heap of snow had fallen from the upper rocks on the dead ox, and advanced so close that I was only twenty paces from it before discovering in my supposed snow-heap two enormous white bears who were rending the body asunder with their giant claws as one might rend a chicken, and were devouring it with all the gusto of an appetite whetted by the frosty air.

To add to my dismay at this unexpected rencontre, I perceived close by, some portions of a human body, half-devoured—red, raw, and appalling!

A horror came over me, suggesting that this victim might be either Paul Reeves or Hans Peterkin; and it was not until some time after, that I was assured, by fragments of the dress which remained, that the unfortunate was a Greenlander, whom they had crushed to death and dragged away. Pausing in their banquet, these savage brutes, which were of enormous size, uttered a hoarse growl, and while their black nostrils seemed to snuff the breeze, their deep-set eyes surveyed me ominously.

My gun had but a single barrel, thus if I killed one bear I might fall a prey to the other before there was time to reload; and if my first shot missed, my fate would be sealed by both, as they were certain to crush and devour me between them!

Turning, I fairly fled up the rocks towards the three pinnacles, pursued by the bears, whose progress was slow, as they were evidently gorged by their double repast on the dead man and the musk-ox.

Twice I stumbled in my flight, and fell heavily on my hands and face. My breath came thickly and fast, and my long seal-skin boots and overalls, which were strapped up to a waistbelt, greatly incommoded me; but love of life and dread of a horrible death are sharp incentives to exertion and activity; thus I struggled to gain a cleft in the rocks, from whence I might turn and shoot down these unwieldy monsters at vantage and at leisure, while they trotted laboriously after me, uttering a succession of deep and menacing growls.

I had left them nearly fifty yards behind, while

clambering up the slope, terrified every instant lest by slipping on the ice-covered rocks I might roll down under their very paws. Already I was within twenty feet of the cleft, beyond which the dazzling gleam of the Aurora played, when a hoarser growl saluted my ears; and there—there—above me in the cleft—in the very haven I was toiling to reach, appeared a huge brown bear, squatted on his hams, licking his great red lips, and quietly waiting my approach!

Bewildered by this new enemy, taken in front and rear, for a moment I remained irresolute, with my rifle cocked, but not knowing which to shoot before I met the rest with my weapon clubbed; and now to add still more to my dismay and peril, a *fourth* bear appeared, advancing from another point!

The monster in the cleft above me, now began to utter hoarse and savage roars, in anticipation of my destruction, which seemed certain; for those northern bears are so cruel and rapacious, that the female secludes her cubs (of which she never has more than two at a litter) from the male, lest he should devour them during the first month of their blindness. I leave the reader to judge of my emotion on finding my single self opposed to *four* such antagonists; for the white Greenland bears are double the size of

those melancholy looking brown brutes whom one
may see dancing in the streets at home, being generally about twelve feet long.

I was blindly desperate, yet my heart did not
entirely fail; and I felt forcibly " how an influence
beyond our control lays its strong hand on every deed
we do, and weaves its iron tissue of necessity."

Clambering up the flinty face of the rocks to elude
the three, finding footing where, under circumstances less exciting, I might have found none, I
ascended resolutely towards the bear which stood in
the cleft snuffing the air, roaring, and showing his
glistening teeth.   Already his hot and fetid breath
began to taint the air about me.   I was within six
feet of him, when, taking an aim there was no
doubt would be true, I fired, and the conical ball
pierced deeply into his vast chest.

Maddened by pain, Bruin made a wild bound at
me, but missed his mark, as I crouched low; so he
rolled, dead I suppose, to the bottom of the rocks, in
his progress tumbling over one of those which were
in pursuit of me.   Springing into the cleft he had
so lately occupied, I hastened to reload, and defend
my position, for only one brute at a time could
assail me, unless there were, as I feared, others
among the rocks in my rear.

Now what were my emotions on discovering that in my exertions, while struggling up the rocks, the strap of my shot-belt had given way, and that I had *lost* it, with all my ammunition!

A wild perplexity filled my heart, and a cold perspiration burst over my temples; but at that moment of desperation a happy thought occurred to me.

Remembering that I had a long clasp-knife, which opened and shut with a spring, I applied it in bayonet-fashion to my rifle, and with my handkerchief lashed it hard and fast to the muzzle and ramrod head. This was barely accomplished, when one of the bears had its fore-paws on the edge of the rock whereon I stood, and by the light of the stars I could see his fierce red eyes, his long white teeth, and enormous claws, while burying my impromptu bayonet thrice in his great broad breast, and then the blood flowed darkly over his pure white coat. The wounds were not deep enough to kill him at once, so uttering roar after roar, the infuriated bear scraped away with his hind feet, making vigorous but ineffectual efforts to reach me, till by a furious kick I drove one of his paws off the ledge of rock. The other relaxed immediately, and then Bruin rolled like a great featherbed to the bottom, about thirty feet below, where he moved no more.

But in a moment a second bear took his place. Emotion almost exhausted me ; but in my confusion when charging him, fortunately my knife was thrust into his right eye.   He uttered a hideous cry, between a bellow of rage and a moan of agony, and fell down the rocks—also dead !

The weapon had evidently penetrated to the brain, and killed him.

A wild and joyous glow now filled my heart.   It was a triumphant emotion, a lust for destruction and revenge, after the terror I had endured ; and I believe that had a whole army of bears appeared, I should, without fear, have encountered them—one by one.

Uttering a " hurrah" just as the fourth bear arrived at my feet, I was about to charge him as I had done the others when—oh, terror !—the knotting of my handkerchief gave way, and the knife dropped from the muzzle of my gun, and fell to the bottom of the rocks.

Clubbing the weapon, I rained a torrent of blows upon the great head of this new assailant, which seemed the largest and most ferocious of them all, as he probably had neither partaken of the poor

Greenlander or of that most unlucky musk-ox, the slaying of which had no doubt brought me into this perilous predicament ; but my blows fell on his fur-covered skull as harmlessly as they would have fallen on a bale of cotton.

Furiously I struck with butt and barrel at his broad black nose and great round paws, the deadly claws of which grasped the rock with the tenacity of iron hooks. Bruin uttered neither roar nor other sound, but concentrating all his energies, drew up his hams, made a vigorous spring, and in a moment I was dashed to the ground—his hot and horrible breath was in my nostrils and on my face, while his weight pressed me down as he prepared to hug or crush me to death. But now a gun-shot rang between the rocks of the deep chasm, and I found myself suddenly freed. Pierced through the heart by a single well-aimed ball, the bear rolled over me dead, a quivering mass of flesh and fur!

So severely was I stunned by the shock of Bruin's attack, and so confused by the whole combat, that some minutes elapsed before I had sufficient strength or breath to thank my preserver, to whom I might as well have spoken in Greek or Choctaw, as he proved to be a poor Greenlander who had never heard a word of English before.

CHAPTER XXIV.

WOLMAR FYNBÖE.

AFTER various efforts to make ourselves mutually understood, he said something in a kind of jargon which resembled German, and as I had learned that language at home for commercial rather than literary purposes, we contrived to converse, though not with great fluency, using grimaces and signs when words failed us, which was a circumstance of frequent occurrence.

He informed me that he had been searching for a friend who came forth to hunt for a musk-ox, which had been seen in their district, and who he feared had fallen a victim to its horns or the bear's paws.

" I shot the musk-ox," said I ; " and as for your friend, I fear your surmises are only too correct, for the half-devoured remains of a dead man are lying at the foot of these rocks just now."

He hurried to the base of the precipice, where I was too exhausted to follow him, and by the sounds of rage and lamentation which preceded his return, I was assured that his friend or kinsman had been the victim of these rapacious brutes. This comforted me, however, with the conviction that the remains were neither those of Paul Reeves nor old Peterkin, our second mate.

But, meantime, where were they?

The Greenlander rejoined me, with my shot-belt and gory knife, which he found among the rocks. He thanked me for so amply avenging his friend's death on his destroyers, and proceeded at once to calculate the value of the four skins and eight hams of the bears. He invited me to his house, which he said was not far off, adding that his name was Wolmar Fynböe; that he was a merchant who exported to Europe seal-skins, the horns of the sea-unicorn, whalebone, and blubber; bartering these, and the skins of blue and white foxes, hares, and bears, for knives and guns, shot, tobacco, barley, beer and brandy, &c.; that he had once been as far as Kiobenhaven,* but did not like the manners of the *kablunaet* (foreigners), who were but half men when compared to the Greenlanders; for national vanity is a great characteristic of these poor people, as it is of many others even less civilized.

Copenhagen.

Like the Lapps, he wore a long pelisse of un-
tanned reindeer skin, having a hood like a friar's
cowl attached thereto, and buttons of walrus teeth.
His hose, boots, and breeches, which were all in
one, were of the same material, but decorated at the
sides by bunches of thongs and tufts of white bear-
skin. Thus, but for his fair complexion, he might
have passed very well for an Esquimau of the
Labrador coast.

I gladly committed myself to his guidance.

We soon reached his house, a dwelling of singular aspect, built on the slope of a snow-covered
hill which overlooked the Fin Whale Strait, on the
waters of which the rays of the northern Aurora
were still playing with wondrous beauty; and from
thence he dispatched some of his men to bring home
the remains of his friend, the dead bears, and the
head of the musk-ox.

We were received at the door by an old servant,
a woman of fearful aspect, also dressed in skins;
but these were adorned by stripes of red and blue
leather to indicate her sex. She was aged, and
being of "the *old* school"—for there is one there,
even in Greenland—she was tattooed as completely
as if she had been a denizen of Nootka Sound.
Aloft in her hand, which resembled a crow's talons,

she held a lamp to light us into an inner apartment, where Wolmar Fynböe introduced me to his
daughters, two girls dressed in skins ; but these
were neatly adorned with variously-coloured leather,
especially about the moccassins which encased their
trim legs.   Their dresses were cut low at the neck,
either to reveal its whiteness (for females have
vanity even in that region of ice), or to display
their under garments, which were formed of the
skins of little birds, ingeniously preserved, sewn
together, and worn with the soft feathers next the
skin.

Wolmar Fynböe was the tallest man in Greenland, yet he measured only five feet; and though
deemed handsome, he had all the peculiarities of his
race—to wit, a paunchy figure, a broad flat visage,
of a brown brick-dust colour; small eyes, thick lips,
and coal-black locks, that waved upon his shoulders
like those of a gnome.   Nevertheless, his daughters
Grethe and Alfa had rather regular features, clear
complexions, and long brown hair, their mother
having been a woman of Iceland.

They were preparing a supper of *grod* (Danish),
a species of food made of oats or barley, and
eaten with butter and milk, when their father's entrance with a *stranger*—a being more seldom seen

than mermaids and gnomes, by common report—startled them so much, that some time elapsed before they could resume their occupation, and swing upon the fire the great pot-stone kettle containing the aforesaid *grod* with my assistance—in proffering which I won the hearts of all, politeness to females being rather a rarity on the shore of the Fin Whale Strait.

The large fire burned brightly and cheerily, being composed of drift-wood; for upon that barren coast, in addition to the stranded wrecks of Scottish and Russian whalers, are found at times the spoil of the Great Gulf Stream, the palmettoes of South America, and, covered with weeds and barnacles, the vast logs that whilome cast the shadows of their foliage on the lovely Bay of Honduras. By this strange current the spoils of Virginia and Carolina are also cast on the shores of Iceland, and by it the mainmast of H.M.S. *Tilbury*, which was burned in Jamaica, was thrown upon the western coast of Scotland.

After having fed so long upon the spoils of the ice—the odds and ends of seals and blubber—I made a veritable banquet with the worthy merchant and his two daughters. Then we had the luxury of hot brandy-and-water thereafter—the Ganymede who served us being, ugh! the old tattooed woman.

I have mentioned that the mansion of Wolmar Fynböe presented a curious aspect, but this arose from the circumstance of its being (as he informed me) built from the remains of an old whale-ship of large dimensions, which had been cast away in the Fin Whale Strait about one hundred and fifty years ago. Her ribs and timbers formed the roof and uprights of the walls; on these the outer and inner sheathing were bolted or pegged anew, and filled-in between with moss and turf. The lockers in which her cabin stores had been placed were our seats, the beds were her berths; the room of the fur-clad Grethe and Alfa was merely separated from ours by an old bulkhead, in the centre of which a cabin door was hinged. The four stern-windows were framed into the wall, a luxury, a piece of splendour, in Greenland, where the casements are usually formed of the entrails of seals and dolphins dried, and neatly stitched together. Some faded charts were nailed on the wall as pictures. An old musket or two, and a pinchbeck watch, were nearly all that now remained of the spoil found in the ship, which had been deserted by her crew; but from none of these relics could her name or country be discerned, though I supposed her to have been English from the circumstance of a Bible and little book in that language having been found in her by the grandfather of Wolmar Fynböe, who built his house from her materials.

The "little book" Wolmar showed me. It was a curious black-letter pamphlet, printed at London in the time of Charles II., and in Dutch types. I took a particular fancy for it, as it contained the relation of a perilous voyage performed by a ship which belonged to the Seven United Provinces.

Wolmar Fynböe offered to barter it for the horns of the musk-ox; but I assured him that he was welcome alike to the entire head, the bears' skins, and hams to boot. To this he agreed at once, conceiving, probably, that one who parted so readily with spoil did not deserve to possess any; so I retired with my literary acquisition (the contents of which I shall give to the reader elsewhere), begging Wolmar Fynböe to have me summoned betimes in the morning, as I was most anxious to reach Cunninghame's Haven, and rejoin my friends on board the *Leda*.

CHAPTER XXV.

ADIEU TO THE REGION OF ICE.

NEXT morning I was up early, my bed not being exactly so luxurious as I could have wished; and there was about everything that overpowering odour of blubber which pervades a Greenland household. For breakfast, Grethe brought in a gaily-painted Muscovite bowl, full of warm milk, and a hot barley-cake, made by Alfa. Her father soon after brought my gun, cleaned and oiled; and then bidding adieu in rather symbolical language to his daughters, we set forth into the clear, cold atmosphere of the young May morning—for we were now in what is deemed in kindlier climes the second month of summer—but as yet no sun was visible.

Far away in distance stretched the Fin Whale Strait, towards Kalla Fiord, which opens into the Icy Sea; its broken scenery, its splintered crags, its lofty bluffs and pinnacles, exhibiting the most singular combinations of light and shadow in the yellow blaze of the yet unrisen sun. The summits seemed tipped with fire, while the bases which rose sheer from the still, deep waters of the waveless strait were dark and sombre as ebony.

Waveless it truly was, save where broken by the knoblike head of a blackfin-whale, as he swam *against* the wind, and blew clouds of water into the air.

As we proceeded, I could perceive that Wolmar Fynböe, though merry and good-humoured, like all Greenlanders was deeply imbued with superstitions dark and gloomy as those of the Scandinavian Edda. Leaning on his hunting-spear, he pointed to a rock in the strait, saying that his mother's sister Alfa (from whom he named his youngest daughter) was wont to see a handsome young merman seated thereon, every time she came to the beach to gather shell-fish or dry nets.

"A merman!" I reiterated, believing that I had not heard him correctly.

"A merman," continued Fynböe, emphatically. " His curling beard was green, and his features, like those of the *Innuit* (Greenlanders), were as soft and pleasing as his manner was mild and persuasive. He took her by the hand, and after their fourth meeting led her under the sea, where she lived with him at the bottom of the Fin Whale Strait for a great many years, and never grew less beautiful, though she frequently pined for the dwelling of her mother, whom at times she could behold from the windows of her watery home, every summer when the ice-floes floated out to sea, and the young whales came to play about the headlands in the sunny waves.

"One summer came, but the old woman appeared no more on the slope of the hill; and then Alfa knew that her sorrowing mother had gone to the Island of the Dead.

"Alfa dwelt with the merman, till one night as he was sporting about in the moonbeams amid the waters of the strait, Grön Jette, the wild huntsman, who once in every year comes over the sea at midnight out of Denmark, slew him by a blow of his lance, as he sped with his yelling hounds and fierce black horses over land and ocean towards the north, where the bright streamers were dancing.

"The spell was thus broken; and the young girl found herself turned suddenly into an old woman, seated on the same rock where, twenty years before, the merman had wooed and won her; but now seven well-grown children with fish-tails, and hair that was half green like her husband's and half golden like

her own, were swimming about in the flood before
her, weeping for her return. So, to rejoin them, she
plunged in and was drowned—for the spell of the
merman's presence was no longer around her. Next
day I found her body floating in the strait, and by a
string of crystals round her neck, knew her to be the
sister my mother had lost twenty years before. We
bore her to the Island of the Dead; and as we use
no coffins, like the red-haired Danes, we heaped up
stones to hide her from view; but a bear swam off
from Sermesoak, tore our gathered heap asunder, and
devoured her!"

Wolmar Fynböe rehearsed this strange story with
the utmost good faith; for he was simple enough
to believe that Torngarsück, the God of Greenland
—a spirit which, though no larger than one's thumb,
at times assumes the form of a gigantic white bear—
dwelt at the bottom of the Whale Strait, with his
wife the Demon of Evil, guarded by droves of nar-
whals and ferocious seals, and surrounded by vast
lamps filled with train-oil, in which the sea-birds
swam by night.

With many a strange story of witches, and con-
flicts with whales, walruses, and with devils that sailed
through the air and changed themselves into snow-
drifts to overwhelm belated hunters, he beguiled the

way, until we reached Cunninghame's Haven, where I found Paul Reeves and Hans Peterkin awaiting me in considerable anxiety, and irresolute whether to put off for the Bear Isle and report to Hartly that I had been lost, or to return once more in search of me.

I now gave the honest Greenlander two crown pieces, as neck amulets for each of his daughters (among whose descendants they may become heir-looms for ages), and bidding him farewell, we stepped into our boat, which was well stocked with game—a large white bear, a pile of hares, and several brace of birds shot by the two mates. Then we shoved off to join the *Leda*, and Wolmar Fynböe, ever and anon pausing to look after us, slowly ascended the cliffs, assisted by his harpoon-shaped hunting spear, and at last disappeared on the path to his half-barbarous and wholly secluded home.

In two hours after, we reached the *Leda*, which had her courses loose, a signal for sea. Our quota of provisions proved a very acceptable addition to those obtained by Hartly from the Danish resident.

" Bravo, Jack!" said he, as we hoisted the bear on board, " our victualling department is complete now, and if this wind holds we shall weigh an hour before sunset."

P

" But the victualling—of what does it consist ?"

" The dainties—the luxuries of Greenland !"

" Indeed," said I, doubtfully.

" In exchange for a few hundred seal-skins, and some kegs of rancid blubber, we have got pickled bear's flesh, bull-heads, gulls and belugas, salmon-trout, and reindeer tongues, hares and partridges in pickle, with a few tubs of whortleberries, preserved in oil. We shall have the white bear in the cabin to ourselves."

" Why ?"

" Sailors won't eat white bear hams ?"

" But why ?"

" They assert that the flesh makes their hair grey. We have also a cask of sorrel preserved in blubber."

" Ugh! of course ; but for what purpose ?"

" As a preservative against scurvy. And now up blue-peter, man the windlass, and heave short on the anchor!"

We sailed an hour before sunset ; and ere the pale white moon rose from the sea, the jagged pinnacles of Sermesoak and the stormy bluff of Cape Farewell were melting into the brilliant sky astern, while our sailors sang cheerily as they hoisted the working anchor on board, unbent the chain-cable and stowed

it in the tier.   The mouth being May we had the
light of the sun nearly all night, though in the
daytime he only rises thirty-three degrees above
the horizon.

However, we lit our binnacle lamps when he set,
the sails were trimmed for a south-west course, and
now we fairly bore away into the mighty ocean, and
bade adieu for ever to the REGION OF ICE.

CHAPTER XXVI.

A SHARK.

FOR the fourth time during our rambling voyage, the *Leda* was again free and under sail upon the blue and boundless sea.

I cannot describe the emotions of joy with which, after our recent long imprisonment amid the waste of ice we gazed upon its buoyant ripples shining in the sun of May. Its broad vast bosom of resplendent blue—a blue so indicative of immensity—that spread far away beyond the dim horizon, flecked with tiny floes of ice, seemed as the mirror wherein we could trace the future.

It was freedom, it was the high road to our homes, to sunshine and the genial south. Everything was set that would draw—royals, flying jib, and studding-sails, as we bore on with a breeze, which, though keen, cold, and cutting, enabled us soon to leave the clime of frost and suffering, bears and icebergs far astern.

On the second day we passed a ship waterlogged and dismasted, battered, and abandoned. Her boats, bulwarks, and everything had been swept from her decks. We bore down upon her, but there was no sign of life on board, so we hauled our wind again and left her to drift, where she would no doubt prove a prize, on the sterile coast of Greenland.

One day a shark followed us with singular pertinacity, eluding every shot we fired at his black dorsal fin from our rifles and sealing guns, till Hans Peterkin, who was skilful in the use of the harpoon, evidently wounded the monster by a well-directed blow over our stern quarter, after which our enemy disappeared. Old Hans exulted considerably in his victory, but awoke that night in the midst of a frightful dream, and alarmed all his shipmates by crying out that a shark was devouring him.

" Take care, Hans," grumbled Tom Hammer, as he turned in his hammock, annoyed on being roused from a sound sleep, " don't be falling overboard, for it is my belief that Jack Shark is in the dead water astern yet, looking out for his revenge."

This passed as a joke at the time, but next day it had a singular sequel.

We were almost becalmed. From being light and variable, the wind had nearly died away. The sea was smooth as if oil covered all its surface ; the listless canvas hung asleep, or flapped heavily as the masts swayed to and fro, the reef points pattering, as the *Leda* rolled lazily on the long glassy ridges that swelled up and shone in the meridian sun.

Amid the general apathy which such a state of matters produces on board of a ship, we were roused by the cry of "a dolphin alongside;" and though these fish are generally met in droves, when the waves are breaking and the wind blowing fresh, one was seen rising and sinking, as if sporting in the sunshine.

Immediately Hans appeared on the bowsprit, armed with his Orkney harpoon, a long spear pointed with barbed iron. Rapidly he bent the line to the foreganger of his weapon, and grasping it, with a handful of slack in his right hand, he slid under the bowsprit, and along the martingale stays which are stretched taut to the end of the jib-boom. Clasping the vertical spar of the martingale with his left arm, he took a steady aim at the dolphin, and launched his harpoon with all his strength.

The stroke was followed by a shout from the crew, who crowded into the bows and forerigging, for poor Hans had overstruck himself, and after swinging violently round the martingale, fell

into the sea, missing the dolphin, which instantly
disappeared.

"My dream—oh, my dream!" cried old Hans in
terror, as he rose floundering and sputtering to the
surface.

Then came the appalling cry of "A shark! a
shark!" and in the very place where the dolphin
sank, the short crooked fin of this great monster of
the deep was seen making straight towards Hans,
who, though an expert swimmer, a hard-a-weather
salt, accustomed to all the hardships and terrors of
Ultima Thule and his native Orcades, was struggling
wildly for life, having got entangled in the slack line
of his harpoon.

"Captain Hartly—man overboard! a rope—a
rope!"

"Cut away the life-buoy!"

"Lower away the stern-boat!"

Such were the cries on every hand, while the
current soon swept Peterkin past the brig, till he
was nearly fifty yards astern.

Old Hans uttered a cry of despair, echoed by a
groan from all, and sank!

Regardless of the shark, which was then double
the distance of Hans from us, Hartly, who had
rushed on deck at the first alarm, with the rapidity

of thought, threw off his coat, knotted a line round his waist, lowered himself into the mainchains, and joining the palms of his hands together in the cut-water fashion of a diver, urging the while his agile body by a sharp push from the chain-plate, sprang into the sea, and vanished amid the ripples. Then in half minute or less he reappeared with Hans, whose grey locks he grasped firmly, as he cast upward a glance of mingled hope and terror—hope of aid from his crew, and terror of the monster, which was shooting towards them; for though the ring of Mother Jensdochter was to save him from drowning, the good dame omitted all mention of sea-lawyers.

"Down with the stern-boat!" cried Reeves.

In a moment the falls were cast loose and the boat was lowered from the davits, manned, and shoved off with a rapidity which nothing but the discipline of the crew and their love for Hartly could have ensured! Save those in the boat, all held their breath—all were paralysed by the scene, and our complete inability to aid or to protect our friends. However, the splashing of the half-drowned Hans somewhat scared the monster, and kept him off.

The boat soon reached the spot; they were

drawn on board, and just in time, for the shark's nose was close to Hans' heels, while a hearty hurrah greeted him and his gallant preserver.

Ere the boat was again dangling at the stern davits, the shark, which had now recovered his surprise and the alarm Hans' splashing had occasioned him, was seen darting furiously to and fro in search of a victim; and but for the celerity of our boat's crew, one or other must have perished in his horrible jaws. Though the shark has rarely the power to bite a man in *two*, he can *strip* the flesh from his body in such a manner, that death is sure to follow.

The wind freshened after this, and the ship's course was resumed; but as night came on, the studdingsails and royals were taken in. Hans appeared in very low spirits after his recent adventure, so Hartly excused him from deck duty for that night. Then, as we sat over our grog in the cabin, the deck being in charge of Tom Hammer, Hartly said—

" By the bye, Jack, you said something of finding an old printed yarn about a shipwreck in Skipper Fynböe's house in Greenland."

" Yes—a queer old story it seems."

" Let us have it, then; read it aloud. Cuffy, trim

the lamps; bring another case-bottle from the
locker, and shut the cabin door. Pass word for Mr.
Reeves and Hans Peterkin to step down—Mr.
Manly is about to spin us a yarn."

I soon produced my little story-book, of which
(as it was an authentic narrative) I shall give the
exact title; though I prefer to rehearse the contents
in my own manner, as the language and spelling of
its author are somewhat quaint and antiquated.

It was called "The Wonderfull and Tragicall
Relation of a Voyage from the Indies, printed at
the Black Raven, in Duck Lane, A.D. 1684."

The *substance* thereof was as follows.

CHAPTER XXVII.

THE FATAL VOYAGE OF THE HEER VAN ESTELL.

IT was in the month of August, 1670, that the barque *De Ruyter*, bearing the flag of the Seven United Provinces (then under their High Mightinesses the States General) and named after Michael Adrian de Ruyter, Admiral of Holland—the same valiant mariner who beat the English, burned Chatham, and bombarded Tilbury—left the port of Pernambuco, in Peru, for Rotterdam, tacking carefully to avoid the shoals and rocks which made the Portuguese of old name it the "Mouth of Hell"—*Inferno-bocca* —hence its present corrupted name.

She was manned by Captain Koningsmarke and sixteen seamen; she carried four brass guns, and had her stern decorated by the lions, spotted sable and gules, which form the arms of Rotterdam. Her mate was an Englishman named Carpinger, a brave and skilful seaman.

As passengers, she had the Heer Van Estell, his wife Gudule, their two little children, Erasmus and Cornelius, with Dame Trüdchen, their faithful old nurse. The Heer was a native of the Low Countries, who, after a long residence in the Dutch colony at Brazil, had amassed a magnificent fortune, and risen to be a Director of the Company of the Great Indies, a dignity which no one could attain unless he vested twelve thousand guilders in the old stock. Now, having amassed all the wealth he deemed desirable, with his wife and children—little curly-haired Erasmus, whom he had named after the great philosopher of Rotterdam (towards whose statue in the Bürger-platz he gave a thousand rix-dollars), and chubby little Cornelius, whom he had named after Cornelius de Witt, who, with his brother, was so barbarously assassinated by William of Orange (and afterwards of England)—he was returning to his native city to spend his days in peace and quiet, with the three beings whom he loved most on earth.

The day was cloudless and clear, the wind was fair, but light, and while the bark, with all her canvas set, from her flying-jib to her spanker, and with the colours of the Seven Provinces flying at her gaff-peak, passed in safety the flat sandbanks of St. Antonio, and that long reef which receives the full force of the sea, and guards the town of Recife, the tall and portly Heer, with his beautiful wife and chubby little ones beside him, sat in a cushioned chair on the warm deck, enjoying a long pipe of tobacco with all the ease and complacency that became a wealthy Hollander and Director of the Great India Company.

Without any emotion, save joy that he was returning, he saw the hill of Olinda, the tall slender spires of the town, and the grim batteries of Cinco Pontas, melt in the distance astern, as the *De Ruyter* bore away into the Western Ocean.

For more than a month the voyage was delightful and prosperous; but adverse winds came anon, and storms too; and Captain Koningsmarke was blown out of his course; moreover, he lost his reckoning, as the sky remained obscured by clouds, and for weeks both quadrant and sextant were used in vain.

His anxiety and that of the Heer became great, for provisions were becoming scarce—so much so that, ere long, all on board received but a scanty allowance. Then Van Estell and Dame Gudule beheld with secret agony the roses fading from the cheeks of their children, their pretty faces becoming blanched, and their once round forms attenuated.

Week after week rolled anxiously, mournfully away!

Still the winds were adverse, and still the *De Ruyter* tacked and tacked again, like the fabled ship of Vanderdecken, but without meeting a craft that might assist them, till at last there fell a death-like calm upon the sea ; and then, for many, many days under a hot sun, and in the breathless nights that followed, the helpless vessel lay like a log, with her blocks and cordage rattling, and her loose canvas flapping until it was frittered aud frayed on the blistering yards and masts, while the sea chafed her rusting chain-plates and the pitch boiled from her planking—yet " she lay so that, for several weeks, they could scarcely tell whether they were forwarded a league's space."

And now a deadly pest broke out on board— a malignant fever, which covered its victims with livid blotches, like the spotted lions, gules and sable, on the ship's stern ; and among those who perished were Koningsmarke, the captain, and eight of his crew. They were thrown overboard, and for days their bodies remained in sight, with fishes sporting about them, and obscene birds of the sea lighting on them, as they floated on its still and waveless surface.

Provisions were now dealt out more sparingly than ever. Strong men grew wan, and gaunt, and feeble; for as their strength failed and hope faded, so did their spirit die within them; and then even the most superstitious ceased to *whistle* for wind.

At last they were reduced to a half biscuit and single morsel of meat per day; the latter failed, and then the half biscuit; and now they looked grimly and terribly in each other's hollow visages and blood-shot eyes, while wondering what was to become of them, for although lines had long hung overboard, the sea had refused to yield them fish.

" To wait with hope is nothing, but to wait with DESPAIR is worse than death!"

So did the Heer Van Estell wait, and his wife Gudule—now no longer the beautiful Gudule, for she was wan, wasted, and sinking, having given her pittance of food for several days to sustain her little ones. All his wealth all the riches acquired by years of prudence in the Indies, would the unhappy Van Estell have given gladly to purchase a single biscuit, to sustain for one day more the lives of those he loved so well.

At last little Erasmus and Cornelius died, passing away without pain or a murmur, having become of late too weak even to weep for food.

They passed away, and the Heer and his wife remained by the pretty corpses as if transformed to stone!

Four days passed after this—still no food—no hope—no wind in the air, no ship upon the sea!

Gudule could not consent to cast her dead children into its mighty depth; but anon she repented of it bitterly, for the eight seamen who remained, after a long conference on the forecastle, and frequently casting glances aft towards the cabin—glances like those of wolves—came in a body, and demanded that the dead children should be surrendered to them as *food!*

The entreaties and tears of the parents were vain. The Heer (now shorn of his strength) and his miserable helpmate were thrust into their cabin, while the wasted bodies of their children were borne away and laid on the drum of the capstan, where they were cut to pieces by the cook's knife, and then devoured raw. Hunger seemed to make the sailors insane, and able to overcome all aversion for food so unnatural; but whether it was that they ate immoderately, or that with satiety came a horror of their meal, I know not, but they were immediately assailed by a dreadful sickness, which left their bodies weaker than ever.

Gudule lay in a stupor on her bed, but the Heer loaded his pistols, though scarcely knowing for what purpose; and exerting all his strength, he contrived to burst open the cabin door and stagger on deck, when the crew, whom the hunger of another day assailed again, had just concluded the last of a second dreadful banquet—a banquet on his children!

On the capstan there lay the head of one. It had the fair curly locks of little Erasmus.

"Oh, madness and agony!" groaned the miserable Van Estell, as he took it in his tremulous hands, kissed it tenderly thrice, and slowly and solemnly dropped it into the glassy sea.

He could not weep—his hot dry eyes refused a tear, but groans burst from his overcharged breast and parched lips, and he swooned on the deck. There he lay, and so another day passed. When he recovered it was about the time of midnight, and a full round moon was shining on that now neglected ship of death and of despair.

The atmosphere was mild and warm.

The Heer stole into the cabin, and saw that his poor, sad, childless wife lay very still and motionless. Tremblingly he drew near, lest she might be dead; for then he had resolved to cast her and himself into the sea, lest her fair form might also

Q

be devoured by the madmen on deck. But she was
in a soft sleep, dreaming, perhaps, that her lost little
ones were alive, and seated by her side in a palm
grove of Peru, listening to the voice of the cam-
panero, or sweet bell-bird of Brazil. The deep
slumber that follows long hours of mental and
bodily suffering had fallen upon her.

The poor man wept and kissed her tenderly, but
at that moment the mate, George Carpinger, entered, and roughly ordered him to come forward to
the capstan head, where he and his comrades were
deliberating on what was to be done next.

Heer Van Estell assured himself that his pistols
were still in his pocket, that they were primed and
loaded, and then he obeyed. As these nine men
stood round the capstan, they resembled spectres
rather than human beings, when the cold lustre of
the moon fell on their pallid visages and bloodshot
eyes that glared wildly from out their sunken sockets.

Eleven persons were still on board, namely, the
Heer, his wife and servant, the mate, and seven
seamen; it was evident that one must be sacrificed
to prolong the existence of the rest, and mentally
they resolved that whoever became the victim,
should be cooked, lest the flesh might sicken them
again. . . . . . .

CHAPTER XXVIII.

" I AM aware," says the author of *Antonina,* " of
the tendency in some readers to denounce truth itself
as improbable, unless their own personal experience
has borne witness to it." In this spirit, some may
denounce the fatalities of the Heer's voyage as
improbabilities, though the hideous circumstance of
human beings in extremity of hunger destroying
each other for food, has been too well and too terribly established in many instances—such as the
wreck of the French frigate *Medusa;* when the
British frigate *Nautilus* was lost on a solitary rock
in the Mediterranean ; during the famine on board
the American ship *Peggy;* and on many other occasions.

But to resume our little quarto.

The mate conducted the Heer Van Estell to the
capstan, where the starving seamen stood in a silent

group, and then he informed him in a hoarse whisper—

"That unless they contrived a means of furnishing themselves with food, they must all die of starvation; it was impossible for them to subsist for another day. That there were eleven persons on board, and they had come to the resolution of determining by lot who should die that the rest might live."

"*Eleven* on board!" reiterated the Heer, faintly, for his poor wife Gudule was one of these.

"Eleven," added a seaman named Adrian Crudelius, with a wild glare in his eye; "if one dies, ten may live. Bring your wife on deck, sir; she must take her chance with the rest. There must be no distinction here."

"Nay," said George Carpinger, "we may excuse her presence, and so spare her some of this horror; but her husband shall draw for her."

"Sirs," replied the poor Heer, "I thank you. Even here she finds the privileges of her sex accorded her."

Then with tremulous hands the mate tore a sheet of paper into eleven pieces, and numbered them from *one* to *eleven*. He folded and placed them in his hat. It was then agreed that he who drew number *one* was to die, and that he who drew number *two* was to be the executioner. After shaking the fatal pieces of paper, amid a silence that was awful—the silence of horror—for food or want, death or life, were on the issue, every glassy eye was fixed, each nether jaw relaxed, while with hot and feverish hands that trembled, they drew forth their lots—the Heer taking two in succession. He opened them hastily, smote his forehead, uttered a wailing cry, and reeled against the capstan.

He had drawn numbers "one" and "two," so it was the lot of him to die, and by the hand of Gudule, or *vice versâ !*

The unhappy seamen had scarcely foreseen a chance so terrible as this. Carpinger urged that the wife should be spared, or that lots should be cast once more; but those who by risking their fate had escaped death, were loth to tempt it again, and with sullen murmurs declined. Propping himself against the capstan, the unfortunate Van Estell summoned all his energies, and thus addressed them :—

"My good companions in misery, you have seen our sorrow and despair for the loss of our dear little children ; and though I know that death would be a relief and refuge to my poor Gudule, neither she nor I can perish by the other's hand. Thus I offer

myself freely and willingly as the victim and sacrifice. When I am dead, I charge you—I pray you
be kind unto her. Conduct her to her friends, her
home, her country, and be assured that if ever you
are happy enough to see the waters of the Maese,
and the old spires of Rotterdam, she will have
wealth enough to reward you all. May Heaven
bless you! Gudule, farewell—my poor Gudule!"

At these words he drew a pistol from his pocket,
shot himself through the head, and fell flat on the
deck. Some appeared stunned by the whole affair,
but two threw themselves upon the yet quivering
body like wild animals, and sucked up the blood
that oozed from it.

In the weird light of the moon, that bloody deck,
that silent group and fallen corpse, presented an
awful scene to Gudule Van Estell, who tottered from
her cabin, being roused by the sound of the pistol;
but now Carpinger the mate, Adrian Crudelius, and
her old nurse, bore her back into the cabin, and
fastened the door to prevent her seeing the dreadful
scene that was sure to ensue, when the famished
men, in their voracity and fury, almost tore the
clothes from the body of the Heer, being rendered
more mad than ever by the contents of a single case-
bottle of Geneva which had been discovered. They

hewed the body to pieces, cast its head into the sea, and again the horrible repast commenced—a repast which rendered two raving mad, for with loud yells they sprang overboard and disappeared.

All the rest became insane, save the mate and Adrian Crudelius, who endeavoured to control their extravagance. One proposed to scuttle the ship, or set her on fire, that all might perish together; another raved and blasphemed Heaven for with-holding the wind; a third denounced the craft as being under a spell, and thus fixed to one part of the sea, from whence she would never stir till her timbers rotted and her planks opened; and all, save the mate, were unanimous that next time the wife of the Heer, upon whom one of the lots had fallen, should perish for their sustenance if a sail came not in sight.

That day passed as others had done; the glassy sea without a ripple, the hot sun overhead, the sails flapping against the masts; the banner of the Seven Provinces, inverted as a sign of distress, hanging listlessly downward from the gaff-peak; the sky without a cloud, the horizon without a sail, and the hearts of the cannibals on board the *De Ruyter* without hope!

Gudule Van Estell was still surviving. The kind

mate had caught a couple of mice; these he gave to the nurse, who cooked them in secret for her mistress and herself.　But now, towards evening, four of the crew, who were bereft of reason, approached her cabin door, and were attempting to force it open, for the purpose of dragging her to the capstan head, when George Carpinger, armed with a cutlass, rushed forward, and drove them back.

They soon procured arms, and howling like wild animals, attacked him, staggering the while like drunken men with weakness.　Crudelius now joined the mate, and there ensued a conflict in which two were slain, and their bodies were cast overboard by the survivors, who were already so glutted by their horrible food as to have no desire for more.

By the noon of the next day, all had perished by exhaustion, save the mate and the Dame Van Estell.

Night was coming on, and the poor solitary seaman was sitting on the windlass in a species of stupor, when an unusual coolness in the atmosphere roused his attention, and, with a sailor's instinct, he felt the coming breeze.

First there came a gentle catspaw upon the darkening water, then a ripple, and now a whitening of the wave-tops at a distance.　He stretched his tremulous hands towards them, and wept in joy !

Anon, clouds came banking up in dense masses to leeward, and rain—blessed rain! began to fall, while the wind of heaven blew the long neglected rigging out in bends, and filled the flapping sails.

A brace of lazy gulls suddenly appeared wheeling about; and a bird—a land bird—perched on the end of the studding-sail boom alongside.

The haggard eyes of Carpinger swept the horizon, and saw afar off a spark, which he at first supposed to be a star, but, ere long, discovered to be a light; yet whether it shone on board of a ship, or on the shore, he knew not; so he lashed the helm, and rushing to the lifts and braces, strove to trim the sails and shape the vessel's course towards it.

The bunting began to shake at the gaff-peak; ere long it floated out upon the wind, while a wake whitened astern, a bubble rose under the bows, and the *De Ruyter* walked through the water as of yore.

The breeze continued, and next morning she was close in upon a bleak, rugged, and mountainous coast, which proved to be the Lizard Point in Cornwall, the most southern promontory of England.*

---

* It must be borne in mind that the mouth of the Channel was less frequented by shipping in 1670, than *now*.

George Carpinger had the Dame Van Estell conveyed ashore in the stern-boat, together with a
casket of valuable jewels; and the *De Ruyter*, after
drifting about the coast, escaping the Cornish
wreckers, who deemed a wreck "a Godsend," was
taken into Plymouth and sold. Gudule Van Estell
was afterwards conveyed to Rotterdam, where she
found herself one of the wealthiest widows in the
city; and as a reward to George Carpinger for
defending her life so valiantly in the fated *De
Ruyter*, she bestowed her hand and guilders upon
him.

"They lived long and happily together; and he
died Burgomaster of Rotterdam in 1720, when Anne
was Queen of Britain."

"So ends this story," said I.

Hartly filled his glass of grog, and emptied it in
silence.

Then I could perceive that the perusal of the
history of this fatal voyage had a most unpleasant
effect upon all who heard it, for Reeves, Hartly,
and Hans Peterkin, frequently recurred to it
afterwards.

" That little black pamphlet came from a wrecked

ship," said Hartly, one day —" 'a fated craft'—I can't help wishing you had never brought it on board, Jack."

" Why ?" I asked.

" It is such a devil of a horse-marine yarn about these Dutchmen eating each other."

" How ?"

" I always think about it."

" I can easily put it out of existence by stuffing it under a kettle in the cook's galley ; it may aid Cuffy in cooking the dinner."

" No, no," said he, hastily, " that would be worse."

" In what way ?"

" I don't know," said he, thoughtfully ; " but such things are like the Flying Dutchman's letters, which must neither be taken or refused when the wind blows them on board."

Some days after this, Hartly lost his *ring*—the ring given him by old Mother Jensdochter—the amulet which, until that moment, he had never been without. It was torn from his hand while assisting to haul the maintack on board, and dropped over the gunnel.

This trivial event, and the story of the *De Ruyter*, together with the past evils of our voyage, affected

Hartly and Reeves more seriously than I could have imagined. From the cabin, Cuffy Snowball soon carried the vague fears forward among the seamen. Hans Peterkin began to shake his white head ominously, for old mariners have, they know not why or how, strange instincts and presentiments; so our crew, without any just reason, became more than usually solicitous about their duties, and anxious for the termination of the voyage.

CHAPTER XXIX.

ADVENTURE WITH A WHALE.

NEXT day the wind veered due west, and we trimmed the *Leda* to lie close to it, making long tacks to the southward, as we had been driven so far to the north-east.

Hartly and I were leaning over the weather-quarter, chatting and gazing listlessly at the white water that bubbled like a flooded mill-race under the brig's counter, while Mother Cary's chickens came tripping lightly after us, when suddenly a huge whale (like a ship's hull, bottom uppermost) rose from the waves close by us, with the water pouring in torrents from its dusky and shining sides. Its appearance was so sudden and alarming, that I started back; but Hartly laughed, saying,

"Don't mind him, Jack; he is not coming on board."

For a full minute he floated in the water, keeping

pace with the brig, to the great admiration of our old Orkney whaleman, Hans, and then sank slowly down—down far below. We could see his vast bulk shining as he passed *under* us, and came up on our other side, so close that he almost grazed the copper of the *Leda*.

This monster of the deep was nearly as large, at least as long, as the brig, and his aspect was calculated to inspire awe in those who were less familiar than we now were with the denizens of the sea.

He was a common whale, and the head being, as usual, out of all proportion, was one-third the entire size of the fish, while the eyes were no larger than those of an ox. The smooth and slippery skin, from which the foam dripped, was mottled; and it—or *he*, as we named him—swam not as whales generally do, *against* the wind, but with us.

Our friend was evidently in a playful mood, as he repeatedly rose and sank, plunged and surged up on each side of the *Leda* alternately, and twice grazed our rudder.

"He smells the blubber and sealskins aboard, sir," said Hans Peterkin, "and they make him frolicsome, you see."

"Look out, sir!" added Reeves, who was in the

mainchains; " by Jove, he'll be foul of us in his next gambol!"

"And we may have our rudder unshipped—I don't like this at all," replied Hartly. "Cuffy, bring me a sealing-gun, with powder and a handful of slugs."

In half a minute Hartly stood in the boat at the stern davits, with the long gun loaded and charged with ten square junks of lead, each larger than a rifle ball. Then, just as the whale, for the fifth or sixth time rose under the stern, he fired.

The whole charge entered one of the great spiracles, or blow-holes, which are situated in the middle of the head, about sixteen feet from the nose, and through which this fish can spout to a vast height when wounded or annoyed. The moment the gun was fired, our whale sank like a stone.

" There he goes, for ever I hope!" cried Hartly.

" We have not seen the last of him, sir," said old Hans, as he got astride the boom of the fore-and-aft mainsail in his excitement to see the whale again; " he has a long way to go *down*, before he'll come up again. Why, Lord love you, sir, I have known them in the sound of Yell, when struck by a harpoon, descend head-foremost for eight hundred fathoms, (at the rate of eight knots an hour, till the line in the bowpost smoked, ay, blazed with friction,) and then come up with their jawbones broken, by running foul of a rock at the bottom. That one has gone down fully four hundred fathoms."

"How do you know, Hans?"

"By the eddy—he'll be up to *blow*, directly."

"Where?" said I.

"On our weather beam, I think. See! there are the bubbles of his blowing already!"

Hans was right; even while he spoke, the whale rose to the surface, about fifty yards from us, and from his blow-holes shot a vast spout of water streaked with blood into the air, and then it pattered like rain as it fell into the sea. After lashing the water furiously with his tail till it boiled in foam around him, and the air above became filled with vapour, he threw himself into a *perpendicular* position, and stood for a moment like a pillar, from the sea.

It was a strange and exciting scene!

He now flapped his mighty flukes, which were perhaps thirty feet apart, till they cracked like a gigantic whip, and then sank from our gaze in a deep eddy, around which the concentric waves heaved and broke for a considerable time; but we saw him no more.

"Well, Hans," said I, "how do you like this adventure?"

"Not much, Master Manly," replied the old Scotsman, shaking his white hairs; "'cause you see, sir, when a whale takes to dancing about on his nose in this fashion, after lashing the water with his flukes, a *storm* is sure to follow. A whale knows better than a human creature when a close-reefed topsail breeze is coming, by a pricking pain that comes over their bodies, and so, after dancing about as that fellow did, they run right away from that quarter of the sea to another. I have known o' this many times, when I was a wee bairn at home in Whalsoe. I'll stake a trifle we have our topgallant yards on deck before the sun sets."

And old Hans proved correct.

CHAPTER XXX.

LOSS OF THE "LEDA."

ON the night after our adventure with the whale I had turned in to bed betimes; but was roused about two in the morning by the noise made by Hammer, our carpenter, Cuffy Snowball, and others battening the deadlights of the stern windows. At the same moment I became sensible of the unusual motion of the vessel, of the tremendous din that reigned on deck, and of the furious manner in which my cot, the brass cabin lamp, and the tell-tale compass swung about.

"What is the matter?" I asked, starting up, while the prophecy of Hans flashed on my memory.

"Matter, sir! faith, if you were on deck you would soon find out!" was the somewhat impatient response of Tom Hammer, who was drenched to the skin.

"Is it blowing hard?" said I.

" 'Twill nebber blow harder, Massa Tanly, till him blows himself right out," grinned Cuffy Snowball.

" A regular hurricane! the brig is almost under bare poles, and we sound the pumps every half-hour," added Hammer, who seemed indignant at the soundness of my past slumber.

On hearing all this, I leaped out, dressed **myself,** and hurried on deck.

A wild gale, in short, a tempest, was roaring through the rigging and straining the shrouds of the *Leda;* she lurched and pitched heavily, as she rushed through mountains of seething foam; for amid the black obscurity on all sides we could see its whiteness, and the snowy surf, which was torn by the wind from the wave-crests, and swept, like smoke, along the sea.

The brig was driving right before the wind, under a foresail, foretopsail, and fore and aft mainsail, all closely reefed. Everything was done that might render her snug. The deadlights had barely been shipped before she was struck by a wave which buried her in the black trough of the sea—tore her stern-boat from the iron davits, and swept it away like a leaf shred from a twig.

Hans and Paul Reeves were at the wheel. Hartly

stood by them pale and excited, as I could perceive by the glimmering lights of the binnacle. All hands were on deck, and muffled in their glazed storm-jackets and dripping sou'-westers, so they seemed as drenched as if they had come up from the bottom of the sea.

"Take care of yourself, Jack—take care!" cried my friend; "every sea she ships sweeps something off the deck, and we have already lost one man from the fore-yardarm."

"Good Heavens—when?"

"About an hour ago—poor Bill Bradley!"

I grasped one of the mainshrouds, for the deck was so slippery, the gusts of wind so fierce, and the force of the seas, which broke ever and anon across the brig, so overwhelming, that I could never have kept afoot for a moment without some support.

On, on careered the *Leda*, through wind and waves—on through whitening foam and tossing wrack—on through drenching rain, darkness, and obscurity, with the storm roaring and whistling amid her straining spars and rigging, while she groaned in every timber, and seemed to quiver to her backbone, as the ponderous waves pursued and burst upon her.

Once or twice the gloom around us was varied by sheets of lightning which gleamed luridly at the far horizon ; and then for an instant the black waves seemed to be washing *against* the reddened sky. Elsewhere to the northward, when the black flying scud was torn asunder in heaven, we saw the long flickering rods of the " merry dancers" playing athwart the sky. Then the crape-like rent would close, and all again became pitchy darkness. The sea which tore away our quarter-boat had started the sternpost. Tom Hammer and his mates rushed to sound the pumps, and reported that " the water in the well had risen *four feet !*"

Hoarse orders were bellowed by Hartly through his trumpet, and the clank of the pumps rang incessantly, for it was evident she had sprung a leak somewhere aft, the *clear* water having replaced the bilge ; so a fresh gang was required every quarter of an hour. Here was a place in which I could make myself useful, and take my " spell" with the rest ; and where, though the dread of perishing was strong in my heart, I worked hard but mechanically, like one in a terrible dream.

Hammer, with all the hands that could be spared from the deck, hurried below, but soon reappeared, to announce—why I know not—that to get at the leak was impossible !

" Do we gain upon her ?" was the constant question of those who toiled at the pumps; but Hammer was too full of hopelessness to reply; so for hours the monotonous clanking went on, till the chains and leathers of the pumps became almost useless, and then the water rose rapidly in both the fore and after hold!

We threw our large anchors and carronades overboard to lighten her by the head; but without much avail. Pale and composed—resolute yet anxious—poor Hartly had stood by the pumps, encouraging us by his voice and example. He was, however, sad and gloomy. That the loss of his *ring* affected him was evident. How strong and yet how weak is the mind of man!

The water continued to rise rapidly, though we toiled till our knees and arms ached; grey dawn began to brighten in the east, but there was no symptom of the storm abating.

"If she ships one sea more, such as that which struck our quarter," said Hartly, "she will founder!"

The words were scarcely uttered, when a mighty mountain of black water reared up like an arching cliff, fringed by foam, came hissing and roaring towards us, and burst in thundering volume on our decks, sweeping poor Tom Hammer the carpenter, another seaman, and all the spare booms, spars, buckets, and everything that previous waves had left, overboard—starting the longboat from its lashings, and dashing it with such violence against the larboard bulwarks, that a vast breach was made in them. The gang at the pumps were all tumbled in a heap into the starboard scuppers, and returned to their work with difficulty. The iron sling of the mainyard gave way at the same moment, and the spar with the handed sail fell heavily with all their gear into the sea.

Under this shock the *Leda* literally *stood still*, as if paralysed in her forward progress.

Another fatal volume burst upon her quarter, and *then*, alas! she began to settle down into the trough of the sea. She had lost all her buoyancy and was sinking! Her rudder was torn away—the stern frame shattered, and so she filled with perilous rapidity.

"Clear away the longboat, Reeves—unship the compass in the binnacle," ordered Hartly; "Hans, get up a beaker of water, a bag of bread—in oars and blankets—we must quit instantly and shove off!"

" In such a sea as this ?" asked Reeves, with wildness in his eye, as he clung to a belaying pin. "No boat can live——"

"Ay, Paul, even in such a sea as this; we must quit the ship, or sink with her. Stand by, my lads, and throw her head to the wind."

"The foremast will go like a reed—but see—the wind has already done what you wish."

The loss of her rudder had rendered the *Leda* (her chain plates were now in the water) unmanageable, but, with the promptitude and decision of brave and desperate hearts, some of our men hurried to the braces, to strive and keep the vessel's head to windward, while others got the longboat cleared of all that endless *débris* and rubbish which usually accumulate there during a voyage—launched it, and by fending, with no small exertion of skill and strength, prevented it from being dashed to pieces against the side of the foundering *Leda*. A cask of water was thrown in, also the binnacle compass, which, unfortunately, was broken during the confusion. The oars were luckily lashed to the thwarts; the mast, yard, sail, and rudder were also there, and we prepared at once to leave.

Wild though the wind, the atmosphere was dense and full of vapour and obscurity; the mingled rain and surf were so blinding, that one could scarcely see one's hand outstretched at arm's length. To keep our feet in such a howling tempest was almost impossible; thus in passing forward or aft, we were obliged to drag ourselves along by clutching belaying pins, cleats, and ring-bolts, while many of us were severely injured by pieces of broken wreck that floated about the deck, and were dashed to and fro by the waves.

Two or three of our men were stunned, and on falling overboard were seen no more; but in less than three minutes after the longboat was launched, we had all left the ship—Hartly being the last to do so—and to the number of fourteen in all (including Paul Reeves, Hans Peterkin, Cuffy Snowball, and me), committed ourselves to the mercy of the sea and storm, in that small craft, which was tossed like a cork upon the billows.

For a time the boat was rasped so furiously against the side of the brig, that all our united strength was requisite to get under her shattered stern, and fairly shove off. We worked in silence—the silence of black desperation !

But on falling astern of the sinking brig, the boat became exposed still more to the fury of the sea.

" Pull her round," cried Hartly ; " keep her bow to the break of the sea, or we shall be swamped. Pull to windward of the *Leda !*"

As we did so, a single wave nearly filled the boat,

and we had nothing for it but to bear away before the roaring blast.

Through the black drift we could see the brig, from which we were only a few yards distant, sinking deeper and deeper; at last the waves rolled in fierce tumult over her deck; still not a word escaped us. Our hearts were too full for utterance; but a pang of sorrow and dismay thrilled them when the poor little *Leda*, with her masts still standing, went down into the waste of waters and disappeared for ever!

Hartly now took off his sou'-wester, and briefly told us "to be of good heart, for God would be sure to protect us."

All present untied and took off their hats, and listened to him in silence, though he could scarcely be heard amid the wild fury of the gale. Then Paul Reeves, who pulled the bow oar, shouted—

"Three cheers, my lads, for our captain!"

And they gave them with all the heartier will that he was now as poor as themselves, for all that Hartly possessed in the world had gone down with the *Leda*, as she was not insured. To keep the boat from being swamped, with incredible difficulty we now stepped her mast, hoisted a little of the sail, and bore away before the wind; but when we

were in the *trough* of the sea, it flapped against the
mast, and the next instant, when we rode on the
summit of a wave, the wind almost tore it to shreds.
Then the wild water bubbled over her stern, often
immersing the steersman to his ears, and obliging
us incessantly to bale with our hats; but the increasing light of dawn, and an evidence of some
abatement in the tempest, encouraged us to persevere in our efforts to save our lives; and so we
struggled manfully with the warring elements.

CHAPTER XXXI.

THE CRY.

THE wind and sea went down together as day brightened on the cheerless scene. After the night we had passed, how grimly pale and wan our faces seemed in the cold grey dawn of morning!

This catastrophe occurred in the middle of May, when we were about three hundred miles from St. John, our destination. Our compass was broken, but we continued to steer south-west and by west, as well as we could determine.

The gale having abated, we hoisted the sail to the masthead, shipped our oars, and after receiving about a tablespoonful of rum per man, endeavoured to make the best of our way towards Newfoundland, in the hope of being picked up, ere long, by one of the many outward or homeward bound traders.

When day was fully in, we swept the sea with anxious eyes, but not a sail was visible!

Cast thus helplessly on the wide ocean, with a few biscuits, a small beaker of fresh water, and a gallon keg of rum, at a distance of three hundred miles from land, our prospects were gloomy in the extreme; and amid them all, the horrible story of the *De Ruyter*, and similar miseries endured by those of whom I had heard and read in such situations, haunted me.

Exertion warmed us: we now got our clothing wrung out and dried, the boat thoroughly baled, and by midday we were as comfortable as men so circumstanced might be. Cuffy, who had saved his violin, the only article of property he ever possessed, now proceeded to enliven us, as he had often done before, by singing a negro melody, to his own accompaniment; yet this was but ghastly mirth at best.

Our biscuits being soaked by the brine, excited a thirst which we were without the means of allaying. Moreover, the *idea* of being upon allowance in itself excites a thirsty craving; thus by the noon of the second day, the water in the beaker was nearly consumed, and we had no hope now but for rain.

I believe some hours elapsed before we were fully aware, or had realized a true sense of our dreadful situation

How shall I describe the days that passed—and how the nights? Morning after morning only dawned to raise our hopes of success; and these faded as the day wore on; and then the nights were dark monotonous hours of bitterness and despair.

Yet they were the short nights of May; and it must be borne in mind that however warm they are upon the land, and in more temperate latitudes, they were cold and chilly when passed in an open boat, upon the mighty Atlantic. The evening of the fourth day deepened, and still not a sail was in sight. About nine o'clock, one of our forlorn party, whose clothing was thinner than the rest, and who had suffered much from hunger and exposure, died in the bottom of the boat, and we silently committed his body to the deep.

There were neither prayer nor funeral service, but we all stood up, and uncovered our heads, while Hans and a seaman launched the poor fellow into the sea.

Our last drop of water was now expended, for it had been poured between the parched lips of this sufferer, in vain.

Our bread we dared scarcely eat, even in the morsels in which it was doled out, lest it might excite that awful thirst which we had no liquid to assuage, and which the summer sun, when blazing over our heads at noon, rendered worse by a thousand degrees, making us long for night, when the moist dew would fall on our parched lips and arid visages; then night made us long for day, in the hope of seeing a sail, as we were in terror lest one should pass us unseen; and I am assured that more than one must have done so.

Amid his own bodily misery, poor Hartly frequently reproached himself for having, as he said, "lured me from a quiet occupation into a career so fatal and disastrous."

The older seamen sought to encourage us by relating how often they had been wrecked, and yet had escaped death.

"I remember," said Hans Peterkin, "when the *Brenda*, a bark of Kirkwall, was wrecked on her voyage from Jamaica. The night was rough, and we were under close-reefed topsails, when a sea struck her, and unshipped her rudder, just as she sprang a leak. All hands were ordered to the pumps, and to the thrumming of a sail; but the loss of the rudder hove her dead in the wind's eye, so her mainmast went by the board, bringing with it the fore and mizen topmasts, making her a useless wreck in a moment. I was washed overboard; but there was no time to look after me, so I rode on the mainmast all night. When day broke there was no ship to be seen—she must have foundered in the dark. Three days and two nights I rode upon that shattered mast, till a Spanish schooner, bound for Rio, picked me up; yet I never lost heart, shipmates, for I knew I should be saved."

"How?" said Reeves.

"Because we have a saying among us in Orkney, that he who eats of the dulse of Guiodin,* and drinks of the well of Kildingie, will escape everything but the *Black Death;* and many a time I have eaten of one and drunk of the other."

On the fifth day another man died, and was committed to the deep. No one stood up this time, we were becoming either too weak or too callous.

"Water—water," sighed Paul Reeves; "when ashore, I will never drink aught but pure spring water again."

"Bide ye, messmate, and dinna gut a swimming fish; or, as we say in Orkney, cut up nae herrings till ye have them in your net. When you are ashore!—ashore indeed—when shall we ever see the shore?"

---

* The creek of Odin, in Stronza.

Even the strong mind of the hardy Hans was wandering now. The wind kept tolerably fair, and though by alternate spells at the oars we toiled day and night to add to the speed of our sail, we had no means of ascertaining the distance we ran; and now the pangs of hunger were alternately maddening or paralyzing, but they were trivial when compared with those of thirst. By skilfully striking with his oar, Hans contrived to kill four petrels when they came tripping by close to our boat. Since the days of Clusius and Pliny, tradition has foolishly made these poor birds the precursors of a storm; but the elements had done their worst upon us, so we cared not. They were soon plucked and demolished.

We found them very fat and nutritious, as the whole genus of petrels have a singular facility for creating and for spouting pure oil from their bills in defence of themselves and their eggs if molested; and of this oil they can produce plenty, as they feed on blubber and fish. The quantity in them astonished all but Hans Peterkin, who had been wont to harry the nests of the *skua*, as the petrel is named in his native isles, and who told me that whales were often discovered in the Firth of Westra and the Sound of Yell by the flocks that followed in the hope of a gorge of blubber.

"My father was drowned by a *skua*," said he.

"Drowned—how, by a skua?"

"Ay, for so they called the petrels in Orkney once, and so they call them in Faroe now."

"But how was he drowned?" asked Hartly.

"He was a bold fellow who could climb the steep rocks that overhung the most furious sea, to get eggs and catch the petrels *asleep* if possible; for the skua or fulmar supply us with feathers for our beds, medicine in illness, and oil for our lamps. My mother used to make the whole bird a candle by passing through its mouth a wick, which the fat of the body fed. My father, Magnus Peterkin, was, I have said, a bold fellow, though he wore a *glain neidr*, or adder-gem, an old amulet of the Druid days, and believed that while it hung at his neck he was safe. On a stormy night he swung himself over a rock in Pomona to pull some petrels out of their holes, but one squirted a billful of salt oil right into his eyes—just as I might a quid—which so confused him, that he quitted hold of the rope, fell upon the rocks three hundred feet below, and perished miserably—poor man!"

The fifth night was calm and beautiful—too calm for us, as the wind had almost died away, and a clear moonlight was shining on the silent sea, when a singular and startling event occurred—one that filled us with vague terror and awe.

Six of us, faint, worn, and half-asleep, were tugging monotonously at our oars; four slept in the bottom of the boat, and Reeves was steering by a star, while honest Cuffy Snowball, whose native good-humour and cheerfulness even the horrors of our situation could not repress, was playing sweetly on his violin, and, to keep our spirits from sinking, sang a negro song which he had picked up during the years of his slavery in South Carolina—and sung it while his tongue clove to the roof of his mouth with thirst. I leave the reader to judge how in such a time and place the soft melody and grotesque pathos of a hackneyed popular air sounded in the ears of the starving and the dying!

> " All round de leetle farm I wandered,
>   When I was young ;
>   Den my 'appy days I squandered,
>   Many de songs I sung.
>
> " When I was playing wid my brudder,
>   Appy was I ;
>   Oh take me to my kind old mudder,
>   Dere let me lib and die.
>
> " All the world am sad and dreary,
>   Ebberywhere I roam ;
>   Oh darkies, how my 'art grows weary,
>   Far from de old folks at 'ome !"

Alas, it was grotesquely horrible!

The calmness of the night, the sickness of my heart, the weakness of my limbs, and the sweetness of the violin as its notes floated far over the moonlit sea, together with the monotonous sound of the oars, made me fall into a waking doze—yet I still tugged mechanically on, though dreaming.

At times I imagined that I was in a dense fog off the harbour mouth of St. John. I heard the booming of the fog-guns from the battery on the mountains, though they sounded faint and far off. Then followed the welcome voice of the gunner on the low rocky point of Fort Amherst, challenging as usual—

"What ship is that?"

I strove to answer as we ran in through the Narrows, but my tongue refused its office.

Again, I was at my desk, engrossing in giant ledgers, with the snorting voice of old Uriah Skrew grating on my ear. Anon I was in my father's rose-covered villa at Peckham—in London, amid the roar and gaiety of its streets—its evening bustle and lights—in the theatre—at the opera—galloping out of town on the Derby-day. Then I was in a silent forest—but lo!

My dreams were broken by a shriek which made us all start as if electrified—the oarsmen at the oars, the sleepers at the bottom of the boat. Cuffy dropped his violin, and Reeves his tiller, as we all sprang up, looked in each other's sunken eyes, and on the glassy sea, that rippled in flat immensity far away in the moonlight.

"What is it—where did it come from?" we all gasped.

But none could answer correctly.

"It seemed to rise from the sea, far away on the starboard bow," said Reeves.

"*The starboard bow!*" repeated Hartly, shuddering.

We gazed intently around us, and though one of our men insisted that he could see a large figure like that of a man swimming towards us in the moonlit water, the rest could discern nothing.

This supernatural cry or sound seemed to belong neither to earth nor heaven; it rent the air and penetrated to our inner hearts; its cadence, too, was horrible, and unlike anything we had ever heard before. Its source occasioned us endless surmise, and we never discovered it; but the circumstance affected us all variously, and for a time we forgot our thirst, our hunger, and our danger, in the mystery and vague fear it occasioned.

That it could be given, as one surmised, by a drowning seaman who had escaped from some wreck, was impossible, for under the brilliant moon of the early May night, the whole sea was visible to us as at noonday. Hans of Orkney declared it to be a spirit of the sea, a water-bull, or the ghost of a man, whom we had unwittingly deserted in the foundering wreck. Cuffy moaned out that it was a warning from the Obi man. An Irish batman muttered something about a Banshee, but poor Hartly was too careless now, or too desponding, to suggest anything, and remained silent.

I can scarcely conceive that this cry, so strange, so wild and thrilling—so appalling to those who were in such a solemn and terrible situation—and which was heard by us all at the same moment, was the combined effect of imagination ; but whether it was some phenomenon—a sound brought through the air from a vast distance, by some unknown cause —the echo of a crime committed elsewhere, or a jarring of the elements that affected our over-strained organs of hearing, I know not.

I merely relate the event as it occurred ; but never, while life remains, shall I forget the bewildering and terrifying effect of that appalling shriek, when it rang in our ears, across the otherwise silent sea on that most mournful night.

CHAPTER XXXII.

THE TWELFTH DAY.

THE sixth day dawned as the wind freshened and
the waning moon went down in clouds; it dawned
upon an angry sea, a leaden sky, and with a cold
breeze that bore no ship—no hope of release towards
us.

On this day two more of our men, who had been
lying in a torpid state for three hours, died, and
were cast overboard. We were completely callous
now. About eleven in the forenoon, Hans Peterkin,
who was steering, suddenly uttered a hoarse cry.

"See—see!" he exclaimed, pointing a-head, while
glaring with haggard eyes; "a sail—a sail! Thanks
be to God," he added, pulling off his fur cap; "we
are saved!"

We that were rowing turned, and those who were
dozing between the thwarts sprang up; and there
sure enough, hull down about eighteen miles off, we

saw a large ship under a cloud of dark canvas, which
had evidently been wet by rain overnight, running
close-hauled upon the starboard tack, and going with
great speed through the water.

Oh the ecstasy of this sight!

We trimmed our little sail anew; we hoisted all
our neck-ties at the mast-head, as a signal; we pulled
with the strength of madmen—madmen, who were
dying and despairing—towards her; but she saw us
not. (I dare not say that her crew *heeded* not.)
Though for a time we seemed to gain upon her, the
wind freshened so much that she was soon out of
sight; and once more, after all our prayers, our long-
ings, and our joy, we were left alone upon the sullen
sea—alone amid emotions too terrible to delineate,
for hope and life went with her!

Some of our strongest men wrung their hands and
wept. Three days after this, those who had re-
strained the maddening desire to drink of the sea,
now gave loose to their burning thirst, and heedless
of the appeals of Hartly and the warnings of
Peterkin, plunged their wasted hands in the brine,
and drank it in great quantities.

The sequel soon followed—a delirium and insanity
which rapidly became infectious.

All were soon raving. Hartly talked of his dead

wife—of their little ones, and the green churchyard, where they lay under an old yew-tree; then of his lost ship, and the ring of the Iceland witch.

Hans sang Orkney songs in a guttural dialect— half Scottish and half Norse; and believed himself to be whaling in the Pentland Firth, and Sound of Yell. Paul Reeves sat with a serious but fatuous aspect, writing an imaginary log with his fingers on the boat-thwart; Cuffy played scraps of negro-melodies on his violin; and believed himself to be in his caboose, cooking a sumptuous dinner for those in the cabin.

Some raved of rich repasts, and with idiot joy enumerated the viands that smoked before them, or the cool draughts of spring water that gurgled over mossy rocks and under broad green leaves in shady woods—and of luscious fruit that grew in ripe clusters, but which they strove to reach in vain, as, like the gushing spring, it always eluded them. In pursuit of one of these illusions, poor Hans Peterkin fell overboard, and, without an effort to save himself, sank like a stone. Alas! the holy well of Kildingie and the blessed dulse of Guiodin, availed him nothing now!

At last we ceased to row, for the strongest among us " caught crabs" from time to time, and had the oars twitched out of their hands by the sea, for we were helplessly and hopelessly worn out.

The haggard features of some became rigid; the black fur of fever gathered upon their cracked lips; and their wild, sunken, and blood-shot eyes assumed a snaky glare. Their wasted forms seemed to dwindle before me; then they grew and dwindled again like a species of phantasmagoria, as I sat bewildered and half torpid among them; then a lurch of the boat would throw some of them off the thwarts motionless and dead!

On the *Twelfth* day after we had abandoned the *Leda*, there remained in the boat only four alive, including Hartly, Reeves, a seaman named Jones, and myself. All the rest had been thrown overboard in succession as they died—even poor Cuffy Snowball, clutching his violin to the last.

In their delirium some had been very violent—proposing to scuttle the boat; others threw the oars overboard and unclasped their knives to slay their messmates. One sprang into the sea, with a husky cry, and ended his miseries at once.

Grim and fearful as they were, I thought the calm aspect of those who died was to be envied. They seemed so free from every ill and storm that might assail them, while those who yet lived and lingered were the most helpless of human beings. I know not why or how it was that so many strong and hardy men perished, while I survived.

Reeves, Hartly, and Jones the sailor, lay prostrate in the bottom of the boat; and at times I knew not whether they were alive or dead, save by an occasional spasm that twitched their features, or a quivering in their limbs. After a time even these symptoms of existence ceased.

I felt the slumber of long exhaustion stealing over me. Lest the boat might capsize in a squall, I remember having just sense and strength sufficient to enable me to let go the halyard, and lower the sail, or rather, let it fall by its own weight, when I sank down in the stern sheets, and must have lain there for hours.

A drizzling rain refreshed me, and when I awoke, the silver moon was shining on the sea.

Another night had descended upon us !

I baled out the boat with a hat, for the forms of my passive companions were half-covered by water. As I did so, I thought Hartly spoke—at least, that his white and bloodless lips moved; but this might be fancy. My mind was a chaos of gloom, misery, and terrible forebodings.

Anxious to learn whether life yet lingered in my

friend, or whether I was quite alone—the *last man* —with the dead upon that silent midnight sea, I stooped close to Hartly; but at that moment the boat gave a sudden lurch, which threw me violently among the three bodies. In falling, my head struck against one of the thwarts, and happily I became senseless.

     *   *   *   *   *

CHAPTER XXXIII.

WHAT FOLLOWED.

AFTER that night a long time of dreamy stupor seemed to elapse, before any distinct sense of existence forced itself upon me. Then I seemed to wake from a heavy slumber (which had frequently been crowded by dreadful images), and found myself in bed, and in what appeared to be a little state-room that opened off a ship's cabin.

The roof seemed close and near my eyes; but the bed was soft and screened by green curtains, which hung upon a brass rod. The little panelled apartment had shelves crammed with books and bundles of papers; a gun, a cutlass, and telescope were hung on hooks; and from the deck above, a bull's-eye threw the sun's rays vertically down upon me. I saw all these details at a glance, but believed them to be portions of a dream—that I was still tossing in the open boat, with my dead or dying companions

rolling about in the bilge-water below the thwarts
—so my last thoughts of loneliness, of despair, and
coming death recurred to me in all their bitterness.

Gradually, however, the warmth and softness of
the couch on which I lay became too confirmed and
real to be doubted ; and now a hot but soothing
liquid, like mulled wine, was poured between my
lips. I drank deeply, and not until the draught
was ended did I open my heavy eyes, and again
look round me, fearing to dispel the delicious
illusion of imbibing a liquid, for the wild agonies
of unassuaged thirst were still in my memory.

A jolly and bluff-looking seaman, well tanned by
exposure to the weather, and well whiskered ; squat
in figure, merry in eye, and hearty in voice, wearing
a straw hat and pea-jacket, with a handsome gold
ring to secure the ends of his black silk neck-tie,
was holding back the green curtain, and surveying
me with some solicitude of manner.

" How do you feel yourself now, my lad?" he asked.

" Weak—giddy—ill—Hartly—Bob Hartly, keep
her head to the break of the sea, or we shall be
swamped," said I, incoherently.

" By Jove, I thought the mulled port would bring
you up with a round turn and make you speak if
nothing else would."

"Where am I?" said I, partially recovering again.

"On board ship at last."

"Which—what ship?"

"The barque *Princess* of London."

"Thank God—thank God!" I exclaimed; but though my breast heaved with wild emotions of joy, not a tear would come, for even that fount of tenderness seemed dried up within me.

"We picked you up when in an awful plight, my poor fellow! Your boat was half full of water, with two dead bodies washing about in it."

"Two!"

"Yes—two, and you were lying in the stern-sheets looking as pale and as stiff as the others. We were just about to send you over to leeward with a cold shot at your heels, when, fortunately, some signs of life escaped you."

"And you, sir——"

"Am the master of this craft—Captain John Baylis—I think you wont forget the name," he added, smiling.

"Forget it! Oh, sir, how shall I ever forget it?" I groaned. "But Hartly—poor Bob Hartly!"

"Who was he?"

"*Was*—is he then dead?" I exclaimed.

"I cannot say, until you tell me more."

"He was Master of the *Leda,* and my dear friend. She foundered in a tempest, and those you found in the longboat were the last of twenty-five stout fellows who sailed in her from St. John's, New-foundland, on the 17th of March."

"Is he about my size; with very dark whiskers and short curly hair?"

"Yes."

"Then he is getting on famously, and lies in my chief mate's berth—but you must not speak any more at present, try to sleep; a little time, and I will be with you again."

This was joyous intelligence!

In short, I learned by degrees that Hartly and I were the sole survivors of the crew of the *Leda.* Paul Reeves and Jones the seaman had been found dead in the long boat by the crew of the barque, who buried them in blankets, each with a heavy shot at their heels. After this they scuttled the boat, as the sight of her suggested unpleasant ideas.

The vessel which picked us up proved to be the barque *Princess,* a stately Blackwaller of sixteen hundred tons register, Captain John Baylis, from Quebec, bound for the Cape of Good Hope, with a general cargo. Our poor boat, tossing on the sea, had been descried about daybreak, by a man who was at work on the maintopgallant yard. She immediately bore down upon us, and hence our rescue at a time so critical. I must have been insensible for about four hours when her crew found me; and but for their ministrations, could not have survived another.

Fortunately for Hartly and me, the jolly and hospitable captain had his wife on board, and she nursed us with the tenderness of a mother. Indeed, honest Baylis and his whole crew vied with her in their attention to us.

Our feet and legs were so soddened by the bitter, briny water in which they had been so long immersed, that for some days mortification was dreaded; but as Mrs. Baylis had six goats on board, she made, and skilfully applied, poultices of bread and milk, which ameliorated the symptoms and our sufferings.

Food and liquids were administered to us in homœopathic doses at first; and several days elapsed before our interiors became accustomed to receive their usual quantities. At times we were both somewhat bewildered in mind—especially when the vessel encountered rough weather, and rolled much. Then Hartly and I were sure to imagine ourselves again in the longboat on the desolate sea, with the starving and dying around us; and long the voices of poor Hans Peterkin, of Paul Reeves, and the notes of Cuffy's violin, lingered in my ear, especially in dreams.

In about a fortnight—thanks chiefly to the kindness and nursing of Mrs. Baylis—we were able to sit on a sofa under an awning on the poop-deck; for we were now in warmer latitudes, and a protection from the sun of June was necessary. We greeted each other like two kinsmen who had escaped death; but Hartly mourned the loss of the *Leda* and of her crew, as they were all picked men, whom he never paid off on entering a port, but who had sailed with him to all parts of the world, and would as readily have thought of attempting to fly in the air as of leaving the poor old *Leda*.

For many days her loss, and the anecdotes connected with it, formed a staple subject for our conversation, until other thoughts, with returning health, forced themselves upon us: for those who are in the world must live for it.

The *Princess* was bound, I have said, for the Cape of Good Hope, where she would, perhaps, take a freight home for London; but there was an equal probability of her being chartered for Bombay, Hong Kong, or anywhere else, so that on reaching Cape

Town there would be an immediate necessity for Hartly and me looking about us, and seeking means for returning to the great metropolis.

As we approached the line, the heat increased rapidly, awnings were spread over the decks, wind-sails were rigged down the hatchways, and skeets over the sides were resorted to daily.

The latter are pieces of grooved wood, for throwing water over the planks or outer sheathing of a ship, to prevent them from being rent by the heat of the sun in warm climates.

For some weeks Hartly and I were totally unable to make ourselves of any use, so great was the lassitude which succeeded our recent sufferings, and rapid transition from starvation and misery to comfortable quarters, and from the Regions of Ice to those of the burning sun; for after passing St. Jago, the most southerly of the Cape de Verd Isles, we rapidly approached the line; and then Captain Baylis, his wife, Hartly, and others, prepared letters for home, to be left at the Isle of Ascension, or given to the first ship that passed us for England.

Day after day I reclined listlessly under the awning, watching the shining sea, on which many an argonauta now was floating; and, in a warm latitude, singularly beautiful are those little "Portuguese men-of-war," as our sailors term them, when whole fleets of them may be seen sailing past, with their purple sails up and rowing swiftly, with all their tentacula or feelers out.

But, on being approached by anything, in go the tentacula, and down sinks the miniature sail, as the fish concentrates itself in its shell, and both vanish together, like a fairy in the sea.

CHAPTER XXXIV.

THE SAILOR'S POST-OFFICE.

WE crossed the line on the last day of June. I need not rehearse the description of a hackneyed ceremony known to all—how curtains were rigged amidships—how Father Neptune with his hempen beard came on board, seated on a gun-carriage, and how roughly all who had *not* crossed the line before were tarred, scraped, shaved, and soused by his whimsically attired barbers, courtiers, and Tritons, to the great delight of the older salts—a ceremony which I only escaped in consequence of my recent sufferings.

Two days after, we passed St. Matthew, a little desert isle on which the Portuguese formed a settlement so early as 1516, and which lies " amid the melancholy main," at a vast distance from the African coast. It is the abode of sea-birds alone.

Then we completed our bag of letters, which were

all duly gummed up—*wax* will not do in the tropics
—for delivery at Ascension, which, after three
hundred miles' further run, we sighted on the evening of the 9th July, for we had a fine wind, and the
Princess carried her studdingsails night and day.

I was not without hope that we might find some
homeward-bound vessel at Ascension, on board of
which we might be transferred, as I was most
anxious to return home to tranquillize the minds of
my own family, whom I knew must long since have
numbered me with the dead; but this hope was
dissipated when we came abreast of the roadstead,
which was *empty*, and let go our anchor about midnight, in fourteen fathom water, on a red sandy
bottom.

The anchorage of this solitary isle is a sheltered
creek, overshadowed by a high pyramidal mountain,
having on its summit the remains of two great
crosses, erected of old by the pious and adventurous
followers of Juan de Nova, a Portuguese mariner
who flourished in the days of King Alfonzo Africanus.

The heat was so great now that the atmosphere
in the cabin rendered one absolutely breathless;
and with pleasure, Hartly and I, clad in light
clothes, with broad straw hats, furnished to us by
kind Captain Baylis, accompanied him and his wife

ashore next morning after anchoring, and landed at
the little town, which is fortified, and the harbour of
which frequently forms a rendezvous for our African
squadron. The longboat with her crew afterwards
came off for fresh water and turtles. The super-
intendence of collecting these was left to the chief
mate, while with Hartly (who had been there before),
Captain Baylis and I set forth on a ramble over the
island, which is only nine miles long by six miles
broad.

An undefinable interest is excited when landing
on a lonely little island after a long sea voyage; and
for ages Ascension has been a species of halfway
house, or resting-place for ships between Europe
and the Cape.

We resolved to visit the *Sailor's Post-office*, a
cranny in the rocks, known for ages to the mariners
of all nations, who were wont to deposit their letters
there, closed up in a bottle, to be taken away by the
first ship which passed in an opposite direction—a
custom which the Dominican, Father Navarette,
mentions as being *old*, at the time of his visit in
1673.

The little isle is barren, but having been rent by
volcanic throes, it has hills of pumice-stone and
calcined rocks, with abrupt precipices overhanging

sterile ravines that are full of black ashes. Here
and there a solitary goat might be seen cropping the
scanty herbage, or perched upon a sharp pinnacle,
snuffing the sea breeze that waved its solemn
beard. Where a spring gurgled from the rocks into
the sea the turtle were seen in plenty, and there our
boat's crew came in search of them. There also lay
the skeletons of great numbers, which seamen, in
mere wantonness, had turned on their backs, and
left thus to die.

From the summit of the pyramidal hill which
overlooks the anchorage we could survey the boundless ocean, spreading away towards the distant shores
of Africa, the still more distant coast of Peru, and the
unexplored waves of the Southern Sea, all glassy,
heaving, and vibrating like a mighty mirror under
the vertical glare of the tropical sun.

Fanning ourselves with banana leaves, for at
times we gasped in the heat, we trod among ashes
ankle deep, and over rocks where the power of the
sun had turned to fine salt the spray cast upon
them by the sea.

At last we reached the Sailor's Post-office, and
examined the cleft in the rocks, where the bottles or
cases containing many a letter that carried to the
hearts and homes of generations long since gone to

dust, hope and happiness, or it might be sorrow and woe—the tidings of loved and lost ones far away in lands and seas that were then so little known and so little traversed; and then combining prose with poetry, we sat down to discuss some light sherry, pale ale, and sandwiches, which the worthy Captain Baylis insisted on conveying for us in a travelling-bag slung over his shoulder.

As evening drew on, the sterile rocks and impending bluffs, the great rugged pyramidal hill that towered over the anchorage, the little town of Ascension, with its battery and gaudy Union Jack, all assumed a dusky red hue; and when the sun sank westward, the shadow of the *Princess* at her anchor was thrown far across the bright blue water of the creek. Our last boat with turtle, bananas, fish, and fresh water, was to leave the harbour at sunset; so we were preparing to descend, when an object lying among some stones at the bottom of the cleft in the rock, caught Hartly's eye.

Scrambling among ashes and black pumice-stone, he reached, and drew it forth.

It was a stone jar, shaped like a ginger-beer bottle, tightly corked, and covered over the mouth and neck by thin sheet-lead, which was paid over with old tarred spunyarn; but it was so thickly encrusted with

lichens and dust, which the sun and dew had baked
upon it, that it had quite the colour and aspect of
the stones that lay around it.

"Now, what the deuce is this?" asked Captain
Baylis.

"A bottle," said Hartly, turning it over.

"A bottle in the Post-office!"

"It must have lain here a long time, if we judge
by its outside," said I.

"Letters have never been deposited here since
1816," observed Baylis, "when the British built the
town and battery yonder."

"So if it has lain here one year, it must have lain
fifty."

"Shake it, Hartly," said I.

"It is full of something that rattles!"

"Letters, probably; but few folks can care about
them now."

"Faith! the man's head does not ache that un-
twisted this spunyarn; it is at least seventy years
old!" said Captain Baylis, fraying the strands with
his fingers; "but we'll crack the bottle when we get
on board, and see what the contents are."

We joined Mrs. Baylis at the landing-place. She
was reclining in the stern of the gig with a large
white umbrella over her head, and could scarcely

repress her curiosity to discover the contents of the old stone jug, or bottle, till we got on board.

Then we broke it by a blow of a hammer, and there fell out, not letters, as we expected, but a roll of paper, consisting of leaves stitched together, and closely covered with writing, containing a narrative, or something of the kind, which had been deposited in that strange mode and strange place by some waggish or eccentric person, in the hope, perhaps, that if ever discovered, by the mystery enveloping their literary production, it would assuredly be given to the public.

It was without date; but fortunately the hand-writing was plain and legible, though the ink was dim and faded, for the stone bottle being porous, the paper had become damp, almost wet, and had to be carefully dried in the sunshine, which curled it up like crisped leaves in autumn, so the preparation of it for perusal was consigned to my care by Captain Baylis, who had discovered that I was, as he said, "a regular-built bookworm."

"It is a history," said he, as he lighted his long clay pipe in the cabin, after the *Princess* got under weigh next evening, and stood out of the anchorage under her courses and topgallant sails, with her royals, spanker, and gaff-topsail set.

"Or the narrative of an unfortunate voyage," suggested Hartly, thinking, doubtless, of his own.

"Or the revelation of some dreadful crime, or unfortunate love-story," lisped Mrs. Baylis, all impatience, pausing and looking up in the act of pouring out our tea.

"It is none of these," said I; "but seems to be the translation of a Portuguese legend, connected in some way with the discovery of the Cape of Good Hope."

And so, while the good captain lounged in his shirt sleeves on the cabin sofa, and puffed away with his long clay pipe, while his buxom wife made tea for us, and Hartly lit his Havannah, I commenced to read the MS. we had found so singularly; and it ran thus—but requires a chapter or two to itself.

CHAPTER XXXV.

MS. LEGEND OF EL CABO DOS TORMENTOS.

IT is written—says the Spanish Dominican Friar
and Missionary Priest, the Padre Navarette—that
the first time reports reached Europe of a spectre
haunting the Cape of Storms, was by the narratives
of certain Portuguese adventurers, who sailed into
the Southern Sea, with the Senhor Bartholomew
Diaz, in the early part of the fifteenth century, when
Dom Joam II. occupied the throne of Portugal.

His cousin and successor, King Emmanuel, fired
by the discoveries made in the reigns of his pre-
decessors, who had planted their flag and cross on
the shores of Madeira, the Azores, and Isles of the
Cape de Verd, resolved to accomplish what they had
failed in, and with praiseworthy zeal despatched an
admiral to discover a passage to India by sea.

After a long absence this cavalier returned and
reported that he had found the *southern* extremity of
the mighty African continent; but, that his ships

had encountered great perils when off a flat-headed mountain of wondrous form, which he had named *El Cabo dos Tormentos.*

The King of Portugal suggested that " *El Cabo de Buena Esperança (i.e.,* the Cape of Good Hope), would be a better term ;" and it was at once adopted by his courtiers, though the mariners of the Admiral adhered to " the Cape of Torments," as they alleged that, not only had they nearly been swallowed by the waves of a black and stormy sea, but that they had seen a stupendous form, resembling a human figure, riding upon the whirling scud above the Table Mountain, and spreading his giant arms as if to clasp them in his terrible embrace, and hurl them into the yawning deep.

They insisted that this dangerous promontory was the *end* of the habitable world—the abode of devils, spectres, and torments—a place wherein nothing human could dwell; and that the seas which washed its shore should be shunned by all future navigators.

They ridiculed the title of *Buena Esperança,* and urged that no mariner in his senses would visit the place again ; for the old salts of those days devoutly believed in tales of

> " That sea-snake tremendous curled,
>   Whose monstrous circle girds the world,"

and that the earth was girt with fire at the Equator; that whoever passed the tempestuous Cape Bojador, which was first doubled by the Portuguese in 1433, and which forms the southern limit of Morocco, was doomed never to return, as a mysterious breeze (the trade wind?) blew for ever against them; that ships got into currents that ran *down hill* — currents against which they might beat and struggle in vain, till their shattered hulls were cast upon Bermuda— the "vexed Bermoothes" of Shakespeare, which, as Stowe tells us, "were supposed to be inhabited by witches and devils"—an iron shore where perpetual storms raged, and fated ships were dashed upon the rocks.

Despite these terrors, animated by a spirit of adventure, Vasco da Gama, a valiant mariner and cavalier of Alentejo, resolved to sail in quest of this terrible cape, accompanied by many of his friends, among whom was a noble young hidalgo, named Vasco da Lobiera, grandson of the gallant knight of that name, who fought at the battle of Aljubarotta, and received his spurs on the field from King Joam of good memory, at whose feet, in after years, he laid his famous romance, "Amadis de Gaul."

From his grandsire young Vasco inherited a love of wild adventure; thus his mind was full of tales of

" The days when giants were rife
    With their towers and painted halls,
And heroes, each with a charmèd life,
    Rode up to their castle walls—
When gentle and bright ones with golden hair
    Were wooed by princes in green,
And knights with invisible caps to wear,
    Could see, and yet never be seen."

Notwithstanding the alleged terrors of the spectre or storm fiend which haunted the Cape, the brave Da Gama and his friend Lobiera resolved to set forth upon these mysterious waters, and to double the promontory of Southern Africa. So the former, as Captain-General, hoisted his banner on board the *San Gabriel*, of two hundred and twenty tons; while Paulo da Gama, his brother, commanded the *San Rafael*, of one hundred tons.

Vasco da Lobiera had the caravella named *Nossa Senhora da Belem* (or Bethlehem), with Joam da Coimbra as pilot, and Gonsalo Nunez had their great storeship laden with provisions.

All these vessels were built of the pines which were planted in the forest of Marinha by King Denis the Magnificent, and were manned by one hundred and sixty chosen mariners.

King Emmanuel made them a farewell oration, and gave into the hands of each commander a white silk banner of the military order of Christ, together with his royal letters to an imaginary potentate, who was supposed to dwell beyond the Southern Sea, and was named Prester John of the Indies, Lord and Emperor of Ethiopia ; and so, with the prayers of all good Portuguese for their success, the little squadron sailed from Lisbon, on the 8th July, 1497, when it is recorded that " thousands remained weeping on the shore, until the last traces of the receding fleet had disappeared."

Among their own crews, as well as among those of the other two ships, Da Gama and Da Lobiera found men averse to touching at the Cabo dos Tormentos ; and these urged, that to double this dreadful promontory, they should stand further out to sea than the adventurers of Dom Joam's days, and then visit in safety the realms of Prester John on the *other* side.   Gama and his friend heeded neither their remarks, their exhortations, or their fears, but bore away steadily to the southward.

After a long and perilous voyage, and after anchoring in a great bay which they named Angra de Santa Elena, the crew of *Our Lady of Belem* first saw the land of Table Bay on the morning of Saturday, the 4th of November, when, in obedience to Dom Vaseo da Lobiera, the ship's company donned

U

their gayest apparel, discharged a volley from their culverins, and blew all their trumpets ; but, as they stood towards the shore, they were compelled to lessen their canvas, for the wind, which had hitherto been moderate and favourable, now changed to the south-east, and increased to a gale, while the sun set in dense clouds, and turning from light green to black, the waves began to froth and break as they alternately rose into hills or sank into valleys.

And now as night and mist descended together on the sea, and on the Cabo dos Tormentos, light-nings began to play about the awful summit of the Table Mountain, which rises for more than three thousand two hundred feet above the shore. The four ships which prior to this evening had kept close together, were compelled by the violence of the gale to separate, lest they might be dashed against each other; and in the murk and gloom they continued to beat against the headwind, with their topsail-yards lowered upon the cap, their courses close reefed, and their spritsails stowed.

When the vessels last saw each other, the Senhor Vasco da Lobiera was much chagrined to perceive that his caravella had dropped far astern of her companions. He had ever prided himself upon the swiftness of her sailing, and now he burned lights, and strove to come abreast of the Captain-General, who had beat far to windward, and who he feared might attribute his drifting so much a-lee, and towards danger, to want of skill or seamanship.

He set as much canvas as he dared, and *Nossa Senhora da Belem* tore through the angry sea with her foresail and foretopsail close reefed, and her jib and spritsail set, while the waves lashed her worn sides, and burst in foam over her carved and lofty prow at every furious plunge.

The seamen told their beads, lit candles before the shrine of Nossa Senhora in the great cabin, shook their heads, muttered under their long black beards, or maintained gloomy silence, fearing they knew not what, but anticipating all the terrors that had beset the followers of Bartholomew Diaz in the same waters.

And now wave after wave broke in thundering volume over her decks, till Lobiera was fain to cast overboard the brass culverins which had been consecrated by the Bishop of Lisbon, and his men averred that each uttered *a cry* as it sank into the sea.

By midnight they were, as Joam da Coimbra stated, about six miles from the mouth of Table Bay.

Hoarsely roared the wind through the strained shrouds of the labouring caravella, as she rolled and pitched wildly amid the black and fearful waste of water, and ere long she was driving under bare poles with only her jib and staysail to lift her head from the sea, which rushed upon her like a succession of watery mountains.

With all the firmness of true mariners and cavaliers, Vasco da Lobiera and his friend Joam stood at the tiller, crossing themselves ever and anon when they shouted a command through the trumpet, or invoked our Lady of Belem. The deck had long since been cleared of every loose spar, bucket, or other material by the waves; and more than one poor mariner had been swept overboard to perish miserably in the midnight sea, for no human hand could assist them.

Some there were who asserted that they had seen the claws of a giant figure start from the black waves, and drag their shipmates down below by their beards and trunk hose.

"We make no progress," said others, rending their hair; "a mighty magnet, buried deep in the sea, holds us to one accursed spot!"

"Nay," said Joam da Coimbra; "'tis the teeth of a mighty fish that grasp our keel."

" Be of good cheer, I pray you, my friends," said Vasco, pointing to the Southern Cross, which was then visible through a rent in the fast flying scud; "behold the sign by which we shall conquer! What says the motto of our country?"

" *In hoc signo vinces!*" exclaimed Joam da Coimbra, throwing his hands towards the south.

" Amen," responded the terrified crew, and still their ship bore on.

" Thou art right, Joam," said Vasco da Lobiera; and the courage of the crew revived, for their pilot was a mariner of great experience, and, like Chaucer's shipman—

" By many a tempest had his beard been shaken,"

CHAPTER XXXVI.

LEGEND CONTINUED—THE CATASTROPHE.

THE moon, which had hitherto been concealed in
dense vapour, now glanced at times through the
flying clouds. It was one of those stormy moons
well known in that quarter of the world. She
seemed small, but keen and bright, gilding with
whitest silver the ragged edges of the torn vapour,
which fled past with such speed as to give her literally the aspect of sailing through the sky.

A mournful and moaning sound now came upon
the wind which traversed that dashing sea, and the
mariners of Lobiera, who had never looked on such
a scene, nor beheld such lightnings as those that
girdled like a fiery belt the flat summit of the Table
Mountain, were becoming more bewildered and faint
of heart, when a cry of dismay burst from Joam da
Coimbra, and now even the resolute Vasco stood
speechless and aghast.

Above the Table Mountain the clouds rapidly rolled themselves into a denser and darker mass, which assumed the outline of a human figure that grew in volume while they gazed upon it, until it towered into the sky, against the moonlit blue of which it was defined with terrible distinctness.

"The spectre—il demonio del Cabo dos Tormentos!" said each in his heart, while it continued to tower, with mighty arms outstretched, as if to clutch the devoted ship, or bury it in the sea that seethed around this dreadful cape—the great promontory of the southern world.

With one foot planted on Table Mountain, and the other on the Devil's Hill, with a head that darkened heaven, stood this mighty form, which appeared to have the power of curbing and of loosening the elements, for at every wave of its threatening arms the sea increased in turbulence, and the wind in fury, for the thunder appeared to be his voice, the lightning the flashes of his eye, the tempest the breath of his nostrils!

"Madre de Dios—our Lady of Belem!" prayed Dom Vasco.

"Dei genetrix, intercede pro nobis!" was the faint response of his quailing crew.

"Courage, comrades," he exclaimed; "I have

still the blessed banner which our Lord the King gave me, and it shall yet float above the storm."

"But the ship has become unmanageable!" cried Joam da Coimbra.

"Nay, say not so—Heaven forefend! *Nossa Senhora da Belem* is as gallant a craft as ever came from the woods of Marinha, and she shall bear us yet to seas beyond the power of this resentful demon!"

Vasco da Lobiera would have said more, but a burst of thunder drowned every other sound; lightning filled the entire sky with lurid flame; the wind bellowed, and the blinding rain descended in a solid sheet upon the trembling sea with such power as almost to still its waves. He ordered the masts to be cut away; only two of his crew heard the order, or had the courage to obey it. The rest were crouching in a group, stupified by despair and fear.

Three blows of a sharp axe were alone required, the tempest did the rest, and the stately masts with all their yards and gear vanished alongside. The rudder was torn from its iron bands, and now the boasted *Lady of Belem* floated like a log upon the waves, which incessantly broke over her, washing the crew in succession away. Now it was that the heart of Vasco da Lobiera began to sink, and he gave himself up for lost !

In a few minutes more he found himself struggling in the sea, for his ship was hurled upon the rocky coast and dashed to pieces.

Clutching a piece of wreck, he was tossed up by a vast wave, that cast him stunned, breathless, helpless and alone, upon the desolate shore of that terrible promontory ; so his holy banner availed him nothing.

And there he lay as the sea receded, wave after wave continuing to hiss and roar behind him, as if loth to lose their prey.

*   *   *   *   *

CHAPTER XXXVII.

LEGEND CONCLUDED—THE SEQUEL.

WHEN the Senhor Dom Vasco came to his senses, says the Padre Navarette, morning had dawned. All nature was calm, and the warm rays of the rising sun were shedding light and gladness on the land and sea.

Above him rose in sullen majesty the triple crest of the Table Mountain, the Devil's Hill, and the Hill of Lions; and undisturbed by a single ripple before him lay that treacherous sea, which, but a few hours before, had destroyed *Nossa Senhora da Belem.* With some surprise, Vasco found that his doublet and hose were dry; and that his bruises were not so severe as he might have expected, under all the circumstances.

He arose, invoked Heaven on his knees, and surveyed the watery plain with anxiety, to discover whether any fragment of the wrecked caravella was floating there; but not a vestige was to be seen, and apparently none of his crew had reached the shore save himself, all had perished.

The forlorn cavalier could not repress an exclamation of bitterness and grief, on realizing the full horror of this catastrophe; for he loved his crew, and also the little caravella in which he had sailed so gaily from the Tagus, on that auspicious 8th of July.

Distant from his native land many, many thousand miles, without a hope of rescue or release, he was about to abandon himself to despair, when in the vague hope of meeting another survivor, he traversed the plain which lies at the base of the Table Mountain, and which was then covered by white lilies, gorgeous tulips, and almond trees, all growing wild.

To add to his grief and terror, here he found the remains of his friend, Joam da Coimbra, half devoured by lions or wolves, who had dragged him from the beach. Dom Vasco shuddered, and was hastening on, when a deep voice that seemed to fill the whole welkin, cried,

" *Stay !*"

He turned, and beheld a copper-coloured man of wondrous stature, and savage, yet noble aspect, who

held in his right hand a hunting spear, so long, that
it was twice the length of any Vasco had ever seen
—aye, thrice the length of the lance his grandsire
had carried at Aljubarrota—and in his left a reeking
skin, which he had just torn from a lion—perhaps
one of those that had been feasting on the hapless
pilot. His aspect was alike sublime and terrible;
his black beard was of majestic length; his bright
eyes wore a sad and gloomy expression, and his hair
which rose in great curls, like those of the Phidian
Jove, resembled the mane of a sable lion. But what
is stranger than all, this wild man spoke very good
Portuguese.

"In the name of Heaven," said the cavalier,
"who and what are you?"

"The spirit of the Cabo dos Tormentos—the
demon of the storm which rent your ship asunder,
and cast it on yonder shores, dashed to a thousand
pieces," replied the form in a deep, but melodious
voice.

Vasco—continues the Padre Navarette—doubted
the evidence of his senses. This was like one of the
adventures with which the history of "Amadis de
Gaul" had filled his mind—one for which he longed;
but he felt the reality the reverse of pleasant.

"I have ruled these regions since the ark rested

on Mount Ararat, and since the land was parted from the waters; but never until now, has the foot of man invaded them; and had my power prevailed in the storm of yesternight, instead of being here, thou too shouldst have found a grave where many other adventurers lie, in yonder rolling sea."

"Terrible spirit," said Dom Vasco, "is the presence of a mere mortal so hateful to you?"

"Yes," replied the demon, shaking his mighty locks with gloom and sadness; "for now my power over these seas, and shores, and clouds, must end where thine begins. Elsé, wherefore did I bury ship after ship in that tempestuous sea, or split them by the flaming bolts, that all on board might perish? Many have sought to pass my promontory, to reach the golden realms of Prester John, but none have escaped me save *thee!* I have had the power of assuming what form I please. To-day I am a man, to-morrow I should tower to the skies astride the Table Mountain, or ride the wild blast that comes from the arid desert of Zahara, to bury some barque in the distant sea; but that my power is passing away from me. I tell thee, O most fortunate and valiant cavalier, that from this day the Cabo dos Tormentos shall be a Cape of Storms no more, but one of Good Hope to all the mariners of the earth—

for so it was ordained by the hand which placed Adam in Eden and gave such wondrous power unto the Seal of Solomon."

As the spirit concluded, his voice became fainter; his broad and dusky chest heaved as he sighed deeply, and he gradually appeared to dissolve into a thin white vapour, which floated upwards and melted away on the summit of the Table Mountain. But the power of the spirit lingers there still; for over the same spot where he vanished from the eyes of Dom Vasco, a *thin white cloud*, which rises from the hill, is unto this day the sure forerunner of a storm.*

Next day, the *San Rafael*, the vessel of Da Gama, which had been greatly shattered by the tempest, appeared off Table Bay, and on Vasco da Lobiera making signals, a boat was sent for him and he was brought on board, more dead than alive after all he had undergone.

To the wondering followers of his friend, he related his adventure. They deplored the loss of his

---

* In summer, when the S. E. wind blows, a cloud called *the Tablecloth* appears on the mountain, and always indicates a tempest. This cloud is composed of immense masses of fleecy whiteness. — *Arnott.*

caravella, and of so many good and pious Portuguese ; but they shook their long beards doubtfully when he spoke of the spectre, though the unusual calmness of the weather about the Cabo dos Tormentos seemed to verify his story and the promises made to him.

On being joined by the vessels of Paulo da Gama and Gonzalo Nunez, they bore away to the eastward, and named the coast La Terra de Noel (or Natal) having anchored off it on Christmas Day. Sixty leagues from the Cape, they found a bay, which they named San Blaz, and in it an island, full of birds with bat's-wings.   (Penguins.)

Thus the passage of the Cape of Storms was fully achieved and the spell broken by these valiant Portuguese ; but they could nowhere discover the realms of Prester John, so the royal letters of Dom Emmanuel remained unopened.

On his return to Lisbon, Dom Vasco applied to the King of Portugal for a gift of the Table Mountain, and money to colonize the land about it, in virtue of his interview with the spectre ; but he was laughed at by the courtiers, and especially by the priests, who proved his greatest enemies.

The King, after this, styled himself Lord of the Seas on both sides of Africa ; Lord of Guinea,

Ethiopia, Persia, India, Brazil, and many other lands; but how fared it with Dom Vasco da Lobiera?

Fury, pride, and mortification turned his brain; but he survived till the reign of King Joam III., when he was last seen, an old and impoverished man, with a white head and threadbare doublet, hovering in the Rua d'Agua de Flore in Lisbon, at the gate of the Estrella, or at the chapel of Nossa Senhora da Belem, raving to the passers about the friendly Demon of el Cabo de Buena Esperança, and the colony of which the King had deprived him.　　.

So—says the Padre Navarette—ends this wild story.

CHAPTER XXXVIII.

WE LAND IN AFRICA.

AND now to resume my own more simple narrative.

The barque *Princess*, which, until we touched at Ascension, had been favoured with singularly fine weather, now encountered strong head-winds. She was driven out of her course, and had to run well in, on the African coast.

After long beating about, on the 2nd of August we saw the great continent on the southern shore of the Gulf of Guinea.

The winds had become light and the weather cloudy. On this day I remember the crew were variously employed, and the carpenters were busy in making two new topgallant masts, to replace those injured in the rough weather we had so recently encountered.

About six P.M. the weather became squally. Captain Baylis ordered the studding-sails to be taken in, and the chain-cables bent to the anchors. At midnight we took in the royals and flying-jib.

At four o'clock on the morning of the 3rd, as we required fresh water, we came to anchor in a little sheltered bay of the Rio Gabon, which lies between the Bight of Benin and Cape Lopez Gonsalvo.

The wondrous transparency of the atmosphere here exceeded all I had seen—even in the pure region of eternal ice; for amid the clear splendour of the heavens, the eye could observe without a telescope many a lesser star unseen in the north; and on this morning when we were coming to anchor, two of the fixed planets shone with a refulgence so brilliant as to cast the shadow of the ships far across the estuary.

By this time, the hot vertical sun of the tropics had peeled all the paint off the blistered sides of the *Princess.* Her anchors and ironwork had become mere masses of red rust, her once white paint had been turned to orange colour, and her tar to dirty yellow, while the caulking and pitch had boiled out from her planks and seams.

Captain Baylis had no intention of remaining here longer than he could avoid, as the climate is unhealthy. Though the hills which overlook the river are of considerable height, the land between it and them is but a series of swamps, where the gigantic

water-weeds of Africa and the wild mangrove-trees
flourish in rank luxuriance, and where the hideous
crocodile squatters in the slime, or crawls along the
sand, where its eggs are hatched by the hot sun, if
they are not previously stolen by the ichneumon.

While the chief mate went off in the long-boat to
the Pongos—as the little isles at the mouth of the
estuary are named—to fill several casks with fresh
water, Captain Baylis proposed a visit to a negro
village on the coast, for the purpose of procuring
some elephants' teeth and leopard skins, and having
a *palaver* with the natives, many of whom, though
extremely savage, have picked up a little English by
the frequent visits of our ships, particularly those of
the African squadron.

With a view to barter, he placed in his gig four
old rusty muskets, some well-worn table knives, old
coats, pots and kettles, while, to be prepared for any
emergency, four rifles, carefully loaded and capped,
were concealed in the stern sheets, and Mrs. Baylis,
Hartly, and I accompanied him on this expedition,
which was the commencement of a series of
disasters, that ended in the destruction of nearly all
concerned.

For the lady's comfort, an awning was rigged over
the stern of the gig, which, being rowed by eight

oars, ran rapidly close in shore, where we saw a
number of black fellows in a state of semi-nudity,
gabbling, gesticulating violently, and watching our
arrival with considerable interest.

Some of their actions seeming to indicate hostility
as they brandished long spears and asseguys, Captain
Baylis stood up in the boat and displayed his old
pots and kettles, making signs that he wished to
trade or barter with them.　On this they uttered a
simultaneous yell, and disappeared among the mangroves, which fringed all the bank of the river, and
formed a species of natural arcade by their branches
arching over from the solid soil, and taking root in
the slimy water.

Of this unsatisfactory result we could make nothing; but in no way daunted, Captain Baylis
(though saying that he "wished he had left his good
wife on board") steered for a little creek, on entering
which, we lost sight alike of the Pongo islets and
the *Princess*, which lay at anchor in the estuary,
about four miles off.

Beaching partly the sharp-prowed and handsome
gig in the soft sand, Baylis, Hartly, and I sprang
ashore, and looked in every direction among the tall
weeds and mangroves for our sable traders; but all
was silent and still.　The breast of the broad river

was undisturbed by a ripple, and seemed to sleep in the sultry sunshine; the silence of the mighty forests that grew along its banks was unbroken by a sound; and the vast baobab or calibash trees, with their gigantic yellow fruit and wondrous horizontal branches, covered by foliage, were drooping listlessly in the hot and breathless atmosphere of the tropical noon.

" I don't understand this, and, moreover, I don't much like it," said Captain Baylis, in a low voice to Hartly and me; " for when I was here before I found the darkies ready enough to 'make friends,' as they term it, and to exchange their elephants' tusks, panther skins, and camwood for any rubbish we could collect on board."

But he knew not that, at this time, one of the crew of an American ship which sailed on the previous day had wantonly shot the fetisher, or priest of a village, and thus inspired the people with hostility to all white strangers; and it is not improbable that they conceived the Yankee and the *Princess* to be one and the same vessel.

After looking about us for some time, and finding that none of the natives returned, Baylis proposed that we should pull a little higher up the stream, to the village of the Rio Serpientes—or Snake River, as it is called in the charts—a tributary of the Gabon.

The giant size of the plants, shrubs, and trees, their wonderful greenness and luxuriance, the brilliance of the flowers, the loud hum of insect-life, where insects are as large as birds at home, the depth of the forest dingles, and the overpowering heat of the atmosphere, all served to impress me with novelty and strangeness; while mingled emotions of wonder, pleasure, and apprehension filled my breast.

With deep interest I trod this wondrous soil, of which so little is known. "For three centuries," says some one, "our ships have circumnavigated Africa, and yet, with a few exceptions, our knowledge of its districts is very incomplete; while the interior presents to the eye a *blank* in geography—an unsolved problem, in moral as well as physical science." Though nearly four thousand years ago the valley of the Nile was the cradle of art and commerce, we know no more about the Mountains of the Moon than old Ptolemy himself knew.

We were about to re-embark, when the united yells of more than a hundred negroes rent the clear welkin, and starting from the leafy seclusion of the mangroves into the blaze of sunlight, a horde of black and naked savages rushed upon us with long asseyuys, bows, clubs, and knives; and in a moment we found ourselves their prisoners.

Two seamen in the bow of the gig, while attempting to shove her off, were struck through the body with poisoned spears, and slain on the instant; the rest were dragged out, the gig itself was lifted fairly out of the water, hoisted on the brawny shoulders of nearly twenty men, and borne with yells of derision and exultation up the bank, where they hurled it high and dry ashore among the mangroves ; while at the same moment, poor Baylis with horror saw his shrieking wife dragged by others into the jungle.

After being beaten with asseguy-shafts until we were nearly senseless, our clothes were rent from us roughly, and in a state nearly approaching nudity, covered with bruises, and in some instances with blood, we were dragged into a thicket, and brought before the King of the village, who was seated on a grass matting, which was spread under the umbrageous shadow of a baobab-tree, where he was smoking a great wooden pipe.

All this passed in less than five minutes; and I was so stunned by the rapidity of the transaction, as well as by several blows received on the head from lance-shafts, that the whole affair resembled a terrible dream !

CHAPTER XXXIX.

THE KING OF THE SNAKE RIVER

In that district of Africa every village has its petty monarch, and these are all vassals of the King of Gabon, who, in turn, is vassal of the King of Benin; and Zabadie, the sooty sovereign of this empire, had just died about this time.

The town, or capital (of his Majesty of the Snake River), if it could be so named, in which we found ourselves, was composed of some six hundred huts or so; and these resembled a large collection of beehives, being constructed with meshes, twigs, straw, and turf.

I was dragged to the door of one, while a savage, whom I conceived to be the proprietor, and who wore a large coin at his neck, threw in my hat, coat, vest, and trowsers, of which he had violently possessed himself, being a person in authority and near relation of the King. While he grasped me by a

thong which secured my right wrist, I could perceive within that his dwelling consisted of one
apartment, the appurtenances of which were only
mats, calibashes, a stone mortar for pounding millet,
and a cauldron of earthenware.

Closing the door, which was composed of basket-
work, he dragged me to our forlorn group, which
stood before the King, who for some time permitted us to be pelted with stones, decayed gourds,
and pulpy water-melons, by the women and children
of his capital; and under this treatment and her
terror, poor Captain Baylis saw his unfortunate wife
about to sink without being able to yield her the
least assistance, as the point of an asseguy menaced
his throat at the slightest movement.

As an accessory to the alarm our situation excited
within us, close by where his Majesty sat was
a negro, on whom a sentence of his had just been
executed.

This miserable wretch had been tied to a stake,
disembowelled alive, and had his body thereafter
filled with hot salt. Despite the terrors of our own
situation, his dying agonies suggested terrible
thoughts of what our own fate might be. At last his
contortions and quiverings ceased for ever, and then,
on the hoarse beating of an old Arab drum, the pelting

was stopped, the King of the Snakes laid aside his pipe, and while all his sable subjects, save those who guarded us, prostrated themselves on the turf, he commenced to address us; and Baylis, who knew something of his jargon, replied, and translated the conversation to us.

The Captain earnestly deprecated our treatment, as we had come among them with the peaceful intention of trading. He pled especially on behalf of his wife, and offered a great store of bottled rum, old firelocks, pots, kettles, brass buttons, and iron nails, as ransom for us all.

At these offers his sable Majesty, the Solon of the Snake River, before whom had been laid the entire contents of the gig, with the bloody garments of the poor fellows slain in her, only grinned from time to time, and then uttered a diabolical laugh, which boded us no good.

This savage chief presented a dreadful aspect. Black as ebony, tall, strong, and muscular in form, he had a horizontal slit in his nether lip (a custom of his people) through which he could loll his tongue at pleasure. This unusual aperture was so large as to give him the appearance of having *two* mouths; thus, when he grinned, the white teeth appeared at the upper, and the red cruel tongue through the lower. He wore long splints of wood through the lobes of his ears; one eye had a fiery red circle painted round it, the other a yellow. He wore the skin of an ape in front like an apron; and this, with a pair of sandals, formed of elephant hide, completed his attire. His weapons were a long asseguy of tough teak wood, having a point of iron; and a short sword of iron, curiously fashioned, with a great leathern tassel at the end of the sheath, hung on his left side.

Behind him a savage held the bridle of his dromedary, which was covered by a multiplicity of barbaric trappings.

"It is the law of Empungua," said the King, " that he who slays a man shall have a public trial in face of the tribe; and if he cannot justify the act, he and all his adherents are doomed to die."

"Then," replied Baylis, "I demand justice on those who slew two of my men, and plundered our boat."

"But how know we not that one or both killed the fetisher, who was at worship in the Wood of the Devil?" demanded the King, with a dreadful expression in his yellow eyeballs.

"Ya—ya—ya—yah!" chorused the tribe.

"I swear to you that we know nothing of the

act you mention," replied Baylis, with great earnestness.

"The white men are liars!"

"If we had known, or been guilty of it, would we have ventured ashore to trade or barter with you like brothers?"

"Yes; because the white men are all liars!"

"It was done by the ship of another nation."

"All the white men belong to one tribe, and one big canoe is very like another. You are liars who come over the Sea of Darkness."*

Baylis, on finding that all his assertions of innocence met with utter disbelief, bent all his energy to bribe our release; but his sable Majesty only grinned through *both* his horrid mouths, and said—

"Enough! the King of the Snake River will keep what he has got, without trusting to getting more. The white men are false. Who of my people would venture to your ship when we know now what we never knew before?"

"And what is this?"

"Accursed dog and son of a race of dogs!" thundered the King, spitting a quid of something like beetel-nut full in the face of Baylis; " we have

---

* The Atlantic.

learned that you white men take our people away in shiploads to fatten them for food, in a land far beyond the sea!"

On this, a yell similar to that we had first heard made wood and welkin ring. Violent hands were again laid on us, and we expected instant immolation; but their purpose at present was merely to denude us more fully of anything we had about us.

On having his shirt torn from him, poor Hartly endeavoured to protect or conceal a little gold locket, which contained the hair of his dead wife and of their little ones, and which was hung at his neck by a black silk riband. But he received a blow from a carved war-club which covered his face with blood; he reeled backward, and the prized relic was instantly appropriated by the King, who, no doubt, deemed it the white man's fetish, a "great medicine," or amulet.

Mrs. Baylis became insensible, and was delivered over to a crowd of women, who shouted and laughed like devils as they bore her into a wigwam, while her husband, Hartly, six seamen, and I, were, by the King's order, conducted through the town of huts, and driven like a herd towards the summit of a high mountain, where we fully expected to be put to death in some barbarous fashion.

Mounted on his dromedary, the King accompanied his savages, one of whom, brilliantly smeared over with ochre, was an esquire of the royal body, I presume, as he sat behind, and held outspread a broad umbrella of grass matting.

CHAPTER XL.

THE GABON CLIFF.

A SAD series of barbarities, suffering, danger, and death make up the remainder of my story.

We were in the hands of a tribe addicted to fetishism of the lowest kind. Worse than the ferocious Bisagos, who pay divine homage to a dunghill cock, or the people of Benin, who worship their own shadows, they adored the devil and all snakes, from the little adder to the great cobracapello, and maintained temples and priests in their honour ; remaining, in this age of steam, gas, and electricity, as ignorant as the people mentioned by Ælian, who worshipped flies, and offered up full-fed oxen on their shrines!

Amid a yelling horde, who, by their menacing tones, seemed full of animosity, and no doubt were pouring upon us their whole vocabulary of abuse, though we understood it not, we were led up the

steep rough slope of a mountain, which rose at a
very sharp angle to a great height. The side on
which we ascended was covered with loose stones,
amid which the wild coffee and tobacco plants, with
innumerable thorny trees—the *persea* of Theo-
phrastus—grew in tangled masses, with serrated
grass, having blades as sharp as knives, with many
a nameless bramble that tore our tender skins, while
gnats came upon us in swarms, and well-nigh drove
us mad; and all this we endured, while the well-
armed crew of the *Princess*, in ignorance of our
fate, were within a few miles of us!

On reaching what we supposed to be the summit
of a mountain, we found ourselves upon a green
plateau that terminated abruptly in a precipitous
cliff nearly four hundred feet in height, and overhanging some rocky shelves, which sloped down to
the bed of the Gabon River.

Here the King dismounted from his dromedary,
and squatted his sable person on a piece of grass
matting under the royal umbrella, while several of
his chief men seated themselves at a respectful
distance, after knocking their woolly heads upon the
earth, in token of their slavish submission.

From the brow of this cliff we could see our ship
at anchor in the estuary, but alas! far beyond the

reach of signals. We could also see the little green Pongos, which stud the bay formed by the great sweep of the Gabon.

Afar off on the other hand towards the east, we could discern where, between groves of strange trees —the plantain, banana, and the baobab—with many a giant plant and mighty flower upon its shores, the great river of Guinea, the Rio Gabon, rolled from its distant source, in the unexplored land of Ungobai—a stream so broad and deep that a sloop of war has ascended it for more than seventy miles.

Transparent though the air was around us, a hot sunny haze shrouded those green forests through which the Gabon came rolling like a mighty flood of gold towards the west—rolling through a vast plain, covered by a leafy wilderness, where the lordly lion with his shaggy mane, the cruel panther with his stealthy step, and the ponderous elephant, roved in *herds;* and amid the luxuriant flowers and lovely fertility of which, the scaly cobra-capello, and a hundred kinds of dreadful reptiles, with tongues that teemed with poison, lurked; where every fruit and herb were gigantic in proportion to the mighty continent which produced them ; where the crocodile squattered in the green miasmatic slime, and the hippopotami, huge, mis shapen, and pre-Adamite in form, swam like the great tusky walrus of the icy regions I had left so recently.

All these natural wonders were contained in the vast plain at our feet — a plain that seemed to vibrate under the cloudless glare of the burning sun; for the heat at noon must have been somewhere about 107° in the shade, and our tender skins were blistering under it.

But the thoughts this scene inspired for a moment were soon diverted from it, by the terrors about to be enacted there.

A hideous old negro, whose barbaric ornaments announced his rank and character as a *fetisher*, proceeded to examine, with gipsy-like care, the various lines on the palms of our hands.

What he affected to gather therefrom we could not divine, but the lines proved fatal to three of our companions, whom, with yells of satisfaction, he thrust aside from the rest, and the work of torture and death at once began by order of the King.

Three strong and handsome young seamen had their hands tied behind them by a thick thong.

To this a rope was attached; after this they were thrust over the cliff, and a piercing cry, which curdled the blood in our hearts, burst from each, when, by the violence of the jerk and their own weight, their arms were torn round and upward, and dislocated in the shoulder socket.

In this horrible situation they swung at the extremity of the suspending lines, which were made fast to the roots of a palm-tree; and there with a pendulous motion, they swayed to and fro in mid-air, over the sharp edge of that impending cliff, with the rocky bank of the Gabon four hundred feet below.

Need I say their shrieks and cries for pity were piercing and unheeded?

Unable to yield them the slightest assistance, we gazed in speechless horror; while, as their strength waned, their sad moans arose from time to time to the plateau on which we stood.

The hungry cormorants, in anticipation of their coming repast, came out of their holes in the cliff, and with flapping wings, wheeled and swooped up and down about them.

To protract the mental and bodily agony endured by these poor fellows, they were permitted to hang thus for nearly half an hour, when the King gave a signal, and a score of tum-tums, or drums, were beaten. On this, the cords were parted by three blows of a sharp hatchet, then the bodies of our companions fell whizzing through the air, and vanished from sight far down below, where no doubt the river crocodiles, the greedy cormorants, and the wild ducks would soon rend their poor corses asunder.

So perished these unfortunates!

We looked into each other's haggard eyes with blank dismay; and it may readily be supposed that such an episode made us still more spiritless and timid.

"Oh, my wife! my poor wife!" exclaimed the unfortunate Baylis from time to time. "Death is but the birthday of *another* life, the parsons tell us; but I think with horror of her fate among such cowardly dogs as these. God help her! God help her!"

A series of prolonged and exulting yells now announced that our captors conceived they had appeased the spirit of the fetisher whom the Yankees had slain.

"Let them die! let them die!" (Baylis told me were their shouts;) "they are but white dogs who worship neither the sun nor moon, nor the big snake that lives in the wood."

There were now but six of us remaining, and our fate was soon decided. The King selected Hartly and Baylis as slaves for himself, assigning the four others to different chief men of his town or territory.

"My poor friend," said Hartly, "this is from bad

to worse! Why did we not perish with the *Leda?* We shall never weather these fellows, I fear!"

I fell to the lot of the savage with the coin at his neck, a personage whom they named Amoo—the same supple fellow who had first pounced upon me when we landed in that fiendish country.

As we were separated, Hartly and I had only time to exchange a farewell glance. My hands were still secured by the thong, which was tied so tightly that the flesh of my wrists was becoming blue, livid, and swollen almost to bursting, so my aching arms were powerless. By blows with the shaft of his asseguy, Amoo drove me down the hill, and conducted me to his wigwam, when the tribe separated, and save on *one* occasion I never again saw any of my poor companions in misfortune; though I afterwards learned the miserable fate of Captain Baylis and his wife.

CHAPTER XLI.

HOW THE CAPTAIN PERISHED.

I HAVE mentioned that the gentle Mrs. Baylis— she who had nursed us so kindly in our helplessness —had been carried off by the women of this tribe of devils, who confined her in a wigwam.

On perceiving the whiteness of her skin, and the great length and softness of her hair, which was of a fair auburn colour, forming thus a strange contrast to their sooty exteriors, and the short, poodledog-like tufts of wool with which their own round skulls were covered, they diligently proceeded to *make* her as like themselves as possible.

A species of gum and certain herbs were boiled in an earthen pipkin, and with this decoction they rubbed her whole face and body, until they became black as ebony.

They next rooted out the whole of her soft and beautiful hair, making her perfectly bald. Her head was then smeared thickly with gum, and coated over with green and crimson parrot's feathers. They then streaked her breast and shoulders with red and yellow paint. This process occupied two entire days, during which she remained a passive victim in their hands, and at the close—when these ladies of the Rio Serpientes thought they had made the unhappy woman as fiendish in aspect and as like themselves as possible—they placed a kind of hoe in her hands and dragged her into a plantation of millet to work with them; as the naked warriors and lazy husbands of Gabon, like those of other savage districts, disdainfully leave all manual labour to their slavish helpmates.

Despair and exhaustion rendered Mrs. Baylis unable to work; so the negresses beat, scratched, and bit her, till she sank under their hands at the root of a date-tree, where she lay inert and reckless alike of life and death; but the horrid hiss of a serpent close by, aroused her.

So great is the instinctive love of life, that on beholding this hideous reptile, which was of the venomous kind and some six or eight feet long, rearing its head to attack her, she uttered a shrill and piercing cry for aid.

Two white prisoners who had been hewing wood

in an adjacent thicket came forth on hearing this;
but the negresses, who laughed and danced on seeing
the poor woman assailed by one of their holy snakes,
met the two men with their hoes in a hostile
attitude, and barred their advance to a rescue:
while the white men, conceiving the shrieking victim
to be a mere savage—so darkly was the skin of
Mrs. Baylis dyed by the decoctions of her tormentors—were not over anxious to interfere.

In one of these white prisoners, worn to a skeleton,
haggard in eye, and covered with sores and bloody
bruises, she had nearly as much difficulty in recog-
nising her husband, the once plump and jolly captain
of the *Princess*, as *he* had, in tracing in the face of
that dusky and copper-coloured squaw, with her
gummed wig of red and green parrot's feathers, his
pretty English wife, with her once snowy skin and
silky auburn hair; but she cried aloud,

" Save me, Baylis—Oh, save me! I am your poor
wife, your own Annie!"

The unfortunate Baylis trembled with mingled
rage and horror, and snatching a hoe from a negress
rushed upon the poisonous serpent, which had
already bitten its victim thrice, and beat it furiously
upon its flat head and scaly body; but while doing
so, the frantic cries of the negresses, who deemed this

an act of sacrilege, brought to the spot Amoo, with a crowd of savages, one of whom pierced Baylis through the heart with his asseguy, and mercifully slew him on the instant.

The negresses then rushed upon his wife, and by repeated blows of their implements upon her head, face, and bosom, soon ended her miseries.

On beholding this scene of double barbarity, the seaman who had been at work with Baylis, and who, like him, was also a mass of sores and bruises by the ill-usage he had undergone, became filled by a species of frenzy. Wresting an asseguy from Amoo, he ran three of his followers through the body in quick succession, and killed, or mortally wounded them, as all these weapons are poisoned; but he was soon overpowered by numbers, beaten down, secured, and condemned to death by tortures, almost too horrible for narration.

His eyes, mouth, and nostrils were forced open and filled with hot pepper. He was then enclosed in a strong basket of cylindrical form, full of long sharp thorns, and this was rolled for hours about the town of wigwams, until he became a shapeless mass of flesh and blood, which dropped through the wattling of the cage; and during this dreadful torture, under which he must soon have perished, if he uttered cries they were unheard, as they were unheeded, for the whooping, yelling, and beating of tum-tums, might have made one suppose that Pandemonium had vomited all its denizens on the bank of the Gabon River.

While this was going on, I was at work among the plants which grew in a patch of ground adjoining the wigwam of Amoo; but I could in no way discover *who* this last victim was. However, as Baylis and Hartly had been condemned to slavery together, I was full of deep sorrow lest the sufferer might be my friend.

CHAPTER XLII.

AMOO.

AMOO, the savage who wore the amulet or coin at his neck, proved to be the King's brother; and when first dragged to his miserable dwelling he informed me, by signs—pointing to the earth which I was to till, and to the trees which I was to hew—that I was to be his obedient servant or slave, and by placing the poisoned point of his asseguy in dangerous proximity to my throat, he menacingly indicated that death would be the result of the least attempt at resistance or escape.

I understood his grim pantomime in all its terrible minutiæ; but in no way daunted thereby, resolved, whatever froward fate might have in store for me, to leave no means untried to fly his thraldom and reach the coast, in the hope of escaping to any vessel that might come in sight, or anchor off the Pongos on the same unfortunate errand as the *Princess.*

I could no longer hope that *she* was still there, as the chief mate, after the lapse of a week, would suppose we were all murdered, and so continue his voyage to the Cape of Good Hope.

Amoo, though savage and exacting in the tasks he set me, was nothing in severity when compared to his wife, for this Brave of the Rio Serpientes had "a helpmate meet for him," who hoed his rice and maize, shared his matted hut and couch of skins, and who scraped in thankful silence what he was pleased to leave her after meals at the bottom of his calibash; who shared with the house-dog his half-picked bones, and nursed a frightful little imp about a month old. They had three others, and Amoo doubtless fondly hoped (to quote Ossian) "they would carry his name and fame to future times."

By an anomaly in savage life, Amoo was very much attached to his four children, while their mother was tolerably indifferent about them, and often forced *me* to carry her black bantling, which I did, with an exhibition of all the solicitude I could assume, and with as little disgust as possible, conceiving that if her good will and confidence could be won, they might improve my chances of escape; but I strove in vain, and might as well have caudled the cub of a she-bear.

My mistress was a negress of Guinea, and of un-usually horrible aspect. Her lower lip was slit, and had a long wooden peg inserted in it so curiously, that the end thereof dangled upon her breast. Her great ears, set high upon her woolly head, had pon-derous rings of metal, which dragged them down-ward to her shoulders. Her teeth were dyed blood red by some native herb, known to the fetishers alone, and her whole body, where revealed by her only garment—an apron of grass matting—was covered with a species of tattooing, and always smeared with a thick unctuous grease, in which the embedded gnats and flies could revel undisturbed.

To eat repasts which were cooked by her odious hands excited a loathing which hunger alone could conquer; but anxiety for the future, and the intense heat of the atmosphere, made me generally averse to animal food; hence I found the yams, which there grow like turnips (and shoot out long leaves like French beans), my most pleasant food, as I could cook them for myself, either by boiling them in a pipkin, or roasting them among cinders. The inside is white as flour, and sweet and dry.

For many days I lived on these, with such fruit as I could find when at work near our wigwam, and Amoo gave me at times a little olive oil and palm wine, but in secret, for this warrior, though fearless in other respects, was civilized enough to be afraid of his wife.

My days were spent in hoeing yams, cutting fuel, carrying water in calibashes, selecting long and straight reeds for baskets, or boughs and bark to keep the wigwam water-tight. My mistress would have had me dive into the bay in search of sea-eggs, but to this I would by no means consent, and my refusal caused an open and standing feud between us.

At night, in a corner of their wretched dwelling, I coiled myself up on a panther skin, and for hours would lie awake in the dark, revolving plans of escape. To push a passage through the wattles, and make off under cloud of night, would have been an easy task, could I have silenced or circumvented the herd of ferocious dogs which guarded the town, or rather village, after sunset, and the yells of which, on the slightest movement, raised an alarm that would soon cause their being unleashed and let slip upon my track.

The negroes among whom I was cast worshipped the sun, the moon, and the devil; and in many instances, with singular barbarity, offered up their youngest children to the latter, that rain might fall in due season to make the yams big and the bananas grow.

Amoo strove in vain to lessen the severity of his wife, who frequently beat me with a hard club, till I grew weary of existence, and my heart swelled with savage thoughts of revenge.

Among the glass beads, feathers, rusty nails, and other trash which Amoo wore as a necklace, was his great amulet, a curious coin, which he one day permitted me to examine, but which he would have yielded up less readily than his life.

It proved to be a piece of the reign of Servius Tullius, sixth King of the Romans, and consequently must have been more than twenty-three centuries old. How came it there, and what was its history? So this prize, which half the savans of Europe would have rejoiced to possess, hung, and, for aught that I know, still hangs at the neck of an African savage, who found it on the sea-shore.

It was several ounces in weight, and bore on one side the head of Minerva, on the other an ox, as plain as if struck yesterday; and accoutred with this "great medicine," Amoo rushed fearlessly to encounter alike human enemies and the wild beasts of the forests which bordered the Gabon and the River of Snakes.

In the course of three weeks I picked up several words of the native language, which is full of rather musical sounds, as most of the words end in a vowel. The desire for escape added to the care with which I studied it.

One day when Amoo, with other savages, was hunting in the forest, and his better half was paddling about in her canoe on the river fishing, she suddenly uttered a shrill yell, which arrested me at my work among the yams, where I was hoeing under a broiling sun.

She was only about forty yards from me, and was pointing frantically to a huge baboon, which had squatted itself close by where her youngest child was asleep, under two large plantain leaves, the stems of which had been stuck in the turf as a species of sun-shade.

The baboon was of the ursine species, larger than a Newfoundland dog, and though common enough in South Africa, I now beheld it for the first time. It was a hideous brute, covered with shaggy brown hair, except on the hind feet and hands, for its forepaws are literally *hands*, and bare as a man's, being constantly employed in climbing rocks and trees, pulling fruit, or grubbing up roots and esculents for food. Its head resembled that of a dog, but its hind feet were rather human in form.

These baboons are so strong and bold, that they

will attack a leopard or hyæna, and by their teeth, which are an inch-and-a-half long, and their sharp fore-claws, can rend the throat and·jugular vein with ferocious dexterity.

The woman uttered yell after yell, and pointing to her nursling with one hand, paddled vigorously towards the shore with the other, while I gazed at her with irresolution; thus, before either of us could come to the rescue, the grisly she-baboon had snatched it up and bounded into the forest!

Though I had no great love for the tribe of the Rio Serpientes, the natural impulses of humanity, together with a dread of the vengeance that might fall upon me for neglect, caused me instantly to rush away in pursuit.

CHAPTER XLIII.

THE RESCUE OF HIS CHILD.

SOME time before this, I had fortunately made for myself a pair of long sandals, formed of panther's skin, which I wore as Bryan O'Lynn did his breeches—

" With the skinny side out and the hairy side in."

Indeed these, and a kind of shirt of grass-matting, were all the garments I possessed; for the savages, on our capture, tore all our clothes into strips, that each might have a portion; thus, every coin and button found upon us were appropriated; even our watches were broken up, and the wheels and springs of them were worn in their noses and ears as ornaments.

These sandals enabled me to run with ease and safety through patches of prickly yams, among serrated blades of grass, wild vines, dense creepers, and all kinds of thorny bushes.

Two warriors, on hearing the alarm, joined me in the pursuit. One soon passed me, but went upon a false trail; the other stumbled and hurt himself severely; so relinquishing my wooden hoe for his asseguy, I continued the pursuit alone.

Encumbered by her prey, the baboon could only run upon her hind legs, thus I easily kept her in sight after seeing her again. She was making straight towards those steep and lofty rocks which overhang the Gabon river—the same fatal rocks where three of our boat's crew had perished so miserably.

But her progress was soon impeded by a wall of gigantic reeds about ten feet high, through which a passage seemed impossible, as they grew close and dense amid a deep miasmatic quagmire, which covered all the plain at the base of the rocks, and amid which myriads of water-snakes lurked, and poisonous reptiles squattered. Here, too, there was no air—not a breath could be inhaled with freedom, for the density of the reeds obstructed every passing current; and, gasping and bathed in perspiration, as I drew near the savage animal she turned, and was about to make a hostile, and perhaps most fatal spring, in which case all had ended with *me* then; when suddenly perceiving a narrow opening in the reedy wall, she changed her intention, and entering, again vanished with the child.

Further pursuit seemed impossible!

I sank under a tree, and for some time fanned myself with a large leaf. While thus employed, I heard a strange railing cry at a distance, and on looking round perceived the baboon, about a hundred yards off, clambering up the face of the rocks, where it entered a hole, and disappeared.

Though I could scarcely hope that the child of Amoo would be alive or undevoured, I marked well the locality of the crevice its captor had entered, and making a detour, reached the end of the reedy marsh, and then proceeded boldly to ascend the rocks.

In some parts the climbing convolvoli and papyrus grew in such masses, and were so interlaced, as to form a rampart, against which I toiled in despair, and had my skin torn in innumerable places, ere I could burst through them. One feels so helpless without clothing.

At last I reached the vicinity of the hole, and after pausing for a time to recover breath, advanced with the asseguy charged breast high, lest the fierce brute might spring forth upon me; but on peering into the den, I saw its eyes glancing, and its grim satyr-like visage grinning at me, while uttering a hoarse cry.

The infant was alive, and its captor was kindly fondling it; having been probably deprived of her own offspring by some hunter's shaft, the act of abduction had been prompted by a strange and erratic maternal emotion in herself.

Amoo explained this to me afterwards as being no uncommon occurrence. I had no thought of it then, but rushed upon her with the long and sharp asseguy, and thrust it deeply into her breast. Coiled up in her little den, and thus rendered incapable of active resistance, she could only howl, bite, and writhe upon the tough teakwood shaft; while her life-blood smeared all the little black infant, and ebbed away among the well-picked bones of the small monkeys and wild ducks, which strewed the hole that formed her lair.

The poor baboon expired just as I drew forth the asseguy for a finishing thrust; and at that moment Amoo, with a crowd of other savages, came rushing up the rocks, and joined me, with excitement expressed in all their wide mouths and glittering eyeballs.

Breathless and drenched in perspiration, overcome by exertion, and somewhat sickened by the cries and death agonies of the half human-like creature I had slain, I sank upon a bank of turf, incapable of further exertion.

Amoo, after holding up his offspring by each leg alternately, and viewing it over as one might do a dead duck or rabbit, to ascertain if any of its bones were broken, found that it had suffered only a few scratches, on which he uttered sundry shrill howls expressive of paternal satisfaction, and patted me kindly on the head and breast, in token that henceforth we were friends, and in amity.

"You are brave—you are brave! Yah—yah!" said he repeatedly. "You are the brother of Amoo."

Thus did I achieve the very end I had in view—to win the confidence of my savage task-masters!

We returned to the wigwams in triumph, bringing with us the skin of the ursine baboon on the point of an asseguy; and the circumstance of a creature so agile and ferocious having been slain by me, the poor despised white slave, was evidently the cause of much marvel to that dingy community.

From this day there was a sensible alteration in the bearing of my mistress towards me. I cannot say that I gained more of her confidence, or had fewer tasks set me, but when beating me with her club, she entirely ceased to strike me on *the head* or face, as she had been wont to do. But the reason of this unusual forbearance was explained to me by Amoo, and proved a very cogent reason for hastening my departure from the unpleasant vicinity of the Snake River.

CHAPTER XLIV.

THE GRATITUDE OF HIS WIFE.

In two instances she patted my head and smiled on me, till the corners of her mouth went up to her ears

On the last occasion she gave me a large iron knife to sharpen, indicating by various signs that a very fine edge must be put upon it.

"She is grateful to you for saving her child," said Amoo, who observed her.

"I am glad of it," said I, with a sigh of mingled bitterness and impatience.

"She means to show you and the tribe that she is so."

"The tribe too, how?"

"Yah, yah," said Amoo, as he placed one hand on my head, and drew the right forefinger of the other across his throat, in a way that was unpleasantly suggestive. Then he laughed and pointed to a gaily painted canoe that lay among some reeds by the river-side.

"She will assist me to escape in it to a big ship at the Pongos?" said I with a glow of hope.

Amoo frowned, then he grinned and shook his head.

"What then?" I asked anxiously.

After a good deal of pantomime, with which he endeavoured to aid his explanations, at last the horrid truth broke upon me!

She wished my caput as a figure-head to her canoe, for which purpose, after being duly prepared by gums, balms, and herbs, she could make it suitable. Amoo flatteringly added that such had been her desire from the first, as "I was the youngest and best-looking of the prisoners."

Here was a pleasant prospect!

"And it was for this purpose she gave me the long knife to sharpen so carefully?"

"Yah, yah," replied Amoo, while a glow of rage filled my breast; "and even now she is gathering herbs on the borders of the wood to boil in the stone jar with it."

"It—what?"

"Your head."

"I must watch."

"It is of no use to watch," replied Amoo; "some-time, when you are not thinking of it, she will give you some red berries, that will cause .you to sleep *very sound;* and then with her knife or a sharp shell —yah, yah!" he concluded by a guttural laugh, and again pressed his finger round his neck.

"Oh, Heavens!" I exclaimed, "aid me to escape from this atrocious squaw!"

I asked Amoo if he, in gratitude to me for saving his child, would aid me to escape; but he shook his head, adding:

"I am the brother of a great king, and must keep my slave."

"Why?"

"To punish the white men, who fatten up our brothers beyond the Sea of Darkness, and eat them."

After reiterated applications to his gratitude and pity for freedom or assistance, finding that he was gradually losing his temper and becoming sus-picious; that his snake-like eyes were beginning to gleam and his thick red nostrils to quiver, I aban-doned the subject, and resuming my hoe, went to my daily task in the patch of garden where our yams and other esculents grew, and affected to work as usual, conscious that, for a time, my savage owner was eyeing me with vague doubts, and while playing ominously with his long reed-like asseguy, was probably repenting that by his admissions he had put me on my guard against the artistic views of his better half.

After a time he disappeared, yet I dreaded that it was only to conceal himself under some of the bushes, or the leaves of the creeping gourds, to watch me, so I affected to hoe industriously—yes, and to whistle too, though my heart was sick and full of dreadful apprehensions.   One thing I had resolved, come what might, never again to commit my head to sleep, or to pass a night within the same wigwam with that horrible woman.

While revolving in my mind, and almost blind with desperation, what measures I should take to save myself, to escape from my present danger and misery, I saw her pass from the wood towards the town of wigwams.   In one hand she held the knife I had sharpened so nicely for her, in the other a basket filled with herbs—herbs, I doubted not, for my especial behoof; and she " grinned horribly a ghastly smile," as she walked on with that shuffling gait peculiar to these negresses.

My heart swelled with so much rage and hatred at this hideous creature, that I had some difficulty in repressing a vehement desire to beat her down with my hoe; but such a proceeding would only have ensured and accelerated my own destruction; as I knew not what number of watchful savages might at that moment be eyeing me from amid the jungle of leaves, flowers, and fruit which bordered the patch wherein I worked, under a sun so vertical that I had scarcely a shadow.

Lest such a surveillance might be maintained, I resolved as soon as she disappeared to adopt something of their own subtlety.

I seated myself under a tree among some weeds, as if tired, and then, after a time, affected to sleep; though keeping watch with open ears and half-closed eyes, lest any one might approach; but all remained still around me, save the monotonous hum of the millions of insects that revolved in the shade of the adjacent wood.

On being assured of this, I crept on my hands and knees into the jungle, dragging my hoe after me, and going feet foremost on my face for nearly a hundred yards or so, that I might with my fingers obliterate all traces of a *trail;* and in this, I was very successful by raising the crushed grass and shaking the bruised twigs.

At last I reached a runnel, the waters of which I

knew would destroy all scent of my footsteps, and baffle the keen nostrils of those ferocious dogs, which would certainly be let slip in search of me the moment I was missed.

Assured that this runnel of water would be a tributary of the Rio Serpientes, I proceeded *up* its course for several miles, and in my anxiety to escape the human race forgetting all about the ferocious denizens of the African forest—the snakes and other dreadful reptiles with which the woods, the water, and the bordering deserts teemed.

I must have proceeded about ten miles without meeting either man or beast to molest or obstruct me, when evening was beginning to close, and I found myself nearly exhausted, but within a pleasant thicket of orange, citron, and chestnut trees, which bordered a pretty lake, and flourished amid the thousand flowering shrubs of this luxuriant wilderness.

The necessity for rest forced itself upon me; but I dared not sleep on the earth lest snakes might assail me, and even in a tree I was not safe from the panthers, yet I chose my couch in the latter. Furnished with a large stone, as a missile for defence in any emergency, grasping the hoe by my teeth, I clambered into a chestnut-tree, scaring therefrom a whole covey of kingfishers, copper-coloured cuckoos, and green and flame-coloured parrots.

Then selecting a place where the leafy branches were forked out from the stem, and grew in such a form that I could rest upon them with ease, and without fear of falling, I deposited the stone in a hollow of the tree, and after an hour of anxious and exciting watchfulness, gradually felt sleep stealing over me—a sleep to which the "drowsy hum" of the insects, the balmy air of the evening, the lassitude produced by my recent travel after a day's toil under a burning sun, all conduced; and so, heedless of everything, at last I slept profoundly on my awkward perch.

CHAPTER XLV

FLIGHT.

In this precarious situation I must have been asleep for some hours, when awakened by a dreadful sound, and with a start so nervous that I nearly fell from my roost upon the long, reedy grass below.

This sound was the roaring of a lion!

I had heard it often in menageries at home; but there the sound was feeble as the bay of a house-dog when compared to the dread roar, which rolled along the ground and rent the still air of the morning in that lone African forest. A terror possessed me; yet, grasping my hoe, while quivering in every fibre, I gazed with keen anxiety between the leaves of the chestnut-tree for the approaching enemy.

Ignorant alike of his powers of leaping and scenting, I knew not whether the lion might, on discovering me, at once spring up like a tree-leopard, which can pursue its prey, like a cat, from branch to branch.

Oh, how I longed for a good rifle—a sharp sword—a dagger—for any other weapon than the miserable wooden club (for the hoe was no better) with which I was armed at that moment.

The lilac light of dawning morn poured through the thick green vista of the wild forest, and the little lake which lay near my chestnut-tree shone white as a sheet of milk, bordered by countless gaudy tulips and opening flowers.

The sun was yet below the horizon, but every dew-drenched herb, and leaf, and tree, were distinctly visible in the clear pale light that overspread the sky.

Every pulse quickened, and all my energies became wound up to the utmost pitch by excitement, when I saw the mighty lord of the wilderness—a vast dun-coloured lion, with his large round head and shaggy mane, powerful legs, his close round body and tufted tail, that shook wrathfully aloft as he trotted past swiftly, bearing a dead sheep in his mouth.

Passing almost under the tree, and round the margin of the lake, he disappeared in the forest; but a *sense* of his terrible presence seemed to linger about me still. My doubts and irresolution wer·· increased; the dangers of the wilderness in which ï wandered, alone and unarmed, became more vividly impressed upon me, and for a time I almost regretted that I had left the coast, and the protection of my savage task-masters. But then the wife of Amoo, and her hideous desire for possessing my head!   .

"Hope is the bounty of God!" thought I, and as the forest remained still and quiet—at least, as no sound reached my ear, save the increasing hum of the myriads of insects warming into life and sport in the light and heat of the rising sun—I resolved to descend from my perch, and follow the track of any stream which might lead to the coast, for by the sea—the open, free, wide sea—lay my only hope of escape from this dangerous and detested shore.

Remembering the geographical form of Africa, as represented on the map, I knew that if I could, by any means, proceed westward for about two hundred and fifty miles or so round the Bight of Benin, I should be so near our settlement at Cape Coast Castle as to be in safety. But *how*, in such a country, was this to be accomplished?

I had already begun my descent from the tree, when the noise of something coming rapidly through the forest made me scramble into my perch again. And lo! a savage, armed as usual with a long asseguy, but mounted on a swift dromedary, came from amid

the trees, and paused by the lonely lake to give his
great misshapen nag a drink ; and while he did so,
in his brawny form and tasselled apeskin apron and
sandals, his eyes with their circles of red and yellow
paint, the slit under his mouth, his hideous aspect
and barbaric trappings, I recognised the brother of
Amoo—the King of the Rio Serpientes !

Were both upon my track, or had chance alone
brought him here ?   I knew that if retaken, I had
met with more mercy from the lion than from either ;
and the image of the wife of Amoo, with her sharp
knife and basket of herbs and gums, seemed to rise
before me.

The savage looked around him, and suddenly
turning his dromedary, rode straight towards my
place of concealment.   I grasped my hoe, resolved,
if he *had* seen me, not to yield up my wretched
existence without a desperate struggle ; but all un-
conscious of my presence, his sable majesty dismounted, placed his asseguy against the chestnut
tree, spread a grass-mat at its root, and seating himself, proceeded quietly to light a species of hubble-
bubble, or pipe made from a reed and a nut-shell.
Stuffing therein some dried herbs, he applied flint
and steel, and began leisurely and literally to enjoy
his morning *weed*.

At his neck I could see poor Robert Hartly's gold locket glittering.

The vicinity of this ferocious and tremendous personage, with the chances of his horde being all within hail, like the band of Roderick Dhu, so greatly alarmed me, that fully a quarter of an hour elapsed before I rallied sufficiently to conceive the idea of appropriating his quiet and docile dromedary (which was cropping the herbage close by), and using it as a means of reaching Cape Coast Castle, the western goal of all my hopes.

I knew that this animal was deemed a miracle of swiftness even in that burning clime, where they will travel with ease fifty miles per day.

The savage King seemed to be asleep, or in a waking doze; but I knew that by habits of danger, activity, and a life spent in the open air, the senses of these people were so acute, that the slightest sound would revive him; and that, if once discovered, he could crush me like a shrimp in his powerful grasp.

"Can I not kill him?" thought I, as furious thoughts began to fill my mind; "my hoe is too light—ha! the stone!"

I snatched the stone, which with difficulty I had conveyed up the tree overnight, as a missile against wild animals, and poised it in my hands. It was nearly twelve pounds weight, and the woolly skull of the King was immediately below me; but it might be thick as that of an elephant, so the missile would prove more harmless than a ball of worsted.

If I missed, death to me was certain; if I slew or stunned him, I had an equal certainty of escape. Then I thought of poor Captain Baylis, of his tortured wife, of Hartly, and of that horrible butchery by the steep rocks of the river Gabon, and a glow of merciless fury filled my soul!

The stone shot from my hand, and, bathed in blood, quivering and senseless, the brutal King of the Snake River rolled among the long dry grass, with foam issuing from his mouth, and the aperture below it.

Swift as lightning I descended the tree—all cramped and stiff by a night passed amid its branches; caught his dromedary by the bridle, sprang upon its back, snatched up the asseguy as a weapon for defence, and, without casting a glance to ascertain whether I had been guilty of actual regicide, or had merely given him a crack upon his imperial crown, urged the animal I bestrode westward at furious speed, through a grove of pale green orange trees, where the rich dewy fruit hung like balls of gleaming gold in the light of the morning sun.

CHAPTER XLVI.

FLIGHT CONTINUED.

STEERING my course westward, so closely as I could judge, I rode rapidly through wild and pathless places; and when mounted on an animal so sure and swift of foot, I felt more confident of escape from any savages in whose way I might fall.

I was not without a dread of wild animals, for the furious lion and the stealthy panther roam everywhere through the forests of Africa; and though nearly the whole day passed without meeting one of either species, hundreds of pernicious serpents, black, or brown, or green and scaly, with glaring eyes, hissed at me from amid the long rank grass; while brightly pinioned birds flew about me, and horrid baboons and monkeys, of all kinds and sizes, leaped and frisked on every hand, springing from branch to branch of the trees, where they swung madly to and fro by their tails as I passed.

At a distance rose the smoke of fires, with the dome-shaped wigwams of three negro villages; but these I avoided by keeping far off, and without tarrying a moment for food or refreshment, pushed on westward, through a broad plain where the maize, cassava, and pulse were cultivated in little patches. On, on where the banana, the papaw, the lemon, orange, and tamarind trees grew wild in thickets; where the spotted giraffe, the striped zebra, and the graceful little antelope, made their lair, and trembled when they heard the roar of the lion of Libya.

On, on I rode to reach the castle of Cape Coast, and urged the dromedary to his utmost speed.

Leaving the plain, at the end of which the sun was setting now, I continued my way still westward across a long tract of desert sand; and now for the first time I paused to look around me.

On the borders of this desert grew some wild lotus trees. Dismounting, I took some of their farinaceous berries with joy to assuage my hunger, and found their flavour to resemble sweet ginger-bread.

After a draught of water from a runnel—water that was actually tepid—I remounted with difficulty, as my strength was nearly gone now; having ridden the livelong day under a burning sun, which left the sand so hot that it scorched my feet, while the finely pulverized grains of it were floating in a cloud about me, and filling my mouth and eyes as it whirled in eddies when the faint evening wind passed over the arid waste, rippling up its surface as if it was water.

At a distance appeared some bustards and long-legged cranes; but no other living thing, as the setting sun, vast, round, and blood-red, after shedding a steady crimson glare across the desert waste, sank beneath the horizon.

At the quarter of his declension, I perceived a grove of trees, and fearing to remain all night on the open waste, rode swiftly towards them; but they were farther off than I imagined, and seemed to recede as I progressed, so deceptive is the distance of a level sandy desert; thus night was far advanced when I reached the shelter of their foliage, and overcome by a lassitude—a total prostration—there was no resisting, I had just strength sufficient to throw the bridle of the dromedary over the branch of a tree, and to roll off his back upon a bank of soft turf, when a heavy sleep fell on me.

Waking next morning, stiff, cramped, and drenched with dew, I looked round for my four-footed friend, but he had disappeared, and not a trace of him remained.

Thus, after all the toil and travelling of the past day, my prospects were little better than before.

But the forest scene was lovely! It was full of scarlet and golden blossoms, all bright as the glossy plumage of the parrots that nestled amid the foliage; while the perfume of the orange and lemon trees, which the dew of the past night had refreshed, filled the morning air with delicious fragrance; and now the mighty hum of a myriad great insects loaded it with monotonous and perpetual sound.

On the outskirts of the wood, between me and the far-stretching vista of the white sandy desert, my eye suddenly detected the tall dark figure of a savage, stalking about with a long asseguy in his right hand. He was naked, all save a scanty scarlet grass-cloth around his body.

Coiled up in my lurking-place, I watched with considerable interest the motions of this man of the wilderness. Supple, brawny, and strong, he had the form of a bronze Hercules, the agility of an antelope, and the eye of an eagle. He had detected the footmarks of the dromedary, and gliding about, with a light stealthy step, and a keen prowling eye, he tracked them with his face near the ground, until he came close to where I lay, but never, the while, did he venture *within* the actual boundary of the wood.

Suddenly his eye fell upon me!

He started; uttered a shrill cry, and poised his long asseguy, as if about to launch it; then he lowered it, and uttered a whoop, which brought some twenty or thirty other savages around him.

They all pointed to me in a manner and with expressions that seemed to indicate surprise or rage; they gesticulated violently, and by what they said, I could learn that by being *within* the forest, I was guilty of an act of sacrilege. Their language seemed a dialect of that spoken by the tribe I had fled from, on the north bank of the Gabon.

CHAPTER XLVII.

THE WOOD OF THE DEVIL.

MAKING signs that I was a friend, or wished to be considered one, by casting away my asseguy, and placing my hands upon my head and breast, I advanced with a resolute aspect, but with a quaking heart, towards them.

By what I heard then, and learned afterwards, I had violated the sanctity of a holy place—the abode of a fetish—as this wood had for ages been dedicated to the Devil, whom these savages, like those of Benin, worship as a dreadful spirit, not to love, but to conciliate.

No one entered this wood, which was composed of giant chestnuts, palm, orange, and lime trees, all growing wild for many leagues, as the spirit of evil was alleged to harbour in its inmost recesses.

Here then, on its skirts, a mother and her infant were sometimes sacrificed with tortures too terrible for description, to propitiate this dark spirit ; though in some rare instances a husband might ransom his doomed wife with a poor female slave, captured from a hostile tribe.

So sacred is this wood deemed, that if a person accidentally enters it by one path, he must force his way through it to the very end without turning or looking back—a feat none ever performed, as it teems with wild beasts, whose fangs and claws speedily dispose of the intruder. Even a foreign *negro*, or his wives, dare not enter it; then, what punishment was due to me, a white man, for having ventured to do so ?

Dapper, a very old traveller, and a bold fellow, too, mentions that, to ridicule the faith of the people in this forest, he went shooting into it, and deliberately turned *back* when about half way through.

"What will the Devil think of this ?" he asked the negro priests, who were scared by his audacity, and confounded by his return in safety.

"He does not trouble himself about white men," was their response ; and, singular to say, our traveller was permitted to go unscathed, for savages generally admire courage and temerity.

However, the negroes into whose hands I had

unfortunately fallen seemed of a different opinion from Mr. Dapper's friends; and after a noisy *palaver*, to which I listened with an agonizing interest, my life being in the balance, they laid violent hands upon me.

I was dragged to a tall palm-tree, which grew on the verge of the forest, with some of its fibrous roots extending among the grassy border on one side, and into the dry sand of the desert on the other.

I was placed with my back against the stem; and there they bound me hard and fast by drawing my arms round it and tying my wrists securely by the tendrils of a convolvolus—one of the climbing kind, which, when tough and green, is strong as a new inch-rope.

They then retired, mocking and grinning, and ever and anon threatening to launch their asseguys at me; thus I fully expected to be martyred like St. Sebastian, as we see him in Guido's picture at Dulwich; but they left me, and disappeared round an angle of the forest, abandoning me to my fate and my own terrible reflections.

It was midday now, and above me shone the blaze of an almost vertical sun; thus I found the shade of the drooping palm branches grateful and pleasant—a boon, a blessing.

Lest the savages might be watching me from a distance, I did not attempt to release my hands; but after nearly an hour elapsed, fearing that strength might fail me from the cramped manner in which my arms were bound backward round the tree, I strove to rend the green withes which fettered me to it.

Vain task!

Strain them as I might, the tough and unyielding tendrils of the convolvoli only seemed to tighten, and to cut me as I tore, wrenched, and struggled without success.

The horror of being left thus defenceless at the mercy of the wild animals with which the forest teemed was so great, that I forgot alike the pangs of hunger and those of thirst, which are greater still ; and again and again strove frantically for freedom, until, with the futility of each successive effort, the conviction forced itself upon me, that without human assistance I could never be released, but might perish of starvation, or be devoured alive.

Human assistance! who, then, would be disposed to aid me? And, if so, who would come in time?

And so the hot day passed breathlessly, slowly, and terribly on!

As the burning sun revolved towards the West, the lengthening shadows of the wood went round in the reverse direction, until the level sunbeams cast them far across the arid desert I had traversed so swiftly yesterday; and as the light of evening sank, the hues of that white glistening waste changed to yellow, then to brown, and then to amber.

My arms ached till they seemed in process of being rent from my shoulders: so, panting, hot, breathless, and half dead with thirst, I reclined against that abhorred tree, from which I could in no way free myself.

As evening deepened, the hum of insect life lessened, and the bright-plumed birds of the wilderness were seeking their nests in the foliage above me; but on me their beauty was lost. Even the cock of the Libyan forest, with his purple breast, his crimson and green pinions, was unheeded, as he picked up a few grains of millet at my feet, and passed to his mate in the orange tree.

A raven or two, soaring through the blue immensity of the sky, suggested dreadful thoughts of what I *might be* on the morrow.

Then little snakes came from amid the long grass to writhe and wriggle on the sand, which was yet warm with the sunshine of the past day; and they made me think of the dreadful cobra-capello, with his flamelike tongue, charged with poison and death —the hooded serpent, which, when in fury, has been known to rear its horrid front, and spring at a man on horseback; and then of the berg-adder, which I feared still more, because it is so difficult to discover, and which I had no means of avoiding if it approached me.

My past reading had given me, moreover, a somewhat exaggerated idea of the number of wild animals in Africa. At Ascension, I had seen a narrative of a *Voyage à l'Isle de France*, by a person who styled himself an *Officier du Roi*, and who stated that, in the forests of Africa, "there were to be found whole *armies* of lions."

Later travellers have ridiculed this idea, but be that as it may, the distant roaring of a lion now added to the accumulating dangers which surrounded me, and filled my soul with emotions of horror so great that I could not summon even a thought of prayer, and memory refused to supply me with the most hackneyed ejaculation of piety.

Bound and helpless, without means of defence or flight, I now heard this terrible animal approaching me, crushing the shrubs and branches in his native forest as he came.

On hearing this sound, so fraught with danger, a zebra and several antelopes bounded out of the wood and paused to listen. Again that prolonged cry rang upon the still air. The zebra cowered and shuddered, and after crouching for a moment, sprang away into the desert of sand, followed by the fleet little antelopes (which were of the kind called Guinea Deer, having legs no thicker than a tobacco-pipe), and they were all soon out of sight.

The roar was singular in sound. Hoarse and inarticulate, it swelled upon the air like a prolonged O, that seemed to come from and pass to a vast distance. It never became loud or shrill, but the *idea* it suggested of the animal itself, made it seem to pierce the very soul ; and all the tales I had read or heard of the lion, and all the terrors I had conjured up as being embodied in his tremendous person, came upon me like a flood.

There are some who aver that if he has once tasted human flesh he will for ever disdain any other.

With great bewilderment of mind—like one in a dream that is full of nightmare—I beheld a great and dark-skinned lion, with an enormous dusky mane, run out of the wood about a hundred yards off, and, after looking about, he came straight towards me, for by some strange instinct he became sensible of my vicinity in a moment. In his mouth he bore a zebra (about the size of a Shetland pony), which he grasped by its crushed back, and the legs of which were trailing on the ground as he bore it along, with all the air and all the ease of a cat carrying off a large rat.

On beholding me he dropped his prey, which was quite dead, and after uttering another hoarse roar, continued to approach, with his nose close to the ground, while switching his tufted tail and shaking his shaggy mane, preparatory, as I imagined, to making a spring upon me; then I closed my eyes, and with a heart that died within me, resigned myself to my fate.

Onward he came, step by step, for I could hear his footfalls on the ground!

Onward yet, and now every pulse seemed to stand still!

Then a warm and fetid breath played upon my face, I felt his whiskers touch my breast, and there was a strange snuffing sound in my tingling ears.

Opening my eyes, I beheld close to mine the tremendous visage of the lion, the enormous upper lip, in form so suggestive of cruelty and rapacity, and all studded with wiry hairs, bristling out fiercely on either side; the low flat forehead and impending brows; the wild orbs that seemed to glare from amid the masses of his tangled mane; the open jaws and sharp teeth, reeking and steaming with the warm blood of the zebra he had just slain!

After deliberately snuffing at me in this manner for a second or so—a time which seemed an eternity, so much agony of thought and tension of the heart were compressed within it, he quietly *turned about*, took his dead zebra, as if he deemed it the most preferable supper of the two, trotted into the wood and disappeared.

The agonies of a lifetime seemed concentrated into that minute!

All I had endured now proved too much for me. A sudden insensibility sank like a cloud over all my senses, and a sleep—the sleep of utter prostration of mind and body, fell upon me. Thus, the noon of the next day was far advanced before I became again conscious, or aware of my miserable existence.

CHAPTER XLVIII.

RETAKEN.

RELEASED from the tree, but still benumbed and sore after being so long bound to it, I was now stretched upon the grass, under the shadow of its great fan-like branches. Many persons were moving about me, and the hum of their voices filled my ear.

Raising myself slowly and heavily upon my hands, I saw around me hundreds of negroes, and close to mine was the ugly visage of— Amoo.

"Oh," thought I, bitterly; "this is too much! A prisoner again, and after all the dangers I have dared—the friends I have seen perish—the miseries I have undergone! Will fate never weary of persecuting me?"

But Amoo was not such a wicked fellow after all.

Producing his gourd bottle of palm wine, he mixed it with cool water from a shaded spring, and forced me to imbibe a long draught, after which I sat up and looked about me more collectedly.

I was in the midst of a species of negro bivouac, consisting of many hundreds of men and women, with camels and dromedaries laden with various stuffs and rudely fashioned weapons and utensils, made up in bales with grass matting and cordage.

They were cooking at several fires, and in various modes, the flesh of an elephant which they had snared, as Amoo informed me, in a pit on the other side of the forest on the preceding day, and the meat of which is esteemed in these latitudes as a veritable dainty—a right royal luxury. He pressed me to eat a slice or so, but in my weak state, and the fever of my spirit, the odour and the aspect of it were more than enough for me, so a mouthful or two of boiled yam and palm wine sufficed.

The negroes were all well armed with asseguys, swords, bows, muskets, and targets, as if proceeding on a hostile expedition. Among them were many who were better clad and more civilized in aspect than the painted savages who dwell by the Snake

River, and these, Amoo informed me, were subjects
of the King of Benin.

After relating how his companions had found me
bound to the tree, senseless or asleep, he inquired
how it came to pass I was there.

"I fled to escape your wife," said I, looking
round fearfully.

"Yah, yah," said he, laughing; "I was sorry
for the loss of my white slave, but am glad you
escaped her knife; for she wished much to ornament
her big canoe, so she got the head of another white
man."

"Another—who—which?"

"Amoo does not know; he tried to steal a canoe
and escape to the Pongo Islands, but was retaken,
and so my wife got his head for her canoe. She
boiled it in a stone pipkin, with gums and herbs,
stuck fish-bones in its nose and ears, and now it
will last for many, many suns and moons, without
decay."

(Who was this *other* unfortunate that had
perished so miserably? He might be my friend
Hartly—if indeed it was not he who was so cruelly
destroyed in the basket of thorns.)

"Never mind who it was," said Amoo, divining
my thoughts, "since you are found again."

"To be your prisoner?" I sighed.

Amoo grinned, leered cunningly, and shook his woolly head.

"What then?"

"To be reserved for something better than being my slave."

"*Better!*" I reiterated, with perplexity; "how —where?"

"Yah, yah—you will learn in good time."

"When?" I exclaimed, with impatience.

"On our reaching the capital of Benin."

"You are going there with all these people?"

"Yah."

"For what purpose—to fight?"

"No."

"What then?"

"To bury Zabadie, the king, who is dead."

I was somewhat comforted by this, as everything added to the chances of escape; for I knew that European vessels frequently anchored in the Bight of Benin, and I associated ideas of greater civiliza-tion with that quarter of Africa, though it bordered on Dahomey—that barbarous land of blood and terror.

It was evident that Amoo knew nothing about my encounter in the wood with the King, his brother, or the manner in which I had borrowed the royal dromedary; for he informed me, in the course of our obscure and somewhat pantomimic conversation, that on his return he would probably find himself King of the Snake River, as his brother was not expected to live.

I inquired why.

"As he was asleep under a tree, a great baboon let a big stone fall upon his head, and nearly killed him," replied Amoo, with perfect unconcern, and I cannot plead guilty to feeling the smallest compunction in the matter.

This species of caravan was proceeding from the territory of Gabon, whose king is a vassal of the monarch of Benin, with a tribute of female slaves, baskets, gourd vessels, panther skins, elephants' teeth, and gold dust, to assist at the funeral of the late royal defunct, or to lay at the feet of his successor; and I was pleased to find that we were to proceed as nearly as possible along the coast.

I resolved to take the first opportunity of securing arms—a musket and knife if possible—of leaving the cavalcade, and concealing myself in a wood near the sea-shore, there to await a ship; but the hope was formed in vain, for Amoo, who frequently spoke of the "great future in store for me at Benin," never lost sight of me for an instant, either by night or by day, when we halted.

When we did so, we warily lighted a circle of large fires to scare wild animals from our bivouac, and thus could sleep in security.

CHAPTER XLIX.

THE CARAVAN.

THE whole of the coast there is broken by innumerable river estuaries, the banks of which are covered by bright green reeds, and broad-leaved weeds and canes of mighty growth. Thus our progress was slow, as we had frequently to embark in canoes on those frowsy waters, whose miasma is so pestilential by night, and which are ever rendered dangerous by the alligators and hippopotami that lurk in the oozy holes along their banks.

At a place where we were about to cross, the black scouts, who formed a species of advanced guard, returned in haste and excitement to state that one of the last-named animals (one of great size, too) was asleep on the bank.

On hearing this the caravan halted, and Amoo, being a brave and hardy warrior, and moreover the brother of a king, claimed the privilege of assailing it. Armed with a spear made specially for the purpose, he advanced to the enterprise, accompanied only by one companion and by me, to whom he relinquished for a time his gaily painted bow and quiver of poisoned arrows.

I had heard so much of those fierce and unwieldy monsters, that I followed him with considerable interest and curiosity as we shouldered and pushed a passage through a dense and leafy jungle of gigantic weeds, prickly yams, serrated grass, and reeds of enormous height, which flourished amid the deep quagmire that bordered the broad bosom of this majestic but nameless river, whose waters are now rolling, as they have rolled for ages, into the Gulf of Guinea.

On forcing our way through a wall of reeds, we suddenly came upon the hippopotamus, which was lying on his left side, asleep in the sunshine, and stretched at full length upon a piece of greensward, where, probably, he had been grazing overnight.

The aspect of this mis-shapen monster, which was about fourteen feet long—his singular form, a great round body with short elephantine legs, a broad, square head and stunted tail—was as repulsive as the size of his great cavernous mouth with its terrible incisors was appalling.

He slept soundly, however, so Amoo, gliding stealthily as a serpent, approached until within seven feet of where he lay, snoring heavily, and basking in the hot and breathless sunshine.

With a dexterity which my poor old friend Hans Peterkin would have appreciated highly, Amoo, with a line, attached to his spear a light wooden float, which serves to show where the animal lurks when he takes the water after being struck; then, while the attending warrior stood near to hand a second lance, Amoo raised his sinewy form on tiptoe, poised his barbed weapon, and hurled it, whizzing, with singular force and dexterity, full at the sleeping animal.

Deep through the thick, dark hide sunk the pointed spear, until its iron head was completely buried. At the moment it left his hand, Amoo, an agile and practised huntsman, sprang backward several paces; but not so his unfortunate companion, on whom the awakened monster leaped with the weight of an elephant united to the fury of a panther, and in an instant crushed him to death in his enormous jaws, doubling up the body and grinding ribs and legs together till they were churned into a mass of blood.

Then plunging into the river, he disappeared,

leaving the water covered with froth and bloody ripples, that ran in circles to either shore ; but still the little buoy attached to the spear or harpoon floated and bobbed up and down to indicate where he lay writhing among the weeds and beds of bright blue coral far down below—for the coral *is* blue there.

Amoo's shrill cries brought several negroes to his assistance ; and these, enraged by the sudden death of their friend, began to haul sturdily on the line, which was a good English rope, obtained from some passing ship by theft or barter ; this irritated the wounded animal, so he came surging, bleeding, and frothing to the surface again, when a dozen spears, whizzing through the air, were launched by unerring hands, and he was soon slain, and amid exulting yells, whooping, and beating of tum-tums, was hauled close in shore among the reeds, and there, as he was too bulky to be pulled entirely out of the water, was cut up in large pieces and placed in baskets on the backs of the camels, dromedaries, and slaves.

Amoo declared this prey was too full-grown, and consequently too fat for eating ; but added, that his " skin would make excellent whips."

This was the *fifth* he had slain—thus he equalled Commodus who slew five in the amphitheatre.

The country through which we travelled was low, flat, and thickly wooded; thus we seldom saw the sea; yet, when glimpses of its bright blue waters, stretching to the horizon far away, came before us at times through the groves of orange, lime, and palm trees, or through valleys where the white tufts of the cotton buds flecked the greenness of the luxuriant scenery, how anxiously, how affectionately I gazed upon it, for it was the high road to my home —the way to freedom and dear old England!

After travelling many days, until I was almost sinking with fatigue, by the intense heat of the atmosphere and the number of things I was compelled (as a slave) to carry, we came at last in sight of the great city of Benin, which stretches far along the right bank of the river Formosa.

I hailed it with emotions of undisguised joy, for Amoo had been daily recurring to the liberty and honours that were in store for me there.

CHAPTER L.

WE REACH THE CAPITAL.

I RESOLVED while life remained to persevere to the last in attempting an escape.

" 'I shall never succeed,' is often the parent of failure" (to quote Isaac Taylor when writing on character). " 'I will not try any more,' ensures disappointment. 'It is all *chance*, and I am not in luck,' most commonly leads to disgrace."

Calling his words to memory, I resolved to trust to *none* of these fatal phrases, for I had passed through too many perils not to hope that a few more might be surmounted.

An old writer says, "The King of Benin has men in pay to furnish travellers with water, and these keep great pots full of that which is fresh and clear at convenient distances, with a shell to drink it out of; but no person must take a drop without paying for it; and if the waterman is absent, they drink, leave the money, and pursue their way."

It may have been so when old Dapper wrote or romanced, but not a drop of water found we on the weary track to quench our burning thirst, save in stagnant tarns by the wayside.

It was towards the close of a day when we had been nearly choked by the sulphurous heat which filled the air after a violent thunderstorm, that we approached the city of Benin, and saw its long lines of huts, or wigwams, each one story high, covering for many miles the right bank of the Formosa, one of the greatest estuaries which disgorge their waters into the Bight of Benin.

Groves of beautiful wood, orange, lime trees, cotton and pepper bushes, spread along the banks of the river, and many floating islets, covered with flowers and unknown fruit trees, are constantly borne past by its waters, from the unexplored lands through which they flow.

The city and its walls too were unlike aught I had ever seen before; yet their extent was great, and the dusky hordes that peopled them are probably unnumbered and unknown.

We were admitted through a wooden gate in the ramparts, which were composed of the trunks of trees

pegged together, as palisades are in America, but
loopholed for arrows or musketry; and the guard at
this gate, as at all the others, was composed entirely
of women armed with bows, lances, and old firelocks,
for, like his royal brother of Dahomey, the sovereign
of Benin has somewhere about four thousand wives,
whom he has armed and formed into troops, and who
—when off duty—make crocks, pots, and pipkins
of clay, from the sale of which he derives his prin-
cipal revenue.

They were all stout and handsome negresses,
attired in a species of petticoat which reached below
the knee, with a vest to cover the breast; their hair
was dyed into alternate red and white locks, and
they had great rings of polished metal on their
otherwise bare arms.

Through this guarded gate our long cavalcade of
laden camels, dromedaries, negroes, and slaves,
passed down a populous street of great width, and
nearly three miles in length. The houses, or huts,
on either side, were alike singular in aspect and
construction, being built of red clay, and having
behind or around them spacious gardens and shady
groves of lime and orange trees. Vast crowds of
male and female blacks followed us, but in solemn
silence, as the cavalcade bore a double tribute to the

dead king and his successor, towards whose royal palace—if the odd collection of fantastic buildings could so be called—we now proceeded.

We passed through a kind of square, which Amoo described to me as the market-place; and there the king's female guards were exposing for sale great quantities of their clay pots and pipkins, gourd bottles, calibash basons, wooden spoons and ladles of all sorts and sizes, at their *own* prices; for these industrious Amazons enjoyed the entire monopoly of this branch of trade; and as a hint that none might interfere with them, there hung by iron hooks upon a gibbet the headless bodies of four men, in a frightful state of decay, with turkey buzzards feeding on the fragments that dropped from them, as they sweltered in the burning sunshine.

In the centre of this market-place rose a pyramid some twenty feet high, formed entirely of human skulls, bleached white as snow by the alternate rain and sun—a ghastly and terrible trophy of barbarism and cruelty, which reminded me of stories I had read of old Mexico, where similar monuments adorned the cities of the Incas; or of the tower formed of the skulls of slaughtered Christians, now standing in the Mohammedan isle of Gerba.

Fascinated by this revolting spectacle, I passed

o c

on with the dusky multitude; and Amoo informed me (while all prostrated their ugly faces in the dust) that we stood at the gate of the king's palace!

It was a vast collection of rambling wooden houses, which formed the dwellings of the sovereign, his wives, fiadoors, or officials, stables for his horses and dromedaries, dens for slaves or prisoners (a commodity with which he seldom troubled himself), magazines for stores and plunder. These edifices extended for nearly a mile before us; and on all those quaint buildings, which were barbarously adorned with the bones and horns of animals, a grinning human skull was the chief ornament.

Through a barrier *manned* by a motley multitude of female guards, many of whom were armed with bayonets and old brass-butted Tower muskets, which may have done service under Moore and Wellington, we were conducted into a court surrounded by copper figures, so monstrous in aspect and conception, that the eye laboured in vain to discover whether they were meant to represent men, beasts, or birds.

The crowd who followed were all well armed with spears, bows and arrows, which, as Amoo informed me, were duly poisoned by the *fetishers*, or priests.

Many of the fiadoors wore gay dresses of Dutch scarlet cloth, caps edged with civet fur, and necklaces of jasper and fine coral, or rings of yellow copper, bracelets of lions' teeth, and bucklers of rhinoceros hide.

Round this court were wooden pillars, curiously carved and painted, and, in some instances, covered with plates of engraved copper—the hieroglyphical records of battles, victories, and massacres — the edifices were roofed with palm canes, and had many fantastic pinnacles, surmounted by human skulls, or birds dried and prepared, with their pinions outspread.

In the centre of the court, about twenty negroes, captured from some hostile tribe, were digging a deep hole, like a vast grave, with wooden shovels; and they grinned at us malevolently as we passed them.

Amoo now told me "that the time was come to which he had so often referred, when a great honour would be conferred on me, and when we must part."

I knew not what all this meant, but bewildered by the scenes through which I had passed, the strange places in which I found myself, wearied by the toil of our journey, choked by dust and heat almost to fainting, I resigned myself to the custody of the negress guard, and left Amoo, whom hitherto I had considered a species of protector. Perceiving the dejected state I was in, he gave me a draught from his gourd bottle; and as I was thrust into my prison, and the door of it closed upon me, I saw for the last time save once, the dark visage of this friendly savage, who never forgot that I had rescued his child from the baboon.

The wooden door was secured upon me; the hum of guttural voices died away as the cavalcade passed on to some other portion of this vast and rambling habitation of barbarous royalty; then I was left to my own reflections, and partly in the dark; at least, there was just sufficient light to enable me to see a pile of straw, or dried river grass, on which I threw myself in weariness, if not in despair, as I knew not what new misfortune fate had in store for me.

Sleep, oblivion, I courted in vain. I was now, though exhausted, in too high a state of nervous excitement for sleep; and as my eyes became accustomed to the dim twilight of my prison, I could perceive the chamber to be fashioned of the trunks of trees, squared, smoothed, and pegged together, and then painted with barbarous figures. Above the door by which I had entered were three human skulls, placed upon the hoofs of hippopotami, as brackets.

A sound as of something rustling in a distant corner attracted my attention. I approached, and saw upon a pile of straw and dry leaves a white man extended at full length, and almost destitute of clothing.

I drew nearer softly, for I knew not whether this new companion in misfortune might be alive or dead.

Then imagine what were my emotions on discovering him to be my friend, sunk in a profound slumber—my old friend, Robert Hartly, captain of the fated *Leda.*

CHAPTER LI.

AN OLD FRIEND IN A NEW PLACE.

THE pallor of his countenance, his wasted form, and sunken features shocked me, for I was quite unaware or heedless that he would find an equal ravag· in my own appearance. His beard and hair grew in matted masses about his sunburnt face, and his once stout and manly hands were thin and wan as those of a consumptive girl.

I shook his shoulder; he awoke, and turned listlessly to me at first; then with a strange cry of mingled joy and grief, he exclaimed—

"Jack!"

"Bob—Bob Hartly!"

Such was all we could utter for some seconds as each clasped and shook the hands of the other.

"Oh, Jack Manly," he exclaimed, in a broken voice, "I would rather see you in your grave than in this place with me!"

" How—why—what do you mean ?"

" My poor lad, you know not for what we are reserved."

" Not—not to be killed and eaten ?" said I, in a low voice of dismay

" Oh, worse than that.   Do you not know ?"

" No."

" My poor friend—my poor friend !"

" What on earth can be worse than that ? Amoo told me——"

" Who is Amoo ?"

" A chief, the brother of the King of the Rio Serpientes."

" The savage brother of a savage ! And he told you——"

" That I was reserved for the greatest honours."

" Honours indeed !" reiterated Hartly, with a bitter laugh.

" Yes."

" Did he add, you should have *liberty* to enjoy your honours ?"

" No."

" Air—breath—sunshine—light—life ?"

" No !"

" I thought not, for these accursed savages are as subtle and severe as they are cruel and sanguinary."

"What *do* you mean, Hartly?"

"That we are reserved for *burial alive.*"

"Alive!"

"Yes—with their king who is just dead. It is the custom here to celebrate the obsequies of royal personages—of kings especially—in a frantic and barbarous manner. Oh, Jack! after all we have seen and suffered together, is it not cruel of fate to persecute and finish us thus? And is it not strange that in this age of a civilized world such things *can* be?"

"I will fight to the last!" I exclaimed, furiously.

"We have not a single weapon."

"But these female guards have plenty."

"The weakest among them is stronger than both of us put together *now*," said he, despondingly.

"We must not perish thus, Hartly—we *shall* escape!" said I, emphatically.

"But how?"

"Time will show—we were nearly as desperately circumstanced when foul of the iceberg, or beset in the field ice."

"We have still a few days for deliberation; but meantime, tell me how you came here."

"I was brought to Benin by Amoo, who saved me from dying of hunger, or by the teeth and claws of wild animals in the Devil's wood, where some savages found me concealed, and bound me hand and foot by withes to a tree."

"Tell me all about this, Jack."

I related briefly all that had occurred to me since we had been separated at the cliff above the Gabon, where three of our hapless party perished; the destruction of poor Captain Baylis and his wife; and how I feared that he, Hartly, was the seaman who had been tortured in the basket of thorns; of my slavery with Amoo, and his squaw's felonious intentions with regard to my head; of my flight and recapture—to all of which he listened with varying expressions of anger and honest grief, for the loss of so many brave English seamen.

" And now, Bob," added I, " for your own story "

" I have little to relate that is not similar to what you have told me. On that fatal day when our boat's crew were captured, and we were separated, I was given by the King to a fetisher, or priest, a hideous old fellow who was covered with tattooing, and wore a copper ring in each of his ears, and had the dorsal fin of a shark through his nose, in sprit-sail-yard fashion.

" He employed me as his ' slavey,' in making and pointing arrows for the warriors, as the manufacture of that commodity is a perquisite, or portion of the priestly trade in Gabon, for the tips of the arrows are poisoned by a combination of herbs, of which these fetishers alone possess, or pretend to possess, the knowledge, and with true priestcraft take especial good care to keep the secret among them-selves. If the monstrous negro race hereabout have any religion, it consists of an adoration of the Devil, to whom they never tire of sacrificing wild animals, and occasionally each other—which is a sacrifice of much less consequence."

"Have they no belief in a Supreme Being?"

"They know that some power superior to them-selves created the skies and the earth; but because He is not an evil, but a good spirit, they deem it better policy to appease the Devil, and so they work in *his* service with all their might; and from all we have seen, they seem to have the gift of doing so to the utmost. My old master, the fetisher, professed to be on very intimate terms with Whirlwind Tom, and by his aid could always foretell what was to happen."

"How?"

"He had an old pipkin perforated by three holes, through which he alleged the Devil spoke to him in whispers. He was a vicious old wretch, and on one occasion *bit me,* which was no joke, as his teeth were all filed, till they were sharp as those of a tiger cat.

" When not employed in selecting and cutting reeds for arrows, or feathering, or pointing and poisoning them, this fetisher made me fish for him in a tributary of the Snake River, on the bank of which he lived in a wigwam, which stood amid a grove of mimosa trees ; and it resembled a huge punch-bowl or beehive, as it was built entirely of reeds and turf, plastered over with mud, which the sunshine had burned as white as Kentish chalk.

" There he led me a dog's life, for he was an ill-tempered old savage, who hourly reviled, kicked, beat, and spat upon me, and as my beard grew, he was wont to snatch and tear it, a proceeding, you must allow, very trying to one's temper.

" I perceived that we dwelt in a secluded place ; that, save a warrior who came from time to time for a bundle of arrows, no one ever approached us, so I resolved to escape. In my fur socks, and a species of cummerbund which my master permitted me to wear, I secreted a good stock of fishing apparatus, and selected a strong javelin with an iron point, well steeped in those precious poisonous stuffs which he was wont to brew in a pipkin.

"On the day I had finally made up my mind to slip my cable and be off, we were cutting reeds for arrow-shafts on the summit of a rock above the Gabon River. It was a lovely place, covered with feathery fern, bright scarlet geraniums, and flowering reeds, but I thought it looked very like the place where I had last seen you, and where our three shipmates perished in so barbarous a manner. My heart became filled with wild and dark thoughts, and I was neglecting my work, when suddenly my beard was grasped by the old tattooed fetisher, who squirted a whole quid of some stuff full in my face, while raining a shower of blows upon my bare back with a *sjambok*, or supple-jack, of rhinoceros hide, which he always carried for my especial benefit.

"Flesh and blood could stand this no longer.

"We were close to the brink of the rock which overhung the stream that rolled about a hundred feet below, so I gave his sooty reverence a vigorous kick which shot him over like a crow, and souse he went through the air, with arms outspread.

"Whether he swam, sank, or fed some hungry crocodile, I know not, as I fled into the adjacent forest, and after lurking there long—sleeping at night in the trees, as many a time I had done on the swinging topsail-yard—I began, like you, to make for the coast to the westward, in the hope of seeing a ship venture into the Bight, or bearing toward the Pongos for fresh water.

"For many days and nights I wandered through forests of oak, cypress, myrtle, and mimosa trees, enduring constantly the terror of being devoured by wild animals, or falling again among savages who might force me to render a severe account of the blessed fetisher I had kicked into the Gabon, till at last I found myself in a stately wood of sea-pines and *then* I saw the ocean—the brave old ocean, Jack! —the broad turnpike that could lead us home—the same ocean whose waves swept up by the Nore and Greenwich Reach, to mingle their waters with the Thames—and I laughed with joy, though its bosom was glistening under the vertical sun that scorches the coast of Guinea.

"All the memories of home and Old England swelled up within me as I gazed upon the girdle of her shores. The sea! that

"—— glorious mirror where the Almighty's form
Glasses itself in tempests ; in all time,
Calm or convulsed—in breeze, or gale, or storm,
Icing the pole, or in the torrid clime
Dark-heaving ;—boundless, endless, and sublime !"

CHAPTER LII.

MARTIN'S STORY.

"When night fell, I came out of the lonely forest to gaze upon the moonlit sea—not that the forest was very *lonely*, after all, as there seemed to be at least fifty thousand baboons, monkeys, and squirrels, which jabbered and leaped as if they had all gone mad, the whole night, from tree to tree, and more than once the roar of a lion came hollowly from a distance, under the lower branches of the pines.

"I sat upon a piece of detached rock, and, to seek for food, dropped my fishing-line into the water. There I soon caught a fish, on which I breakfasted next day, after spreading it, split open, on the rocks, where it was half cooked by the burning sun. As for salt, there was plenty of that to be found among the crevices, where the heat had burned up the spray of the sea.

"For three nights I fished there with success

and safety. On the third, I found at my line a fish of strange aspect, and, sailor-like, had some doubts about breakfasting on it, but hunger soon ends all niceties. When morning came, I sought a secluded part of the wood, and thought of lighting a little fire by rubbing dried branches together that I might broil my fish.

"Now, unless I could produce ocular proof of what I am about to say, you would laugh at me for telling you a forecastle yarn, but the proof shall not be wanting.

"While opening and cleaning the fish at a spring, previous to broiling it (an almost epicurean process to me), I found in its entrails—what? MY RING— the ring given me by old Mother Jensdochter, in Iceland, and which, as you remember, I lost a few days after we left Sermersoak, when lending a hand to haul the main-tack on board the *Leda*."

"Your ring!" I exclaimed; "this is like a bit of a fairy tale."

"My ring," he continued; "and here it is, hid among my hair to conceal it from these greedy negroes, who would at once deprive me of it, and keep it as an ornament or amulet."

"This is most singular!"

"Singular indeed, but on beholding it a new glow

of hope filled my breast. I resolved to persevere in my efforts to escape, and so became too bold, for, venturing upon the open beach next day, I was seen by some savages belonging to the King of Biafra, who pursued and soon made me their prisoner. The rest of my story is nearly the same as your own, as my captors were with a caravan on their way to Benin, to attend the funeral of King Zabadie.

" I was severely treated by them. Under a burning and vertical sun, they employed me constantly in loading and unloading their dromedaries, or in pulling up esculent roots for them, and this was a serious task even to a hard-handed sailor, as these roots lay among thorny leaves and serrated grass, the blades of which were like newly-sharpened saws.

" In the desert, the sand was so hot that it baked or roasted the eggs I stole or found at times, and was fain to eat in secret. When my work was over, I was always malevolently treated by the women, and more especially by those little black imps, the children of the caravan. Their chief occupation was spitting at me, reviling and pelting me with stones, bones, rotten gourds, and every missile that came to hand.

" The women had a particular animosity to my beard, and the men hereabouts, like other darkies, not being troubled with much of that commodity, joined them in the general desire for having it uprooted, but I contrived to weather them by singeing it off.

" Every way I endured great misery. I was not even permitted to drink of spring water, save from a calabash, which some of their dogs had used; and to tell the truth, I preferred to drink after the poor doggies rather than after their beastly masters.

" Well, it would seem that His High Mightiness, the King of Biafra, is a vassal of that more illustrious nigger the King of Benin; so, five days ago, I was sent here, with many other miserable wretches, to be—to be——"

" What ?"

" Immolated on the grave of the late king, or buried within it."

" Is such the custom ?" I asked, with indescribable dismay.

" Benin borders on the kingdom of Dahomey, and all the world knows *how* the people there celebrate the obsequies of their kings."

" How ?"

" Frequently by the massacre of thousands."

"Hartly! Hartly—we seem to go from bad to worse!"

"I have been in the Pongo Isles, along the coast of Guinea, and in the Bight of Benin before, and know all about the fiendish ways of their inhabitants. Jack, did you observe a great hole in the courtyard without ?"

"Yes; and I can hear the shovels of the workers among the earth even now."

"When a king dies here, his body is laid in a kind of great hall, which, like that at Dahomey, has a ceiling ornamented by the jawbones of his enemies. There the very sleeping chambers of royalty are paved with human skulls, and have cornices entirely composed of them! Zabadie, the King of Benin, is just dead, and his son proposes to inter him with unusual splendour."

"In that hole ?"

"Yes."

"But what is all this to us ?"

"Oh," groaned Hartly, "do you not understand —have I not told you ? When a king dies here, a great grave is dug somewhere near the palace, and it must be hollowed so deep, that the diggers are drowned by the water which bursts in upon them, and there they lie, after concluding their work.

In this great hole the fiadoors place the royal corpse, dressed in all its barbaric finery, with a lance, sword, bow and arrows. With the dead king are placed all his favourites and servants, who are supposed to follow him to the other world, and serve him there; and so proud are they of this distinction, that it occasions the most violent disputes as to who shall have the honour of entombment, so blind and idolatrous is the veneration of these creatures for their dingy monarchs. When the last man has descended into the hole, an immense stone is placed over it; this is removed a few days after, and one of the great fiadoors inquires what are the tidings from beneath, adding,—

" ' Who has gone to serve the king ?'

" Then the poor wretches who are expiring below reply according to circumstances.

" Day after day the stone is removed, and the same questions are asked, until all in that horrid pit have 'gone to serve the king,' and are dead of starvation and the noxious miasma of the vault. When *no* voice responds to the inquiry of the fiadoor, the great stone is securely built over, a mighty fire is made upon it, a great festival is held, and the flesh of an elephant is roasted and given to the multitude."

"And we—we——"

"Are to be placed there among the slaves of the dead Zabadie."

I remained silent, oppressed by the horror of what was before us; but Hartly spoke again:—

"When a year has passed and gone, these wretches, in honour of their dead king and his dead followers, make a dreadful sacrifice of men and animals, till about five hundred are destroyed. Most of the human victims are malefactors, or slaves taken in war. If enough of either are not to be had, the king sends his female guards into the streets at night to decoy and seize men till the number is made up."

This was a cheerful account of the state of society in the realm of Benin, and it afforded ample food for thrilling reflection and fruitless surmises.

CHAPTER LIII.

THE FEMALE GUARDS.

YAMS, bananas, plantains, even boiled potatoes, and pipkins of pure spring water were liberally provided for us by our black female guardians, six of whom appeared once daily with our food and then retired, securing us with great bars of wood fastened outside in some fashion known only to themselves.

These Amazons were all well armed, and some were richly clad in braided vests and petticoats of Dutch scarlet cloth. Among them were several veteran female warriors, whose skins, by the process of time under a tropical sun, had become spotted yellow and brown, like the hides of the leopard and panther.

Light was admitted to our prison by a small square hole cut through one of the trees which formed the wall, and from thence, when each sup-

ported the other on his shoulders, we could see by
turns the progress of the diggers of the royal grave
in the courtyard, and to judge by the quantity of
earth and stones thrown up, the depth must have
been immense; and it seemed as if King Zabadie
was going to the other world accompanied by all
his wives, slaves, dromedaries, and diabolical courtiers to boot.

We knew not *when* this dreadful interment and
immolation were to take place. When day dawned
on us, we knew not if we should be permitted to see
it close; when it closed, we knew not if we should
ever behold another dawn.

So the wretched hours passed slowly, wearily on;
and the close of the third day found us still
captives, and still unresolved on any expedient to
free ourselves.

Sailor-like, Hartly was fertile in schemes and re-
sources; but the former were no sooner proposed
than they were abandoned as impracticable.

One time he suggested that we should endeavour
to procure a light by friction, set fire to the old
wooden den in which we were confined, and then
seek an escape amid the consequent confusion; at
another, he proposed that we should close with our
guards, wrest away a musket, kill one or two of

them, and fight our way off; but how could we attack women?

"If once free of the palace, the town, and its suburbs——" resumed he.

"Free! how can we remain free, Hartly, in a land where our colour, which there is *no* disguising. renders us constantly liable to recognition, to attack, and recapture?"

"True; but if we could only reach the coast, after having so dearly learned circumspection, we might lurk in the woods."

"Without arms?"

"We have done so before. Then we might steal a canoe, or fashion one, and put to sea."

"But the tools and the skins?"

"We could steal both, as these fellows wont lend."

"Escape from this is necessary first: and in the pilfering visits you suggest, we should certainly be retaken, together or singly; and then how miserable would be the reflections of the survivor."

"Tut, Jack! unless we venture we shall never win."

"Ah, Hartly," said I, "at last I have lost all hope!"

"Do not say so; we are both too young to

despair," was the sturdy response of the English sailor.

We thought of the old stereotyped modes of escape—by ropes or ladders manufactured from shirts and trowsers, and by ample melodramatic mantles ; but such were impossible to us, who were nearly as nude as when we came into the world ; by drugging our guards or sentinels; by bribing, coaxing, or assassinating them ; but these, and all the thousand other modes by which heroic and romantic gentlemen, when in trouble or durance, effect escapes in novels and plays, were useless or impracticable there.

Hartly, indeed, proposed to make love to one or two ladies of the royal guard, and by gaining their confidence, to effect the appropriation of their muskets and ammunition. But those dingy Amazons seemed of a very unapproachable nature ; and moreover, were so thickly smeared with war-paint and vegetable oils, as to be too hideous in aspect and repulsive in odour to render the attempt at all pleasant.

So the darkness of the third night closed upon us, and undecided as to any mode of escape, we sat gazing with longing eyes on the little bit of blue sky that was visible through the hole, which by day afforded light and air into our den.

A single star of uncommon brilliance shone through it now, and so brightly as to cast the form of the loophole upon the floor like a little white patch.

"If once we were out of this place," said Hartly, for the twentieth time, "I would certainly trust to my two hands and pair of heels for doing the rest."

"The town walls seem a high palisade."

"Yes. I had a good view of them for an hour and more on the unlucky day I first arrived in Benin. And yet, Jack," he added, kindly, "I am glad those devils brought me here, after all—we should never have met again else. The town walls are a double palisade, sparred over on the outside and in—double sheathed a sailor would call it—and then the whole is plastered over with red clay."

" Their height——"

" Is not less than twelve feet; and at those parts of the town which are without a rampart, there is a ditch of great depth, full of slime and poisonous serpents, and bordered by an impassable hedge of brambles, through which fire alone could make its way."

If I attempted to sleep, I was haunted by visions

of being buried alive in that enormous tomb, from
which there could be no escape—buried amid a heca-
tomb of hideous and sweltering negro corpses and
the dead royalty of a savage race.   The pictures my
imagination drew of the future nearly distracted
me ;   and I began to consider whether it was
not better, by rushing barehanded and unarmed
upon our captors, to provoke a more speedy and
merciful death under their knives, asseguys, or
muskets ; and failing an escape, Hartly agreed with
me that it was a wiser alternative ; but Heaven
lent us its helping hand ere the third night was
passed.

CHAPTER LIV

ATTEMPT TO ESCAPE AGAIN.

On this night, for more than an hour, there was an unusual beating of tum-tums, and the chorus of some barbaric songs stole upon the wind at times from that quarter of the royal dwelling in which the wives of the late King Zabadie were enclosed.

During the past day the digging in the court-yard had ceased; and this circumstance, together with the sounds we heard (the adoration of some great fetish, or idol), made us tremble in our hearts lest the following day might see us placed in that more horrible prison, from whence there could be no release but by death.

We mutually expressed our fears of this; and so absorbed were we in this terrible surmise, that some time elapsed before we perceived that the blue of the sky and the light of the stars had disappeared; that a thick vapour had overspread both: that rain was pattering heavily on the flat roofs of the wooden city; and that thunder, the deep, hoarse thunder of the tropics, which sounds as if it would rend the earth in twain, was roaring athwart the darkened firmament.

The rain now poured down in such mighty torrents, that we listened to the din of its fall in silent wonder; for it seemed as if once again that " all the fountains of the great deep had broken up, and the windows of heaven were opened."

Ere long we felt the drops descending upon us, tepid and sulphureous, as the clay coating that covered the split canes, or lathing, which formed the roof of our prison, soon became a puddle; while the straw and leaves on which we usually sat or reclined, were reduced to a mass of wetted mire.

For nearly an hour this continued, till our den became so thoroughly wet, that when the rain was over not a single dry spot could we find; and (as Hartly said) King Zabadie's trench in the court-yard would have the water some fathoms deep in it by this time.

On the rain ceasing, and the clouds dispersing, which they did as suddenly as the storm had come on, we saw the stars shining through a breach which the moisture had made in the roof, and something like a branch that was waving to and fro fell on my upturned face.

I grasped it.

It was the strong sinewy tendril of a climbing convolvulus, which had fallen through the aperture. I drew it down, so far as it would come, and then *another* branch fell in. On this I called joyously to Hartly, that "here were the first means of escape!"

Without a moment's hesitation he grasped them, twisted them together, and with sailor-like agility swung himself up, hand over hand, till he reached the crevice through which they had fallen.

Supporting the whole weight of his body by the left hand, with the right he tore down a mass of the fragile roof, and swinging himself up, passed through and at length stood upon the outside.

"Now, Jack," said he, "come up in the same fashion, hand over hand—it is just like going through the lubber's hole, instead of over the futtock shrouds. Bravo ! we'll weather this dead devil of a king and his armed wenches to boot."

I dragged myself up by the twisted tendrils, but when near the hole should have fallen to the ground, had not Hartly's strong and friendly hands grasped and dragged me on to the roof, where for a little time we lay flat on our faces, panting alike with exertion and excitement, and listening anxiously to hear if any guards or watchers were near us.

By the starlight we could see the long rows of flat wooden huts which composed the palace divided into various courts. At the distance of three hundred yards from us, on our right, a ruddy glow that deepened into crimson, then wavered, sunk, and flashed up again, revealed the outline of a monstrous fetish, or wooden idol, of hideous aspect, which the young King, his fiadoors, guards, and people were worshipping; and we could see the woolly heads bowed before it packed thick and close as cannon balls in Woolwich arsenal.

The long vista of the great street of huts, which stretches the entire length of the town, and is alleged to be three miles long, lay upon our left.

We had no guide to the ramparts or outskirts; but as the long extent of this street seemed empty and silent, our best chance of ultimate escape lay through it.

Again grasping the tendrils of the convolvulus, we slid down from the roof and reached the ground. Robert Hartly dropped first. When I was following, the tendrils gave way, and I fell heavily, making thus a noise which roused a large dog in an adjacent shed, where it barked furiously ; but as we lay close and still, it gradually ceased, and growled itself off to sleep again.

We were in a garden attached to the King's residence; and being (by our white skins) liable to immediate pursuit, capture, or destruction, the moment we were seen—a contingency that would become a certainty when day broke—we hurried through it, getting our legs and feet severely cut and torn by the flowers and prickly plants ; but of this minor evil we had no heed at that time.

A paling of split canes was soon surmounted, and once more we found ourselves in the long street of Benin.

CHAPTER LV

THE FORMOSA.

" IF once we are free from the town," said Hartly, "we can find concealment during the day, and by travelling at night may reach the coast. Then, if we can but obtain a canoe, and pass over to one of the little isles in the Bight, we might remain there snugly enough, till some ship ran in on the same unlucky errand which brought poor Baylis here."

" I pray it may end as you say."

"Courage, Jack! Energy and faith will work miracles !"

" But I imagine——"

" Don't talk of imagination ; it may only paralyse you by the fears it fashions, the danger it suggests ; but hush !"

At that moment the fire before the idol flared up broad and redly, and then the mingled roar of many voices swelled upon the night air.

High above the hedge-rows or kraals for containing cattle, and the lines of countless huts, formed of turf, of wickered cane, and other rude materials which the wild vines, creepers, and convolvuli concealed, rose the lurid flame that blazed before the misshapen god of Benin; and far across the flat city it cast the shadows of the tall giraffe trees, which grew in rows around the palace wall.

This red light mingled with the pale white lustre of the moon, which was just rising at the horizon, from whence its splendour cast long and steady shadows across the streets, and thereby favoured alike our concealment and escape.

As we hurried along the empty thoroughfares towards the town wall, Hartly found at the door of a hut, a war-club, of which he immediately took possession. It was formed of teak-wood, black as ebony, ponderously heavy, and its knob was covered by elaborate carvings.

While our hearts alternately glowed with hope, or sank with apprehension, unseen we reached the high wall of wood and clay, and ran alongside it, in search either of an outlet, or some means of surmounting it; but no wild creepers, no gourd vines or climbing convolvuli were permitted to grow there.

We had been out of our prison at least half-an-hour without being met or seen by a single negro.

At last we reached a place where, for more than a hundred feet, the wall was breached by the recent storm of wind and rain, which had overturned and beaten its ruins flat on the ground.

With mutual exclamations of joy, we were proceeding to clamber over the fallen piles of rotten palisades and clay, when a wretched negro, who appeared suddenly, on perceiving the whiteness of our skins in the bright moonlight, uttered a loud cry of wonder or alarm!

In an instant we heard the clatter of steel, and at least a dozen of the King's armed women issued from a kind of wooden tower which stood near the fallen wall.

Hartly uttered something very like an oath; he struck the negro to the earth by a blow of his club, and crying—" Follow me, Jack !" sprang over the scattered ruin, and rushed into the mooonlit country beyond.

Swift of foot and active as these " fair viragoes" were, they proved no match for us in a race for life or death, especially when encumbered by their muskets, asseguys, and red petticoats, which were covered with heavy beads, lions' teeth, and grass braiding.

Two shots were fired after us, but where the balls went, Heaven only knows; fortunately, they fell far from us.

On we ran in the full blaze of the moonlight, bathed in perspiration, now floundering among wild gourds and creeping plants, where little snakes started up to hiss at us; anon over waste tracts, where lilies and geraniums covered all the wilderness; then among long and serrated grass, which cut our shins like saws and sabre-blades. Next we tore a passage through dense masses of wild canes, then through fields of maize, or rice, or millet, and often through cattle kraals, till we reached a wood, where, after taking the precaution of running in *one* direction in the full light of the moon, we turned and, hare-like, doubled in the *other*.

By this manœuvre, I believe, we baffled our *fair* pursuers, as we saw no more of them for the remainder of that night or the following morning, during the long hours of which we lay close to the earth, buried and hidden under a cool and shady mass of leaves and jungle.

And there, without water to quench our thirst, and without other food than a few wild berries that

grew within arm's length of our lurking place, we
lay concealed during the whole of the next day.

When night fell, Hartly climbed into a chestnut-
tree, and after looking carefully around him, uttered
an exclamation of delight.

"I see the way we must steer, Jack," he added.

"You can see the ocean?"

"Ay, or a large river, rippling in the moonlight
to the horizon far away."

A sigh of joy escaped me.

"And so, Jack, if our company is necessary to
complete the happiness of King Zabadie in the next
world, I am sorry for him, as he is likely to take
his long voyage without us."

The chestnut was lofty, and from it Hartly could
see on one hand the distant hills which form the termination of that mighty chain, the mountains of
Kong, and end at the river Formosa. On the
other hand, beyond the flat and open country, he
could see the great river itself, flowing towards the
Bight of Benin, along whose shores and by whose
waters lay all our ultimate hope of escape.

We bathed ourselves in a limpid pool to freshen
and brace our nerves; I armed me with a cudgel
formed of a young tree torn up by the roots;
Hartly had still his war-club; and resolving to

travel only under cloud of night, as cautiously as possible, and to avoid all negro camps and villages, we found the highway—if it could be called so— which leads from the city of Benin towards the Waree.

CHAPTER LVI.

A PERILOUS JOURNEY.

In our ignorance of the wild country through which we travelled, our sole guide towards the sea was the course of the river Formosa, which rapidly widened into a mighty estuary, along the left bank of which we proceeded with the utmost circumspection; and inspired by the triple dread of being recaptured and killed by the natives, devoured by wild animals, or sinking under the heavy miasma which exhales from the marshy creeks and isles of the uncounted river-mouths which there pour their muddy tides into the Bight of Benin, laden with the decaying vegetable débris of an unexplored world.

By various sounds which the wind swept after us at times, such as the baying of dogs, and notes of cane horns, we feared a pursuit by the people of Benin, and the sequel proved that our fears were but *too* true.

We were frequently bewildered by seeing large lakes, which we conceived to be the sea, till dawn of day would reveal their size, and the gigantic trees or walls of wavy reeds which surrounded their stagnant waters.

Hartly often beguiled the way by relating strange stories he had heard or read, and by the margin of one of those silent lakes in the wilderness he told me of the shattered hull of an ancient ship being found, beached upon the bank of one of those inland waters in the continent of Africa.

"How came it to be cast up there?" I asked, with surprise.

"Some alleged that it came through a subterraneous opening, a channel in the bowels of the earth, connected with the same vortex or whirlpool which had sucked it down long years ago—the Maelstrom, perhaps, though many say that, like Charybdis, no such place exists. But it sounds very like a bouncing yarn, such as one may hear at the Royal Society, or under the leech of the foresail of a fine night, Jack, when the middle watch are spinning their *twisters*."

We spent a whole night wearily and anxiously circumnavigating the banks of one of those lakes whose waters were full of thick green slime, of

sturdy reeds, and leaves of wondrous size and form ;
falling into black quagmires and deep holes made
by the clumsy hippopotami, and every instant in
danger of being pounced upon by a panther or a
poisonous snake for our intrusion upon their secluded
domains.

It is in these lakes of Benin, and in those of the
kingdom of Angola, that the quaint old writer
named Dapper (who must have been a very fanciful
or credulous personage) relates he saw "water
animals which the negroes call *ambisiangula,* and
the Portuguese *pezze-moueller.* These monsters
are both male and female. They are eight feet
long and four broad, with short arms and long
fingers of three joints, like ours. They have
an oval head and eyes, a high forehead, a flat
nose, and great mouth. Snares are laid for them,
and when caught, they sigh and cry like women
till they are killed by darts. Their entrails and
flesh are like those of hogs in scent, taste, and
form. 'Tis said the filings of certain skull-bones in
the males, if mixed with wine, are an excellent
remedy against gravel, and the bone which extends
towards the membrane of the ear is good against
bad vapour, if we may believe the Portuguese."

Master Dapper then goes on to state, that of the

ribs of this wonderful fish, particularly those on the
left side, surgeons can make a powder which will
effectually stanch bleeding, and that bracelets
made of them were worn for the preservation of
health. Another account, published in 1714, adds,
that in the Cabinet of Rarities at Leyden one of
their *hands* is preserved, and two others were in the
Musæum Regium at Copenhagen.

We, however, never saw aught but the fibrous
leaves of enormous aquatic plants, large as table-
cloths, floating on the water of these lakes, under
the clear lustre of a lovely moon, that cast the
shadows of the feathery palm and bending orange-
trees from banks where the alligator dozed amid the
slime, or the hippopotamus came to crop the herbage
and bask in the rays of the sun when he rose above
the foliage of the vast untrodden forest.

Manfully we struggled on, supporting nature by
such fruits and esculents as we found, especially
yams, and on the sixth night after our escape, with
a prayer of thankfulness, we found ourselves under
the friendly shelter of a chestnut grove, and close
upon the shore of the mighty sea.

We were now so scorched and burned by the
sun, and so embrowned by daily and nightly exposure, that we might very well have passed for a

couple of mulattoes, and so have claimed kindred with our tormentors.

We had now left the territories of Benin, and were in the land of Waree, which has a dingy sovereign of its own. The whole of this district is covered by wild forests, which in the wet season are frequently converted into lakes and marshes, where the stems of the trees are submerged for two or three feet in water.

Opposite to where we lay concealed, and at the distance of a mile from us, we saw a little green island, having upon its summit a negro village, some of the inhabitants of which, when day broke, came over to the mainland with four canoes, which they moored or beached in a creek not three hundred yards distant from where we lurked among some long grass.

These negroes were sixteen in number, all armed with asseguys, muskets, and bows, and they proceeded into the forest apparently to hunt.

We climbed into a leafy chestnut for security, and passed the entire day amid its branches, thus escaping the hunting party, several of whom passed underneath us, on their way back to the canoes, in which they embarked, and returned to the island laden with game.

These canoes were large; each appeared to be a single tree hollowed out, and flattened in the bottom. Hartly, who announced his intention of borrowing one *sans* leave on the first available opportunity, said, that after being scooped out, straw was burned in them to save the wood from being spoiled by worms. They can be rowed swiftly, and are steered by a long spar, which acts as a rudder. The oars are usually made of teak-wood, and fashioned like spades.

Each of these canoes had a round knob on its prow; and by this they were pulled ashore with ease, and beached high and dry upon the thick mangrove leaves of the creek.

When night fell again, I sank into a profound sleep among the branches of our chestnut tree. There was no danger of a tumble, we had become so accustomed to roosting on such perches.

Day dawned again, and we looked about us.

Ah! what were our emotions *then* on seeing in the blue waters of the bay, and about two miles from the green island, *two vessels at anchor*— one a brig, with American colours flying; and the other a stately ship, with the broad scarlet ensign of Britain floating at her gaff peak!

There they rode proudly at their moorings; but we were destitute alike of means for reaching them or making signals; as yet all their boats were on board, and we could perceive no sign of any of them being despatched ashore. Their topsails and top-gallant sails were handed; but their courses were only hauled up, and some of their fore and aft canvas hung loose in the brails.

We gazed at them with tearful and haggard eyes, our hearts swelling the while with mingled hope and fear—hope that they might yet save, and fear that they might unwittingly sail and abandon us.

While we were debating what was to be done, the four canoes with the sixteen negroes again shot off from the island village, and disappeared among the mangroves of the creek; and soon after we saw them, as on the previous day, pass, armed, into the wood to hunt.

"Now is our opportunity, Jack—now or never!" cried Hartly, as he dropped lightly from the tree; "let us make a rush at the canoes, seize one and shove off!"

I instantly followed his example; but, alas! we were too rash in our desire to embark, for at the same instant we dropped from our perches, we found ourselves confronted by two of the savages, whom the suddenness of our appearance seemed to fill with astonishment and irresolution.

CHAPTER LVII.

PURSUIT AGAIN.

WITHOUT pausing for a moment to express friendly or other signs, we rushed down with headlong speed towards the creek, where the canoes lay beached upon the thick fringe of mangrove leaves, and eight of the sixteen hunters pursued us; but notwithstanding the swiftness of foot they possessed—a swiftness acquired by a savage and roving life—we distanced them with ease, for despair seemed to lend us the strength and speed of ostriches as we rushed towards the beach.

An asseguy, aimed with almost fatal precision, glanced over my left shoulder, and shivered as it sank into the turf beyond me. Then a war-club, thrown with fatal force and dexterity, struck poor Hartly between the shoulders, and nearly prostrated him; but in less than two minutes we were in the creek, and had one of the largest canoes afloat.

" In, in, Jack—leap in !" cried Hartly, while he lightly and adroitly pushed the other three into the water, and setting them all afloat to cut off pursuit, sprang in after me.

His presence of mind was most fortunate, for on the steep brow of an eminence which overhung the creek on the side opposite to our more immediate pursuers, there suddenly burst a storm of shrill yells and discordant shouts, mingled with the beating of tum-tums and the snorting of ferocious dogs, as a number of Benin savages, who doubtless had tracked us thither with the most fell intentions, rushed to the shore in pursuit—but thank Heaven, happily too late !

Hartly's sinewy hand had shot two of the canoes some thirty yards or so from the beach ; and while towing a third by its bow-knob, he proceeded to row most vigorously with one of the spade-like paddles which lay in our craft.

Ere we got out of the wooded creek its water smoked and boiled under the shower of missiles— arrows, asseguys, clubs, and stones—which were sent after us, while five negroes and several dogs plunged in to pursue or to slay.

These tracking dogs were animals of strange aspect—sharp-nosed, with skins spotted black and white, or red—they had slender legs, sharp tusks, and a low, but ferocious bark.

While four of the negroes busied themselves in bringing back the drifting canoes—an operation during which one of them was shot by the musket of some blundering comrade—the fifth, a man of fierce and resolute bearing, having red and yellow circles painted round his eyes, and a knife in his teeth, swam after us, accompanied by a dog, the most formidable of the whole.

Swiftly though our canoe shot through the water, and vigorously though we paddled, they were soon alongside of us. The dog had his fore paws, and the man his black hands, upon the gunnel at the same moment.

The time was painfully critical!

I struck the dog with my paddle, and broke both his fore legs; unable to swim, he floated away sinking, yelping, and drowning; while Hartly relinquishing the canoe he was towing, dealt the painted savage—in whom I recognised Amoo, my former master—a tremendous blow on the head. Though the latter proved *harder* than the hard wood paddle, which was split and splintered, Amoo sank with a yell of rage and pain.

After the danger was past, I was pleased to see

that he rose to the surface again and reached the shore; for this negro chief was not, in some respects, and apart from a general inclination to homicide, ungenerous.

The three canoes were quickly crowded by armed warriors, and rowed out of the creek at a speed that bade fair soon to overhaul us, though we paddled away, each on his own side, with all the rapidity our strength and our desperation enabled as to exert.

We were now entirely clear of the creek, and about a quarter of a mile from the shore, when a hearty English cheer rang across the water towards us.

On turning and looking ahead, we saw two large and well-manned boats, which had been put off from the ship (the craft nearest the shore), pulled rapidly towards us; while two rifles from the headmost one were discharged into the canoes, as a hint for their owners to sheer off, which they immediately did with great expedition.

We were soon alongside of the nearest boat, the crew of which pulled us on board, canoe and all, continuing to cheer the while so lustily, that some time elapsed before we could inform them that we were countrymen.

The steersman then inquired whether there were any more fugitives ashore.

We replied " No ;" on which the boat's head was turned towards the ship; the oars again fell into the water, and the creek soon lessened and melted, as it were, into the general scenery of the wooded shore.

The vessel by which we were so providentially rescued, proved to be the *Havelock*, of London, a fine clipper ship of a thousand tons register, belonging, by a singular coincidence, to my father—at least, to the firm of Manly and Skrew, homeward bound from the Cape; but which had been, like the barque of poor Captain Baylis, driven out of her course by the hurricane of the other night, and had anchored in the Bight to procure fresh water, and repair some trifling damages.

Soon her spars and hull (old England's wooden wall), a welcome sight, rose higher from the water as we pulled towards her; and as they rose, the low, level, and marshy shore we had left, with all its mangrove creeks and reedy lagunes—its wildernesses of giant leaves, and long and fibrous creepers—its dense jungles, where serpents hissed, monkeys chattered, and crocodiles laid their eggs; where the great yellow gourd and coarse serrated grass flourished under the feathery palm and broad baobab trees, amid slime and miasma, that carry death to the vitals of the European—soon all these diminished and sank astern, as our boat sped through the shining sea; and, ere long, Robert Hartly and I shook each other's hands with honest warmth and joy, when we found ourselves among our own countrymen, treading a deck of good English oak, with the old scarlet bunting floating from the peak halyards above us.

Three days the *Havelock* remained in the bay; and during that time, you may be assured, neither Hartly nor I had any wish to venture on shore.

I shall never forget the glow of happiness that thrilled through me, when, on the third evening, the Captain gave orders to hoist the boats on board and prepare for sea.

"Man the windlass!" was the cry; "hands, up anchor!"

The bars were inserted by sturdy hands in the huge beam, and then the pauls clattered cheerily, while the iron cable rattled as it was dragged aft along the deck, and soon the great clipper ship came round with her head to the wind.

"Cast loose the courses; away aloft—shake out the topsails, and let fall!"

And anon the snowy canvas fell like white curtains on the lower spars, as the topsail yards ascended
to the crosstrees.

"Heave on the cable—weigh!" was the next
order.

Tight as if its iron rings would snap like pack-
thread grew the mighty chain, for strong hands and
muscular arms were tugging with united strength
at the bars of bending ash.

"Together, lads — together — hurrah!" cried
Hartly, who had supplied himself with a handspike.

> "Uptorn, reluctant, from its oozy cave,
> The ponderous anchor rises o'er the wave."

And soon the great iron flukes were dripping with
glittering brine, as the ring rattled at the cathead;
then the yards were trimmed; the larboard tacks
were brought on board, and with a fine spanking
breeze, that came from the burning shores of Benin,
our fleet clipper ship bore away for Old England.

    *   *   *   *   *

CONCLUSION.

Such were my adventures in the lands of snow
and sunshine—the latitudes of ice and fire!

On the 17th of December, exactly nine months
after the day on which Hartly and I had sailed

through the Narrows of St. John, we found ourselves bowling along the crowded and busy streets of London in a hackney cab, with our African canoe — all the property we possessed—lashed on the roof thereof.

We separated for a time at the Bank ; he to look after another ship, and I—like he of old, who came to the husks and the swine trough—to return to my father's house at Peckham (a tamer and wiser youth than when I left it) and to the circle of my family, who had long since gone into mourning for me.

I am delighted to add that my worthy Robert Hartly soon got another vessel. As sole survivors of the crew of the *Leda*, we obtained, after a world of trouble with the Red-tapists of the Circumlocution Office, the 500*l.* offered by the Governor of Newfoundland for the destruction of the *Black Schooner*.

My share I made over to Hartly, who invested it in the capital of his new owner.

He still preserves, with religious care, the ring of old Mother Jensdochter ; and undeterred by all he has undergone, sails from Blackwall for China on the 10th of next month.

THE END.

Paper Covers.	Limp CL Gilt.		Picture Boards.	Hf. Roan.
		FONBLANQUE, Albany, Jun.—		
—	—	The Man of Fortune	2/	2/6
		GERSTAECKER, Fred.—		
—	—	Each for Himself...	2/	2/6
—	—	The Feathered Arrow	2/	2/6
—	—	Sailor's Adventures ⎫	2/	2/6
—	—	The Haunted House ⎭		
—	- -	Pirates of the Mississippi ...	2/	2/6
—	- -	Two Convicts	2/	2/6
—	- -	Wife to Order	2/	2/6
		The Set, 6 vols., half roan, 15s.		
		GRANT, James—		Hf. Roan.
~	- -	Aide de Camp	2/	2/6
—	—	Arthur Blane ; or, The Hundred Cuirassiers	2/	2/6
—	—	Bothwell : the Days of Mary Queen of Scots	2/	2/6
—	—	Captain of the Guard : the Times of James II.	2/	2/6
—	—	Cavaliers of Fortune ; or, British Heroes in Foreign Wars ...	2/	2/6
—	—	Constable of.France	2/	2/6
—	—	Dick Rodney : Adventures of an Eton Boy	2/	2/6
—	- —	First Love and Last Love : a Tale of the Indian Mutiny	2/	2/6
—	—	Frank Hilton ; or, The Queen's Own	2/	2/6
—	—	The Girl he Married : Scenes in the Life of a Scotch Laird ...	2/	2/6
—	- —	Harry Ogilvie ; or, The Black Dragoons	2/	2/6
—	- -	Jack Manly	2/	2/6
—	—	Jane Seton ; or, The King's Advocate	2/	2,6
—	—	King's Own Borderers ; or, 25th Regiment	2/	2/6
- —	—	Lady Wedderburn's Wish : a Story of the Crimean War	2/	2/6
- —	—	Laura Everingham ; or, The Highlanders of Glen Ora	2/	2/6
—	—	Legends of the Black Watch ; or, The 42nd Regiment	2/	2/6

Paper Covers.	Limp Cl. Gilt.		Picture Boards.	Half Roan.
		GRANT, JAMES—*continued.*		
—	—	Lucy Arden ; or, Hollywood Hall	2/	2/6
—	—	Letty Hyde's Lovers : a Tale of the Household Brigade ...	2/	2/6
—	—	Mary of Lorraine...	2/	2/6
—	—	Oliver Ellis : the Twenty-first Fusiliers	2/	2/6
—	—	Only an Ensign	2/	2/6
—	—	Phantom Regiment : Stories of " Ours "...	2/	2/6
—	—	Philip Rollo ; or, The Scottish Musketeers	2/	2/6
—	—	Rob Roy, Adventures of ...	2/	2/6
—	—	Romance of W--; or, The Highlanders in Spain	2/	2/6
—	—	Scottish Cavalier : a Tale of the Revolution of 1688	2/	2/6
—	—	Second to None ; or, The Scots Greys	2/	2/6
—	—	Under the Red Dragon	2/	2/6
—	—	White Cockade ; or, Faith and Fortitude	2/	2/6
—	—	Yellow Frigate	2,	2/6

James Grant's Novels, 31 vols., half roan, £3 17s. 6d. ; boards, £3 2s.

		GLEIG, G. R.—		Hf. Roan.
—	—	The Country Curate	2/	2/6
—	—	The Hussar	2/	2/6
—	—	Light Dragoon	2/	2/6
—	—	The Only Daughter	2/	2/6
—	—	The Veterans of Chelsea Hospital	2/	2/6
—	—	Waltham	2/	2/6

The Set in 6 vols., half roan, 15s.

		GOLDSMITH, Oliver—		
1/	—	The Vicar of Wakefield	—	—

		GRIFFIN, Gerald—		
1/	1/6	Colleen Bawn	—	—
1/	1/6	Munster Festivals...	—	—
1/	1/6	The Rivals	—	—

Griffin's Novels. 3 vols., cloth, 4s. 6d. : paper, 3s.

Paper Covers	Limp Cl. Gilt.		Picture Boards.	Hf. Roan
		GORE, Mrs.—		
—	—	Cecil	2/	2/6
—.	—	Debutante	2/	2/6
—.	—	The Dowager	2/	2/6
—	—	Heir of Selwood	2/	2/6
—	—.	Money Lender	2/	2/6
—	—	Mothers and Daughters	2/	2/6
—	—.	Pin Money	2/	2/6
—	—.	Self	2/	2/6
—	—.	The Soldier of Lyons	2/	2/6

The Set, 9 vols., half roan, £1 2s. 6d.

		GREY, Mrs.—		
1/	1/6	The Duke	—	—
1/	1/6	The Little Wife	—	—
1/	1/6	Old Country House	—	—
1/	1/6	Young Prima Donna	—	—

The Set, in 4 vols., 6s., cloth gilt.

		HALIBURTON, Judge—		
—	—	The Attaché	2/	2/6
—	—	The Letter-Bag of the Great Western	2/	2/6
—	—	Sam Slick, the Clockmaker ...	2/6	3/

Haliburton's Novels, 3 vols., half roan, 8s.; paper covers, or boards, 6s. 6d.

		HANNAY, James—		
—	—	Singleton Fontenoy	2/	—

		HARLAND, Marion—		
1/	—	Hidden Path	—	—

HARTE, Bret—
See page 23.

		HAWTHORNE, Nathaniel—		
1/	1/6	The House of the Seven Gables ..	—	—
1/	1/6	Mosses from an Old Manse ...	—	—
1/	1/6	The Scarlet Letter	—	—

		HEYSE, Paul (Translated by G. H. Kingsley)—		
1/	—	Love Tales	—	—

Paper Covers.	Limp Cl. Gilt.		Picture Boards.	Hf. Roan.
		HOOD, Thomas—		
—	—	Tylney Hall	2/	2/6
		HOOK, Theodore—		
—	—	All in the Wrong...	2/	2/6
—	—	Cousin Geoffry	2/	2/6
—	—	Cousin William	2/	2/6
—	—	Fathers and Sons...	2/	2/6
—	—	Gervase Skinner	2/	2/6
—	—	Gilbert Gurney	2/	2/6
—	—	Gurney Married	2/	2/6
—	—	Jack Brag	2/	2/6
—	—	The Man of Many Friends ...	2/	2/6
—	—	Maxwell	2/	2/6
—	—	Merton	2/	2/6
—	—	Parson's Daughter	2/	2/6
—	—	Passion and Principle	2/	2/6
—	—	Peregrine Bunce	2/	2/6
—	—	The Widow and the Marquess ...	2/	2/6

Hook's Novels, 15 vols., half roan, £2 ; Sayings and
Doings, 5 vols., half roan, 12s. 6d.

Paper Covers.	Limp Cl. Gilt.		Picture Boards.	Hf. Roan.
		JAMES, G. P. R.—		
—	—	Agincourt	2/	—
—	—	Arabella Stuart	2/	—
—	—	Black Eagle	2/	—
—	—	The Brigand	2/	—
—	—	Castle of Ehrenstein	2/	—
—	—	The Convict	2/	—
—	—	Darnley	2/	—
—	—	Forgery	2/	—
—	—	The Gentleman of the Old School	2/	—
—	—	The Gipsy	2/	—
—	—	Gowrie	2/	—
—	—	Heidelberg	2/	—
—	—	Jacquerie	2/	—
—	—	Morley Ernstein	2/	—
—	—	Philip Augustus	2/	—
—	—	Richelieu	2/	—
—	—	The Robber	2/	—
—	—	Russell	2/	—
—	—	The Smuggler	2	—
—	—	Woodman	2	—

The remainder of the Works of Mr. James will be published in
Monthly Volumes at 2s. each.

NOVELS AT ONE SHILLING.

By CAPTAIN MARRYAT.

Peter Simple.
The King's Own.
Midshipman Easy.
Rattlin the Reefer.
Pacha of Many Tales.
Newton Forster.

Jacob Faithful.
The Dog-Fiend.
Japhet in Search of a Father.
The Poacher.
The Phantom Ship.

Percival Keene.
Valerie.
Frank Mildmay.
Olla Podrida.
Monsieur Violet.

By W. H. AINSWORTH.

Windsor Castle.
Tower of London.
The Miser's Daughter.
Rookwood.
Old St. Paul's.
Crichton.

Guy Fawkes.
The Spendthrift.
James the Second.
Star Chamber.
Flitch of Bacon.
Lancashire Witches.

Mervyn Clitheroe.
Ovingdean Grange.
St. James's.
Auriol.
Jack Sheppard.

By J. FENIMORE COOPER.

The Pilot.
Last of the Mohicans.
The Pioneers.
The Red Rover.
The Spy.
Lionel Lincoln.
The Deerslayer.
The Pathfinder.
The Bravo.

The Waterwitch.
Two Admirals.
Satanstoe.
Afloat and Ashore.
Wyandotté.
Eve Effingham.
Miles Wallingford.
The Headsman.
The Prairie.

Homeward Bound.
The Borderers.
The Sea Lions.
Heidenmauer.
Precaution.
Oak Openings.
Mark's Reef.
Ned Myers.

By ALEXANDRE DUMAS.

Three Musketeers.
Twenty Years After.
Doctor Basilius.
The Twin Captains.
Captain Paul.
Memoirs of a Physician. 2 vols. (1s. each).
The Chevalier de Maison Rouge.
Queen's Necklace.

Countess de Charny.
Monte Cristo. 2 vols. (1s. each).
Nanon.
The Two Dianas.
The Black Tulip.
Forty - Five Guardsmen.
Taking of the Bastile. 2 vols. (1s. each).
Chicot the Jester.

The Conspirators.
Ascanio. [Savoy.
Page of the Duke of Isabel of Bavaria.
Beau Tancrede.
Regent's Daughter.
Pauline.
Catherine Blum.
Ingénue.
Russian Gipsy.
Watchmaker.

By MRS. GORE.
The Ambassador's Wife.

By JANE AUSTEN.

Northanger Abbey.
Emma.

Pride and Prejudice.
Sense and Sensibility.

Mansfield Park.

By MARIA EDGEWORTH.

Ennui. | Vivian. | The Absentee. | Manœuvring.

Published by George Routledge and Sons.

4

ROUTLEDGE'S SIXPENNY NOVELS.

By CAPTAIN MARRYAT.

The King's Own.	Pacha of Many Tales.	Frank Mildmay.
Peter Simple.	Newton Forster.	Midshipman Easy.
Jacob Faithful.	Japhet in Search of a Father.	The Dog Fiend.

By J. F. COOPER.

The Waterwitch.	Homeward Bound.	Precaution.
The Pathfinder.	The Two Admirals.	Oak Openings.
The Deerslayer.	Miles Wallingford.	The Heidenmauer.
Last of the Mohicans.	The Pioneers.	Mark's Reef.
The Pilot.	Wyandotté.	Ned Myers.
The Prairie.	Lionel Lincoln.	Satanstoe.
Eve Effingham.	Afloat and Ashore.	The Borderers.
The Spy.	The Bravo.	Jack Tier.
The Red Rover.	The Sea Lions.	Mercedes.
	The Headsman.	

By Sir WALTER SCOTT.

Guy Mannering.	Peveril of the Peak.	The Abbot.
The Antiquary.	Heart of Midlothian.	Woodstock.
Ivanhoe.	The Bride of Lammermoor.	Redgauntlet.
The Fortunes of Nigel.		Count Robert of Paris.
Rob Roy.	Waverley.	The Talisman.
Kenilworth.	Quentin Durward.	Surgeon's Daughter.
The Pirate.	St. Ronan's Well.	Fair Maid of Perth.
The Monastery.	Legend of Montrose, and Black Dwarf.	Anne of Geierstein.
Old Mortality.		The Betrothed.

By VARIOUS AUTHORS.

Robinson Crusoe.	Artemus Ward, his Book.
Uncle Tom's Cabin. *Mrs. Stowe.*	A. Ward among the Mormons.
Colleen Bawn. *Gerald Griffin.*	The Nasby Papers.
The Vicar of Wakefield.	Major Jack Downing.
Sketch Book. *Washington Irving.*	The Biglow Papers.
Tristram Shandy. *Sterne.*	Orpheus C. Kerr.
Sentimental Journey. *Sterne.*	The Wide, Wide World.
The English Opium Eater. *De Quincy.*	Queechy.
	Gulliver's Travels.
Essays of Elia. *Charles Lamb.*	The Wandering Jew. (3 vols.)
Roderick Random. *Smollett.*	The Mysteries of Paris. (3 vols.)
Autocrat of the Breakfast Table.	The Lamplighter.
Tom Jones. 2 vols. *Fielding.*	Professor at the Breakfast Table.

Published by George Routledge and Sons.